Game of Life

BELLE BROOKS

Published 2018
ISBN 978-0648377016

Game of Life
©2018 by Belle Brooks

Published by
Obie Books
Po Box 2302
Yeppoon Qld 4701
AUSTRALIA

Cover design by Tracey (Soxie) Weston.
Editing and Proofreading by Karen Harper and Lauren McKellar

For:
Jack, Mia and Alyvia
I'd never give in to my fear.
I'd always fight to come home to you.
Mumma loves you, forever and always xx

A NOTE TO THE READER

These books have been written using UK English and contain euphemisms and slang words that form part of the Australian spoken word, which is the basis of this book's writing style.
Please remember that the words are not misspelled. They are slang terms and form part of everyday Australian vernacular.

"Hell hath no fury like a mother's love for her child. I will fight until my last breath escapes my lips, and my heart beats no more. I will never lie down and say 'die'."

Prologue

The Wolf

The howls of dingoes fill thick air. They're ravenous, and their need to kill is strong—so is mine. I lie listening to their hunger for blood; it's intoxicating. I will have her and release my demons when I get my feed. Patience is the key.

Her long brown hair — matching brown eyes — she's all I see. Well, apart from the thick black numbers spotting each blade on the fan circling above me. One through to five. Her tests.

The sense of elation coursing through my veins comes from the hunt, and never knowing the exact moment I can claim her. It won't be long now—she's letting her guard down and becoming reckless in her self-protection. This pleases me.

One, two, three, four, five becomes inked to her skin in my mind. That flawless silk covering, protecting her flesh, is now tainted. She will never beat me—her weakness is displayed for all who take the time to observe her.

My revenge is close. I can taste its sweet tang on my tongue. She will pay for what she's done, and I will finally get the satisfaction owed to me when I scratch her name from the list of bitches who had this coming to them.

Women disgust me. She fucking disgusts me.

My ultimate prize is all but a moment away.

"Be patient," I breathe.

The stickiness accompanying another humid summer night only intensifies the hatred whirling deep within my soul, causing my fists to clench tight and my teeth to grind.

"Close your eyes and picture all of her. Do it now." I manage to relax as her curvy silhouette and her pretentious and corrupted innocent smile rush into view.

Morgan's blood will be spilt … soon.

Chapter One

Morgan

His breath coats my flesh as he kneels behind me, his body hunched and covering mine. Rough fingers pull away strands of wet hair glued to the side of my face, exposing my neck completely. His nose runs along its length, sniffing loudly as he goes. I cringe with fear from his touch.

Please don't touch me.

"Your skin is soft, smooth and pale, just like skin ought to be on a woman," he says with lust. He twirls his finger into my hair. "Brown hair and big brown eyes … yummy," he swoons, as his lips tug at my earlobe.

I whimper softly, continuing my downward glare,

keeping my eyes focused on the ground as previously instructed.

Stop touching me.

Panting, I'm urgent in trying to supress my need to scream bloody murder at this invasion. The storm, still supplies moderate sprays from above, and every inch of my body trembles even though I will it to cease immediately.

I want to go home. Who the hell is this man? The devil? "We're going to play a game. Do you like games, Red?"

I can't find any words to answer. Even if I could, my throat is tensed so tight, no sound would project.

"What are we, deaf now?" he snarls, pulling my matted locks, ripping my head backwards. The rain stings my face.

"No," I breathe.

Letting go, he pushes my nose into the rocks.

Pig. I think the word, but my heart isn't in it to say it aloud. Closing my eyes tightly, I beg internally for help.

"I will ask you again. Do you like to play games, Red?"

"I don't know," I whimper. Tears, mix with the raindrops flowing along the length of my face until they drip from my quivering jaw.

"I don't know. Good answer," he says.

The combination of gravel and sharp jagged rocks crunch beneath footsteps, growing more distant. I contemplate running, but in every crime show I've watched, running gets you nowhere but *dead*.

Thud.

Something drops to the ground. I jolt, catching what I believe to be a backpack from the corner of my eye. *When did he come back? Why didn't I hear him coming back?*

"You'll be needing this," he says, before an eerily haunting laugh booms. "Now remember, I'm always watching. Follow the path leading into the bushland, and you'll find the first piece of your puzzle."

My eyes dart upwards, trying to locate the bushland he's referring to, but I struggle to see anything apart from shadows being casted by the moonlight. With one hard swallow, I flick my eyes back down swiftly.

No, don't do this to me.

He whistles a slow drawn-out sound. The hairs stand on the back of my neck. A shiver travels the length of my spine. *He's going to dispose of me here. In the pitch black of the night, whilst it's raining.*

A car engine starts, and the sound of tyres moving along the macadamized road has me drawing a large mouthful of air. It doesn't take long until the sound can no longer be heard. I remain frozen before finally finding my voice and screeching out loud. "Help me! Somebody!"

I tremble with fright. Sniffling in between every sob.

I'm going to die here.

I can't feel any pain in my head or on my knees

from my previous injuries. The only pain I feel is the breaking of my heart, until a dull ache finally crawls like an invasive maggot under my skin, attacking every nerve ending in its wake.

Attempting to reposition onto my bottom from my knees proves difficult. My pencil skirt is a straitjacket, hampering the action. I try desperately to stand, but my legs don't have enough strength to lift my weight upright on their own. Eventually, I plummet onto my bottom with a needy gasp, and as I thump down on the ground, I hear the loud rip. My eyes search for the location of the rip, only to find my leg now poking through a split in my skirt that wasn't there before. At least my legs are no longer constricted even if my hands remain bound in front of me with duct tape. Rotating my head, I stare at the bag I'm unable to reach, laying beside me only centimetres away. *Is there a knife in there so I can cut the tape?* Shaking my head, I note how pathetic this thought is. I'm pretty positive a man who wants to play games, would not supply a weapon.

Trying to break the tape, I move my wrists up and down vigorously, but I don't make any progress. I huff, experiencing a raw burning sensation that grows intense at my wrists the more I struggle. I'm desperate to get this tape off and to free myself from these binds.

Okay, Morgan ... you need to focus if you are going to have any chance of surviving. Think Morgan ... what do you remember about duct tape? I still, with a nagging sense to run hampering me, whilst playing images from crime shows I've watched in my head. *How to Survive the Un-Survivable*—I remember watching this program with my best friend, Linda. It showed a step-by-step guide for the exact situation I'm facing. *Duct tape-bound hands.* Raise your hands above your head, and with all your force bring them down in front of you, whilst pulling your arms outward. *Yes.*

"God, I need for this to work," I plead, in the hope that I can follow these instructions correctly.

Quivering legs hold me up as I manage to find rocky ground and stand. I raise my hands high above my head and I yelp when my right shoulder clunks as if it's dislocating from the joint. Breathing heavily, I secure my hands into fists and with every bit of strength I can summon, I throw my arms downwards, ripping them away from each other simultaneously. The tape snaps. My hands are no longer joined. I groan, easing it past my lips in relief, before the force of my previous movement sends me hurtling back to the ground with a hard crash. A bark explodes through my pained lips, one reminiscent of an injured dog, and it causes my breath to linger in my throat as my eyes squeeze tightly shut. Willing air to rush into my lungs helps me endure the agonising pain of the jagged rocks, littered throughout the gravel, digging into my tender flesh.

"Please help me." The long strand of mucus hanging from my nose has me wiping with my palm as I cry so hard my shoulders shake from the force.

I'm really hurt.

Agony is the only way to describe how every inch of my body feels, and with each echoing howl I release, my fear intensifies.

Allowing my eyes slowly to part once more, I spy the bag. I'm saddened by its small size, but take not a minute longer before reaching out my shaking hand, and sliding it to my side. A zipper, cold to my touch, is situated at its back and another shines under the moonlight on a pocket at its front. I'm instantly reminded of the small backpacks our children had when they were little. However, this particular bag doesn't appear to have a cuddly Elmo or Dora picture embedded on it to provide a feeling of warmth and safety.

With caution, my fingers slide the wet zip around, hoping whatever is inside will help me figure out how in the hell I can escape from this mess in one piece. Imagining the contents to contain a dry jacket and long pants brings hope, because my teeth chatter to a crazed beat and not even my numb fingers pressed against my lips can calm them. Sadly, I still have enough sense to know it won't.

Placing my hand into the bag's opening, I remove its contents one by one. The first item is a small canister. It swooshes as I swirl it from side to side. *Water? Poison? Water mixed with drugs?* Whatever liquid resides inside, I can't drink it, even if my mouth is begging for moisture.

I reach in again, this time retrieving a small black torch with a button on its end. My jittering fingers press down, resulting in a single stream of light.

A torch. This is at least something.

Soft raindrops are more tender against my pained skin as they slide the length of my arm. I again shift my hand in the direction of the bag. A compass, bandage, pen and hard-covered notebook soon follow and I wonder what this all means. Why did he leave these things for me? Are they a part of this game?

The backpack is empty when I dip my fingers in once more, and the disappointment that it doesn't contain a mobile phone overwhelms me with faster flowing tears.

I need to get out of here.

My head shifts from left to right, before I gather the items in a hurry and attempt to throw them back inside the bag. The notebook slips from my grasp, landing with the cover opened on the ground. It's a scrawled inking that has me scrummaging to take the torch back into my possession. What does it say? I hover the light over the page.

Welcome to the Game of Life. This is not like the game where you get a husband. You already have one of them. Or have babies. You already have two of them. And it's not a game where you build a happy life for yourself. You used to have that, Morgan.

I cringe as I read my name. He knows who I am. He knows I'm married. He knows I have two children.

He's been watching me.

This is a game for saving your life. You are my number thirteen, the most important of them all. You are the ultimate prize to collect. My irreplaceable thirteenth contestant to play. Will you be lucky? Or unlucky? Only time will provide an answer to this question. I cannot wait to find out. Sadly, I must inform you, the twelve who played before you never did reach the end of the game and never made it home alive.

Teardrops slide uncontrollably down my cheeks, dripping onto the paper below. I close the cover in a snap. Burying my head between my knees, I weep for the loss of my freedom and the game I'm set to play against my will. *Have I somehow entered hell and am I ever going to leave here? Am I ever going home?* Reid, will always think I was angry with him—will always remember our last times together fraught with tension. Our children will always believe I never loved them and that I've abandoned them.

Why is this happening to me?

Craters tear into my heart, and I know I need to silence them before they engulf me—but I *can't.*

I've failed.

I shouldn't have said I'd stay late today to finish that stupid Strassman file. I shouldn't have even gone back to work in the first place. So, why did I?

"I don't want to play a game for my life!" I scream. "Take me home. Let me go home."

I want to be in my husband's arms more than I've ever wanted to be there before, tucked safely in the crest of his shoulder, smelling his intoxicating aftershave and body wash while running my fingers across his warm tanned skin. I need a chance to say sorry.

"I'm sorry, Reid," I say softly. "Reid, I need help. Find me. Please find me, I'm so sorry. I need the chance to tell you I love you." I beg this to the gloomy sky above, too frozen to run away, too frightened to enter the bushland, to petrified to even draw air.

Chapter Two

Reid

This is the third night this week I've cooked dinner, put the kids to bed, and cleaned up alone afterwards. This is the third time this week she's promised to be home and hasn't made it on time. I feel Morgan's doing this deliberately to punish me for all the years I had to work late or travel. I wouldn't put it past her—not considering how Morgan's been behaving lately.

I miss my wife, the one who was here to greet me in the evening and see me off in the morning. The one who doted on our family.

Sighing, I run my thumb around the rim of my now empty and oversized wine glass once filled with

Morgan's favourite red, then place it heavily onto the table. I wanted to show her tonight we will get through this rut we're in. Offer her an olive branch. *But now?*

Her glass of wine sits awaiting her arrival across the table from me. A candle burns with a dull flame, giving a tranquil calm to the room—it smells of lavender, her favourite scent. I look at the chair where she promised to be sitting, but it remains bare. Morgan is pulling away from me, drifting in slow motion just out of arm's reach.

I think she's going to leave me. Why do we always fight?

My stomach churns as I rise from the table and grab the bottle of wine from the bench before pouring myself another. I look around our almost-tidy kitchen, light odours from dinner still lingering in the air. The dinner I prepared. The one Morgan never made it home to eat, her favourite—chicken risotto with shredded parmesan cheese. A shaky breath parts my lips when I stare at her plate rested against the bench, covered in a single layer of clingwrap I applied to keep it protected. My jaw clenches tight, simultaneously with my hands. Why does she keep pushing my buttons like she does? Well, if she can't be bothered being here, she can forget about eating it. I throw the plate with its contents in the trash. It's dramatic, but is it symbolic of where our marriage is heading?

"Morgan, are you cheating on me?" I whisper as if

it was being done against her lightly blushed cheek.

Turning my attention back to the kitchen, I survey all the modern appliances and the many things my wife just had to have, and I become even more agitated. I've tried to satisfy Morgan's every desire, her every need. After all, her smile has always been the best gift I could have asked for in my life. And her laugh? Priceless. There is no monetary value for such a sound. Tender kisses from my wife are nothing short of a dream I never want to wake from. I've worked hard to give her everything she needed—no, wanted—and now she doesn't need or want me anymore because she has it all. "You're being crazy, Reid. Stop this now," I mutter, unsure as to why I'm always so frazzled.

Why the fuck isn't she here? Is Morgan really not my girl anymore? Is she not happy? Have I ruined us?

Sitting heavily back down on the wooden chair at our ten-seater dining room table, my heart constricts. This is the table Morgan wanted. The one matching the polished wooden floors, the flooring she couldn't live without.

I feel bitter towards Morgan. I've never felt this way towards my wife in our entire sixteen-year relationship, yet here I am, confused, angry, and hurting. How I wish she'd never gone back to work. We don't really need the money. We could have made do.

Am I jealous of her working again?

One year ago, our life was her only existence. She breathed us and only us. Now she has this job, and we've been shoved to the back seat. She loves the kids, there's no doubting it, but I don't know if she still loves me. Honestly, I doubt it.

Finishing off another glass of wine, I note the time on the clock hanging on the wall. Nine p.m.

"Fifteen minutes away, my arse," I scoff out loud. "This is bullshit." I bet she was never fifteen minutes away when she called, and the whole tyre blowout was a scam, an act of disguise so she could rendezvous with her new lover.

I'm so fucking over this.

Reaching for my mobile on the bench, I'm ready and raring to have it out with my wife, but I stop myself. If she wants to play silly games, then silly games we'll play. My nostrils flare in the reflection of the toaster before I sit down and pour another glass of wine and I think about where we went wrong.

I wait for her like a lost fucking puppy. I stare at her empty place ... there's still no Morgan. Leaning across the table, I skull her glass of wine too.

Blowing out the candlelight that flickered hope as a soft and peaceful glow in the room, I head up the stairs to the master bedroom. *What the fuck? Ten p.m.* She's still not home. Maybe she won't ever come home. My throat becomes strained at such a notion. Morgan's never done anything like this before. Why tonight? I said I was sorry for yelling at her on the phone, didn't I? My stomach knots as my heart thrums loudly in my chest. Is Morgan in trouble? I shake my head telling myself that I'm tired and my muddled thoughts are just unfounded insecurities hell bent on plaguing me.

The water is hot and stings my skin once I step under its flow. Usually I'd run a cooler temperature when showering, but I'm so numb right now, this little bit of a burn tells me at least I'm breathing. I should have gone to her. Why did I leave her out there in this storm? *Guilt.*

A sudden loud bang comes from the direction of downstairs. It's loud enough to be heard over the water's spray.

Morgan!

I'm quick to reef off the taps before lunging out my arm in retrieval of my towel. It's swiftly wrapped around my waist. Running, I nearly slip on the steps when my wet feet meet polished wood. The kitchen is all but a few steps away as my breathing quickens and I fly past one of the chairs that's been tipped over. *Is she drunk?*

"Morgan, where the hell have you been?" I'm mad as hell, and I'm not going easy on her, as I eye the open fridge door. I'm even angrier than I realised.

"Sorry, Dad. Was just getting a drink."

My body relaxes when I see Brax. "Sorry, mate. Hope I didn't startle you." I wrap my arm to his head and pull him close, kissing the top of his scalp.

He pushes me away. "You scared me, Dad. And you're wet. Get off," he huffs. "Is Mum not home yet?" His brown eyes glaze with a look of sadness. He has the same brown eyes as his mother. This saddened look is all too familiar to me—it's identical to the one his mother flashes when heaviness overcomes her. I sigh at my observation. *Where the fuck are you, Morgan*?

"Not yet, mate. She's had to work late. It's okay though, go back to bed. Mum should be home soon."

"You're angry at Mum, Dad." I'm not sure if he's asking a question or making a statement, but those gloomy eyes are searching for an answer.

"A little, but it's because I'm worried about her, that's all. I'd say she will be pretty tired by now. Brax, I promise she won't be far away. I'm going to wait up until she's home safe. I promise you'll see her in the morning."

Brax glares at me like my nose is growing and the words coming from my mouth are complete lies.

The kids sense our recent unhappiness. I know they do. Hell, anyone who has been in our company over the last few months can.

"Go back to sleep, Son. You have a busy day tomorrow."

He manages to cock his lip in a half-smile before moving past me towards the stairs.

"Brax," I call out, jogging in his direction.

He stops, just short of where I halt.

"Be careful walking up those stairs. I don't want you to trip. They have water on them. I'll dry them off."

"Okay, Dad," he replies, waving his hand at me, while gingerly making his way to the second level.

Dropping my towel to the floor, my leg moves backwards and forwards, my foot handling the task of wiping the water off each step as I make my way slowly up the staircase. If Morgan were here, she would have purred seeing me like this. Well, I can be certain the old Morgan would have. In those days, even a flicker of my bare skin would send her crazy. Morgan has always admired my body through tender eyes, and I hers. We're fit, healthy people. I'm not all bulging muscles, but for a father of two who's well over thirty, I'd say I'm looking pretty damn good. For a mother of two, she looks more than amazing—she's still hot to trot.

It's been a few weeks since I've been allowed the opportunity to explore her body—been allowed to let my fingers trace along her tender skin and my lips to skim her neck in the subtle way she likes. Now I'm invisible. Now Morgan stays covered.

Why is she so withdrawn?

Pulling on a pair of long checked pyjama bottoms and a plain white T-shirt, I head back to the dining room, turning on the lights in wait of her homecoming. The front door is my target and my eyes never stray, until I search for the time once more. The clock reads 10:27 p.m. "Oh, for fuck's sake, Morgan, why are you doing this to me?"

That's it, I'm calling her. No more games.

Taking my mobile off the charger in the kitchen, I press Morgan's number. It rings. Voice mail.

"Hi, you've reached Morgan Banks. I'm not available at the moment, but please leave a message and I'll call you back soon. Have a great day."

I press call again. It rings out. I listen to the same voice message before redialling. What am I doing? Why am I doubting her loyalty? Is it because she's been turning a cold shoulder in my direction every chance she's had of late? Or is it because I've once been tempted to bite into the apple of infidelity myself? I never told Morgan of that night, and although I walked away without breaking our wedding vows, I fear I treated her in this same way upon returning home. I was distant. I was cold. Morgan didn't deserve that from me, and as I stand here lost, running these thoughts through my head, my hands become clammy. Quickly, my throat restricts as if I've swallowed a glass marble and it's shifting to block my airway. I clear my throat and when my hand launches to my lips I taste my own guilt. Am I wrong? Is it my own past mistake creating a non-existent one for Morgan?

Why didn't I go and get her? Hell! Why have I left it so long before I tried calling? I'm such an arsehole.

My fingertips press hard into my scalp. My gut ties into hangman's knots as heat burns a path up my throat. *Panic.*

Even though things aren't great between us, Morgan's never been out this late, and she has never not called to give an update or an estimated time she'd be arriving.

I'm guilty. Morgan's not.

Oh shit, has something happened? "Reid, you are a dick. What if she's had an accident?" I mutter under my breath.

Sweat slides in a drip down my eyebrow as my heart asks me if the woman I love with all my heart is in trouble ... *danger.* Shaky fingers meet each key as I dial 000.

"Police. Please." There's no calm in my tone, there's no hope, only shuddering fear.

Chapter Three

Morgan

Three hours earlier

The door to my office cracks open slightly, followed by a light knock against the wood. A head full of thick blond hair, followed by big blue, familiar eyes peeks in.

"Hey, Morgan, can you look over the Strassman file before you leave today? We have to present the proposal in the morning." Brett's voice is controlled in its usual manner, and as he treks into my office, brushing the lapel of his dark suit jacket as if a piece of lint hitchhiked a ride, I smile.

"Sure, Brett, not a problem," I reply, with probably too much enthusiasm. As soon as the words leave my mouth I realise this *is* going to be a problem, a *big* problem.

The sound of the door latching behind him on exit, turns my once moderately sized office into what feels like a small cardboard box. The walls begin closing in, attempting to swallow me whole. Reid is not going to be happy. Not one bit. Maybe my office swallowing me in one gulp probably won't be a bad thing after all.

You could have said no, Morgan. You're your own undoing.

I cross my arms defensively releasing a drawn exhale. My head drops to my desk. I lift it slightly and then let it drop down again. "Stupid. You're stupid, Morgan. You promised you'd be home on time today," I whisper.

Crap! This will be the third time this week I'll have to call Reid. I shiver at the thought of picking up the phone, but there's no point delaying the inevitable. Without any further hesitation, I prepare for my husband's wrath. Somehow, I think simply going through my standard breathing exercises to bring calm to the situation is not going to be enough. The wretched Strassman file, situated on my desk by the phone, stares at me. *Even it is cursing me.*

"Morgan. Let me guess. You have to work back," he snaps through the speaker. *Yes, he's angry. Again.*

"Hi to you, too, honey." My eyes roll, even though I know he can't see me. "Yes, I do. But I promise you it won't be too late tonight." I try to make my voice sound cutesy, willing it to dampen his vexed mood.

My breath hitches in my throat, hopeful this schoolgirl ploy works.

"Whatever, Morgan. So I'm picking up the kids from vacation care again?" His irritation towards me is evident.

"Please don't be mad. Just today ... I promise. I've got it tomorrow ... No working back. Cross my heart."

The Strassman file is now clutched in my desperate hands, and is creasing from my mistreatment as I scramble to improve our situation. "I know they wanted me to collect them and they're going to be upset I couldn't make it again. I know this. But, please Reid. Can you handle this for me today?"

"When are you going to make time for us? For them? For me?"

I sigh. "Maybe we could arrange for a sitter and go out tomorrow night? Just you and me. A date? I know I've been tired lately and we could do with some alone time together, or we can go out somewhere nice as a family." My voice is hesitant as I wonder if my husband will accept my latest peace offering.

His breathing is harsh and quick, but this drawn-out pause in our tense conversation generally means he is relaxing. "Okay. And of course I'll get them. They're my children. I wouldn't just leave them there. What time will you be home?"

According to the clock high on the wall, it's already 4:45 p.m. *When did it get so late?*

"About—" I stop, making sure to give a realistic calculation. "Seven, no later."

I wait for his reply. It's delayed as it always is when we have these conversations. They're becoming so frequent now that my stomach knots into a tight ball every time I need to call and tell him I'll be late. Ultimately though, I hear disappointment in his tone. *What more could I expect?*

"Okay. Can you promise you'll be home for dinner?"

A soft sigh escapes me as my polished nails begin to press harder into the document folder. I hold my breath as I prepare to supply him with the answer he wants to hear. "Of course, Reid. I promise."

With no farewell, the line falls silent as Reid disconnects. It's not a comfortable silence either. Reid's not himself of late. But, then again, neither am I.

The Strassman file falls to the desk with a soft thud. I stare at the manila folder thinking about all the promises I keep making to Reid and our children. Lately, breaking them has been my greatest downfall. Why I keep doing it—making them, and rarely following through—is beyond me. Is it because the words "I promise" deliver a sincere indication of my intentions of being there? I shake my head in confusion. Slow, shallow breaths become the only sound I hear as my tired brown eyes fall to the table. My hands lift, removing the clawed clip from my hair, allowing the mass to fall free of its binds. *How I wish I could fall free too. Juggling work and family is not as easy as I expected.*

"Strassman file," I whisper, as my breath slowly escapes through still-tense lips. I already know when the kids are in bed tonight we will be at it again, arguing about every little thing.

When did my life go from blissfully happy to one full of stress and unease?

Strassman file complete: *Check*

Office locked and secured: *Check*

Numbers floating through my head: *Check*

The corners of my mouth rise into a smile with the realisation it's home time. A feeling of satisfaction fills me as my Range Rover pulls away from the curb. I love being back in the world of finance, and even though I adored being a stay-at-home mum, this last year as a contributor to the household income has been a welcome change. Reid is still adapting, but I know if we keep trying, we will find a balance, eventually.

I turn the music up on the radio when I hear "Sexy and I Know It" by LMFAO. The traffic moves along nicely and I tap my hands against the steering wheel while ripping out a tone-deaf rendition of the song.

My shoulders slump as the music fades. The radio announcer discusses Kim Kardashian's apparent butt implants. My mind, drifts off to thoughts of Reid. No doubt a stormy mood is brewing at home, waiting to explode upon my arrival. I let out a small groan. I hate that he's having so much trouble with the fact sometimes I have to stay back at work.

Suck it up, and take on some household duties, will you? Work with me now. Damn it, Reid! Stop expecting everything from me. Those days are gone. I find myself glaring at the steering wheel gripped tightly between my hands. For twelve years, I took care of everything in our lives—our home, our finances, and our kids. Twelve years of calls from him to say he wouldn't make it home in time for dinner. Twelve years of business trips and airport drop-offs and pick-ups. Twelve years of wiping away tears from two little children's eyes who wanted Daddy to kiss them goodnight, Mummy having to comfort them because he was God knows where.

Now it's my turn, and he pounds on me emotionally about it, even though I've never done this to him. I could have told him how I really felt at times. How overwhelmed I would often be when he was away. How he made me feel so unimportant and lonely at different periods of our life together. How I sought refuge in a glass or two of red wine to calm the fires burning inside me after an exhausting day, or how I would curl into a ball and cry my eyes out deep into his pillow. But I didn't. *Why?* Because he was just doing his job, and I sucked it up like he should.

My hands grip the steering wheel so hard my fingers cramp. *Relax, Morgan, relax.* I inhale to alleviate this sudden tension. Immediately, my grip begins loosening its strangle hold. *You're doing the best you can,* I tell myself in the hope of dispelling my insecure thoughts. I *am* doing my best, even when it doesn't feel like it's good enough.

BANG!

"What the hell?" I shriek as the car swerves off the road. With unsteady hands, I manage to keep control and come to a dead stop in the gutter.

I've blown a tyre. Of course I have. Just my luck. "Arrhhhh!" I scream. With my palms banging the dash, I lean forward and look out the windshield down the long stretch of road leading me home. Knocking my head lightly against the steering wheel, I wonder when life is going to feel easy again.

"Really? Tonight? I have to do this tonight?"

If only that flat tyre was where my bad luck ended.

Chapter Four

Reid

Where are they?

I called the police forty minutes ago, right before I called everybody I could think of who might have a clue where Morgan could be. No luck, and plenty of messages left to voice mail or answering machines. Good old coppers—probably eating donuts and drinking coffee somewhere, meanwhile my wife is possibly lying hurt in a ditch in the pouring rain. There's a summer storm in full force, my wife is nowhere to be found, and I'm a mixture of blood-boiling mad and apprehensive. Shit combination.

The swing on the patio bangs against the rendered walls of our house for the fourth time in the last five minutes and it is annoying the absolute piss out of me as I wait by the door for the cavalry to arrive. I've called every hospital in the area. No Morgan Banks, or any unknown Jane Does for that matter. Where the fuck is she then? Pacing back and forth in angst, I find myself jumping every time the damn swing smacks against the bloody wall.

For fuck's sake!

Stomping through the front door out onto the patio, I'm sprayed by rain, which stings my cheek as I slide the swing away from the foundations holding our two-storey house together.

"At least the banging will stop now," I hiss through a tensed jaw.

Shielding my face, I search the road and with every glance I squint, due to the water droplets being hurled my way from Mother Nature ... It's impossible to see a damn thing out here. "Stop raining, will you? Fuck, I need it to stop raining now!" I shout my frustrations. "Morgan, where are you, honey? Where are you?" I've resorted to begging her to answer me, but all that can be heard is the howling of the wind as it barrels down the street.

The sky is a dome of plasma-grey, mixed with bolts of electricity-infused pulses. I make my way back just inside the house to escape the fury.

Blue and red lights finally appear, and for one split second I relax and allow my shoulders to drop. It's short-lived because a second later, my shoulders launch by my ears once more. The flashing of these lights brings help, but it also brings the reality of the fact my wife is quite possibly missing.

In the hazy cloud the rain creates, it seems as if two police officers are hurrying up the grey stepping stones that lead to the steps and onto the veranda.

"Where have you been?" I snap. "Seriously, do you not realise my wife could be missing? Forty minutes. Are you shitting me it takes this long?"

Two men in uniform quickly take shelter on the veranda in front of me as the wind whips the leaves of two potted palms, on either side of the staircase, crazily.

"Reid Banks?"

"Yes." I scowl.

"I'm Constable Maloney and this is Constable Stratt. Can we come in, please?"

I pause. But comply with a yes. "My wife," I bark once we're inside and the door is latched.

"Can we sit down, Mr Banks?" Maloney's outstretched finger points in the direction of the dining room table.

"Whatever." These two losers have no clue what they're doing. I can tell by the look on their inexperienced youthful faces as I eye them in the light. Where's the real police? Fuck, I should have gone and looked for Morgan myself.

"We've had a report your wife hasn't returned home as expected and you have some worry," Maloney says, finally getting to the matter at hand.

"No shit, mate. I made the report. Go find her." I'm trying to rein in my hurt, but I'm failing miserably.

"Calm down, mate." Maloney's eyes narrow in warning.

"Fine." I throw my hands onto my head and entwine my fingers.

Constable Stratt pulls out a notepad and a pen before his honey-coloured eyes connect with mine. "Mr Banks, when did you last speak to your wife?" His voice is deeper than I'd expected. He's not overly large, yet his voice is so low you would expect someone much bulkier.

"Seven past seven."

"That's pretty exact, Mr Banks. How did you know it was exactly this time right down to the minute?" His expression is questioning. It makes me want to lash out. I don't, instead opting for a strained calm.

"Well, this would be because it was only four hours ago that she called to tell me she had a flat tyre, and I took note of the time because Morgan said she'd be home no later than seven. A mechanic, I think she said, was helping her change it roadside." My jaw flinches as my teeth clamp down in a hard bite and tension continues to pulse through my veins. "She never showed. I can show you on my phone when she called if you need." My arms cross defensively, and my teeth grind together. Why is he looking at me as if I'm to blame? Stay calm, Reid!

"Are you sure she was coming home?" Stratt's voice implies so much more than his words.

Am I sure? Well no, I'm fucking not sure, but she said she was. It's none of Stratt's damn business.

His glare tells me he thinks I'm talking crap, and his sudden changed expression tells me I'm looking guilty as shit right now.

"Yes, I'm sure," I answer in a hard-to-control tone.

"Mr Banks, if the last time you spoke with your wife was 7:07 p.m, and you were expecting her home without delay, why is it then, that you waited to alert authorities?"

I pause. My fingers fiddle nervously in my lap as I sit. "I don't know."

"Mr Banks." Maloney turns his attention to the shiny silver watch secured to his wrist. "It's only 11:02 p.m, so is there any chance Morgan hasn't just dropped around to see a friend or a family member?" The emphasis on friend makes me think by "friend" he means "lover", and by "lover" he is reading my thoughts.

"No, she said she was coming home. She had a busted tyre, it got fixed ... She said she was coming home." As I say this aloud, even I wonder if I'm speaking the truth. My fingers are so contorted it causes pain to shoot through my radius, and I force my hands to relax.

"Mr Banks—"

"Can you call me Reid? Shit. Mr Banks is my father."

Maloney's eyes widen as a ghost of a smile slightly lifts his thinned lips. "Reid, is your wife normally out this late at night?"

His doubtful tone causes my anger to build rapidly. Why is he asking so many pointless questions when he should be out there searching for Morgan?

I swallow the ball of concrete, in my throat. "No, never. Unless she has a function. But I would know if she had a function tonight. I am her husband. I know these things." Why am I being so defensive? Get a grip, Reid.

"Okay, well it hasn't been too long, so let's just relax for now. I'm sure there's been a misunderstanding. Can I ask if the two of you have had a fight today or recently that might have caused Morgan to take some time away? You know, mate—maybe she took some time out for herself? Got some space?"

How fucking dare he? The launching of my head backwards and my pinched lips must clearly answer his question, so he moves on to the next.

"Is there any reason you can think of as to why Morgan might not want to come home?"

"None. Well ..." I pause, trying to replay our phone conversation from earlier this evening through my mind. "The man who helped her, what if he didn't ..." I pause once more, too scared to speak the words out loud. "What if she never left on her own? She said she was leaving, but what if he..."

"We will look into this incident." Stratt writes in the notepad.

"Okay."

"Who is Morgan's best friend?" Maloney says.

"What does this have to do with anything?" Shit. The last thing I need right now is Linda involved in this.

Stratt's eyebrows lift high on his forehead as he says, "You'd be surprised, Reid. Most times we find a quick chat with a woman's best friend results in a speedy recovery of a missing spouse." His blue eyes, are streaked with silver lines, his voice controlled.

But Linda has nothing to do with this.

"Here, mate, just write down her friend's name, address, and best contact number for us." Maloney slides a notebook and pen across the table in my direction.

Extending my arm, I clasp the pen in hand. "Linda's away on business, I tried calling her already and it went to voice mail. Just like Morgan's phone." Maybe they are together. Maybe she took a flight out and was never driving home to begin with. But why lie about the flat tyre then?

"Reid, can you write down your wife's plate number too, please?"

"It's simple to remember," I say writing down Linda's details. "It's B.A.N.K.S.0.2."

How can this be happening?

"We will see what we can find out. If she is not home by the morning, come into the station so we can investigate further. In the meantime, we'll have some officers look into the flat tyre and the alleged mechanic who helped her. Where did you say Morgan punctured her tyre?"

"I didn't."

He shifts his attention from Stratt to me. "Where did it occur?"

"On the highway. About fifteen minutes away from home."

He cocks his eyebrow.

For fuck's sake. My hands start shaking. My heart plummets before going on an erratic sprint, and my stomach drops low. I have to keep it together, but how can I? What if she's hurt?

"Whilst we are looking into these matters, I suggest you keep calling your friends and family to see if she has turned up at any of their homes."

I throw my hands into the air in frustration. "Please tell me you're fucking joking right now?"

"No, Reid," Stratt says bluntly. "At the moment, all we can do is make inquiries. We will find her if she is nearby. Don't worry, mate. We'll go for a look, see what we can find out."

Do they expect me to sit at home and simply wait? Not a chance. My wife is out there, and what if she does need me? Ignoring their lack of concern, I push the chair out with complete disappointment before standing. "I can't wait here and do nothing."

"It's all you can do. It's best you stay here and wait for her like you have been."

I run, flinging open the front door in my haste. The grass is cold under my bare feet as I rush to an adjoining property, the rain still pouring like an ocean being dumped in one bucket load from the sky. I have to find my girl.

Reaching the neighbour's home, I bang my fist loudly against the doorframe.

"Shirley ... John, it's Reid, please open up." My voice is strained from pure desperation. "Open the door John, it's an emergency."

Their outside light switches on before the sound of clicking alerts me to the lock turning over. With a soft creak, it swings wide on the breeze. John stands wearing long pyjama bottoms, wiping the sleep from his eyes.

"Reid! What's wrong, my boy?" His grey eyes reflect a worrisome stare as his hands fall away.

"John. It's Morgan. She hasn't come home."

John shifts his gaze over my shoulder, which in turn alarms me to do the same.

Maloney and Stratt approach with caution.

Expelling a puff of air, I search John's eyes once more. "These idiots are doing nothing about it. I need to go find her. Can you and Shirley come over? The kids need someone to watch them. They're asleep," I add, my feet shifting involuntarily on the wooden surface below.

"Reid, of course." Reaching out his hand, he firmly grips my shoulder, and with his touch, my throat strains from tears suddenly threatening to fall.

"I have to find her, John," I whisper.

"I know, boy. You will. Try not to worry." His aged fingers bear down, applying even more pressure, reinforcing his own worry. "Shirley, come quickly," he calls.

It takes only a moment until the sound of footsteps draw near.

"What's wrong, John?" she mutters, making it to his side. Slipping her glasses out of the pocket of her night gown, she slides them on. Her long nightgown sways with the wind blowing around her ankles and when I flick my eyes upwards I watch her pull a knitted shawl around her shoulders tighter. "What's wrong, John?" Shirley repeats as her hazel eyes finally connect to mine. "Reid, what's wrong, sweetheart?"

"It's Morgan. She's missing—"

"Go boy, go. We'll watch the kids." John doesn't have to tell me twice.

I run back across the saturated grass and I'm quick to move throughout the house, grabbing my wallet, mobile and keys from the kitchen bench. My feet barely meet the floor on my way to the garage.

Pulling shoes on just before I enter my SUV, I devise a plan. Turning the ignition over while drawing a large breath of air, I hope with everything I've got I'll find Morgan safe and sound and soon have her home.

The roller door takes forever to go up. Reversing out with speed, I see John helping Shirley up the stairs to our property. Backing out farther, I get a visual of the two police officers climbing into the cop car. I don't afford them another word, but happily offer them my middle finger stretched into mid-air. Fuck you.

I drive, following the exact route Morgan would normally take on her travels home. Within five minutes, a Range Rover appears in amongst the long grass, a touch inside the estate. Her number plate glows as lightning crashes around it. The interior light is on—it's the first thing to catch my eye as I close in, and then the back end of the car distracts me. Has it been pushed in? How did the cops not see Morgan's car here? Fucking double entry. They mustn't have entered from the highway like Morgan would have, instead they've come in the route from in town. Fuck! She's been so close all this time. Pure panic rattles me.

"Morgan," I yell, turning the car around. Each breath frantic when I pull up not far from her SUV. I sprint the short distance between the vehicles. Her driver's door is open wide.

"Morgan! Morgan!" My desperation is palpable as I race to the driver's door, before looking at her seat through eyes I know are bulging out from their sockets. I hoped … I even said a silent prayer for Morgan to be curled up in a sound sleep. She's not. My heart skips an entire beat by what I can only assume is from frightful fear.

She's not here.

The air bag is deployed. Her handbag and phone rest on the passenger seat. There's blood on the steering wheel. I'm paralysed as I fall heavily onto my knees, trying desperately to stem the multitude of emotions steam-rolling me in one blow, drowning me in despair.

"Morgan," I roar, as a primal noise follows.

Flashing lights fill the gloomy sky when a police car comes to a halt closely in front of me. Dropping my head allows the brutal rain to wash over my slumped shoulders before trickling down my face, a disguise for the tears suddenly leaking from my eyes.

"Morgan," I whisper. "Where are you?"

Chapter Five

Morgan

Two hours earlier

Yep. It's a flat.

"Shit," I mutter as I kick the tyre forcefully. My peep-toe stiletto cracks. And I cuss loudly, hopping around with my foot in hand, clasping at my now throbbing toes.

"Hell," I cry out. *My fricking toes.* I think closed-in shoes would have been a better idea today. And of course, as I sit to check said toe, long pants would have been ideal, too. One never presumes they will be changing a tyre at the start of their day when they are choosing a tight pencil skirt for work.

This. *Blows.*

Hobbling to the back of the Range Rover, I pop the boot and locate the tyre iron. Thankfully, I know what it looks like.

"It's not going to change itself, Morgan, so you better get started," I huff, realising it's best to call Reid and have him come do it. Request denied, rips through my brain. *Yep, always the person hardest on yourself, aren't you, Morgan? When are you going to stop being so stubborn?* I want to tell my thoughts to shut the hell up. Lately, my own mind is driving me insane.

I can do this on my own.

Grabbing my mobile from the console, I open Google. Google to the rescue.

How do you change a tyre? *Search.*

Browsing through, I mumble out loud. "Need a jack ... Lift the tyre off the ... blah, blah, blah ... oh, and somehow you need to loosen those bolts." *Okay, yep, seems easy.*

Throwing the phone on the driver's seat, I scurry to the back once more and locate the jack.

"What in the hell?" It's in two pieces. Google said nothing about this. *Why is it in two pieces?* Stomping back to the front of the car, I mumble profanities under my breath before locating my phone from the seat once more.

The Google homepage screen is redisplayed.

How do you put the jack together? *Search.*

Some light reading and I think I have it under control.

Sliding the now-intact equipment under the base

of the vehicle, I start twisting it round. It begins to rise like it should. Okay, I've got this. See, you can do it. *Easy peezy, right?*

"Now to loosen these bolts," I mutter, while lining the tyre iron up with one of the nuts. It starts to turn but doesn't budge. I push harder. Still not budging. I push with everything I have and it twists around flinging me flat on my arse, ripping the sleeve of my favorite silk blouse in the process.

GREAT! FUCK I HATE YOU, TYRE! GO FUCK YOURSELF! WHY GOD? WHY ME?

And then, to top my night off, the rain begins to fall.

Oh *NO,* buddy … no, you don't. Don't start the rain. I'm sorry for being crude. Please turn it off now. Make it stop, I'm sorry, I plead internally, before tilting my chin skyward. It doesn't work. The rain pours down with more force and before I know it, the beginning of a storm is upon me and I'm drenched.

My silk top is stuck like glue to my skin. My skirt feels like it has turned to cardboard—heavy, stiff, and constricting. I need to get home and out of this storm. Rising from the ground, I walk in the direction of the driver's side door once again.

"I need to get out of the rain. Reid will sort this shit out faster than I can," I moan in defeat.

A sudden loud and drawn-out honking sound startles me. Every muscle in my body tenses. I'm not on the road, so what's the problem? "What now?" I yell, turning—my eyes immediately burning from bright lights blinding me. As the lights fade, I spy a glimpse of a small sedan parked behind mine. My eyelids flutter, attempting to re-adjust my sight to the now darkened surroundings.

"Got a flat?" a deep voice yells.

"Yes."

"Let me give you a hand." A man appears tall and sturdily built as he walks towards me. He closes in, and I notice his grease-stained coveralls and a baseball-type cap, but it's too dark to make out any other details, until a passing car's lights gives me another visual ... possibly early forties. I'm strangely calmed by his presence, which is unusual for me, given the circumstances and the darkness I find myself in. I don't know who he is, and he doesn't offer any introduction, but I'm glad he stopped in this downpour to fix a stranger's tyre.

"Let's get this sorted for you so you can get back on the road." He has a kind expression in his eyes.

"Are you a mechanic?"

"Yes, I am. Looks like it's your lucky night." He seems to grin as he rests his hands at his hips.

I giggle. *Me—lucky? Never.*

"Well, now you're here, I guess it is." For the first time in hours, I find myself smiling with genuine happiness. "Luck is not something I seem to have much of. Maybe my luck is turning around."

The mystery man smiles at my statement. "I'll get to it then."

By this time, it buckets down with ferocity.

I keep a studious watch over him as he picks the

tyre iron up off the ground and crouches down inspecting my handy work. By torchlight, the corner of his mouth rises into a small smirk. Eyes as grey as the stormy sky look up to me. A deep and masculine laugh explodes from his mouth, but he quickly stops and clears his throat.

"What's so funny?" I shyly ask.

His hand rubs over his mouth and chin. "Well, your first mistake, miss, is you've jacked the car up before you've taken the wheel nuts off." He holds back further laughter behind strained lips. "You need to loosen the wheel first, you see, then jack it up." His eyes become glued to mine again, but this time they seem to be a light shade of green. There's something about them that suddenly frightens me, so I shake my head to break contact.

"Yep, I'm clueless," I say, rather embarrassed, before turning on my heel and opening the driver's door. The rain continues its assault with such force I leave my head bent inside the vehicle whilst my body remains exposed to the elements. With teeth chattering and knees shaking, brought on by the sudden gusting wind blowing through my thin top, I admit defeat.

"Must call Reid," I say, through frozen lips. Clutching my phone, I wait impatiently as it rings. "Answer the damn phone already, Reid."

"It's seven past seven, so I guess you're calling to say you won't make it, right?" he hisses.

Has he been watching the clock?

"Well, no ..." His tone annoys me. "I've got a flat tyre, and I'm about fifteen minutes from home. Some mechanic guy has pulled over to help me change it, and as soon as he's finished I'll be there."

"Oh, a flat, right. Nice excuse, but you've broken your promise yet again." His voice is a mixture of anger and despair. *As if I would make this up.*

"I do have a flat tyre, Reid. Stop being so mean." Tears threaten to spill, and my lip begins to quiver as my body shakes from more exposure to gusting and icy wind. *When did he begin to despise me so much?* "I'm fifteen minutes away. I can't go anywhere until it's fixed."

He huffs. "And you didn't think to call me for help?"

"Well yes ... I did. But before I got to the phone, this guy pulled over."

"Sure you did! And that's being really safe, by the way. You know it's pissing down rain, right? And it's dark out, yeah? I can't believe you let a complete stranger come to your aid over calling me ... What were you thinking?"

I don't answer. Instead, I stand there in shock, willing this day to end.

"Where are you exactly? Shit, Morgan, I'm coming to get you."

"No!" I snap. "I can fix this on my own. I'd never put myself in any danger. You know I wouldn't; calm down, please. I will be home soon. It's nearly done anyway." I hoped the conversation would end there. But boy, was I wrong.

"You're still a wife and a mother, Morgan. You need to start getting your priorities right and learn to multitask better."

"Reid, just stop!"

"Dinner is getting cold while we wait for you. Or did you forget about family meal time?"

"Just eat, Reid," I yell louder than I had meant. "I'm almost home." I bite at my still-quivering lip, finally stopping the trembling. A gentle tap on my shoulder alerts me to look back over my shoulder.

"Excuse me, miss, it's all done. The new tyre is on and the flat is in the boot, so you're good to go." His gaze has an air of pity to it. I guess he's heard the conversation I'm having with my very angry husband. I lower the phone and place it down upon the seat.

"Thank you so much; I really appreciate everything you've done. I'll give you some money for your time." I rotate on my heel before tilting my chin downwards. I need to locate my wallet, hoping I have at least a fifty inside, but before I manage to duck my head into the car he speaks.

"No, no, it's fine." He waves his hands in front of him. "If you can't help someone in need, then you're not a nice person, are you?" His eyebrows raise with his question.

"Thank you so much."

"No worries, miss. Hope your night turns around. You better get home and dry off before you catch a cold." His eyes stare into mine briefly before scanning me from head to toe.

I feel awkward when I too shift my sight downwards only to remember my shirt has become completely see-through. *Had to wear a soft silk blouse today, didn't you, Morgan?*

Crossing my hands over my chest to prevent any further exploration, I smile with a degree of unease. "Okay … yes, home. You should get home, too. Sorry for getting you out in the rain." My hands still protect my unplanned exposure as my teeth clasp my lip between them.

He laughs before turning back in the direction of where he parked. "It's about to be a bloody fierce storm, I think," he calls back to me.

I don't answer. Instead, I awkwardly clamber into my car, clasping my phone, and plonking my soaked bottom onto the leather seat. Reid's muffled voice can be heard dimly shouting my name, so I rest the phone back against my ear.

"Reid."

"Sorry, Morgan. I'm sorry; I'm tired. Come home, sweetheart. We will wait for you." Fatigue plagues his own words, and I relax as his tone sweetens.

The phone slips momentarily from my wet hands, but I manage to juggle it into the crook of my neck. "Please, don't wait. It's fine, start dinner without me. Don't let it get cold. It's all fixed up now. It shouldn't take me too long to get home if traffic is on my side." My tired body slumps further into the seat.

"Okay, see you soon, sweetheart. Take your time; it's pouring out there." I'm comforted by his concern.

The seatbelt slides with ease over my chest, and my body continues to shiver as it clicks into place. I extend my arm and turn off the air conditioner due to its cold blast against my wet clothing, before switching the indicators over. A quick shoulder-check has me heading back into the slowed traffic. I'm wet and cold, even with the air conditioner off, but my eagerness to get home to a steaming-hot shower distracts me from my iced state.

"Nearly there, Morgan. A few streets now," I say, through chattering teeth, as I enter the outskirts of our estate. I need a hot shower.

BANG!

My body jolts forward as the car veers into bushy grassland.

"Oh, you've got to be fucking kidding me!" I yell from the top of my lungs before the airbag deploys, smothering my continuing foul rant. Someone has run up the arse of my fucking car. Yep, this night is officially the worst night in history. Swinging open the door in a rage, I attempt to stomp down its length. I stumble and fall as each step finds a piece of uneven ground for me to trip on. All I want to do is give this bastard a piece of my mind.

"You're about to get the biggest tongue lashing, arsehole," I bellow in fury.

A crippling pain thuds in my head, and a multitude of colours dance behind my eyes. *Stay away from the darkness.* It's too strong.

Chapter Six

Reid

Officer Stratt places his hand on my shoulder as I vomit pieces of rice and chicken up onto the grass.

"Morgan," I choke out between one mouthful of my wretched-smelling stomach contents.

"Are you alright, Reid?" the officer asks.

My eyes dart upwards and connect with his dark globes under the dull street lamp. "Do I look like I'm okay?" My voice is strained.

He shakes his head.

"Where's my wife? Where's Morgan?"

"We don't know right now, but don't worry, we'll find her."

"Yeah, great job you've done so far," I hiss. "You

ignored my pleas and insinuated my wife was with a friend—I'm not dumb, I know what you were implying. She's not *cheating* on me. Got it?"

He shakes his head.

"You don't know my wife. You don't know us. She isn't cheating on me. She isn't ..." My heart aches. It's a despondent pain that is constant and a reminder of how much I love this woman. Morgan, my wife. My soul. The missing link to my existence. Without her I'm nothing but a hollow and broken vessel. And as much as I'm defending Morgan in front of these officers, I can't be sure if my defence is warranted. I'm still uncertain if she's been unfaithful, and right now I have no way to ask her, because I still don't know where she is.

"Reid, it's our job to investigate all possibilities as to where Morgan might be. We're taking this matter very seriously, okay?"

I lift my weight with every ounce of strength I can muster. I stand flush in front of Stratt with my finger outstretched and poking it a mere inch from his chest. "You weren't going to do anything until the morning. You were brushing me off. I know my wife. I know my wife," I repeat, my words spitting like venom off my tongue.

Maloney appears out of nowhere, wrapping his hand gently around my finger before lowering it slowly to my side. "Reid, you're very upset and frightened—"

"For fuck's sake."

"Reid." He pauses. I can tell he's trying to think of the right words to say. For me there are none. "You're not helping us find Morgan when you act like this. It's understandable you're pissed off. Hell, if it was me I'd be the same way, but you need to calm down before you do something stupid, mate."

For Morgan, I would do many stupid things.

I grunt, before pacing back and forth. I can't dispel my distress, or is it anguish? My shaking hands find their way into my hair just as the rain softens.

"This is Morgan's car." Maloney's peering through her back window.

"Yes. God, you pigs are frustrating ... Do you think I'd be reacting like this if it wasn't? Would you like me to do your job? It's apparent you have no fuckin' clue how." As I approach, his eyes narrow, his own anger building.

Maloney swallows hard and manages to keep control when he says, "Reid, I'm just stating my observation."

"Fuck," I snap.

He grasps the police radio from the holster on his sleeve and begins to talk into it. "Dispatch, RK-242."

"Yes, RK-242, go ahead."

"Constable Maloney here. We have located the car of Morgan Banks, a possible missing person. Vehicle is abandoned. Mr Reid Banks, husband of Morgan Banks, reported her missing earlier this evening and has now located her vehicle. Plate number is Bravo. Alpha. November. Kilo. Sierra. Zero. Two. There's rear damage––air bag has deployed. We are going to need CIB and Soco here; there's blood on the scene. We will also need the fire brigade to disable the remaining air bags."

The radio makes a crackling noise before a soft female voice comes through. "RK-242, we will get the Criminal Investigation Bureau out and send Scenes of Crimes as requested. Fire brigade has now been dispatched. There's other road patrol units in the area ... they are now on the way to your location. They're responding quickly to this comm call."

"Thanks." Maloney places the radio back into his holster whilst scanning the environment surrounding us. I watch as his eyes shift a swift left and slowly travel to the right.

Leaning against the cold and wet metal street post, I continue to keep my sight planted on Maloney. With a twist on his heel, he starts back in the direction of Morgan's car. Why isn't he combing through it? Why isn't he looking for evidence?

Where's Stratt? I'm unsure how he managed to move out of my line of sight so fast. "You're shitting me," I groan as I find him only a few metres away, on the other side of the street talking on his mobile phone. *Get off your phone, pig.*

It's only a matter of seconds before Stratt lowers his damn mobile, crosses the road, and heads straight over to where Maloney is still circling around Morgan's car with a torch.

"DDO officer is coming, Max."

"Good," Maloney replies.

Who's DDO?

"Who the fuck or what the fuck is a DDO?" I pinch the bridge of my nose as I stand less than a metre from them, not sure if I was supposed to be privy to such information.

"District Duty Officer, Reid. They're our bosses. We're first on the scene. Our job now is to secure this site and wait for the people who handle these types of scenes and the investigations that follow."

"Useless, like I thought."

"Come on, mate. I know you're having the worst night of your life, but this is protocol and what is going to bring your wife home." Maloney remains calm as he tries to settle me. No matter what I've thrown at them, they continue doing their job. Maybe I should lay off them a bit.

Twisting, I look out to the crossroad and find it odd how quiet it is. My legs become heavy like dead weights, and my body has the sudden urge to crumble into a helpless heap. Images of Morgan hurt, flash through my mind and danger alerts within me. I find it hard to control the need to run aimlessly in search of her. I think, wherever she is, she is long gone.

Stratt and Maloney both have torches drawn when I shift my attention back to them.

"I'll get the tape out and seal it off," Stratt says to Maloney, before shining a narrow beam of light out into the open vacant lot.

"What are you doing?" I snap.

"We are going to search and secure the perimeter," Stratt says.

Oh God! Why did I not think to look out into the overgrowth?

I rush toward them. Stratt turns and shines the light straight into my eyes. They burn, and are forced closed from the shine. I'm blinded, and it causes me to stop dead in my tracks.

"What are you doing, Reid?" Stratt's deep voice is stern and forceful.

I place my hand above my eyes to shield them from the light as my head tilts to the side. "I need to look for my wife ... I can help. Six eyes are better than four, right? I'm going to check all this open land here. She might have stumbled out there."

Stratt whispers something to his partner before lowering the torch from my face. "Not a chance, mate. This is a crime scene. Nobody's setting foot through this overgrowth until the teams are here."

"You can't stop me," I grunt.

"I'll arrest you, Reid. Don't make me cuff you—"

"Look, mate, how about you and I have a smoke, calm down and get our head together while we wait?" Maloney interrupts, indicating for me to walk in the direction of his outstretched arm.

"I don't smoke, and stop calling me mate. I'm not your fucking mate. My wife could be in the long grass. She could have been trying to get help and collapsed. I'm looking. Got it?" I march away from his direction.

"Reid. Stop."

"Fuck you."

The smell of wet cement after a storm fills my senses as I continue my lack of care for law enforcement and their pathetic codes and bullshit–– shouldn't they do everything they can to try and help my wife, instead of waiting for more dickheads to arrive? Part of me hopes Morgan's lying in all the overgrown grass. The other part of me hopes she isn't, because if she has been lying out here this long, then it would mean two things—she's unconscious and critically hurt, or dead. As these soul-crushing thoughts register in my mind, I feel that God-awful bile rise up my throat as it tries to seduce the vomit from the pit of my stomach to follow once more. *Reid. Stay in control.* The force of each hard swallow sits like concrete in my oesophagus. The acidity of the bile attempting to escape burns my throat.

"Banks. Don't!" Maloney yells with authority. Feet hit the pavement in a run, so I decide to do the same and try to make my way into the overgrowth, only I don't move more than a few metres before I'm crash-tackled heavily to the ground. I don't make it anywhere that could have helped my wife.

"I warned you, mate." The sound of metal clunking

together tells me one thing. This prick has handcuffs out, and they are going to be slapped around my wrists. My arms are twisted behind my back as my cheek presses into the wet grass. "This is a crime scene. It's important not to go traipsing through it. You didn't heed my warning; I've no choice." He lifts me to my feet as I sneer.

Twisting my head over my shoulder, I see Maloney's glare. "You don't get it. I just want Morgan found, and you're wasting time."

"I do get it. But you're interfering with our work. I'm putting you into the back of my car."

"You can't. I'm not under arrest."

"Don't push it," he scolds.

In my peripheral vision, I catch a glimpse of his narrowed eyes. That's right before I throw my head back and connect it with Maloney's cheek.

"Fuck!" he yelps. "Reid Banks, I'm placing you under arrest for assaulting a police officer." He spits blood out onto the road.

"Hope it hurt."

"Hope it was worth it," he snarks back just as quick. *Fuck, Reid, what did you do?*

"How long until everyone gets here?" I fire out as I'm lowered into the back seat of the cop car. Before he even answers, I see blue and red flashing lights rounding the corner.

"I'd say about right now, Reid."

Before long, massive spotlights are erected over

the area. More cars arrive, and then the barking of dogs has me watching as they enter the vacant lot. There are bloody cops everywhere. A sea of navy blue goes to work in a very structured and practised routine. I sit here, arms aching from their positioning behind my back, staring at the scene playing out in front of me–– one you'd expect to see on a screen in the cinema with actors portraying the horror. *Only this isn't a movie ... this is my worst nightmare in real time.*

Everything begins to speed up, like a hurtling rollercoaster, when officers in dark uniforms bob up and down between long strands of grass. I hear the calling of my name as the door to the car I'm sitting in opens.

Dark-washed jeans and a navy shirt catch my vision. Scanning farther upwards I'm met by a moustache with greying hairs entwined into black coarse hair. The distinctive smell of stale nicotine and cheap coffee wafts from his breath before he rotates his head away from me and orders with authority, "Get him out."

I'm helped from the car, then instructed to turn around by an unknown man. The cuffs are removed and I'm turned back. Using each hand, I rub into either wrist until I'm presented with an outstretched hand awaiting mine to meet in a handshake. I reciprocate.

"I'm Detective Astin West. I'll be handling your wife's case. It will be in your best interest to accompany me down to the station, Mr Banks." I feel his penetrating eyes shifting the length of my body. I gather he's trying to detect any information my body language might supply him. When his eyes rebound to mine, I'm alerted to my own weary nodding. I had no idea I was even doing it.

West swivels on his heel, turning in the direction of a navy undercover car parked distantly from the many other emergency vehicles here. In a march reminiscent of a solider, he starts moving forwards and without hesitation, I follow close behind.

He opens the car door wide before using his free hand to indicate his request for my entry. I hesitate, placing my palm against the slippery roof before looking up towards a full moon, which finally appears from behind the drifting cloud cover the storm created. It's oddly large and seems only a stone's throw away from the Earth. How can something so beautiful exist in a sky after a terrible storm on the night my wife vanished.

"Morgan, I love you. I'm coming to find you—don't worry," I say, my voice barely audible, before ducking my head low and sliding in and across the back seat.

"Reid, your car will either be delivered to the station or back to your residence."

There's a long pause as I rotate my head in an action reminiscent of a shoulder check.

Maloney looks exhausted as he runs his fingers down the quarter glass behind my head. "In case you were wondering," he adds with a heavy-hearted tone.

I don't reply as I shift until I'm hypnotically staring out of the front windscreen. Gulping in a sharp breath, I'm unable to hold in my lungs, I release it with a choking cough.

Where is Morgan?

The hands of time are ticking faster than I can process a single thought, and as I try to keep up with my erratic brain function, I'm also smothered by a building urgency. I'm pleading for someone to fucking find my wife.

Chapter Seven

Morgan

One hour earlier

I can't breathe ... I can't breathe ... Why can't I breathe?

Pitch black has my eyelids blinking with ferocity, willing my pupils to adjust. With each bat of my eyelashes, my head thuds with a heavy pain. It's a sensation I've never experienced before and one I find myself instantly praying will cease.

"Ouuuucccch," I moan, sheer desperation has my quivering hands frantically groping the small space surrounding me. "Where the hell am I?" Panic firmly sets in when my fingers run across what feels to be rough carpet. They scrape the surface beneath me repeatedly. I'm not sure why I hope for the sensation to change, but I do.

My body is curled into a constricted ball and my attempt to stretch my legs leads to an excruciating cramping sensation. There's no room to move to alleviate the agony. A gut-wrenching thump has my heart beating to the pounding rhythm of my head, and every alarm my body possesses sirens in warning. I'm in trouble. *Please stop thumping, head. I can't think.*

It's a rattling sound which first alerts me to the running car engine, followed quickly by the throat-burning smell of freshly pumped fuel. The scent is so putrid I fear the small hairs in my nose have singed. *Instantly nauseated.*

I'm in a car. Is it moving? *Morgan, you need to get out. You need to get out now.*

I try to think back to the endless crime shows that would often give me nightmares. The shows I'd watched all those nights when I was home alone while Reid was away. *Come on brain, work.*

The splitting pain still piercing my skull makes it hard to think about anything. "Don't give up," I whisper, and then the answer comes. *A lever? No, a cord. There is something you pull to open the boot from the inside.* Desperate searching follows; there must be an escape.

"Where is it?" I breathe. I can't find anything. *I can't find it.*

The level of my panic soars, and so do my panted breaths. *SCREAM, MORGAN. SCREAM!*

I do. It's loud, fierce, and projects without mercy as I try to roll from my side, flat onto my back. The space is too tight; it's impossible.

Music begins blaring. It's erratic with the beat of heavy metal, and my brain threatens to explode from its sudden violation. Clasping each hand over my ears to dull the sound doesn't work. It's torturous. I can't help screaming louder and with more desperation, but the music only increases in volume, and the pain I'm experiencing continues to intensify. *Nobody can hear you, Morgan.* Tears rush in a stream down my cheeks. *What the hell is happening to me?*

Squeezing my eyes tightly closed doesn't halt my tears. Instead, they continue to flow like rapids. Lifting one hand, I place it against the side of my head before fanning four fingers out into a matted mass of hair, locks once cleaned and styled professionally.

A thick sticky substance coats my skin––it's warm, yet chalky. *What is it?* Lowering my still shaking hand in a long stroke of my face, I stop by my nostrils. What is that smell? The odour is metallic. Holy shit. I wince––*Blood*. Launching my hand back to its original position in the matted mess of hair without any hesitation, I cry out with a needy roar. Frantically, I work until my fingers move deep down and I finally touch my scalp. It's watery and wet. *My head is oozing fresh blood!* A war has taken place against my body, one I've no memory of fighting in.

This single touch brings with it the sound of an engine revving, visions of my car veering from the road take over. *"You have got to be kidding me,"* I'd screeched on my mission to talk to the driver who'd forced me from the road. Did he take me? Have I been abducted?

"Anybody?" I scream. "Help, somebody! Help me!"

With this plea comes a sudden halt. My body jolts forward. My cheek slams hard into metal. *"Fuck."*

Two loud thuds sound from above and my body jumps from the shock as my breath catches and then hangs in a state of limbo.

"Red, it's in your best interest not to do anything stupid. Do you hear me?"

His voice. I'm sure it's one I've heard before. Definitely male. Calm, yet deep, and––

"Red, did you hear me?"

Who's Red?

There's a short pause, and in the silence, I hear the familiar pitter-patter of rain tinging against the metal. Wherever I am, it's raining. It was raining on the drive home––I remember now. Am I close to home?

"I would like to keep you alive for a bit longer. I've plenty in store for you, Red. It will be such a shame if our time together has to end abruptly."

I lie still as his words bring a fear so intense I swear it stops blood pumping through my veins.

Come on, brain. Do I fight or do I stay frozen? I can't find the answer––my mind is blank. No words leave my lips in response as I continue to lie, trembling violently. I can't stay frozen because I'm not in control of my limbs—my fear is. So, do I fight?

Click.

"Oh my God, please don't hurt me." My throat constricts into a tight strangle as a thin slither of light appears. It's enough light to cause my eyes to squint from the burn to my pupils.

"Red, I'm going to open up. Stay still. If you don't, you *will* feel my wrath." He chuckles deeply.

I know this laugh, but from where?

"Put your wrists together and hold them up. Do it now." He speaks with controlled authority. The confidence in his tone suggests an old hand. Has he ordered such a thing before?

I cringe, but follow his instruction and do as I'm told. A long stripping sound follows—tape pulling away from the roll. I cringe once more. The fine hairs coating my wrists strain from the skin when the sticky substance is wrapped quickly around my wrists, holding them tightly in place.

"Please," I whisper through a tensed throat. "Stop, please. You're hurting me." A whining cry presses past my lips as my body is reefed from the car by my hands. I slide when my knees plant on what feels like uneven ground, ground I assume is covered in slippery sharp rocks due to the agony greeting them. The cramps plaguing my legs intensify from my new position, and I scream as a result.

This can't be happening. Not to me. It hurts so bad.

"Shut up, Red, or I'll shut you up, you hear me, you cowardly bitch?"

"Who's Red?" I mumble through latched teeth.

"Shut the fuck up." He is calm when he says this. Eerily calm.

"I think you have the wrong person. I'm not Red; my name isn't Red." The urgency in my tone is palpable.

"I know." He laughs. It's a smooth and controlled sound.

Pushing my head downwards, he forces my torso to follow. My naked knees continue to pain. The sensation of skin being sliced has me sucking in air. I grit my teeth to stop myself crying out my agony. Instead, I hold it internally and opt for a strained sob. I'm tired, cold, and hurt. I want Reid--I want to go home.

"We are going to play a game," his voice bellows. "A wonderful game with two players. You and me. If you play nice and follow the rules, you will get to go home. If you don't, well ..." He clicks his tongue. "Well, you'll die, Red. It's a pretty simple concept to understand."

"I don't want to die. Please let me go."

"I should tell you, though, you'll have to outsmart me, and a fucking bitch like you has no chance of ever ..." He doesn't finish speaking.

Why?

My lips tremble from fear as he breathes a slow, whistling breath. There's a long delay before a loud chuckle comes out of nowhere. His smug tone combined with my shivering makes me feel ill. *Oh shit. I think I'm going to be sick.*

"Stop your noise." His hand cups my mouth and

presses down hard. I struggle to bring air through my nose in response.

It's quiet, apart from the rain, and I listen intently wondering if these delays are because we're not alone here and he's searching to see if we are.

He releases my mouth slowly. "Now, how could you possibly outsmart me?" He taunts me. Continuing as if he hadn't previously stopped speaking. "Let me tell you a little secret. I'm yet to have a silly woman beat me at my own game, so your chances are not looking good, not looking good at all." His snarky bite causes bile to travel from my stomach to the back of my throat, burning it, before the roll I ate for lunch makes its exit from my mouth with tremendous force onto the rocks in front of me. Saliva drips in a long thread from my bottom lip, which results in hard laughter spewing from behind me.

"Dirty fucking bitch," he snarks.

Rain falls with authority, running over my hunched body. *So cold.* I try unsuccessfully to control my tremors, but the more I try, the worse each shake becomes. My throat is begging for water, the taste of vomit still present. My knees beg for bandages to offer protection from the elements. My head follows, begging for an ice pack and paracetamol, and my fearful heart begs for Reid.

"Help," I moan, my voice barely audible.

Chapter Eight

Morgan

Present

Slowly reopening the cover to the notebook, I swallow with a loud gulp. I know I need to continue reading, but it's hard to imagine how much worse the scripted words will be. Drawing in deep breaths of air, I try to prepare myself for what's about to come, but this delay achieves nothing. Holding the flashlight over the page, it bounces around with the vibrations of my filthy hand.

Why me? Why do I have to be part of his game? I'm a nobody. Who would want me to endure such torment? Better still, why is he calling me Red when he clearly knows my name? My mind is plagued with many questions, ones I want answers to, but I don't have any. *Come on, Morgan, you can figure this out. Think.*

Still nothing.

Good job, Morgan.

"I know," I whisper to my own thought, watching as my hands continue to tremble uncontrollably.

You're talking to yourself, Morgan.

"No shit," I blurt out, in anger. *Get it together, will you.*

I shake my head, in an attempt to silence my subconscious as anger replaces my previous gut-wrenching fear. This anger is telling me, right now, I'm captured by a lunatic who is not only sick, but twisted and sadistic. It also tells me I'm so entangled in his carefully woven web that there is little to no chance of ever leaving this game. I'm going to die here.

The strain around my eyes alerts me to my scowl as I try to visualise what this pig looks like. My vision is blank ... there is no face. How come I didn't see his face? His voice is definitely one I've heard. But *where? When*? I can't help trying to identify a voice with such a distinctive monotone. "Who are you?" With widened eyes, I gasp so loudly, even I'm shocked by the sound.

George Anderson ... It's him. It must be him. Surely our company losing a huge sum of money for a client wouldn't turn the man into a serial killer. And if it did wouldn't he have killed others from the company and I'd have heard about it?

No. It can't be him. *Can it?* George did write a

threatening letter stating every person who'd laid finger to his account would pay. I was one of them. A small part of his losses, but still a part. Surely I'd know if twelve staff members had been killed? People talk in a small organisation. There's no more than two hundred employees in our firm-- there had to have been information handed out if this had happened? The police would know, and I imagine there'd be one big board covered in faces of the people who had died at his hands.

Morgan, you've watched too many police shows. Stop this foolishness. My irrational and rational mind are fighting, and I'm not sure which one of them to listen to as I shake my head again to switch my subconscious thoughts into something more encouraging. It doesn't work. Instead I'm left considering many plausible, yet utterly ridiculous, theories. I sigh at the realisation I'm now not only in a physical battle, but a mental one, with myself. I honestly don't think I have the strength to play any games, even more so, one responsible for my life.

"I can't do this," I croak.

Yes, you can. At least he gave you something. He has given you instructions and a flashlight, which is going to be mighty handy. Read what he's written so we can go home, will you? Now!

"Fine."

I've no choice but to continue reading from where my tears caused me to previously stop.

Morgan, if you want to see your family again, you

are going to have to follow the rules. Here is the list of the rules:

RUN, Morgan, and don't STOP or I will gut you like a pig.

You see, there are no rules. I have full control of how this game will end. I'll be watching you, and I'll always be one step ahead. Well, unless you solve the puzzle. "I know who you are, Morgan Banks, the question is, who am I? Five games will set you free when you can tell me who I'd be."

ARE YOU READY TO TAKE ON THE WOLF, LITTLE RED?

The remainder of my lunch violently makes its way through my taut lips. My body heaves with such force it feels as if one of my ribs pops out of place from the action. I gargle a scream through each upchuck that follows, my throat now wretchedly dry.

"I need water." I beg.

The canister is clasped in my tight grip. Although I know not to sip from it, my need for a drink is strong. If it is poisoned liquid, will it provide a quick death? I'm not sure how long I debate with myself on the appropriate action to take in this situation, but my tongue becomes slick after a few wary sips. It's not much, but enough to bring relief.

Placing the canister into the bag, I click the end of the red pen provided, telling myself I should write down something. With a shaking hand I write my name and, *'I need help. I've been abducted. Alert authorities.'*

Ripping out the page, I scrunch it into a loose ball and discard it on the ground. Leaving a trail of written clues might help me. This is something I can only hope.

"What?" I gasp, when the torch and my eyes swing back to the book.

The following page is not blank like I assumed it would be. Instead, it's titled:

Insert your goodbyes here. I will ensure your family get them once you're gone.

The wolf.

Bone-chilling shudders travel the length of my spine as every individual hair on my body stands at attention. *Morgan, you are going to die here.*

My head falls, then the ground fills my vision from the torch light that follows. Tears I was trying to control burst out from within. I cry with such force my shoulders shake. Mucus drips excessively from my nose and a steady flow of salty warm tears cascade over my cheeks, which I'd no idea were so cold. Fate is hard to face when fear, pain, and despondency pour out from within.

Chapter Nine

Reid

The drive to the police station seems a lot longer than it probably is. My mind is inundated by a million thoughts about what my future could hold without Morgan in it, and every one of them seems dismal. I'd rather die than walk this Earth without her. But then, confliction sets in, because I have been focusing on my selfish wants over the needs of our children. I couldn't do that to them. Frustration brews, causing my heart to beat with tremendous pressure against the wall keeping it safe. I shake my head, pressing my fingertips hard into my temples.

What are you thinking, Reid? You've given up on Morgan already? You've already stuck the tag over her big toe and closed the door on her life?

She's not dead. She's coming home.

As each thought penetrates my mind, my fingers press harder and my eyes squeeze tighter together.

"Mr Banks, follow me please," West says, as we make our way through the front door of the local station. I'm escorted to a room situated behind another three doors.

West saunters with an air of confidence before me, and I can't help thinking, he has already concluded, *"Yep, the husband did it."* I bet he's already working on tactics to secure the confession for my awful, yet unfounded, crime? *I'm not stupid. The husband is always the primary suspect.*

I've never been in trouble with the law, or needed to be in this part of a police station, for that matter. How can a single moment change the course of one's life? It's both a daunting and nerve wracking thought.

I didn't kill my wife, I keep telling myself, followed by, *I want my lawyer*.

I'm directed to a very uncomfortable-looking chair. I attempt to pull the chair outwards only to find it's bolted to the floor.

Shit! Just bring in the shackles and lock me up already.

Two more chairs rest across from mine, a basic table between me and them, and now I'm alone in here, left to wait.

My fingers tap against the table's surface in an attempt to control the tremors. It doesn't work. Slipping them downwards, I tap against my soaked checked pyjama bottoms, and stare at my thumbnail moving to an uncoordinated beat. Grass and mud stains cover both the knees caps on the material covering my legs, and thoughts of what tonight has entailed causes me to swiftly place my hands back up onto the table. Without permission, my fingers again resume a nervous beat, against wood.

Detective West enters, followed by another man. He is in dark-washed jeans and a navy shirt too, and is about three inches shorter than his counterpart, who seems to be my height of six-foot-two. His hazel eyes have a spark of kindness in them. His features are much softer and more cared for than West's, so I believe he's younger. His skin is dark in colour, as is the stubble covering his chin. I'm guessing good cop ... *bad* cop.

My eyes dash around the four white plain walls. A bolted down chair, a brown-topped table, me, and two detectives—this should be fun.

"Mr Banks, this is Roland Gleaton. He is another detective in our unit and will be assisting me on your wife's disappearance."

I lean back into the chair before showing my palm in a half-hearted wave. It's going to be a long night. A worried moan escapes my lips as they begin to stare at me like a man on trial. How quickly the atmosphere in this small room changes.

Detective West shifts his eyes downwards focusing on some crisp white papers he has laid out in front of him. "Mr Banks, we will go through some of the formalities first, collecting essential data from you, and then we will have a chat," he says, as his eyebrows rise and his grey-blue eyes stare hard into mine.

A large lump fills my throat and prevents any sound passing its non-existent lodgement. I nod to indicate I understand his intentions.

"Mr Banks. Can I call you Reid?"

"Please," I reply with a clearing of my throat.

"What's your wife's full name?" He poises his pen over the papers.

I cough to clear my throat once more and then hesitantly begin to speak. "Morgan Amelia Banks."

"How old is Morgan?" He crosses one foot over his knee, his expression relaxes as if he is more than comfortable sitting across from me and we're having a leisurely chat.

"She's thirty-five."

"Your address, please?"

"168 Potter Road, Norman Gardens." My jaw begins to ache as I clench my teeth.

"Beautiful property. I believe it's the one with the tyre swing in the front yard, yes?" His calm and relaxed demeanour mixed with his sudden cold, stony glare is confusing and overwhelming all at once.

"Yes."

"Lovely part of town, too." He cocks his head to the side, his banter delivered in a friendly manner.

"Yes, it is."

"You have two children, Reid?"

"A son, Brax, and a daughter, Aleeha."

"Ages?"

"Twelve and ten," I croak.

"Your full name, please?"

"Reid Elis Banks." He writes down everything I'm saying, and as I watch the cap pressed to the end of the pen forming inkless patterns in the air, the lump in my throat grows more constricting, leaving me slightly short of breath. Why isn't the other detective speaking? What is he thinking? Why does he look so disinterested?

"Age?" West says, snapping me out of my observation.

"My age?"

His eyes scan upwards as I point to my chest. "Yes."

Moving uncomfortably in the chair, I rub at my face to calm myself. "I'm thirty-five as well."

"I see ... Reid, can you tell me in your words what happened tonight?"

I go to speak, but he raises his hand to stop me and turns his head, whispering something into his colleague's ear. Detective Gleaton nods before promptly standing and then exiting the room.

Confusion fills me.

"Is everything okay?" I ask, my voice shakes on my words.

West returns an arrogant smile.

What's their game?

Gleaton re-enters not long after he left. He's holding a small audio machine to his side. Placing it to the middle of the table, he fiddles with it until he nods and steps back.

"Reid, we're going to record your statement. You don't have an issue with this, do you?"

You ask me now, arsehole, after so much effort setting it up?

"Nope." I roll my eyes.

His expression shifts to irritated. "Okay, continue."

"Where do I start?" I'm unsure as to what part of tonight West is referring to.

His glare, and his manner, tell me he is looking for a shortened version of events, over a long-winded and drawn-out one. Or is this what I think he wants?

Watching West inhale, has me following him and repeating his very act. Do I plead my case now?

"Start at the beginning."

I place my hands on my head, and as I fold them on top of each other, I take another large mouthful of air, puffing out my cheeks. Slouching farther into the chair, which is as uncomfortable as a boulder below my arse, I take a moment to close my eyes and think back to the call Morgan made. The one where she would have been drenched by the rain. The one where she was on the side of the road with a flat tyre. She must have been so mad at me. Why was I such an arsehole to her?

"Mr Banks," West says, dryly.

"Huh?"

"What happened tonight?"

"What happened?" I repeat.

"Yes. Reid."

"Morgan ..." One word. My wife's name echoes through my mind.

"Morgan. Yes. Tell us what happened with Morgan."

"Well ... She ... We..."

"Do you need something to drink, Reid? Would you like to step outside for a cigarette? Calm your nerves?" West seems caring in asking.

"No. I'm good. I'm okay. I just needed a minute."

"Okay. Well, when you're ready, tell us what you remember about tonight."

Left. Right. Up. Down. My eyes travel in a bounce from the white walls and roof with nothing pinned to them. Not a picture, or a poster—not even a memo. Eight times I find myself sucking down deep breaths through my nose. I count as I try to remember what happened. "Morgan had to stay late at work tonight." I pause. "I had to pick the kids up from vacation care. Afterwards, I cooked dinner. Morgan had told me she'd be late. I think we had a bit of a disagreement about it."

"You think?"

I shake my head. "No. We did. We disagreed. It was her turn to pick up the kids."

"Okay." West raises his hand again, his indication for me to stop talking. Then he begins writing something down, but I can't see what it says.

"It—it's—well, it's not like that," I manage to finally spit out.

"It's not like what, Mr. Banks?"

Fuck, this man is intimidating. "It's not like we were … Can I start over?" My tongue ties.

"Just keep going please. You had a disagreement. What type of disagreement?"

"The married type," I spew out with force. He knows he's rattling me, and I believe he gets further satisfaction when my hands curl into fists and then drop down loudly against the table. "Stop." My throat is strained from desperation.

After a few lengthy inhales, I straighten my posture to sitting stiff and upright and glare as the corner of his mouth rises slightly. It's as if he wants to smile. I blink, and by the time I look at his mouth again, he's reined back his need and is displaying a completely neutral expression. How does he do that?

There's complete silence. A standoff of wills as I try to calm myself again.

"Look … Morgan had to stay late for the third time this week. I'm not going to lie. I was pissed about it."

He nods.

"I didn't yell at her or anything … I only let her know I was upset by another late arrival home. Come on, you must know what I mean. Wives, they piss you off sometimes."

"Okay," he says, in an understanding tone.

"I cooked dinner for the kids, like I said. They were having showers. We were waiting for Morgan to arrive before eating. But she called. She said she'd blown out a tyre. Fifteen minutes away. She was only fifteen minutes away, she said this. There was some guy, she called him a Good Samaritan, he stopped to help her with the flat—"

"A man stopped and was with your wife?" West has one eyebrow shoot upwards as the other stays in place.

"Yes, but he left. He left before I even hung up. I heard the mumblings, but I swear she said goodbye and thank you before we ended our call."

"Okay, continue." His eyebrows sit squared to each other again.

"Morgan and I had some words. You know how it is. Well, maybe it was just me being annoyed because she didn't call me to come fix the fucking tyre. She normally calls me for stuff like this. I got a bit riled up, and I let her know she needed to be home more, she needed to stop working back so much. Of course, Morgan bit back at me. She said to start dinner without her...but when I hung up, we had both calmed … actually, Morgan might have hung up."

"Okay, what happened next?" West rotates his neck, which results in a cracking sound, and I watch him until he focuses his attention on me once again.

"Nothing happened. She didn't show up. I cleaned the kitchen, poured a glass of wine for each of us, and waited."

"You were drinking?" West seems surprised as he leans forwards, hovering further over the table.

"It's not illegal to have a few nightcaps." *Why did he react this way?* My shoulders involuntarily lift in a shrug. "It was a couple of glasses, you know?" My palms move outwards, gesturing that his overreaction to a few glasses of wine is borderline ridiculous.

"Are you under the influence of alcohol, Reid?"

Is he kidding right now? Of course not. I squeeze the back of my neck, shaking my head, dumbfounded by West's question. "Nope. I'm not. Breathalyse me."

"When did you start to worry something might be wrong?" he asks, matter-of-factly.

"Well, I don't know, I guess—" I stop studying the two officers across from me. "I thought maybe she had gone back to the office, maybe she had forgotten something—"

"Or maybe she was lying and didn't have a flat tyre at all, and it was a ploy to be elsewhere." West's words are so calm when he delivers them, I know my reaction is shocked, due to the fact he just read my earlier thoughts.

I lower my head before moving it from side to side.

"Am I right, Reid?"

I nod.

"Do you think your wife is having an affair?"

"No," I whisper, unsure if I believe it myself.

"Are you sure that's the truth, Reid?"

Jolting upright, I shoot fire daggers from my eyes as anger pumps through my veins. Clenched fists result as steam builds, threatening to explode from my ears and nose. "Morgan's not cheating on me. She's not. Do you understand?"

One punch hard into the desk causes me to

grimace. Neither West or Gleason are startled by my reaction or the sound my fist makes hitting against the wood.

"This is fucked."

Chapter Ten

Morgan

You can't sit here and wait to die, Morgan. If this is your destiny, then at least have the courage to die fighting. *Move, will you?* My thoughts fire rapidly.

Rage surges through my blood as a result. I turn to the next page in the book and write.

Thursday, December 18th

I sigh with sadness as the realisation I'm probably not going to make it through day one becomes my only belief. I wasn't built tough. I was built to nurture.

With a broken heart, I place the book and pen into the backpack and slowly stand up on uneven ground. My visually battered and bruised body aches, and my buckling ankles almost see me fall. Somehow, I manage to find balance on the thin pegs of my shoes. One drop of what I hope is water skirts the length of my nose, causing me to look upwards and straight at a moon much larger than its normal size. The storm once blocking its exquisiteness is now all but a distant memory. Reid would have loved the moon tonight, with its shades of pink ...

Reid.

I search for his ocean blue eyes and when I envision them, they're a welcome imagery. I wish he could hold me securely right now. I'm alone and frightened and most likely going to be killed if I don't move out from this open area. Right now, I'm a sitting duck, waiting to be slaughtered.

I have no strength––I'm so tired. Acid burns a path from my stomach and up my throat before latching onto the back of my tongue, causing me to swallow hard. I don't have the strength to even vomit again. "Please, I can't be sick."

Closing my eyes has me managing to distract myself and with thoughts of Reid and I, sitting on the porch swing at home together after another long day, it finally disappears. The visions of soft swinging bring much-needed peace and have me ready to play a game I have no desire to play.

"Find me, Reid," I whisper before turning towards the bush I have no doubt will house spear grass and a horror I have no choice but to accept.

One step. Two steps. Three steps make me shudder, so I stop moving. I twist my head over my shoulder and look back at the long dirt and gravel track we drove down. I've been sitting in the same spot for a while, and he never came back. Why? Maybe he won't and he's gone, and the game is already over. My mind begins to tick at a rate so fast I have trouble keeping up with its thought patterns.

He's gone, Morgan. Surely, he can't see you. Maybe the reason the twelve women who came before you didn't win was because they should have walked back the way they came in. Maybe this is the way to win the game—never enter it in the first place. I stay planted on the spot, running this theory over and over in my mind. Could it be this easy?

Shaking my head, I whisper it aloud. "Can it be this easy?"

Surely not, but I'm liking this idea much more than the one that has me walking into the overgrowth of death.

Cautiously, I shift my body to turn back towards the path we came in on. One step. Two steps ... it's a tiptoe at first, almost creeping. Three steps. Four steps. Five steps. My pace quickens. Surprisingly, I'm balancing well on my heels and growing more confident as my momentum builds and with it speed follows. What started as a creep soon turns to a jog, and then to a run. How I'm accomplishing such a mission is beyond me. The only plausible explanation is my supermother powers are beginning to kick in right in the nick of time.

Run, Morgan, run, or he will gut you like a pig. My feet heed these words, and I find a faster gear.

The sound of crushing gravel and a car engine in the distance has my heart sinking and my stomach following. I was never alone whilst I sat there—he was indeed watching like promised.

Oh *shit!*

Morgan, you weren't supposed to do this. You should have entered his maze, allowed the hunt to take place and played his game … It was never going to be so easy. My stupid mind lets me down and I halt immediately, shivering as my lungs try desperately to draw oxygen into them. A spray of gravel followed by clumps of mud are slung in my direction, successfully catapulted against my face. It stings something fierce on impact.

Morgan, you didn't even make it past the beginning. You are pathetic.

My heart sprints as I close my eyes and I wait for the ultimate moment … my end.

Tears rush silently down my cheeks as I welcome images of the people I love to flash behind them. This flickering imagery removes all the hellish visions of what could possibly happen to me during the last moments of my life.

The sound of cracking pierces my eardrums, and I jump. My eyes spring open with the force of my fear only to be confronted with a masked man, who has his arm hanging out of the open car window and is holding a bull whip that flashes my sight, not once, but twice. It rises into the air a third time, and I can no longer see it whipping towards the ground. *Where is it?* I run.

Another loud crack has a piercing screech erupting from deep within my soul. It's so loud it brings the taste of blood into my mouth. The bridge of my back burns, like a fire being lit with a single spark of a match. I scream again. This time the projection echoes throughout the empty space surrounding us, bouncing between the different natural elements that currently house my hell.

Another loud crack has me flung with such vigour, my cheek skids along the path, my flesh tearing until I come to a complete halt. My back burns like a thousand fire ants are biting at my skin and I growl to contain the scream wanting to explode through my lips.

Then there's quiet. It's so quiet all bar an untimed thudding in my ears. Every pulsation causes the pain to shoot through delicate nerve endings that send hurried messages to my brain. It's the most excruciating agony I've ever felt in my life. I sob and the previous silence I feared is kept at bay by me, by the noises being forced from my mouth. They are so unfamiliar to me, I can't believe they're even mine. The last attempt to call out my agony is not heard, as my voice fails me and becomes hoarse.

I lie motionless, listening to a squeaking noise which reminds me of an old rusted hinge being worked. There's a loud bang, one I suspect is caused by the closing of a car door.

It starts out softly, yet becomes more powerful—the awful whistling belonging to the man who has taken me. Each one of his footsteps has me trembling with fear, and as they draw closer his whistling intensifies.

Warm liquid runs down the insides of my legs alerting me to the fact that I've just wet myself. I have to stay still. *Stay still Morgan*, runs through my mind. I need for him to believe I'm dead so he leaves and I can get away. I take one large inhale and hold my breath. It's all I can do, and I hope to god I can hold it in long enough.

He kicks my left foot. How I don't tense is a miracle. I somehow manage to remain limp. "Oh, don't tell me the game is already over?" There's disappointment in his tone.

This just makes me blood-boilingly angry. How can a person be this cruel?

"I'd say it was a nice shot from a car, wouldn't you?" he taunts me. A kick follows to my upper thigh, and it has my lips parting wide, yet no sound exits. "How I love a moving target." He laughs. It's a laugh belonging to the devil himself. Only pure evil could laugh like this. "Red, oh Red," he sings.

The eeriness of this keeps me in my frozen state, lifeless against the rough rocks. If I could stop my chest from rising and falling, I would. It's an impossible task, and I inhale a big breath.

"Ladies and gentleman, there we go—she lives!" he announces, just as one would when addressing a packed stadium of fans. This announcement destroys me, along with his merciless laughter, which travels with the blood pumping through my veins.

"Just kill me already," I whisper.

"Well, that wouldn't be fun now, would it? The game has only just begun. I'd hate for it to end so soon." He speaks with such calmness, it makes me want to lash out at him with everything I have. But sadly, I've nothing left in my tank; there isn't even a reserve to tap into. I have no fight. No strength. I'm done.

"That was pretty clever, Morgan. I must say, I've never had any of my women choose the route you did before. Maybe you're smarter than I'd initially given you credit for ... bravo," he congratulates me. The sound of his hands clapping echoes around us.

I hate this obnoxious man.

He clears his throat. "The only problem, Morgan, is you forgot I was watching you. I've always been watching you."

My face is still flush to the ground as he kneels beside me. A distinctive odour––his foul body, mixed with cheap musty cologne—rushes through my senses. If I could spit in his face, I would, but this act would require me to move my head, and the thought of trying to accomplish such a task is too much to bear.

"What am I going to do with you, Red?" he mutters, as his breath coats my sensitive skin, only intensifying my pain. He tuts over and over. "I think you were the best choice for number thirteen. I selected well. Yes, I will savour every bit of this."

My breath snags in my throat and threatens to stay trapped in limbo for all eternity. I wish it would, so I could suffocate on the very thing that began my life.

"How should you be punished? Hmmm ..."

I don't know why, but I can't hold myself back from provoking him, and as the words form on my tongue and croak from my mouth, my mind screams *BIG MISTAKE*. "You should know the answer, you pig." I clear my throat. "After all, it's your"— I clear my throat once more — "messed up game." I'm becoming dizzy, or is it woozy? "Unprepared, are we?"

Why Morgan? Why say such a thing?

A stinging sensation rips through my arse and scorches through the nerve endings attached to my spine. He's crushing my chest ... he's fucking crushing my chest. Pressure is being applied forcefully between my shoulder blades. It feels as if his knee is pressing harder into me as every second ticks over.

"Say that to me now, you bitch," he jeers.

But I can't, because I can't inhale even one breath.

"Cat got your tongue, Red?" he says.

I struggle to draw air as I open my mouth wide. I'm suffocating. My face is boiling hot as it pools with blood, blood he's restricting from visiting the vital organs dependant on its supply. My heart is working overtime trying to pump, but failing miserably. Pressure builds behind my eyeballs and it's a hellish burn that accompanies it. This is it. I'm going to die.

"Fuck you," I mouth.

Chapter Eleven

Reid

Why? It's a word constantly plaguing me. Why is this happening? Why am I here in this station instead of out there looking for Morgan? Why are these fuckwits wasting their time asking me so many bloody pointless fucking questions?

"You do realise you're wasting valuable time in finding Morgan, don't you?" I hiss, as my anger transforms into fury. "Why am I here? Why are you here with me instead of out there doing your jobs, hey?" I yell with full force, standing from the chair and pacing back and forward. "I didn't *kill* my wife," I proclaim, before I even realise I've said it out loud. *Good job, Reid. Now they will think you're guilty, you dick!*

West stands, and with a tone as smooth as butter, he distracts me from my thoughts. "Reid, sit down. Nobody said you did anything." A sparkle appears momentarily in his eye.

Did he want me to say that? Is this a test?

"This is all normal procedure. Officers are out looking for Morgan as we speak, and we promise you they are searching, but we need to start somewhere. You were the last person we know to have spoken to her, so the sooner we get through this, the better it will be. How about you sit down, okay?"

"I'll stand if it's okay with you?"

West shrugs. "Reid, what happened next?"

"Well, I showered, and when I got out I thought Morgan had come home, but it was Brax getting a drink. I watched the clock tick over, and I knew then something was really wrong. I called triple zero." Exhaustion begins to slow my speech.

"Right. So you have not spoken with your wife since around seven p.m?"

"No." I'm deflated.

"Is there a reason you waited before trying to contact her?"

I shake my head as this one question repeats on a loop through my mind. *Because I'm a terrible husband who's selfish*, is what I want to tell him, but I say nothing and drop my head into my hands. Tears build, threatening to spill. I try with all my might to rein them back, but I can't, and without my permission they start to fall. With a tear-soaked face, I whisper, "I love my wife. I love her. I would never hurt Morgan. Please, you need to find her. Please."

Chapter Twelve

Morgan

He bellows a ferocious laugh. I detest the sound. It sends my body into distress at the thought it will be the last thing I hear before I die. I try to close my eyes, but they won't co-operate due to the pressure increasing behind them as they attempt to pop from their sockets. His knee rises and the overwhelming compression lifts as a result, but my heart pains. My head becomes lighter and my sight hazy.

I'm dying.

His laughter stops as my fuzzy head considers its impending shutdown.

"Morgan," his tone eerily calm, "if you pass out, I'll slit your throat."

Hot stagnant air rushes down my ear canal from

his breathy threat, his body pressed firmly against mine.

Trepidation crawls like spiders throughout my veins. These antagonising words activate the needed hammering of my heart.

"There we go … Welcome back." He chuckles, as I gasp with full dramatics and then cough and splutter uncontrollably.

When he rolls me over onto my back, my chest rises and falls in slow motion as my raw and whipped skin is forcefully pushed into the ground. The bones sheltering my heart feel as if they're crushed, and every breath hurts, causing me to wince from the pain. My blurry sight is clearing and when my eyes begin to focus I realise the face of the man who has captured me is yet to reveal itself because it's covered by a black ski mask. All I can see are azure blue eyes and lips sculpted by the devil himself. *How can someone with such beautiful eyes be so God damn evil?*

His hand runs upwards from my knee, travelling along my inner thigh before diverting through the split in my skirt that the previous fall created.

The breath I not long claimed, launches in my throat as he moves higher and higher up my leg. Squeezing my thighs tightly together in protection, a moan of terror escapes my quivering lips. "Please don't …Please, no."

His haunting laugh only terrifies me further as his hand continues to skim along my skin.

"Please no. Don't do this. Not this." I beg, closing my

eyes momentarily.

He groans, and when my lashes flicker open, I'm greeted by a look of lust. His tongue slides slowly along his lower lip, and I tremble.

"Please, please don't." My final plea seems to fall on deaf ears, and it's too much to continue witnessing.

He begins to laugh. "Open your eyes, Morgan."

"I don't want to," I reply with a trembling voice.

"Now, Morgan," he demands, his hand stopping against my groin. Five fingers dig into my skin with painful pressure. I can't watch him while he violates me in the most physical of ways, but I'm forced to obey him, and I open my horror-filled eyes just as he bends his head in close to mine.

"Don't worry, Red. I'm not interested in you like that." Spittle resides on my cheek. "I just thoroughly enjoy watching you squirm. It's payback for what you've done."

What did I do?

His hand runs down my leg stopping exactly where he started, above my knee. "Your skin is very soft ... It's truly beautiful. I will enjoy slicing it from your flesh when you lose my game."

I gasp at his psychotic statement and my flesh ripples in fear. He's quick to stand upright, while my body lies there shaking on the ground from the prodigious amount of fright I feel.

"Get up, Red," he snarls.

I try to peel my back from the ground, but it won't budge. My eyes grow wide as panic increases. *Get the fuck up, body*! It won't comply and continues to lie heaped and useless on the ground.

"Morgan, I will only say this once more. Get off the fucking ground," he yells, before producing a large polished hunting knife in front of my eyes.

The knife does exactly what I need it to do. My brain registers the urgency of the situation and sends the crucial messages to start my limbs moving. Slowly, the broken vessel carrying my soul rises from the ground. The heels of my stilettos are no more when two cracking sounds alert me to their breakage, and I stumble, before I fling each foot in desperation to remove the hanging pegs. It takes no time to send them flying and slanted covers meet the earth in their place.

His dead-cold glare inspects my maltreated body. A finger is placed below my chin, and with gentle care he tilts my head back and his eyes meet my engorged lips.

"I can't see why anyone would want to kiss your lying mouth. If you promise love, you should keep your promise." Spit follows, landing on my nose. My head is left to drop by the sudden absence of his hold, and his five fingers spring open, then swing backward before flying toward me, connecting with my cheek with an angered force. I hear ringing and then a scorching sting when the slap fills my senses. I cry out loud, cradling my cheek in my skinned palms.

"Look at me, Morgan."

I do, through narrowed eyes.

He lunges forward and whispers, "*Boo!* Run now, if you want to live to see tomorrow," before he throws the backpack at my chest.

Slinging the bag over my shoulder, I shift on the spot, turning and stumbling towards bushland. I've no idea how my body is completing such a task, but it is, and I'm getting away from him. A cackle of laughter comes from behind me, and I sense each footstep as he takes chase.

He's behind you! Run faster!

I whimper as stabbing pains course throughout my limbs, and my breathing becomes rapid as my crushed chest expands, regardless of the agony it creates. The footsteps hitting rough terrain behind me suddenly stop and are soon replaced with a drawn-out whistle. Peeking over my shoulder, I catch his retreat and see only the back of him moving farther and farther away from me.

I don't stop running. Instead, I secure an awkwardly shaped overhanging branch to aim for in my sights and run even faster. Stretching my shuddering hand, I take a hold of the awkward branch I made my mission to touch, and shiver as I shift my eyes in the direction of what is awaiting me. The combination of high and low tones coming from within the haunting bushland are chilling, and for a split second I try to convince myself to turn around and give the track back out of here another go. Only problem with this is the arsehole's silhouette is still visible in the distance. He will make sure I do as I'm told this time, I've no doubt.

"Okay, Morgan, you can do this," I mutter, over and over and over through clenched teeth. No matter how many times I tell myself it's possible to survive, I remain still, staring into the unknown.

My breathing is fierce, and my calf muscles burn. "I can't do this," I whimper as my teeth start chattering to a crazed beat. I'm not cold, anymore, in fact, more like overheated, but every part of my body moves uncontrollably now.

Tears begin to fall as I try to scream, "GO!" to myself. I'm not sure if it's because I make no noise, or if it's the paralysing fear taking control, but I don't move my feet at all.

BANG! BANG! BANG!

Three loud gunshots ring out into the night sky, and within seconds I'm no longer grasping onto the awkwardly shaped branch. Instead, I stumble and sob my way through the beginning of a game with no rules.

Muddy earth pulls my legs down. My head bobs and twists as it tries to gauge which way to go. The storm achieved one goal tonight—drenching a bone-dry environment. For the last week, Queensland has endured a scorching heatwave, and although right now the wind carries a slight chill, come morning I know I'm going to be facing a roasting sun and unbearable humidity ... well, that's if I even see the morning. Shifting to the right, has sticks scratching at my arms and the more I pull away from them the deeper they burrow into my flesh. With no real lighting, I fight. I have to fight.

The backpack slung over my shoulder falls to my front, and without thought I fumble until I've caught it with the very tip to my fingers.

Why can't I stop shaking?

The zip is difficult to jerk open, but I persevere and it complies.

Where is the torch?

My touch is the only sense I can use to locate it. I know the torch is in here, yet I can't find it. "Come on," I groan, unable to move freely.

Finally, with a loud grumble travelling the length of my throat, I grasp the torch securely with a curled fist and swiftly press the button in its end. A weak stream of light offers an opening to a trail as I continue struggling against whatever the hell I've managed to get caught up in. Pushing my body forwards, I twinge from a sharp object poking into my side. "What the fuck is this?" Throwing the bag to the ground, I place the torch between my teeth and clamp down. Using each hand, I violently rip away the foliage and with every muffled growl I find myself releasing through my teeth, I grow more desperate. *Please, let go of me.* Another jab below my armpit has my temper escalating, "Aaaarrrrrrhhhh." *Is it thorns or spikes?* One roar bursts my mouth wide, and a forceful throw of my limbs has me stumbling and falling onto my knees. *I'm freed!*

I puff widely, yet cry hysterically. How did I

manage to get caught up in this? My hands begin sinking, and before long mud folds in on itself, wrapping and then compacting around my arms. The sensation of being trapped again has me springing in a single leap skyward.

"I want to go home," I yell.

Where is the torch?

Left, right, left again I move, before circling frantically. I catch a thin slither of light out of the corner of my eye and halt on the spot, only to jump from a pin prink to my bare foot. My slanted coverings completely removed. "Help! Help Me!" I'm not sure why I wail this so loudly, but I do.

The sound of a branch snapping has me pedalling backwards away from the torch I planned to take back into my possession. *What was that?* I move quickly, and although I know I'm leaving the bag with my only supplies, fear shoots my legs forward at breakneck speed.

It's not a gentle shove launching me back to the ground. It's a punch aimed between my shoulder blades.

Rolling my head followed by my body has me coughing and then spitting. I can't see. Madly, I stroke my hands up and down my face, trying to remove mud.

"Who's afraid of the big bad wolf?" It's whispered in song. "Red. Is." A chuckle dances around me, and then there's whistling. His eerie whistle.

"Why are you doing this to me?" I choke out.

"Why?"

"Who's afraid of the big bad wolf?" he repeats in song. "Morgan Banks is."

I cry.

His laugh haunts me. He's a pitiless man. He's my worst nightmare. He's my one fear.

Chapter Thirteen

Reid

Back and forth … they ask the same question, I give the same answer. We dance this tango over and over, and with every passing minute, my heart dies a little bit more. I've no idea what time it is. I've no idea where Morgan is. I've no idea what happens from here. All I know is I'm stuck in a room with these two dickheads who I wish to strangle so I can get the fuck out of here. I'm barely keeping control of the anger bubbling like lava in the pit of my stomach, threatening to explode from a pissed-off spout at any given moment. *Hold your tongue, Reid.*

"Reid. Let's go over this one more time," West says, before Gleaton finally spreads his pressed lips and repeats the same words, "Reid, let's go over this again, one more time."

"Really? You've something to say now?" I spit at Gleaton before thumping my fist hard on the table. Neither of them flinch. "What are we doing here? Please, help me find my wife. Just help me find my wife." Dropping my head to the table, I moan––it's a helpless sound as I will somebody to hear my pleas.

"Reid. I understand your worry ..." Gleaton starts, his voice controlled and pitched with authority.

One breath, two breaths rattle my airway as I attempt to bury my pain. Breathing exercises don't work. Less than a second later, I'm on my feet with my hands placed flat to the table, and my body bent over it. "You understand shit. Has your wife gone missing? Well, has she?"

"No." Gleaton throws his head back as his eyes widen.

"Don't even pretend to understand this. Don't even try to tell me how I feel. Just do me a fucking favour and get me the hell out of this room so I can search for her. Can you just do this for me?" The grinding of my teeth alerts me to my tensed jaw. Pushing myself off the table, I roll my fingers beside my ear, trying to remove the pressure. "Come on!" I yell before kicking at the bolted in chair.

I'm losing it.

"Get the man a drink," West says to Gleaton as I take refuge against a wall with my back turned to the both of them.

"You don't understand. She's my tiny dancer. Morgan is my tiny dancer. I'm responsible for keeping her safe. I'm responsible for protecting her fragility. I'm responsible for calming her wild side. I'm the lead and she's my ..." I can't continue. So, I breathe. I breathe long, drawn-out breaths.

"Go on." Gleaton keeps his tone low and soft.

I take a moment to close my eyes and envision Morgan in the red dress she was wearing the day we met. She looked like a rose in full bloom as she twirled and then proceeded to walk backwards in front of me so I could see her face as she continued talking. God, she is stunning.

"Go on," Gleaton repeats.

I'm not walking with Morgan in the red dress right now. I'm fighting to find Morgan from an interview room at our local precinct.

After a more delayed inhale, I'm ready to continue. "When we met, I could ascertain how graceful Morgan was, you know? Her touch, her walk, her movements ... She was an angelic and tiny ballerina, so delicate and fine-featured. I was drawn to her. I loved her immediately." My shoulders droop as I let the memory steal me. "She has grown tough and resilient throughout the years. She birthed our children. She's endured pain, loss, heartache. But when I close my eyes and see Morgan right now, the only image my mind is allowing of her is this breakable porcelain ballerina. Tell me where my wife is. Can you at least tell me she won't be suffering?"

"No." It's almost a breathless reply from West. "I'll get you a drink, Reid."

"I don't want a drink," I whisper helplessly.

"We're nearly finished our questioning. How about you sit down?"

"Just ask the fucking questions," I growl. My anger returns with full force.

I'm not sure how many times they make me recount what happened tonight, but it's a shitload. I swear in this time they've not only learnt my shirt size but everything I've competed in, listened to, or watched in my life. It's fucking ridiculous. Slumping back into the chair, I have the urge to claim a white flag and wave it in retreat. I cannot take a minute more of this.

Maybe the detectives see a change in my demeanour, or maybe they too hit a level of exhaustion, because suddenly the questioning stops, and the room grows quieter until it's completely still. I'm alone in here.

I lay my head to the table once more and close my eyes, picturing Morgan this morning, her rush to leave due to running late. The sounds of her heels meeting flooring as she scurried from one location to the next. The running of her hands down her sides as she straightened her clothes ... She looked beautiful, even though there was no doubt she was flustered. After a final kiss to the children's cheeks before she wished them a good day and a subtle wave in my direction, she opened the door leading to the garage. She didn't smile; in fact, she couldn't have been more disinterested in me. Why didn't I march to her and take her in my arms, kissing her deeply like I used to? Why didn't I tell her I loved her?

I can hear myself breathing and with each breath sound, I try to hold on to this lasting image of Morgan.

Are we truly broken?

I studied her face this morning and the stressed nature in which she looked at me as she wrapped her fingers around the door handle spelled out her unhappiness. Her love and delightful disposition on life had been all but ripped away.

I'm breaking her heart. I know I am. Why can't she see I'm still me? The man she fell in love with?

Running my eyes over her blouse and down her pencil skirt, I didn't admire her, I turned my eyes away. *Was I being as cold and withdrawn as she was?*

Before long, I find myself trying to change the circumstances of the morning. I try to play out the scenario in a way it should have taken place. I'd wake up to find Morgan beside me and instinctively reach out to cradle her head to my chest. Instead of climbing out of bed and abandoning her without a touch, I should have smelled her hair whilst whispering, "I love you," until her eyes fluttered open. When did I stop doing this?

"Reid." My name is spoken with such distance at first, I ignore the sound and keep running images of Morgan through my mind.

"Mr Banks." The voice grows louder.

"Reid. Are you okay?" Another tone is now registering.

"Huh," I mumble.

"Reid, we need to take your shoes. Can you put them in this bag please?"

"Shoes?" I'm confused.

"Your shoes—put them in this bag. They will be sent off for testing."

Lifting my head, I'm greeted by misty grey-blue eyes and register I'm still with these fucking officers of the law and they've returned to the room.

"Sure," I murmur before reaching down and slipping the joggers from each foot. With no socks underneath, my feet instantly chill from the cold hard floor, and with pure hatred pulsing through my veins, I look to West and say, "Do you want my fucking clothes too?"

Chapter Fourteen

Morgan

Dirt and mud have stolen my vision. I wipe my eyes savagely, trying to return my sight. Each of my knees bear my weight, and I can no longer hear him. Where did he go?

Running is the only way out. It's the only way to find safety, but I'm so frightened, and although my mind screams at me to complete this necessary act of running, my body renders itself helpless and stays positioned as if I'm a carved statue placed in a museum on display.

"Are you forgetting something?" He's taunting me.

Where is he?

The sudden impact to my cheek doesn't cause me to flinch even though pain radiates to my skull.

"Were you looking for that?"

"What do you want from me?" My voice shakes.

"I want you to suffer, you bitch, just as you've caused me to suffer."

I pant, from this confession.

"Are you suffering, Morgan?"

"Yes." It's an urgent reply.

"It's not nice to suffer, is it?"

"No."

I jerk suddenly from a smooth stroking of my head. He runs his hand as if he is patting a chained and obedient dog––I hate it.

"There, there. Everything is going to be okay." He's condescending.

I whimper.

"Here you go. Take it."

I can't see what he is referring to at first, but then there is a dim light which grows brighter until it has me squinting. He shines it directly into the narrow slits my eyelids create.

"You are such a horrible person, Morgan. A fucking beast." He pauses. "Open your mouth."

I hesitate. I don't want to open my mouth.

"If you don't open it, I'll open it for you." He brushes his fingers against my cheek. "Open your mouth," he breathes.

I do and with its wide birth, I involuntarily release a single puffed exhale.

"Here, I'm helping you. You wanted help now, didn't you? I'm going to fulfil your need." As he speaks,

I feel a cylindrical object press between my teeth before continuing farther into my mouth. It's cold and causes me to gag, not once, but twice as it hits the back of my throat. "Clamp your teeth shut."

I do without hesitation.

Warm air washes over my earlobe, and I shiver from the sensation.

"Roses are red, violets are blue, let's play a game where I hunt you," he whispers. His haunting laugh follows, and I grimace, trying to rein in my need to cry.

Forced breathing through my nose seems to control my gag reflex, and with a little work from my tongue, I manage to slide the torch away from my palatine uvula and slow my rapid huffs.

Without warning, he takes my left wrist and gently slides what I believe to be his hand up the entire length of my arm. He repeats the same thing on the other side, and the breathing I just managed to take in slightly becomes loud nasal puffing once more. Complete silence is my reality when my nose is pinched tight, and I'm forced to flare my cheeks and claim oxygen this way.

"Don't be frightened, Morgan. Relax. We have so many more things to share together." And with these words he releases his pinched grip and I try to be quieter even though I'm panicking.

"One," he says calmly. "Two." It's quick to follow. "Red, get the fuck off the ground and hightail it out of here or I'm going to shove that torch down your fucking neck."

I jump before falling forward. I can't move for there is something hanging from my front. *The bag. He was giving me back the bag.*

"Three," he barks, and without another second passing, I crawl, until I find my feet and scurry, removing the torch from my mouth as I run aimlessly.

I'm knocked. I fall. I get back up, only to be knocked down again, and as I continuously find myself in this position, I can't help but think I'm in a pinball machine being flung around for another's entertainment.

There's no air.

I crunch over, my torso folded completely in half as I try to suck oxygen into my lungs ... but it's not working. Slowly, I fall in what seems to be slow motion until I'm sitting down on the ground.

"Just let me go," I mouth, as my eyes follow the stream of light coming from the torch and shining off to my right.

Rustling has my ears pricked, and whistling has my heart hammering at a rapid pace once more. *Holy fuck!* With one leap, I'm upright. How I'm able to accomplish this so quickly in my current condition is beyond me, but I am, and blindly, I try to locate the direction from which he is coming. He's nowhere, only a noise riding on the breeze, and this observation has me taking a few steps one way, before changing direction in a zig-zag pattern. I have no idea which way to go from here. I have no idea where I am.

The whistling that had me back on my feet is brief and I can no longer hear it, but I know he's here somewhere ... stalking me like wounded prey. Slowly and wearily, I place one foot in front of the other. Every few steps I bump into an object and with sluggish reflexes, I shift the torchlight in the direction of the object I've bumped into. My processing abilities have been rendered useless, because I have no clue what anything surrounding me is. Everything seems blurred.

The farther I find myself moving, the more alert I become, and after God knows how long, I see a combination of trees towering above me. They are so high, and they make the snippets of blackened sky seem as if it's a very long way away. Pointing my chin skywards, I locate an outer slither of the pink moon I saw earlier, and I'm compelled to walk towards it. With baby steps, I follow, trying not to divert my eyes for too long in fear I'll lose sight of it. I'm shuffling when a snapping of a branch stops me dead in my tracks.

"I win." He chuckles, before soft fabric is slipped over my head and pressure immediately applied to my throat. "To breathe is to live. To live is to be free. You will never see your freedom, Morgan, because your past can never be erased."

Chapter Fifteen

Morgan

Drip, drip, drip.

The sound of water droplets that ting against metal, have my eyelashes fluttering open as I lay outstretched on my back. The sound of a newborn infant crying, dances around my throbbing head.

Where am I? Whose baby is that?

"It's a boy. Morgan, we have a son, I have a son." Reid is sobbing and laughing at the same time.

"Reid," I choke out through a thick throat as I stare at a blurred white panel.

"Mummy, mummy, did you see me twirl?" Aleeha's happiness echoes around me.

"I think you are the prettiest ballerina." I can hear my voice, but I'm not speaking.

Aleeha laughs. It's truly the sweetest sound.

"Mum, where are you? Why did you leave us?"

"Brax," I breathe.

"Why would you hurt us like this?" His voice trembles with heartbreak.

"I didn't leave you." I'm desperate as I bolt into an upright position, clasping my hands momentarily on either side of my head, hoping to limit the constant thrumming plaguing me.

"I know what you did, Morgan. I thought you loved me?" Reid's words are laced with disgust.

"Reid. I do. I love you. What did I do?" I'm confused as my eyes dart from left to right. My sight remains blurred and my surroundings flash by as if I'm in a car hurtling through a dark tunnel with limited lighting.

There's silence.

Drip, drip, drip.

I blink furiously as I hunch my body into a tight ball and wrap my arms around my knees. I'm frightened. My body is aching all over, and I'm nauseous.

I hear a newborn infant crying, and this sound causes my heart to sprint and my tears to spill.

"We have our girl, Morgan. She's beautiful." I can hear the pride in Reid's shaking voice, just as I did on the day of our daughter's birth. Today is not that day. I'm not sure what is happening to me, but I have enough sense to know ten years have passed since her arrival into this world. I shiver as my breathing becomes rapid. "Help me," I whisper, fearing for my own sanity.

The room grows quiet again, apart from the sound of my heartbeat pounding in my ears, and a whistling noise coming from my nose as I take quick and short breaths. A flicker of light grows brighter, and with its presence, my fuzzy vision becomes slightly clearer.

"Hello," I shudder.

There's no reply.

Rectangular concrete blocks, the colour of a silver bullet, hold me in a stare. I watch as they zoom in and out with my strained sight. *Where am I?*

Drip, drip, drip.

I rotate my head over my shoulder and stop when I locate a metal sink with a rusty tap. Every drop of clear water leaking from the spout has me hypnotised. I'm thirsty, so very thirsty that I run my tongue over my bottom lip and swing my legs off what I now realise is a navy stretcher, but I stop myself midway and place my feet firmly back from where I removed them.

I'm scared.

Scanning the concrete floor, I settle my vision on four thick wooden legs. I swallow hard through my dry throat as I close my eyes and reopen them only after I tilt my chin slightly upwards. *A table.* It's not bare, in fact it looks cluttered.

"I see the drugs have worn off." His voice is calm. The voice of *my captor.*

I close my eyes once more.

"Red, welcome to your room. You won't be here long, but we have work to do before we get back to our game."

"I want to go home," I whisper.

"Well I want to fucking kill you, but I have to be patient, so how about we focus on one thing at a time?"

"Why?" I cry out hoarse.

He laughs. "Look at me, Red. Go on. Can you see a wolf?"

Slowly, I fold back my eyelids and shift my head towards the sound of his voice. I'm halted by a projection screen taking up a large space, covering the concrete blocks at the foot of the bed. Azure blue eyes and full lips are the only features I can see of the man who has taken me, the one who proclaims himself to be the wolf, as his top half fills the screen. A black mask covers the remainder of his face, head and neck, and black clothing keeps his identity hidden.

"What did I do that could make you want to hurt me so bad?" I stare deep into his eyes, wondering how they can look so beautiful, yet be filled with a murderous hate.

"I don't want to hurt you, Red. I want to kill you." He throws back his head with his chuckle. When he regains his composure, he glares at me again through the screen. "But, it wouldn't be fun for me if we didn't play a little cat and mouse chase first."

"Please," I beg.

"Begging gets you nowhere, Red. You never heard the pleas of others, so why should I hear yours?" His tone is eerily calm, not ferocious like someone teeming with hate would normally react.

I gulp, hoping to swallow my fear. It doesn't work, because my fear is not only clawing up my airway, it's swirling in my stomach and filling my blood with each pulsation of my erratic heartbeat.

"Here's your instructions, Red. Listen carefully."

"Let me go home."

"Shut up," he barks. He's instantly angry, and it's as if someone flipped a switch and his previous composure is torn away from him.

I pinch my swollen lips tight together.

"You have one hour. The backpack I put together for you is sitting on the barrel beside the table."

Flicking my eyes from the screen I scan my surroundings until the metal barrel comes into view with the backpack sitting on top.

"Look at me." His words are delivered softly, yet there is no warmth in them — The wolf's heart is sculpted out of ice.

I take in his lips. They are large and shaped perfectly. They appear soft and welcoming. This causes me to tremble, because these lips are reminiscent of those my husband and his brother have been blessed with.

"Red ..." He wears a haunting smile. "You have one hour to write your goodbyes to your family. This is your only chance to leave a piece of you behind for them. Don't waste it."

I shake my head as I sob, "No, no, no ... Please. I can't. I won't."

"You will do it!" he snaps.

"No!" I yell. "I won't. Why are you doing this? Who are you?"

"Shut your fucking mouth or I will tear the lungs out of your body. Or should I stop your beating heart with my bare hands?" He smirks. "Red, I will not rest until you live through the torture that you yourself have created. It's you who made me who I am. It's your fault all those women died. Their blood is on your hands. Their deaths are stained to your conscience."

"I didn't do anything. I've never hurt anyone." My heart sprints faster as I drop my head.

"You've tortured people, Red. I guess we're no different, you and I ... we're made from the same cloth and all that shit." His laughter booms and my body trembles in response.

"Let me go home," I sob.

"This is your home. It houses your mistakes. Fuck! They were costly, huh?" He speaks casually, yet he's smug.

I don't reply. I can't. My tongue won't move to form the words. My throat has seized.

"Morgan Amelia Banks, you took something from me I can't get back, and now I'm taking something from you —your freedom — your life — your forever. Now fucking do as I say or it's game over, bitch."

I cry so hard my shoulders shake from the force, and my nose becomes instantly stuffy with mucus.

"Your one hour will start soon."

I glare at the Wolf through my tear soaked eyes and before I have a chance to speak another word, he's gone, and the screen becomes blank. I open my mouth wide and release a blood curdling scream, a scream that is arduous. My heart shatters into a million pieces. I don't want to say goodbye. I want to live.

Let me live.

The ground is cold beneath my soles when I find the strength to place them on the floor. I want to snatch them back from the chill, but I don't. I need to do as he instructed. I groan as I use my arms to push my body from the stretcher. My knees crack as I stand. My hip clunks loudly when I'm almost upright, and I grimace from the instant ache. I'm battered, broken and bruised.

Shuffling my feet, I slowly work my way towards the small desk. It's excessively littered with paper and books, and this keeps me moving. Maybe there's a clue in this mess.

"I, Reid, take thee, Morgan, to be my wife. To have and to hold, for better, for worse, in sickness and in health, till death do us part."

Reid's voice is loud, so loud I clutch my hands to my ears and squeeze my eyes tightly shut as I halt on the spot. Twisting my neck, I eye the projection screen and see my husband dressed in the same grey tailored suit he wore on the day we exchanged our vows and became husband and wife.

My arms go limp and drop to my sides when I gasp

at the sight of myself adorned in my mother's fishtail wedding dress. I can see the pond with the white lily pads bobbing up and down in front of us, and I can also see my family and friends. I try to reach out my arms. I want to touch them, hold them. But my arms won't budge because they're as heavy as lead.

"Morgan Amelia Cuttings, do you promise to cherish, Reid Elis Banks? Support him, love him unconditionally and without conviction for the remainder of your life?"

Dave Jury, a close friend of my father, and celebrant, speaks these words through a small microphone attached to a headset. My mind screams for him to sense my trouble, and to get my Dad and Reid to come help me.

"I do." I smile as Reid slides a thin gold band down my finger.

Flashing. Lots of flashing has me slowly lowering to the floor and as my bottom meets the concrete, I yelp from a sharp pain shooting up my spine.

"Tinkle, tinkle, ittle tar. How'd I nunder what dew are. Tup adove da world toe high, ike a diamond in da sty ..."

Aleeha is so tiny as she twirls in her black glitter tutu and she sings. Reid is sitting on the lounge chair clapping along whilst a much younger Brax sits crossed legged on the floor beside her, banging two wooden spoons on top of an overturned saucepan.

"My babies. My little babies," I cry out, wrapping my arms around my chest attempting to shelter my breaking heart.

"Daddy. Mummy. I love it. It's just what I wanted. This is the best birthday ever."

Brax is only six years old as he wears his ninja turtle pyjamas and climbs onto a new bike with a big blue bow stuck to its front.

Tucking my head into my arms, I rock. My heartache increases further as I realise this man has my home movies. He's been in my house and invaded my privacy, my life. How else would he have these?

"Oh Red. So many memories. You better get off the floor and write those letters or you're going to leave the people you were supposed to love and protect with fucking nothing. What a terrible mother that would make you."

I dry wretch the moment I see the ski mask and those eyes.

Photographs begin shooting across the screen drowning out the image of the Wolf, until he's completely gone. Picture upon picture continue to layer on top of each other, and they play out my life in snapshots. As much as I want to look away right now, I can't, because I can't leave my family. I can't turn my back on them, not now, not ever. I have to fight.

Chapter Sixteen

Reid

"Can I go now?" My voice vibrates. I'm mad, I'm so mad I'm trembling.

"Yes." West nods.

Knock. Knock. Knock.

"Come in," Gleaton calls.

Maloney stands in the doorway. A clear plastic bag with 'evidence' written in yellow lettering on the front, hangs from his scrunched hand. "I have Reid's belongings," he says in a low tone.

I peer at the silver watch wrapped around his wrist and then shift my eyes upwards taking in his thinned pulled lips. I'm focused on every movement his mouth makes when he says, "Your wallet and phone, Reid."

"Constable Maloney, thank you." West steps

towards him and then outstretches his hand until he claims the bag for himself.

"Do they know where Morgan is?" I find myself holding my breath in wait of a response.

Maloney shakes his head.

"That will be all Constable Maloney," West continues, placing his hand to Maloney's shoulder whilst simultaneously ushering him out. The door closes without delay. "Let's get your fingerprints taken, and after I'll take you home." West moves in my direction, the bag swinging from his pinched fingers.

I nod as I take my possessions from him. "Thank you." My voice is barely audible.

The seal makes no sound as I tear it open. I place my phone into my palm and glance at the screen, *eleven missed calls*, and they've all been made from the one number, my home line. *John and Shirley. Shit!*

"I need to call home first." My voice rattles.

West nods.

My hands are shaking as I press my fingertip against the last missed call recorded in my phone's log, and the line connects. Gleaton who is exiting the room, catches the corner of my eye as I listen to the sound of each ring. "Pick up," I mutter.

"Hello. Banks residence, John speaking."

"John," I say, with a relieved tone. "John, are the kids okay?" I drop the bag still containing my wallet onto the table and proceed to rub my face in an attempt to remain composed.

"They're fine. Sleeping like angels. Reid, my boy,

where are you?" His voice is filled with worry.

"I'm at the cop shop. I'll be home soon. They found Morgan's car; it's not good. I think these idiots think I'm the prime suspect," I speak quietly, turning my back to West.

"Why would they think it was you? You wouldn't hurt a damn hair on that beautiful girl's head. These idiots are crazy if they are trying to pin this on you." After the night I've just had, I feel relieved to know someone can at least vouch for my innocence. "Reid, I'll organise a lawyer for you. Cops can be corrupted and can create their own versions of events. Exercise your right to remain silent and we'll organise a lawyer as soon as possible. I have someone in mind." His voice is writhing with distaste.

"No lawyer. I've complied and answered all their questions." I rotate two fingers on my left temple, trying to release the sudden onset headache ravaging my head. "I've nothing to hide, because I didn't do anything wrong."

"Reid."

"Yes John."

It's a long pause. "Something strange is happening here at the house."

"What do you mean strange?"

"The phone has rung five times throughout the last two hours. The first time Shirley answered it and there was only heavy breathing on the other end. I answered the next four times, and apart from a few growls and huffs, there was nothing, but I don't think it was Morgan. I think it was a man."

"A man?"

"Call it a hunch. It wasn't Morgan, boy. I'd know if it was our girl."

I'm stunned into silence.

"I tried everything to urge whoever it was to talk, but they never replied. I think it's important, boy. I've tried to contact you numerous times, but it just went to your voice mail.

My throat tenses. This is definitely important information and one he should have reported to the police. "Okay. John, don't answer the phone from here on out, promise me." My heart sinks; the ache that follows causes an unfamiliar tightness in my chest.

Morgan's been taken.

"I won't. I promise. Hurry home." There's definite dismay in his tone.

Whoever is calling has Morgan. I know it. "Just do nothing. Keep the kids safe for me."

"They're safe."

"See you soon, John. Don't answer the phone." Hanging up promptly, I twist on my bare heel to face West. His eyes question me immediately; there's no need for any words.

"Morgan ... shit ... fuck." My fist curls into a tight ball as I huff.

"Reid, what happened? You look like you've seen a ghost."

"Morgan's been kidnapped," I blurt out, with full intensity.

West stares hard. "What's happened?" His head cocks to the side. His expression remains firm.

"We have to go now. You need to get to my house. We need to leave right now. I'll fill you in, in the car." I snatch the bag from the table. "Let's go." I snap.

West takes the lead as we hurry back through the doors we entered after my arrival here.

"Roland. We're going," West says as we pass Gleaton who is standing by the front counter in reception already swinging the keys from his finger.

"Right." It's all Gleaton replies before he joins us.

Exiting the front doors of the police station at a pace faster than I could have hoped for, has the three of us entering the unmarked car I previously rode in. Once buckled in, I search the screen of my phone once more. Five a.m., so much time has passed.

"Banks residence." West is direct with his instruction, and Gleaton wastes no time pulling out from the curb. We're on the road before I can even blink. West swivels in his seat, and I wait until his eyes are peering over its top.

"Morgan's been taken."

"Reid, talk me through this."

"There's been phone calls made to my house. John said there was breathing and growling coming from the other end. He thinks it's a man calling, and so far, this has occurred five times.

"Since when?"

"The last two hours is what I was told." I'm breathing heavily. I can hear every breath I'm taking.

"The person who's calling won't say anything. John said he tried everything he could think of to get him to respond. It has to be linked to Morgan, right? What if they're waiting for me? Isn't that how kidnappings work?"

West stares at me, until his narrowed eyes suddenly widen. I know he believes I'm speaking the truth, because not a second after I think this, West shifts in his seat and leans forward flipping a switch. The sirens wail loudly. "Roland, get us there now."

With a sigh of relief I drop my shoulders and relax my tensed jaw. It doesn't last long, because my balls launch into my throat the moment we go flying around a corner at high speed.

The sirens are cut a few streets out from our house, even though we still travel at such a high speed the car bounces over the entrance of the driveway with tremendous force. When the car stops an inch from closed garage doors, I take one moment to breathe before leaping from the vehicle and racing up the front stairs. I don't get the chance to grab the door handle before it opens and Shirley appears. Her shawl is wrapped around her shoulders when she outstretches her arms. I don't know why I do it, but I run right into the gap this creates and find comfort in her embrace.

"Shirley," I whisper as one of her arms folds around my waist and the other lifts until her fingers stroke my hair.

"I know, Reid. I know. It's going to be okay. It'll be

okay. You must be exhausted," she says, releasing her grip and holding me at a distance. "Look at your eyes. They're swollen and bloodshot. Let me make you a coffee."

"The phone, Shirley. Where's the phone?" It's a breathless deliverance.

"Let's take these questions inside, Reid," West says, when he suddenly stands beside me.

The house is quiet. Too quiet. And with every step I take towards the light the kitchen provides, I become more unsettled. A dark cloud hovers above my head. A cloud as charcoal as the ones that accompanied the storm which ripped my life apart last night. Doom and gloom is what is left behind. This is my reality. My wife has been abducted.

I race to the cordless phone perched in its holder on the kitchen counter. I snatch it into my possession and hold the receiver in my tight grip. It doesn't ring, but there's a part of me hoping the moment I put it to my ear, whoever has been calling will talk. There's nothing but a ringtone when I work up the nerve to listen.

Call, you bastard.

"This world can be an awful place at times, Reid. It disgusts me. I know our Morgan and she's as tough as nails. She will come home, you believe my words." Shirley has her back to me as she holds the kettle under the running kitchen tap.

"She will," I reply, choking on my spit, which causes me to cough and splutter as I pass the receiver to West who's holding out his hand.

"Reid." Shirley turns.

I nod as I clear my throat. "I'm fine."

"Sit. You need to sit." Shirley encourages with an outstretched finger, indicating for me to choose a seat at the breakfast bar. I don't move a muscle.

"Do you have more than the one cordless?" West asks.

I nod. "The office. There's one in my office."

"Where's the office?"

"Down the hallway between the kitchen and Morgan's open library there." I point to the open area surrounded in darkness to my right. "Open the last door on the right-hand side."

"Okay." West stands close to Gleaton and mumbles something I can't decipher. It's clear it was instructions to retrieve the handset because Gleaton disappears down the hallway with haste.

"What happens now?" I can't be sure if I speak these words or I think them. West doesn't say a thing, so I assume I never spoke aloud. I'm caught off guard when West hands the receiver he's been holding to Gleaton who has returned as fast as he left. Everything seems so out of place. So wrong. Again, the detectives exchange mumbled words between each other, and I wish for my sake they'd speak clearly and open so I don't need to strain in trying to hear them.

A notepad drops to the kitchen bench with a soft thud, claiming my attention. West opens it wide and turns his eyes downwards. *Where did the notepad come from?* It's not one I recognise. "What happens now?"

West and Gleaton both shift their attention to me, neither say a word in response.

Just answer the question, dammit.

They don't. They continue their muffled whispers instead.

Shifting my eyesight to the unlit staircase, I'm hit with the realisation our children are up those stairs, in their rooms, with absolutely no knowledge of what has happened. Soon they'll awaken and find a horrible mess awaiting them, one I've not been able to fix. How do I tell them what's transpired? How do I take care of them and find Morgan at the same time?

Why is this happening to our family?

"I'm making you that coffee now. Two sugars, yes?" Shirley pauses. "Reid, the kids are fine. I promise. They're still sleeping. John is up there."

I nod. "Two," is all I manage to say.

"Do you two detectives want a coffee while I'm making some?" Shirley continues.

I snap my head towards Gleaton and West.

"No, thank you Mrs ...?" West pauses. I believe he's waiting for Shirley to fill in the blank.

"Mrs Peters, and you be sure to remember that. I don't particularly like being questioned by police, I'll have you know."

West writes in the note pad. "Mrs Peters, thank you. It's a no on the coffee."

I hear footsteps coming down the staircase. I listen

intently for the children, then twist my neck in the direction of the noise. John appears and I follow him as he strides towards me. The second moment of relief I've experienced comes from seeing John. I'm not dealing with this alone, because he's here with me, and there's no mistaking how much of a loyal friend he is to our family. His hand pats my shoulder when he reaches my side, and my relief all but vanishes by the time we make eye contact. I'm not alone in my worry, fear and heartache, but Morgan could be and I can't seem to shake this thought.

"Reid, it's good to have you home." John seems to look over my shoulder. "Who do we have here then?" He continues past me and holds out his hand. "Detective ...?" he waits for a reply.

"West ... Astin West, and this is Detective Roland Gleaton."

Immediately John says, "I hope you have leads on where Morgan is?"

"We are taking this situation very seriously." I watch as West scans his eyes up and down John. "Mr Peters?" he asks.

"Yes, it's Peters, but just call me John. Now, does Reid need a lawyer? If you are trying to pin whatever's happened on him, you're sadly mistaken." John has no fear of their presence and is acting like the dad any child would need in a difficult situation.

My mind darts straight to thoughts of my own parents and then Morgan's. The thought of having to call them, along with my brother, makes my stomach churn. *How do I tell them something like this?* I cup my hands around my mouth and begin to rock back and forth on my heels. I need to find out what happens next.

"Not at the moment, John, he doesn't need a lawyer at the moment."

"He won't be needing one at all. I'm telling you right now, Reid has nothing to do with Morgan's disappearance. We have been their neighbours since before they brought their beautiful boy into this world and their love for each other is the real deal. You would be mindful to remember that." John's words spit out with force and sincerity.

West nods. "Mr Peters. I'm sorry, John, we will keep this in mind throughout our investigation."

"Yes, you will." John hitches his upper lip as he passes West, and then Gleaton, whom I see place one of the handsets he's been holding back onto its base, and the other he lays against the bench beside it. "There's my bride," John says loudly. "Can I get a cup of coffee, my love?" He moves towards Shirley.

Shirley delivers a smile in response, and it's one that could light up the room. This automatically has me envisioning Morgan and the way she used to be so smitten whenever I'd enter the kitchen as she made breakfast. I'd wrap my arms around her waist, kissing her neck, and then I'd wish her a good morning. Why did I stop doing this?

When did we lose our way?

When did we forget to treasure each other?

God, I miss her. I want her here, I need to say sorry. I want to trace kisses up her neck and across her cheeks. I want to wrap her in my arms and never let her go, ever.

"Reid let me fetch you something to eat, breakfast, anything you would like?" Shirley's sweet gaze seems to be begging me to say yes.

"No thanks," I sigh, pulling one of the four stools out from under the breakfast bar where I finally sit.

A freshly brewed cup of coffee is placed in front of me. "Well, drink this and we will think about food again soon." I receive a sad smile from Shirley, and I instantly try to tell myself that this is a nightmare I'm going to wake up from soon and that everything will be okay. The only problem is, this situation feels far too real to be that of a bad dream. I wish it was. I wish I could wake up, race down the stairs and gather Morgan in my arms, confessing my love for her. No more tension, no more woe is me. I'd tell her I'm proud of her and I love her. I need a chance to do this. I need her to come home so I can.

"John, I'd like to ask you a few questions, if I can?" West is oddly abrupt.

"Let's get this over with." John is quick to reply, almost as if he expected West to ask this of him, right here, right now.

"How about we go over there?" West is pointing to the left and in the direction of the room on the opposite side of the staircase.

"That's a loungeroom," John says.

"Good. It will give us more privacy. It won't take long."

"Reid?" John looks to me.

"Just do whatever he wants, John."

"Okay. Let me grab my coffee first."

I've had a moment to shower and to change out of the blue cotton pants and T-shirt that West gave me to put on after they took my clothes at the station and threw them into an evidence bag. I wasn't surprised when Gleaton handed me another zip lock bag before coming upstairs to shower. His instructions: Put the clothes in it and seal it. I did as I was told. Co-operation is going to be the key to finding Morgan.

I slip on a pair of grey sweat pants and a white cotton T-shirt trying to be as quiet as I can, because the last thing I want is to be poking around in my drawers making noise that will stir the children. The evidence bag is scrunched in my hand as I tip-toe past the children's bedrooms and make my way back to the lower level, in the hope of seeing what John's expression is like after his private chat with West. I'm too late because John's already back in the kitchen with Shirley when I drop the bagged clothes on the bench and sit back on the stool I previously occupied.

There's talk all around me. West and Gleaton, John and Shirley ... I listen to bits and pieces of each conversation, well, until it becomes one muffled sound banded together and then I force myself to block them all out. I run my finger around the rim of my coffee mug over and over, and keep thinking about where Morgan could be. I picture every place we've ever travelled. I search my memory for each overgrown piece of land I know exists around these parts, every lake and river … there's so many of them. I'm on edge. I need to figure out how to find my wife. Where do I even start?

Knock, knock, knock.

I instantly startle and leap to my feet.

"Sit down, boy. I'll get the door." John takes charge and marches until he has the door thrown wide open. "More cops," he calls out.

Constable Maloney follows John in, and there are two other officers I've not seen before. Well, if I have, I can't recollect it.

"You three need to do a sweep of the lower level of the house. I want you to look for anything out of the ordinary," Gleaton says calmly.

"Right, boss," a tall lanky gentleman with bright orange hair responds.

"Is that necessary?" I'm not sure why they are searching the house. Morgan's not here.

"This is just routine, Reid." Gleaton says, sounding distracted.

The clock I watched tick over every minute last night, takes my attention; it's 6:45 a.m. It's been another hour and forty-five minutes since Morgan has been missing and my heart still has that god-awful aching sensation ripping through it. I find myself clutching my hands to my chest and praying the phone rings so this prick can ask for his ransom, and I can give him what he wants in exchange for Morgan's safe return ... then this will all be over. Why hasn't it rung yet? A stabbing pain penetrates my chest when I come to think of how very frightened Morgan would be if she's in the hands of someone truly evil. I'll find this asshole and slit his throat if he hurts a hair on her head — I'd kill for Morgan.

Ring, ring, ring.

I'm upright and panting. My throat constricts as my heart pumps with force. I'm instantly terrified by the sound of the phone ringing. I can't move.

"Answer it Reid, now!" West orders as his face appears right in front of me. "Move."

I do. I rush to the handset and take it into my grip. West is clutching the other handset, cupping his hand over the mouth piece. He points to the accept button. "Press it now," he mouths.

I do. "Reid Banks speaking." The words croak from my mouth.

"Good morning, Reid. How are you this morning?" The voice is robotic.

"I've had better," I say, in a tone absent of masculinity.

"Are you missing something? I think you might be missing something."

"Where is she?"

"Who?"

"Morgan."

"Oh, her."

He damn well knows who the fuck I'm talking about. "Just don't hurt her." I try not to sound panicked, but I fail.

"I'm glad you're home, Reid. I've been trying to reach you. It's rude not to answer your own phone. I guess you're lucky though. If you hadn't picked up on this attempt, I might have just slit your wife's pretty little throat. Don't leave the phone again. You hear me?"

"Yes. I'm here. I won't. Please, don't hurt her. I understand."

"She's fine. Don't worry. Right now, she's taking care of a little business and soon we'll play our game."

I listen intently, gulping as I swallow excessively. My balls have launched to the back of my throat and are hanging there in suspension... I'm fucking petrified by the word *game.*

"Reid, I really hope Morgan is much better at my game of life than she ever was when playing life with you." A small laugh follows before the phone goes dead.

"Fuuuuuuck!" I scream at the handset. "Where is she? Where's Morgan? What game?" Detective West takes the phone from my trembling hand and places it onto the bench beside the one he had.

"He's gone, Reid. You did a good job staying calm, well done." His fingers press in to my shoulder.

"Well done. Well done. Some psychopath has my fucking wife and I wasn't here to take his call earlier because of you arseholes." My words fire at him with toxic acrimony.

"Reid, we need to follow procedure. Everything is being done to help Morgan and you just need to trust us. This is another clue and it gives us more of an idea what we are dealing with."

"You're dealing with a fucking lunatic who has my wife ... he has my wife."

Chapter Seventeen

Morgan

Your life depends on you. Red, get up.

This thick black lettering holds my attention as I stare at the projection screen. He knows me. He knows what to say and do to seek a response. This must be someone I know well.

My ankles buckle when I try to stand, so I launch my arm out and stumble until my fingers clasp the edge of the table. The notebook from the backpack is perched on top of a pile of white papers. It's opened in half with a pen laid down its crease, a pen that doesn't disguise the torn edge of where the page I stole from it once was. I bare my teeth and snarl as I scrummage with desperation through the mess, knocking the notebook made for me and the pen provided to the ground. Every item I'd hoped were documents containing some form of information to assist me in figuring out who this creep is, are not. They're blank. The books strewn and buried amongst this clutter also contain empty pages. Why do this? What does this mean?

Inch by inch, I lower myself down, and then I'm sitting against the cold floor. Here I thought this disorder would hold a clue, but it's been created as a charade. Does he just like fucking with my head?

Beep. Beep. Beep.

I search for the sound. Bright red digits appear on a box above the projection screen. A box I hadn't noticed until it was lit. 1:00:00. *One hour.* It's a timer. *Fuck!*

59:56.

59:55.

59:54.

I turn on my side and run my hand across the smooth flooring, taking the pen in a pinched grip. I manage to slide the notebook to my side, using the tip of my pinkie finger. My right hand shakes as I look down at the simple pen and try to breathe through my anxiety. I gasp loudly. *What the fuck?* Rotating my wrist until my shredded and filthy palm is upright, has me staring in horror at my inner arm.

One

Two

Three

Four

Five.

These numbers are inked in bold red cursive letters to the middle of my washed and red sunburnt skin. I rub my fingers over the lettering in hopes of removing it, but I'm forced to stop by the burning sensation this creates. I'm tainted. He's branded me. When did he do these tattoos? How drugged was I?

I cry. I cry so hard, I slump at my waist. Daggers shoot up my spine as my forehead tucks into my stomach. "Fuck," I moan as I lengthen my posture and tip my chin so far back, that I'm focusing on the rectangular panels above me. "Help me. Somebody help me." I'm breathless.

Turning my eyes to the timer with a harsh flick of my head, I continue to sob.

49:33

I'm running out of time.

I scurry on my bottom to the stretcher and utilise it as a writing surface. I grimace as I tuck my legs below it and leer at the empty page now awaiting me.

Reid. I scribble on the first line.

Soft violin music plays softly out of nowhere. It's so distant, it feels as though it's being pushed by a gentle breeze past my face. It can't be though, because where I am is growing more stifling by the minute ... there's no breeze here in this hellish prison. I glance at the clock, *42:41. Fuck!* Morgan, you need to do as he's instructed, but how do I say goodbye?

My grip of the pen is strained to the point the nail bed on my thumb changes to purple, and my hand trembles more rapidly in response. *Breathe, Morgan, breathe.*

My one true love. I scrawl messily before the ink is disturbed by a fallen teardrop that runs in a line down the page. I follow its path in disbelief. I never thought I'd ever find myself in a situation where I'd have to write such a letter, but here I am, doing exactly that.

I love you. I do. I always have. I cry out as each letter forms and my mind races with all the things I want to say, but won't have time to say.

> *I let you down. I lost sight of what mattered in life and that was you and the kids. All I ever wanted was our family. I'm not proud of some of the things I've done of late, and whatever you learn after I'm gone, please try to remember just how much I loved you. I lost my way, and you seemed to have lost yours too. I made a mistake and I'm sorry for not being stronger. I'm sorry for everything. I love you Reid so, so, much. Thank you for choosing me to be your wife. I'll be with you. I haven't left you.*

I do. I love him, even though I stopped showing him.

> *You're a wonderful father Reid, but until recently you haven't been around very much. I know you do, and have, worked hard for our family, and you've given us so many beautiful things, but if I'm no longer here I think these things are important for you to know so you can care for Brax and Aleeha:*

1.) Brax gets eczema behind his ears when he's getting sick. He has since he was a baby. It's a tell-tale sign, so check for that if he seems under the weather. Also, as far as I know, he's still allergic to Penicillin so please don't give it to him. He's had it only the once, but his reaction frightened me. You were in Texas, I was alone. I wish I had more time with you. I really do. Please, no penicillin unless under medical supervision, do not toy with this. I'm sure you remember, but in case you don't ...

2.) Aleeha hides a diary in the back of Mr Giggles, the pink monkey backpack you won her at the carnival. This is how I learn about what's bothering her. Just don't let her catch you snooping.

3.) Hide as many vegetables inside their meals as you can. I know they eat them fine, but you cannot overdose a child on vegetables.

4.) Brax loves football now and I know you love that he plays, but if he wants to give it up let him. Don't forget our number one rule, they live through their own eyes not through ours.

5.) Ballet is Monday nights when dance resumes. Aleeha loves it, try to keep taking her. I wish you had a chance to see her dance before now.

6.) Don't give them too many sweets.

7.) Love them for the both of us.

Reid you're an amazing father and you can do this. Your heart is pure and kind. Our babies are beautiful, thank you for giving them to me, they

fulfilled the empty space I had in my heart. All the beautiful and thoughtful gifts you have given to me throughout the years, have no value compared to the two precious lives you created with me. I love you Reid. Please try to forgive me. Please don't be frightened. Close your eyes when you're unsure and search for me, I'll be there to help you.
This I promise.
Forever ... Your Morgan xx

I flick the page over and flash my sight to the clock *32:08*

All the sadness filling my heart dissipates, and it's as if I've stepped out of my own body to protect myself, from myself. My soul can't bear this and neither can my heart. There's no more pain in my chest. I'm completely numb. I focus.

To my Handsome Brax,

My hand is steadier, and my tears cease to spill. I use the back of my arm to wipe my sticky face and when I close my eyes, it's so dark. My world has gone dark.

One breath. Two breaths. Three breaths have my wet lashes parting.

The light beams onto the page. The pen hovers in await. I'm ready.

I love you. I'm so sorry. Please don't internalise this. You've always been my thinker, my quiet boy, my intelligent bean. Talk Brax. Feel Brax. I'm with you and I'll always love you.

You're going to feel like the weight of the world is on your shoulders and that by no means is the wrong way to feel, but don't forget to come back up to the surface and take air in, or you will drown in sorrow, and the beautiful person you are will be destroyed. I love you my big man. You have Dad to lean on. He'll be there, and those arms give the best hugs. Ask for help and don't deny Dad when he tries to comfort you. Remember, I'm still here with you. I'd never leave you because without you I'm nothing. I've been your mum for twelve incredibly blessed years and I'll be your mum for all eternity. I'm proud of you, Brax. Every day and with every breath you take I will always feel pride. Keep breathing Brax and let the wave of life roll you in the directions and along the paths you're supposed to explore. You're not alone and you never will be.

I love you, to the moon and back and that will never stop.

Love mum xx

Why does it have to be this way?

Why is my time in jeopardy?

I clutch the pen and slowly rotate my head towards the clock *21:01.* I need to stay focused.

A new blank page.

Aleeha,

Mommy, will always love you.

My little princess. If you are reading this Aleeha, it

means Mummy is playing dress ups with the angels now. But don't worry, I can still see you and promise I'm with you. The special thing about a mummy and her daughter is, they never truly part. Even when their body is no longer allowed to stay, their hearts still beat as one, to a bonded rhythm. Mummy is standing right beside you, holding your hand. Every time you feel the touch of warmth against you, don't be frightened, it's just me reminding you that I'm here for you every step of the way, for all of your life. What a beautiful ten-year-old you are. Wiser than your age. Smarter than you should be. Always excelling. Aleeha you've always had this contentment with life and this is something a lot of people never have the opportunity to find within themselves ... You on the other hand were born with it. I know you'll be happy, healthy, successful and you'll find love everywhere you go.

Your heart is going to feel ripped into a million pieces right now, and that feeling is going to stay with you for a while, but it will begin to heal as the years pass by. Just like it did when Prickles your hamster died. It will never fully repair, but you will feel better, I promise. My heart is feeling the same pain as yours. The thought of never holding you, kissing you or having the opportunity to tell you I love you again, brings me awful sadness. But, in time, I'll smile, as will you. Remember you have so many people who love you, so let them wrap you up tightly in their arms while your emotions escape you.

Feeling sad is just a part of life, as terrible as it is, and it's okay to take as long as you need to feel better again.

As you grow, you'll experience so many different things and I wish I could be there to enjoy and help you through them all. Remember, although I'm not physically here, I'm with you. You have your Daddy and big brother to look after you, never shut them out, they are the two most important people in your life, let them be there in the hard times and the good times baby girl.

I miss you and I love you to the moon and back, Aleeha.

Love Mummy xx

A cramp radiating from my wrist to my elbow has me contracting my hand and then releasing it. My eyes squeeze tightly shut and I moan through my pinched lips. My goodbyes are done and with this comes a mind-shattering realisation. I'm leaving my family something like this to read once I'm gone, but I want to give them more of me. I want to give them all of me, in the flesh, right beside them, for many more years. I can't leave them with this. I need to go home, because these letters won't cut it.

I drop my head, as my heart beats one painful thud and then sinks low, so low it's as if I've flown from the top of a rollercoaster and I'm suspended in mid-air. I'm sitting in wait of the deathly plummet that will follow, crashing me in to the ground. I sob softly. I pray, even though I'm not at all religious. I ask for help, and then I spring my eyes open and glare at the blank projection screen.

The music, the home videos and photographs, this whole nightmare, will not compare to the torture that will be awaiting me once I close the cover of this book. I need to be stronger than the Wolf. Wiser. Smarter. Better. I'm going to fucking fight to win this game. The wolf is messing with the wrong Red, because as the white of the screen takes my vision I become angry, so angry a monster awakens from within me. I hear its hungry growls rumbling in my chest, and feel the spark of fire that threatens to burn wildly in the pit of my stomach. I've courage seeping into my veins, and I'm not going down without the biggest fight of my life.

I quickly turn the page and write:

You are the wolf and I am your Red, run you fucker because I'll see you dead. Are you strong enough to take me down, you bastard?

With a fierce hurl of the pen from my hand to the wall, I snarl and clench my teeth together, before my fists curl closed. I'm fuming and all I see is blood … his blood on my hands.

Let this fucking game begin.

Chapter Eighteen

Reid

I breathe in and out rapidly. "What happens next? Tell me what the fuck you're going to do?" I can feel my cheeks puff out and my eyes narrow as I look towards West and Gleaton.

"We look at the evidence collected from last night, and we have all phone calls coming into the house tracked. When the next call comes in, it should lead us to where they're being made. It will give us a perimeter to work with. In the meantime, we'll organise the SES to conduct a search of surrounding areas and set up a media conference to get the word out to the public. This will take little time." His demeanour is strong and open and he seems confident.

"You can locate him from calls? If he calls again?" My voice pleads that this is correct.

"If we keep him on the line long enough, we'll be able to locate where the calls are coming from, yes."

I nod. This is a process I tell myself.

"I've found nothing." Maloney reappears with the two other uniformed officers beside him.

West flicks his wrist towards him and the officers move in closer. He then points in the direction of the loungeroom and they move in a group away from me. I think to follow, but stop myself. If West wanted me to know what they need to discuss, he would have stayed. I have to trust them.

I'm still rattled as I preoccupy myself with the task of taking my mug to the kitchen and tipping the now cold coffee down the sink. Rinsing the mug, I stare at the words, 'WORLD'S BEST DAD', in large letters filling both sides. My mind flashes to Father's Day all those years ago. The look on Aleeha's face as I tore open the wrapping paper was better than any present that laid beneath. This was the first gift she'd picked out for me on her own — Memories begin to flow like a current being swept by strong winds. It's a visual display of magical moments our family have enjoyed together –– the smiles, the laughter, the undying love. This can't be the end of these moments for us, it just can't be. I swallow hard and place the mug in the sink with gentle care, before I hunch my shoulders in defeat and turn around. I'm met with four of the most perfect eyes God created, two blue and two brown.

Their sleepy eyes are filled with innocence and unspeakable beauty.

"Good morning, Daddy," Aleeha says, her long blonde locks matted from a night's rest.

"Good morning, Aleeha honey, did you sleep well?" My lip quivers, I pull it into my mouth with my teeth, trying to hold it together for the sake of my children.

"Yes Daddy, I had the best dream." She starts to stretch until she is on tiptoes, her eyes open wide, and she suddenly shifts her head to the right, so do I. John and Shirley are standing there side by side.

"Hey, little bug," Shirley says sweetly.

"Hi Grandma Shirl," she says, running towards her. "Poppy John." They embrace her tightly.

"Morning Brax," I say, as he enters the kitchen.

He runs his hand down his face. "Hi Dad."

"Did you sleep well?"

He shrugs.

"Breakfast?" I ask, trying to keep some sort of normality.

"Yeah." He yawns.

First, I hear them talking, then I see them. The three uniformed officers have stepped into view, and so have detectives West and Gleaton. They stop speaking immediately and halt on the spot.

"Dad." Brax glares at me. "Where's Mum?"

"Daddy?" Aleeha's voice is high-pitched.

"Dad, what's going on? Who are those men? And why are they here?" I can see the fear swirling in Brax's brown eyes.

Be strong Reid, they need you. Handle them with care. I tell myself to encourage a gentle approach. "We need to talk. Can you come sit at the dining room table, please." I'm dreading this. Morgan is always better at breaking sad and devastating news. It reminds me of the time their hamster Prickles died two years ago, and Morgan said we had to tell them the truth and teach them about death. I just wanted to buy them a new Prickles, and have them be none the wiser, not Morgan, she said death is a part of life and we couldn't hide it from them. I trip over the word death in my mind and its meaning:

Dying or being killed; the end of someone's life.

Uneasiness washes over my skin and knots instantly tie together in my stomach. The death of their hamster will be nothing compared to the death of their mother, and I refuse to believe I'll ever have to explain and comfort them through such a life changing event. I begin to choke up and find myself lost for any words that could help our children. I don't exactly know what to say; I just look at their innocent faces as we sit.

Aleeha and Brax sit across from me. Shirley and John sit either side of them. I nervously twirl the yellow gold wedding band around on my left finger. I can feel the impact of what I'm about to do. I will break their hearts with four little words, words that on their own have no effect, but when added together shatter lives. Four little words. *Your mum is MISSING.*

I inhale and then exhale as the children look to me, and John and Shirley look to the children. I open my mouth and then close it again. I rotate my head in search of West. He nods when I locate him.

Is this encouragement? *Fuck.*

"Brax, Aleeha ––"

"Dad. Where's Mum?" Brax's tone is tense.

"I don't know how to tell you this, just know that we're doing everything we can, okay?" I'm making no sense. I know this because those innocent eyes seem puzzled.

Reid get it together, will you.

"The five men standing over there are police officers and detectives. They're here to help us."

"We need help? Or Mum needs help?" Brax asks immediately.

"Brax, all of us do, your mum is missing."

Aleeha draws a noisy breath of air before gasping out loud. Tears flood from her eyes and it's an instant river they create. She rambles, but nothing she's says can be understood. Shirley strokes her hand up and down Aleeha's arm and I turn my attention to Brax whose face has drained of all colour and glows a pale white.

"We're going to find Mum, I promise you. You just have to believe we will," I say, trying to console him. It doesn't work because soggy tears burst from Brax's eyes.

Aleeha runs towards me, and quickly clambers on to my lap without any warning. Her head rests in the nape of my neck. Her tears soak through my shirt. Placing one hand to the back of her head and the other to the middle of her back, I try desperately to hold myself together. I search for Brax, who drops his head and sobs against the table.

"I want my mummy," Aleeha chokes out.

"I want your mummy too" I whisper, as my bottom lip begins to tremor. "It's going to be okay, sweetheart. Daddy's going to call Grandma and Grandad, Nanny and Pop-Pop, Uncle Cruise and Aunty Natalie, to come, okay?" Her sweet little head nods against me as she howls louder.

"Brax, come here buddy," I say through a tensed throat as I outstretch my arm to the side. He stands before throwing himself at me. Brax is twelve now and he's a tall boy, so I barley manage to hold his weight as I pull him against my side. Raising my eyes, I look for Shirley, my rock, or so I hoped, but she's sobbing into her cupped hands. I dart my attention to John, hoping he can keep me composed. He too is holding back tears as they puddle in his eyes.

I can't do this.

I don't know how long we sit like this, but I don't allow my grip around our children to weaken.

Aleeha suddenly lifts her head and awkwardly removes herself from my lap. She runs at full pace away from me, up the staircase. A loud bang follows shortly after.

"It's okay, Reid. I'll go to her," Shirley assures me in a low tone.

My arm is left bare once Brax's grip is removed, and in a moment of sudden panic I snap my neck in search of him, only to find him holding Shirley's hand as they walk past the police officers and begin taking the staircase together.

I watch every step with a heart heavier than lead. "I can't do this," I say, my voice subdued. "Bring my wife home, please. Just find Morgan because I can't do this," I'm pleading as I make connection with West's eyes.

West nods.

Dropping my head to the table, I squeeze my eyes tightly together and hiss between my clenched teeth, "Who the fuck are you and why do you want my wife?"

Chapter Nineteen

The Wolf

One, two, three, four, five … blur into black lines as the blades of the fan above me spin faster and faster. I smile. It's a smile of victory. I have my Red. She's finally mine. The last trophy. The last name on my hit list. The list that's drawn in red lipstick on the dusty wall beside me. I can't help rolling my head and running my eyes over each name.

~~Daisy Malone~~
~~Cheryl Riddell~~
~~Donna Martin~~
~~Sarah Pilcher~~
~~Christina Monroe~~
~~Elizabeth Shanks~~

~~Lillian Catcher~~
~~Alethia Warren~~
~~Stacey Seymore-Beth~~
~~Octavia Legend~~
~~Anastasia Daughtry~~
~~Katy Hodges~~
Morgan Banks

It's truly a beautiful sight. Every strike through the twelve separate lines spell out my accomplishments. They also reassure me of my power, my endurance and my strength. "Huh." They all doubted my intelligence. *"You'll become nothing. You're nothing."* That's what she said. The dumb fucking bitch whose eyes were the first to glaze over at my hand. I'll never find a more beautiful sight as the one a woman expresses just before her last breath leaves her. It's a mixture of fear, fight and realisation ... it's intoxicating.

It only took two footsteps to catch her. Two. Dumb bitch should have seen me coming. I gave her the chance. I made sure those two footsteps counted and could be heard amongst the leaves. I'm a night stalker. My feet only make a sound when I allow them to, and I like to give my prey one final warning. One final chance. I'm in control of the game. I'm a hunter. I'm a wolf. I'm savage, but I'm also fair.

The early morning is the quietest. Nobody knows about these parts in this bushland. Well, if they do, they haven't dared step foot here. I've not seen a single soul in this area since I've owned this cabin and come to frequent here for the last five years. Well, not a single soul apart from my gamers. But they aren't here by choice, no, they're here because I decided they deserved their punishment. I laugh. It's forceful and pleasing. These thoughts swirling through my head are the only ones to cause me such laughter.

The smell of wet bark and composted leaves wafts through the open window and it's what makes this place home. Sometimes I'm lucky and I get the drifting fumes of a decaying animal that's been taken by another much larger, stronger and smarter animal than it. Other times I reward myself with the scent of decaying human flesh, but that only happens after I kill. I wait to bury my Reds. I wait because I want to play with the law. I give them a shot to do their jobs. They fail, miserably.

It's Detective Astin West's chance to challenge me this time. Dumb bastard. He has no idea all these bodies are buried in his area. He has no idea any of them were even reported missing, I'm sure. Or that their faces are still plastered across flyers offering rewards and information of their whereabouts. If only each law enforcement agency spoke to the other then they could've figured this out a long time ago and Morgan would be safe and sound tucked tightly into her bed.

I'm giving West his chance this time, because I've taken one of his residents, from his town, and apart from my first victim, Morgan Banks is the only person who has been associated with me for a significant period, and the only person who has been snatched from Rockhampton. All my other trophies were just little vixens who thought they could lie, cheat and steal from me during my travels. It's a gift to work for a place that allows you a hefty business account. It also works in my favour that women are so fucking greedy. You promise them the world with all the fine trimmings and they'll follow you anywhere. Even to a cabin in thick bushland. Women are fucking stupid. Didn't their daddies teach them not to talk to strangers? A bellowing laugh projects from my throat at this thought. They are so fucking brainless. Dick, money and jewellery, that's all they want. Love? Nope. They don't want love. They want dick, money and jewellery, and that's what gets them killed.

I can hear her sobs as I look through the screen of the television set up at the end of my bed. Red's curled into a tight ball and rocking on her arse. *How pathetic*. She was writing before, I honestly thought that stubborn wench wouldn't have written a thing, and I'd have finished our game this morning. It seems she might have proved me wrong. She wrote just like she was ordered to. I'm happy about this outcome. I'm happy because we get to move onto step two.

DA-DA-DA-DA-DA.

Times up. The sound of the alarm is like music to my ears. I curl my right hand around the face of my watch and switch off the timer. One hour has passed. Red's allocated time for her first task has come to an end.

Rising into a seated position, I stare at her coiled posture as she rocks on the slab, and I smile. *Game on.* Twisting my neck, it cracks loosening me up. I puff out my chest and pop my sternum simultaneously. I'm ready to battle. The black ski mask is just to my side. I take no time to slip it over my head and roll it down my face. It's tight to my neck and as I adjust its positioning, my finger brushes the top button on my black hunting shirt ... it's come undone again. *What the fuck is going on with this fucking shirt?* I'm quick to rectify the situation and slide the small button through the buttonhole. My arms strain against the soft mattress as I scoot on my arse to the end of the bed. Tilting the camera, I press the stop button on the remote beside it. The music is mute. Lights. Camera. Action.

"Red, oh, Red." Taunting her is heaven.

She doesn't shift from her position, and stays huddled on the floor.

"Where am I, Red?"

Her sobs grow louder.

"Now, Now. It's just words on paper. Nothing to be crying about. You don't have love in your heart anyways. You're a monster."

Her head rises so slowly it irks me. We have much to do and she's wasting my precious time. I thump my hand against the wooden end of the bed frame creating a harsh noise and she jumps. *That's better.*

Her big brown eyes are glazed, wide and swollen

red –– they match the colour and size of her busted lips. I like it. There are so many lines streaked through the dried mud caked to her face; she takes the form of a lost and neglected doll. I like this too. Some of her hair is matted into a massive bird nest on one side of her head. It almost seems as if the strands have morphed into thick straw. I'm pleased. Her exterior now matches her interior … disgusting.

"Please let me go home." She's not begging. She's not whining. It's a forced and strong request. Oh, we have a little fire in the belly. I'm impressed. I keep my eyes focused on hers and delay the shake of my head.

Her middle finger rises as if being controlled by a winding crank. I fight the smile tugging at the corner of my mouth and glare at her. Sliding my hand across the sheet, I locate the remote and pause her image.

She'll never hear me coming. She'll never know I'm behind her. It will be a sudden pinch in her neck and … I click my fingers. Her light will go out. Sleep tight, Red.

Chapter Twenty

Morgan

The smell of bark and dirt are the first to fill my senses. The ground is cushioned below me and as I roll my head, I hear the crunching sound of leaves being torn and crumpled. Instantly, my cheek burns hot in one spot, so I shift my hand and cup my cheek to protect my skin. The need to wiggle my toes becomes strong due to a sudden tickling sensation alerting me to their existence. I moan as I twitch both ankles and then stretch my feet. *God, how I ache.*

A kookaburra laughs and it's the perfect pitch of hysterical human laughter entwined with maniacal cackling. I dart my eyes open, only to close them the moment trees begin spinning. I want to vomit. Let me off this rollercoaster. I'm not sure what's happening.

Am I *dead*?

Chirp. Chirp. Chirp.

Leaves rustle.

My feet tickle once more. I again twitch both ankles before stretching my toes. The sensation increases.

Move, Morgan.

I bend my knees upwards. It doesn't stop the tickle. Something's crawling on me. I jump upright and stumble until I'm lumbering forwards. It's a sharp pinch and then a stinging sensation. I bend and brush my legs. I think I'm being bitten by ants. Everything is blurry and disproportional … I'm breathing hard … I'm smacking at my skin. "Fuck." It's a breathless deliverance of the word. "Get off me. Stop biting me."

I'm running. Pains are shooting through my spine. My thighs are burning. My mouth is hung open and bone dry and then I hear it, something is moving towards me. I halt on the spot. There's bushland in every direction I turn. My heart pumps hard. My head pounds to its rhythm. I twist left then right. I'm searching for somewhere to hide. A thick tree trunk becomes my destination. It's about five metres away from me. I can make it.

I flick my head in every direction. I see nothing, so I sprint until my fingertips brush the bark of the trunk and I fall behind it, landing heavily onto my arse. Every breath I take is dry and hot. But I can't stop breathing, I just need to slow the pace in which I'm drawing air. "Stay away." My mouth grows chalky, my palms are slick from my fear and the words that were disgorged with force from within me.

Mask. Long shirt. Long pants. Boots ... they're all coloured black. I stop when my eyes connect with his.

He shakes his head.

I snap my eyelids closed just as something comes hurtling towards me. It impacts my face hard. I open my mouth to scream, but the result is soundless.

Help.

I curl into a ball, sheltering my head with my arms folded over the top. I wait. I'm waiting for him to grab me. Drag me. Hurt me. He's not. I'm still untouched. I squeeze my eyes tightly together and taste blood in my mouth, my body trembles in response, and all I can do is hold my breath. If I don't breathe, maybe I'll become invisible. I hear nothing. I feel nothing, so I open my eyes to the darkness my hunched body creates. I breathe slow, shallow pants. Something is pressed against my stomach. There's a bulge where a bulge should not be and I'm now alerted to its presence. I take slow movements until I'm uncurled. The sun shines brightly causing me to squint as I try to locate him. There's only trees and overgrowth that spreads far into the distance. He's gone. I didn't hear him leave. He's vanished.

I'm crouching when the backpack falls from my lap to the ground. This is what he hurled my way. I'm quick to unzip it and pull out each item. The bandage. The canister. The torch. The compass. There is no pen. There is no notebook. He's kept my letters.

I ran at first, I ran until my legs become rubbery and don't have enough strength to keep going. Now I've been walking for what seems like hours. Honestly, I think I'm tracking in circles. The backpack, although containing very little, weighs a tonne on my back, and the sun is so raging hot it's burning my skin. Sweat beads flow over my brows and drip from my chin onto my breasts. I need to keep moving. I can't stop. I'm strong enough. I can get out of this maze.

Turning my body towards what I think is a westerly direction, I push through overgrowth which is new to me. It isn't any different in the way it scratches my legs though.

"Fuck!" I huff, hopping toward a sturdy overhanging branch. Placing my foot into my hand, I inspect my sole. Another twig has pricked my skin leaving a small cut. I don't bother wiping the blood sliding in between the webs of my toes away this time. There's no point, because it will happen again in no time.

Letting go of the branch, I take two steps and then something goes shooting past my ear. I hear the whooshing sound it makes as it whizzes by. "These birds," I duck, thinking one has swooped a little lower than it might have intended. If I never have to be around another bird again in my life, I'd be thankful right now. I've no clue about them and I'm wondering why they keep coming so close to my fucking head. I continue to move in the new direction I previously chose. I'm beyond lost. I don't know where to go. I just need to keep moving. It's the only way I'll survive. Or this is what I keep telling myself.

Something goes zipping past my ear again, only this time it stings the tip in its wake. My instincts tell me to bow my head lower; I listen, then crouch down in the long grass.

What in the world?

I rotate my head in every direction. I can't see much, or hear anything, but I elect to stay down at ground level, since it seems like the best option. I know he's here somewhere. He might not make any sound and he may be invisible, but the hairs rising on the back of my neck as well as the feeling of dread flipping my stomach is enough for me to stay still.

Thud!

An arrow splits a groove into the gum tree directly in front of me. It's poking straight out. The red bristles on its end have me swallowing with a hard gulp. *Holy shit. Arrows.* My body tenses at the thought of how close those previous sounds were. Full-fledged fright follows this thought as images of my brains splattering in every direction fills my mind. Anguish becomes the result of this vision and I cringe, as my body shudders.

What do I do? I don't know what to do. I begin to whimper, caught in indecision. My heart hammers at a rate that threatens combustion. I don't know what to do.

Thud!

Another arrow lands in the tree to my left.

I leap upright and instinctively run in a zig-zag pattern until I fall. I spring upright once more and scramble in as many directions as possible over a short distance. Arrows continue to whiz by me, one after another. I hear the whooshing sounds and I feel the brush of air they leave behind. Either he's a terrible shot, or he's an exceptional shot and this is just to frighten the shit out of me. If it is the latter, it's working because fright pulses through me and my heart tries to abandon my body, not wanting any further part of this terrifying situation. I duck, weave and even dive at one point to escape the artillery continually being fired my way. There's no way out. I trip over my feet that tangle and my knees skid along dirt. I scream. I scream loud and then I lay flat and play dead.

I can't breathe and with my eyes wide I see an opening between two large boulders close to where I lie. Another arrow goes whizzing over the top of my head, and I know it's another one because the force of the wind that sailed past my hair was much too intense to be anything else. I scurry along the ground, finding my feet just in time to launch myself into the small opening these two boulders allow.

It's a tight squeeze to wriggle into, but I manage to insert myself and the backpack through the narrow opening. I can feel the colour draining from my face as my heart thumps to a terrifying beat. I try to pinch my lips forcefully together to be as silent as possible, but my breathing is not co-operating and a small high-pitched squeal exits my mouth, one I didn't expect. I'm forced to slam my hand across my mouth to smother the next scream that might follow. I'm crouched and stilled. One of my hands is trying to keep me balanced, and is pressed into the ground while the other remains pressed against my lips. I wait, for how long I'm not sure, but my legs cramp painfully. I know it's not safe to stay here, but nowhere is, and I can't figure out what to do. I twist my feet trying to alleviate the cramps plaguing me, but I lose balance and I fall. I'm falling. I can't grab a hold of anything on the way down, and before I know it my side smashes against something hard. I yelp. "Ouch. Oh. Ouuuch." I clench my teeth together and pant, trying to alleviate the pain in my ribcage.

It's as black as the ace of spades when I manage to roll over and take an uncomfortable seated position. I can't see anything. I'm trying to pull the zip on the bag to retrieve the torch, but I'm shaking so much it proves difficult at first, however I manage to take it into my grip.

Light appears from the torch in my outstretched hand and the beam reveals walls. Cave walls. I gasp. "What?" A picture. It's a picture of my family. All four of us and we're smiling happily. *My precious babies. My beautiful husband.* My stomach knots as my eyes drop saddened.

Slowly, I raise my head and study the image, even

though I don't want to, but I believe it's important. Why else would a photo of my family be stuck to a wall inside a cave? He wanted me to come in here. This is a part of the game. I scrutinise the clothing we're wearing and the palm trees behind us, trying to gauge where this was taken and when. *Cruise's wedding last spring.* I run my finger over our smiling faces, tracing them gently before gulping back my tears and biting at my lower lip. I've not seen this photograph before. Not ever. I can't stop staring at it, wondering where the hell it came from.

As I shift the torch, I catch another image. This one is of me and it was taken when I was in high school. I'm sitting on a grandstand smiling and Matilda, a classmate, has her head rested on my shoulder. I remember this day, that grandstand, and this photograph ... I have a copy in my home album. As I continue to shift the light over the walls I see photo after photo of me throughout my entire life, that is until I clutch my chest and crumble to the ground. An awful cry forces its way from my soul to the ears of God. Reid has his lips connected to that of another. His hands are planted on her arse. Her arms are around his neck. I know the dress she's wearing because I was with her when she bought it. I know the hair clip protruding out of her thick red locks because she purchased it on the same day. I know her pin thin heels. I know her.

"Linda. Why?" I cry shocked.

Chapter Twenty-One

Reid

"Reid, you need to get your kids out of here. Is there somewhere they can go?" West says.

I nod, before racing up the staircase to where John is sitting in the hall. I slide down the wall; my body plops beside John on the floor and I join him in a lean against the frame of Brax's door. I sit for a moment listening to John talk about mindless and trivial things, and he doesn't stop until he's finished talking about the massive fish he caught last summer. Then he turns his head and looks at me with wet glassy eyes. I can feel his sadness and I can see his exhaustion.

"John, something has happened." His narrowed eyes, grow wide. "The kids need to leave the house.

Can they stay at your place until I get their grandparents here?" I know my eyes are pleading with him, because the look he returns to me is sympathetic.

"Of course, boy." His hand reaches over, resting on top of mine. "Our poor Morgan." His voice cracks as the words leave his lips. "You know I think of Morgan as our daughter, and you as our son … you know this, don't you?" The moisture in his eyes builds as he searches me for an answer.

"I do John, I really do." He wraps his arm around my head bringing it into his chest. "We are always here for your family, you hear?"

"Loud and clear."

"Okay, well let's get these kids out of here."

I bang my hand against Brax's door. "Brax, it's Dad, I'm coming in." Slowly, I press down the handle and allow the door to crack open, as I duck my head in first. Brax has my temper and the thought of an item being launched in my direction has me on edge. Nothing is thrown. I dart my eyes from corner to corner of his well-organised room, until they make contact with the side of Brax's face, as he sits on his bed, staring mindlessly out the window, like he's in a trance.

"Brax, it's going to be okay buddy, I promise." He doesn't move so I sit down at the end of his bed "Brax, buddy, I need you to pack some things. I need you to go next door to stay with John and Shirley for a while." I await his reply, but he doesn't respond. I watch him quietly as he scowls, and then he shifts to face me. He isn't happy and I don't blame him. First, he's told his mother is missing and no one knows shit about where she is. Then, he's told he needs to leave his home, his room, his safe place and stay next door for an amount of time nobody is sure of.

"Fine." That's all I get as he shuffles from his bed and opens his cupboard door, pulling out his travel bag. He's quick to put items into the bag, and remains silent the entire time ... The only communication we have is his glares of hatred towards me, those narrowed and glazed eyes, shooting daggers my way. *He blames me! Shit, I blame me.*

I drop my head as my stomach sinks. *I've messed up, bad.*

Bracing myself, I make my way towards Aleeha's room, taking a slow walk down the hallway. Her exaggerated sobs can be heard before I even reach her room. Walking through the open door, I see her wrapped tightly in Shirley's arms. Shirley makes *"Sssssh, Ssssssh, Sssssh,"* noises over and over. The same noise Morgan makes when the kids are upset and she is comforting them. It must be a woman thing.

"Lee-Lee, you need to go stay at Shirl's, okay?"

Aleeha tilts her chin and I'm left with the image of sad, and wet bloodshot eyes. "Daddy," she cries, with her arms outstretched. I wrap her in my arms whilst carrying her to the doorway, keeping my grip firm around her.

"Shirley. Can you put some clothes in Aleeha's

suitcase? It's in the closet. The detective thinks it's better that the kids stay away from the house for now. There's been a call made to the house."

"I'll do it now," she says.

"Don't forget her Raggedy Ann doll. It's still on her bed. I just saw it."

"I know the one. She brings it over when she sleeps there. Morgan always packs it."

I head to the staircase with Aleeha wrapped to me, each step making my blood boil. Who in this world would want to do this to us? This is the ultimate question. Who is it?

Shirley is holding a photo frame containing our latest family portrait at the zoo. We're happy in this photo and I shudder at the site of the frame, the one that normally takes pride and place on Aleeha's duchess. John and Brax walk down the stairs behind Shirley and when they reach my side we exit the house together, walking across the grass separating our homes. John guides Brax inside and I follow with Aleeha nestled into my chest. Lowering her gently onto the couch, I kiss her tear-stained cheek, and pat Brax's shoulder as he comes to sit beside his sister. He doesn't say a word; he only puts his arm around Aleeha and holds her.

"I need you to stay here. I'll be back as soon as I can. All I ask is that you both stay here and listen to everything John and Shirley ask of you." I know they think this is my fault. Who could blame them really? Morgan and I have been fighting so much lately. My throat goes dry and my heart begins to ache at the thought that if I wasn't being such an arsehole Morgan would have called me to help her with that busted tyre. My gut drops. "I have to go," I say, turning quickly … racing out the door.

Shirley is standing on the porch and she stops me by putting her hands on either side of my face. Reaching forward she kisses my cheek. "We will take care of them. Go bring our girl home."

I nod, then turn on my heel and run back to the house and through the double front doors.

"I need to make some calls," I say, pacing.

"Who are you calling?" West seems distracted when he says this.

"My parents. Morgan's parents. My brother. Linda, Morgan's best friend … my boss, probably."

"Okay." West doesn't even look at me; instead his eyes are turned down at some papers he's holding.

I snatch my mobile phone from the counter where I sat this morning with a cup of coffee that chilled before it even reached my lips then pass through Morgan's library until I reach the sliding doors leading out to the back patio.

Where do I even start?

The clock on my phone reads 13:00 hours. Still no Morgan. I slide the door just far enough I can slip through the gap it creates and swiftly shut it behind me. I don't hesitate to press the contact number for

Linda. She better answer. She doesn't. It rings out, and I hang up before the message bank plays. I really need to talk to Linda. Why isn't she answering? Is she in danger too? Shaking my head, I tell myself she's probably busy at work, but I know the police have tried calling her, because they've told me so. Hell, I have too when I was waiting for Morgan to come home. Why hasn't Linda returned any calls?

"Fuck," I growl, as I make the next call to Morgan's parents. It rings three times.

"Hi Reid, honey. How's my favourite son-in-law?" She always says this even though I'm her only son-in-law.

"Is Ron there?"

"Yes." I can hear her smile through the line.

"You both need to come to Rockhampton as soon as possible."

There's no reply.

"Kylee."

"We can come. What's wrong?"

"It's Morgan ..."

"Morgan? Is she upset? Sick. Has my girl caught a tummy bug?"

"She's missing," I whisper. I'm not sure why I whisper it, but I do.

"Missing. She's not missing. Where would she be missing to?"

"We don't know."

"Reid. Where's Morgan?"

"I don't know. The police are here. She never came

home last night. There's been a crash … Kylee, please just come here, okay?"

"Okay." Her voice shakes. "We're coming." I hear her panic.

"I need to ring Mum and Dad … they're holidaying in Switzerland with Cruise and Natalie. I'm going to hang up now. I'll see you soon."

"I'm getting Ron now. We'll get straight in the car."

"Okay."

I hang up and immediately call my dad.

Ring. Ring. Ring. Ring. Ring. Ring. Ring. Ring. Ring.

"Hello." His voice is croaky. It's easy to tell he's still very asleep.

"Dad." One word. It's all I say.

"What time is it?" There's a pause. "Just after five a.m. Son, are you forgetting about the time difference?"

"Morgan's been abducted. You need to come home. I need you." I know I say this rushed, but it's the only way I manage to get the words past my tongue.

"Son. Slow down. Morgan has what?"

"Dad. She's been taken. Some psycho has taken her. Her car got smashed up and she never came home. This morning some man rang … or at least some robotic male voice. I don't know what he wants. I have just over fifty grand in the safe in my office, if it's money he wants, that's all I've got on me. Dad, I need you and Mum to come home."

"Shit. Catherine. Catherine, wake up."

There's moaning. "Woman, open your damn eyes.

Morgan's in trouble."

"Dad.' I pause. "Dad, I have to go." I'm yelling into the phone because I don't believe he can hear me. "Dad."

The line goes dead.

Fuck!

I try Linda once more. It rings out. I hang up before it reaches the message bank. The door behind me slides open and when I turn my attention in its direction, Maloney is stepping out to join me.

"Are you okay? Do you need help with contacting family?"

"It's done," I growl. I'm not sure why I'm growling at Maloney because he's simply offering help. I just am. I'm mad, confused, irritated, agitated ... I'm so many emotions rolled into one and I'm not sure if I'm coming or going. All I keep thinking about is our two children I abandoned next door ... At least they have John and Shirley, so it's something.

"This will be much easier for you when family support arrives." Maloney sounds so genuine. "How long will they be?" he continues.

"Morgan's parents live seven hours away in Longreach. And they're driving here. My parents and brother are overseas. They'll have to arrange flights home. Linda, Morgan's best friend, well, I can't get hold of her and I'm not sure if this should be of concern to you or not. But I'm not sure anyone has heard from Linda since ... well, I'm not even sure. Has she returned any of the police calls?"

"I'll have to check on that, Reid. I will."

"Okay."

"Come back inside." Maloney straightens his arm and shifts it until it's behind my back. "Come on, Mate." He's eyes are kind. His features soften.

"Okay."

The door opens hard, like a strong gust has ripped its hold. My eyes dart to see what has caused this sudden opening, and just as they do, my balls leap right into the back of my throat.

"What the fuck is going on Reid?" she screams, with disdain. Her fiery red hair matches her now fiery complexion. "Where is she Reid? Where?" Her voice raises well over the legal limits for a decibel reader in a residential area.

Both West and Gleaton move towards me as I stare into Linda's rage fuelled eyes.

"Answer me Reid?" she yells.

"Linda, I... just ... can..." I stutter over my words. I really would have preferred a moment to have a discussion in private with Linda, but of course she has to come raging into a fucking room with all guns blazing, seeking blood. Why would I expect anything less? She's a handful at the best of times.

"Reid, who is this?" I hear West ask, but I don't take my eyes off Linda. Instead, I'm trying to use my own expression to discretely tell her to calm the fuck down.

"Reid."

I ignore West.

Linda's hand draws back and then a sharp sting travels through the nerves that control the right-hand side of my face. *Why the hell did she just slap me?* "I told you that if you ever hurt her I was going to kill you and kill you I will." Linda moves desperately towards me, slapping and clawing at everywhere she can reach. Gleaton is quick to rip her off me, allowing me some space. Of course, Linda struggles against him and yells high pitch profanities in my direction.

"What the fuck are you talking about?" I manage to choke out.

"You know."

"I don't. Stop your shit, Linda." I'm mad.

"You stop yours, you arsehole."

"Somebody tell me who this woman is." West's tone is commanding.

"It's Linda, Morgan's best friend." I try to rub the sting from my cheek away, but it remains. "Detective West meet Morgan's best friend and work colleague. As you can see she's beyond angry at me and I've no idea why."

"Settle down, Miss," West commands and just as he does, Linda bursts into a waterfall of tears, slumping her full body weight from Gleaton's arms. Slowly, she drags Gleaton to his knees as she falls against the wooden floor boards. Linda is an average curvaceous woman, with a temper of a wild lion.

"Where's Morgan?" She sobs, "I got the messages.

I'm scared. Where is she?" I feel sorry for Linda as she melts down, I do, and even though I have no idea as to why she lashed out so violently and entered the way she did, I still walk over to her and sit beside her on the floor. I keep my knees bent in front of me and put my arm around her shoulder, hoping to offer some support.

"Linda, we don't know where Morgan is. They're doing all they can to find her. You know I wouldn't hurt Morgan for all the money in the world. I wouldn't hurt her for all the stars in the sky." Linda's head bobs up and down, like one of those bobble head dolls people have in their cars.

"I know Reid. But I'm confused. I have questions. Lots of questions," she sobs harder. "It's just such a shock." She uses her palm to wipe at her face.

"I'm dying here, Linda. I've got no idea. Do you know anything?" I stop and regather myself, softening my expression. "Did Morgan say anything to you?" Her head rises and I stare deep into her wet baby blue eyes. I'm pleading for answers.

"Well, I know you've been acting like a real pig to her lately. Reid, you should be happy for Morgan. She really is enjoying being back at work. She did everything for you while you followed your career ... everything. Why be such a jerk to her? Is it because of that one night with ––"

"Say nothing." My eyes are wide, my pulse is racing. I need to speak to Linda alone. I need her to shut her mouth right now and say nothing. "No!" I bark. My temper is being fuelled by my worry. I glare at Linda trying to tell her what I need to say without speaking the words. Her sunken eyes and flushed cheeks make me want to just up and vanish in this moment. Why did I let Linda kiss me? I can't blame the amount of alcohol we consumed. I can't blame the situation. I let her kiss me, and the guilt from keeping this from Morgan has been eating away at me. It has been for months. I kissed her best friend and Morgan could never forgive me for that. I drop my head onto my knees and think about how much of a jerk I've been of late, and how I wish I could do anything right now to take it all back. I'll confess to Morgan if it will see her alive, well and home safely. Whatever it takes I'll do.

"Reid. Did you have anything to do with this?" Linda speaks softly.

What the fuck? Is she really asking me this in front of the fucking police. "No," I say, lifting my head. "I know I've been a jerk, okay, and if I could take it all back I would, I swear. I was waiting for Morgan to get home from work to tell her how sorry I was. I had her favourite red wine waiting for her. I cooked her favourite meal. I know I was acting an arse, but she's my Morgan. Linda, you know she's my world, she's my universe. I fucked up okay. I was trying to deal with it. But, I'd never hurt Morgan."

Linda leans into me laying her head against my chest. Her snot filled nose, spills all over on my shirt as she releases what I believe to be her fear in my comfort. "She's your Morgan. I'm sorry for what I did.

I know it's my fault you're suffering from so much guilt. Maybe we should have just told her," Linda whispers.

Fuck. This is going to look bad. So fucking bad. I pull Linda up from the floor and practically carry her into the lounge room, placing her gently on the couch. I lean in and whisper, "Do not tell the police anything about what happened in Canberra, yet. I need time to speak to a lawyer and time to think. Linda, say nothing."

Chapter Twenty-Two

Morgan

I thought for sure the Wolf would be waiting for me when I finally managed to climb back out of his cave. He wasn't. But at least he left a tattered rope for me to pull myself out with. It felt like forever before I managed to emerge. Slip, after slip. Fall, after fall. I was far from strong enough to clamber out the first time, or the second, or even the fifth time.

I hate him. I hate this monster for doing this to me. I hate my husband for cheating on me. I hate that I saw the photo of Linda and Reid. The more I've walked, the more I see the Wolf's eyes in my mind. How blue they are. How perfect they are. Reid has eyes like that. Reid cheated on me and the proof was in that photo. Reid can also shoot a bow and arrow and he knows his way around a bullwhip. He grew up on a property. Plus, Reid's been acting strangely. Why am I thinking it is him whose responsible for this game I'm playing? *I have to pay for what I've done.* That's what the Wolf said.

Maybe Reid found out about my addiction, all the prescription meds I've been hiding and popping every moment I get. What started as tablets to help me sleep has turned into a cocktail of anything I can get my hands on. A pinched nerve from working out at the gym supplied me pain meds. The cut I got on my hand after I slipped with the kitchen knife meant a prescription for stronger pain meds, and now I find myself jumping from doctor to doctor, telling any convincing story I can, to get more prescription drugs. Stronger ones. Better ones.

Two weeks ago, I hit the worst of all. A work function in the city had me smoking crystal meth in the bathroom of the conference hall with my colleague, Brett. Crystal fucking meth. The soccer mums' drug. Who am I? How did I get here? These thoughts whirl in my head as I drag my feet and walk in circles, because that's what it seems I'm doing, walking in circles, it also feels like I'm serving my punishment. I'm being punished for my dishonesty. *I'll never take another pill again. I swear, just give me the freedom to prove it.*

It's hot, even though the blazing heat of the sun has

become less harsh as the afternoon draws out. Birds are chirping high in the trees above me, and here I stand, dying of thirst, burnt and telling myself to keep moving. I do, walking aimlessly in the hope of finding any way out of here. Sometimes I find a spark of energy and I manage to run until I think I hear a noise, or the hairs on the back of my neck spring to attention, then I find any refuge I can and hide. I crouch low and stay as still as possible, whilst I try to breathe through the crippling fear I endure. I scream for help every time I find enough courage to yell loud enough to be heard, and at the same time I prepare for the Wolf to hear my cries and come silence me. He hasn't come. Help hasn't come. Nobody comes. Everything I see looks the same — rocks, trees, bushes, paths, vines, overgrowth. I'm starving and my stomach rumbles loud enough to spook me. At first, I don't even recognise the sound is coming from me.

I'm beyond thirsty, but the canister is getting low. I've already helped myself to most of the water, and it didn't quench my thirst; it actually made me thirstier. I'm in so much pain at this point I think about shouting for the Wolf to come and kill me, but then I see my children's faces, and my Mum and Dad ... I want to live. I want to live for them. So, I run until I can't, and then I walk until I'm frightened and hiding. It's a vicious cycle.

I start replaying all my thoughts. I curse the Wolf. I think about his eyes. I think it's Reid. But I always revert to his voice — his voice is different, yet I've heard it before — How can that be if it's my husband? I go through my prescription drug addiction and how this might be tied to the reason for my abduction. I think of Brett, my co-worker, but his eyes are much lighter blue, and for the life of me, right now, I can't remember what his voice sounds like. I see the picture of Reid and Linda and feel anger mixed with sadness. He cheated on me and Linda cheated on me, too. She's my best friend and best friends don't do that. Is the Wolf my husband? Or is my husband only responsible for the Wolf taking me? Is my lie what I did wrong? Is this what he means by I'm the same as him? He lied, I lied, we all fucking lied. Or is it the fact Reid's been acting like an arsehole and I've been so busy with work, the kids, and my drug habit I haven't noticed he's been out killing woman who have wronged him in some way. Shit. Is he a serial killer?

I'm deep in thought wandering through more overgrowth trying to piece this puzzle together, to work out the answer to this sick game. I'm thinking about the times The Wolf has stood before me, on those rocks when the rain beat down hard upon me and I was freed from the car, today with the bow and arrow, dressed in black. Is he taller or shorter than Reid? Is his build smaller, larger or the same as my husband's?

A sudden ripping of my flesh has me screaming so loud, I taste blood at the back of my throat. My face hits the dirt, and it fills my mouth. My legs sting as if they've been sliced open and I spit dirt whilst I pant. "Let me go! Fucking let me go."

Chapter Twenty-Three

Reid

"Reid, we've just received some very interesting information that we want answers to." I try hard to swallow the lump that has formed suddenly in my throat. It's not budging. It becomes even more restricting when I search West's expression to find his eyes cold and his lips pursed.

"I'll help however I can," I reply in a voice that rattles with uncertainty due to this sudden change in West's demeanour. I shift nervously on my feet. They've obviously figured out about the night I had with Linda, the one leading to a make-out session that's had me shaken ever since.

"Reid, can you explain to us why you organised and then removed fifty thousand dollars from your joint account with Morgan, the day prior to her going missing?"

My heart races. *Fuck. How am I going to explain this?* I need to fess up and tell the truth. It's now or never. My eyes grow wide, and I twist my head towards Linda searching for any type of reaction ... she looks furious, her scrunched face says more than any words she could say. I shift my attention back to West to find his eyebrows are crossed and he's waiting for some sort of explanation that will put me in the clear. I'm not even sure what to confess, or even where to start in delivering my confession. I shake my head. "Fuck!"

"Can you tell me why you withdrew the money." West is still waiting. His arms are crossed over his chest. His head is tilted slightly.

I take a deep breath. "I withdrew it because I was suspicious that Morgan, might be planning on leaving me. I didn't want her to drain the bank account and take it all. I also ..." I can't say it. I need to, but I can't.

"Go on."

"I did something I'm not proud of."

"It's in your best interest to tell me the truth here Reid, because this is not looking favourable for you."

"I know." I lower my head and stare at the shag carpeting. *Now or never.* "I thought Morgan might have learnt about what I did. I ... I kissed someone ... It was Linda, on a business trip recently, a couple of months ago." I pause, waiting for something. A gasp. A groan, something, but there's nothing.

"I see."

"Morgan was acting strange after I returned. I gathered she found out what took place. Things have been getting worse between us, so I took most of our savings to keep it safe. Women get angry and want revenge about shit like this. Morgan might have been planning to end our marriage." I hear myself and want to instantly punch myself in the head. I'm so broken, stupid, and exhausted. I wish I could close my eyes and open them again and this will be over. My heart aches. How the fuck could I screw up my marriage like this?

"Linda?" West says.

I look to her for confirmation.

"I kissed him, yes. We never slept together. I didn't tell Morgan. We, Reid and I, decided it was an irresponsible mistake, although harmless, and it's one that should never be spoken of. I don't think Morgan knows like Reid suspects. I'm pretty sure she has no clue about our mistake at all."

I sigh.

"But I thought you said your marriage was fine, Reid? This is obviously not the truth, then is it?" West says.

My fists clench and my jaw tenses. I'm an idiot. I'm the biggest idiot to walk the earth. "The money is here. I didn't use it to do what all you think I did. It's in the safe in the office."

"Where's the office, again?" West speaks calmly.

"This level, down the corridor past the kitchen. It's

the last door on the right, and the safe is inside the cupboard."

"It's best you take us to the safe now, Mr Banks."

Shit! We're back to Mr Banks again.

I'm escorted not only by West, but Gleaton, Maloney and one of the two other officers. The tall lanky one stays behind in the loungeroom with Linda, even though nobody said a word about him doing so. We walk in a conga line down the hallway and when I stop at the office door I know I'm going to be fine, and in the clear, because they'll see the money is there and know I'm finally giving them the whole truth. My hand hovers over the door handle and even though I'm hesitating, I feel letting this skeleton out of the closet will finally end some of the guilt I've been carrying. Secrets make people do stupid shit and this entire situation with Linda has had me making stupid decisions and doing stupid shit.

We enter. I slide open the cupboard door that's positioned directly across from my desk. It's a moderately sized, metal safe and I'm now looking directly at it.

"We saw this on search of the lower level, sir. We have listed it on our form," Maloney says.

"Good," West replies.

I say nothing. With a tensed finger, I punch in the combination, 3.6.5.9.2.1 ... the latch opens. Crouching down, I outstretch my hand and move to retrieve the sports bag of money from the floor of the safe where I left it. My hand runs across the bottom of the metal.

Panic sets in as I fail to locate the bag.

"It's not there," I choke out. "It's gone." The shock radiating through my limbs has my legs growing weak and my arms following suit.

A generic ring tone plays from the pocket of my sweat pants.

I rise slowly from the floor.

"Where is the money, Reid?" West, says. Displeased would be an understatement as to how he looks at me when I come to face him. I'd say, he's about ready to haul my arse down to the cop shop and lock me up for life.

I retrieve my phone taking a moment to glance at the screen. *Morgan's dad is calling.* Morgan must have found the money and hid it somewhere. That has to be it. There's no other logical explanation.

"Reid." Gleaton's tone is clipped.

"I have to take this," I say, softly.

"What could be so important?" Maloney is calm, yet there's a subtle strain to his words.

"It's Morgan's Dad, Ronald. I need to take this call." I'm dazed, confused and downright furious. Why did Morgan take the money?

"Answer it," West orders.

I go to leave the room.

"You can answer it here."

"Hello," I say.

"Put the call on speaker," West instructs.

I immediately switch the speaker on. "Hey Ron."

"Reid, we're delayed. There's been an accident on

the highway. A cattle truck has rolled over. It looks like a pretty nasty accident from where we're sitting. For now, we're stuck waiting. You know what these country highways are like when a truck overturns?"

"Yeah, I do." I scan the room to find eight sets of eyes all focused on me. "Are you two okay though?"

"Yes, we're fine. Now is there any news on Morgan, yet? Have you heard from her? Do you know anything more?" His tone is a mix of despair and worry.

"No, we haven't. Not yet. Linda's here now though."

"Oh, that's good news. Has she heard from Morgan? Does she know what's wrong? Why Morgan hasn't come home?"

"No sir, she doesn't."

"Okay. Can you please ring me if you learn anything or have an update?"

"I will."

"Her mother is beside herself right now and quite frankly I'm worried. I wish we didn't live so far away."

"I know. Me too."

"I'll talk to you soon, Reid."

"Okay."

"I'll let you know when we're moving again." He sighs.

"Drive safe, and I'll see you soon."

"We are. Ring if there is any news."

"I will."

"Bye."

"Bye."

The call disconnects.

The majority of the afternoon is spent being interrogated by the two detectives who no doubt believe I'm their prime suspect. I was allowed to call one person after I spoke with Morgan's dad and that person was my father. He's currently contacting a lawyer and he's pissed as hell at me after I explain everything that's transpired since we last talked. My dad is going to kick my arse when he gets here and I'm going to deserve his boot planted fair up my arse too.

"I don't know where the money is. Morgan knows the code to the safe. She doesn't go in there as far as I know." I pause. "Look, I'm the only one who uses it. I've already told you this."

"So why would --" I cut West off.

"I don't know. All I do know is, Morgan has the code and she could have taken the money out. I can't tell you anything else. I've been telling you this for ages now."

"Where's the money?" West isn't letting up.

"I'm telling you the truth. It was in there. I don't have the foggiest idea where it is now."

Another hail of the identical questions gets hurled my way by Detective West, and soon Gleaton takes his turn of asking them all over again.

"What else can I say? I've told you everything. It's all I know." I feel like a hole has been dug so deep, I'm about to be buried in a very unpleasant way. Twenty-five to life, throw away the key is what my future holds and our children's lives are about to be so royally fucked up, that breathing becomes an almost impossible task.

"I'm going to ask you one more time, where is the money?" West says.

"Where are you Morgan?" I say under my breath, sitting at the very table I sat at last night, awaiting her arrival home.

"Reid, let's go over this again." Gleaton is like a hungry shark who's only mission is to fire questions at me until he penetrates the protective cage I'm trying to find security in.

I drop my head to the table and fold my arms over the back of my head. Why keep asking me these fucking questions? The answers aren't going to change.

Ring. Ring. Ring.

It's the home phone.

My balls instantly launch into my throat and my heart sprints. It has to be him.

"Go. Wait for me to pick up the other line." West is out of his chair as fast as I am.

I nod.

I'm staring at the phone which is gripped in my hand. I'm waiting for West to give the go ahead or a sign to indicate I need to pick up the line. I can see the time on the screen, 5:28 p.m. He hasn't rung again all day. This must be him.

"Go," West mouths with his hand cupped over the speaker and his finger poised over the accept button.

"Hello. Reid speaking."

"Reid, can you do me a favour please?" The accent is British.

Who is this? I narrow my eyebrows and look at West who mouths, "Say nothing."

I don't.

"Could you say hello to Detective Astin West for me. Go on."

West again mouths, "Say nothing."

The line goes dead.

Chapter Twenty-Four

Morgan

Both my shins have sustained deep lacerations. A trip wire placed between two trees inflicted these injuries that are stinging fiercely and bleeding profusely. I swear I can see my bone amongst the tattered flesh, but I'm not sure. I was too caught up in my thoughts to watch where I was going. I need to be more aware of my surroundings. I need to be smarter. He said I wasn't smart enough to win his game, but I believe I am. I need to outsmart the Wolf.

The sight of the injury gives me the urge to vomit through my clenched teeth every time I turn my eyes towards it. Slowly swinging the backpack to my front, I groan in agony. My hands are shaking, as is the rest of my body, and I'm dripping in sweat. The zip slips out of my pinched grip and again, I groan. I just want to lie down and close my eyes. I don't have anything left in the tank. I'm beyond exhausted and my sight is becoming blurry with every blink of my lashes, but I can't give up, so again I try pulling back the zip. This time I have it opened wide enough to retrieve the canister.

Pouring the last drops of water over my open wounds hurts like hell, and I growl through my teeth as the blood mixed with water runs across my feet.

Lord, help me.

The bandage from the backpack, the one he left for me, the one he knew I was going to need is now in my hand. He knew I wouldn't see the trip wire. He knows everything that's going to happen before it even does, and he told me he'd always be one step in front of me. He didn't lie, he is.

One bandage, two open wounds. I must find a way to cut the material, but how?

I leave the backpack on the ground with the empty canister and use my arms to pull my body across mouldy leaves and dry dirt. I search for anything sharp to cut the bandage into two halves, but so far there's nothing. My vision is becoming worse and the nausea I'm experiencing is flipping my stomach so wildly that my will to give in and die is growing strong. For one moment, I contemplate death being the only option I have left. Maybe I should end this game here and now because I can't even walk. Something buried deep down in the pit of my soul keeps me fighting, and I reach out my forearm, press it hard against the ground, and scream my agony as I drag my body a little bit farther from where it was.

A fallen branch catches the corner of my eye. It's not clear to see from this distance, but I believe I can discern a protruding branch poking upwards. Lying on my side I begin to roll my body as if it was being unravelled from heavy carpeting. It hurts like hell, but I'm making ground faster.

Unrolling the material of the bandage, I try to hold it up from the dirty ground below, but it's not working. My teeth become a vice to keep half the length at my height.

I work the fabric over the snapped branch, piercing the middle of the length, halfway down; the threads rip easily. I don't stop repeating this action until the bandage finally splits into two separate parts.

I'm huffing as I attempt to wrap the wounds tightly, it's harder than I anticipated, mainly because my legs are bleeding so badly the bandage is becoming drenched with blood. My sticky fingers are also not helping the situation, but with a determined scrunched face, I somehow manage to secure them in place, tucking the ends inside, at the back of my calf. I don't think they'll stay in place long, but it's something for the interim.

Bang!

It's a loud thunder clap I associate with the sound of a rifle being fired.

Bang!

There's another shot fired.

Bang ...! Bang!

He's coming.

A wild pig comes screeching around a bend, heading in my direction. There's no way I'm going to be able to stand, let alone walk, to get away from this beast. I freeze as my heart gallops and I stare down the boar making ground quicker than I can draw air – – this fucker is going to ram those horns straight through my guts; there's no doubt in my mind about it.

Bang!

I hear a tortured screech, followed by a wild snorting sound and then the boar lies on its side, expelling feral sounds, but not moving.

The Wolf. He slaughtered this animal to save me. Why?

I see him standing far off in in the distance. I know it's the Wolf because he's wearing all black, and he holds the rifle pointed straight in the direction of my head. I scoot backwards. It's not far, but I'm moving, I don't want to screech feral sounds like that boar just did. I don't when a bullet piercing my own skin before ricocheting between my bones and organs.

He takes two steps forwards, and I watch him like a hawk. He begins to walk, until his pace quickens to a jog. The gun still remains in target with my skull.

"Help." It's a drained call. "Help. Someone help me," I whimper whilst continuing my efforts to drag myself to some sort of protective shelter.

The Wolf's running. I can't hear his footsteps as he sprints towards me. It's like he's weightless in his pursuit. How do his feet land so silently? I swallow hard and cry out just as he vanishes from my vision.

Where the fuck did he go?

The backpack is too far from me to grab it, and all I can think is I need to find somewhere to shelter immediately. But where? I can't climb, run or walk. The hairs on the back of my neck stand to attention.

"Red. You have to be faster than that." I feel his breath race down my neck.

He's behind me.

"Move," he whispers with his cheek pressed against mine. "Move," he says again.

"I can't." I cry out.

His touch disappears. *Is he gone?* I fold my eyelids closed just as I feel the barrel of his rifle press into the back of my skull. "RUN!" It's a demanding deliverance, yet it's not anger fuelled. He's in control.

I fall forwards and slide my body away from him using my forearms, that is until I pull myself up onto my knees, and begin crawling. I hear his footsteps coming up my rear and sob hard as I manage to find enough strength to stand on the balls of my feet. I'm hobbling at first, then jogging ... I run. The scream that flies from my wide mouth is the most tortured and painful scream I have ever heard in my life. It's a scream that comes from deep down within a person's soul, my soul. He's destroying me, inside and out. The Wolf isn't going to allow me any mercy. He's taking pleasure from these games, his hunt, and I'm sure he'll get the ultimate pleasure when he guts me like a pig and hangs my skin from his wall as a trophy.

I can't give up. I don't want to be his trophy.

Chapter Twenty-Five

Reid

Kylee stands in the doorway to our home. Her hand is pressed against her beige blouse, right over her breast. Tears leak from her eyes and it's obvious to anyone who sees her she's barely keeping it together. Her face is drained of all colour and her body is trembling as she takes quick short breaths. I wish I could deliver her some news of value to help bring her some calm, but I have nothing to offer. There's no news to share.

I move quickly towards Morgan's mother, and pull her into a tight embrace. All I can do right now is try and offer comfort. Kylee's wispy blonde hair brushes across my lower lip creating a tickling sensation that sends shivers racing down my throat, so I pull my head back and release my embrace. I search her dark eyes that plead for me to do something, but I can't do anything more than I currently am. I don't know where her daughter is and I've no idea where to start looking to find her.

"Reid." Ron holds two small suitcases. He drops them just inside the entry way and then marches towards me. "Reid," he says again in a tone that could snap through the toughest metal. He's strong in appearance, commanding in deliverance, and calm in persona. I outstretch my hand and he takes no time placing his into mind, before I'm pulled into his embrace. "We're here now. Let's find my girl. Let's find her together."

"Okay." It's a tone with no strength. "She'll be coming home; we'll find her." All masculinity has evaded my voice. I'm even more frightened now Morgan's parents have arrived. I'm not sure if it's because their presence makes the situation more real, or if it's because now there is a safety net here to fall into. I need to stay strong and in charge, yet all I want to do is crumble and fall apart.

When I step back Ron says, "Reid, tell me everything that's happened. Don't leave a single piece of information out. I need to hear what's occurred so far … from start to finish. Bring me up to speed."

I nod, leading both Kylee and Ron in the direction of Detective West who's tapping away on a laptop he has set up at the kitchen table. West is trained for this informative shit. I'm not.

Introductions go easy, and West is compassionate as he walks Morgan's parents through as many details as he chooses. I hadn't told Ron or Kylee much before they arrived, and as I listen to every piece of information unfolding, I can see the distress in Kylee's eyes growing wilder. Her tears are flowing rapidly, and she's almost gone through half the box of tissues I retrieved from Morgan's library when they started hearing the circumstances of their daughter's disappearance.

Ron scratches the skin on the bald patch in the centre of his scalp. He does this when he's thinking, but also when he's nervous. I don't know what to say to help him, so I say very little. Ron's a huge man, and his size can be intimidating to most. Ten years he's been working the land and he speaks his mind when it's called for. He's not one to hold his tongue regardless of the situation he's found himself in. Morgan often refers to her dad as a hard man to look at, but a teddy bear on the inside. I'd have to agree. He's not shy in tearing up and expressing his emotions if needed, but right now he's holding it together very well and remaining incredibly calm, even when West goes over the two separate calls we have received and why the children are currently next door.

"I'd like to see the children soon, Reid. Can I see them?" Kylee asks.

I look to West who says, "It's probably best we leave the visits until morning, but we've had a child psychologist with your grandchildren today, and they're being very well looked after by the Peter's. You and Ron have travelled a long way from what Reid's shared with us ... everyone just needs to take some time to rest."

Kylee is nodding. Ron on the other hand has a sullen expression as he stares off into space.

"We've been assured by our trained psychologist that your grandchildren are very comfortable where they are staying presently. I promise you they're being well taken care of."

"I see," Kylee says. Her small shoulders are shaking with the same force as her hands, excessively.

When the matter of the missing money is brought to the attention of Ron, he rotates his head slowly and glares at me. There's an abundance of anger building in his glare and I believe his instincts are burning a raging hot red in his belly. He says seven words to me, "Are you responsible for Morgan going missing?"

"No." I don't break eye contact. I let Ron see my honesty for himself. I know he'll see the truth, because Ron's always been a human lie detector. He can pick a bullshitter from miles away.

"I believe him," Ron says, focusing his attention back to West. "Continue. Reid doesn't know where the money is. Trust me, I know when that man is lying."

"Ronald, did you know your son-in-law and Linda had an affair recently?" West goes straight with a punch to my jugular. *Fuck!*

Ron rotates his head the exact same way he did

only a minute ago.

"That true?" He's angry.

"No sir. Not an affair. A few moments of passionate kissing. I didn't sleep with her. I was drunk, so was Linda. Nothing more happened."

He studies me. I know he's trying to see through me as if I was created from glass.

'You're a dumb arse," he says.

"I know." I don't break eye contact even though right now I'd like nothing more than to look away from Morgan's father.

"We all make mistakes. I believe you didn't do anything else. I also believe Linda wouldn't. Those two girls have been friends a really long time ... since teenagers. You fucked up, Reid."

"I know. I did."

"Reid." Kylee is dabbing her cheeks with a tissue when I shift my attention to her. "You've hurt my girl."

"I know."

"Does Morgan know about this?" Kylee asks.

I shake my head. "I don't know."

"Men are bloody pigs. Ron, he has taken a leaf out of your book by the sounds of this." Kylee glares at Ron.

"No need to bring that up here and now woman. I'll talk to Reid about that at a later time."

"You better talk some sense into him is all I'm saying." She throws the used tissue to the table and slides another out of the box beside her.

"We all make mistakes. It's owning them that

makes a real man." Ron says.

I nod.

State Emergency Service officers are taking up most of the lawn in front of the house. I'm standing less than a metre from them, right beside Maloney. I want to ask questions. I want to know if they have found anything, but I've been forbidden to ask. West said I was lucky to even be allowed to stand this close to them just before he walked in their direction.

Maloney told me early this afternoon they were coming. He also informed me they've been searching through rough terrain most of the day looking for Morgan. Some of the men and women glance briefly in my direction, but most seem to be avoiding any eye contact. I wonder how many of them think I did it and they are wasting their time even being here.

Their orange coveralls are filthy, and their faces wear worn-out expressions. There of different ages, sizes, sexes, heights and races, but they've all got one thing in common, and that is they're trying to find Morgan.

"One last area to search today, the area Morgan's car was found last night, just inside the Norman Gardens Estate. Now our officers combed this land throughout the night and this morning ... it's still taped off and restricted, but I want it combed through again before night fall." West pauses. "Anything, I don't care if it's a cigarette butt. I want it bagged and tagged. Thank you for your duty," West concludes, before turning and walking away from the gathered state volunteers.

I begged, pleaded and made every attempt to be allowed to search this area with the SES, but it fell on deaf ears. All West kept saying was, "If another call comes through you need to be here. You need to help me, help you." It's killing me not to be out searching for Morgan. I feel useless waiting inside the house doing nothing.

Maloney stays beside me as I witness the orange jumpsuits climb back into the many SES vehicles. One petite lady pauses and offers me a slight wave ... I oblige with one in return. Another taller, stockier man with a trimmed beard nods his head slightly in my direction and I offer a strained half smile in return. One man looks sullen, excessively worried even, and I turn my eyes away from him. It's like he already knows this isn't going to end well. I couldn't consider his bright blue eyes for even a second longer. Why is he searching if he shows a face of doubt?

I jump when a car door closes loudly and as I search for the location, I'm staring at a large man who is wearing what appears to be a brand-new set of coveralls. His glare is ice cold. I want to tell him to take a picture because it will last longer, but I don't, I just turn my attention away from him. Another man stops and turns in my direction. He's smiling at me, almost as if he's happy to be here. It's the only thing running through my mind as I make connection with his eyes.

Do I know him? Is that why he's smiling? I think about how familiar he seems as he runs his hand over his pickled face with one hand, and the other he brushes over his short blond hair. His smile disappears when he puffs out his cheeks and then releases the air that expanded them. Maybe I do know him. I nudge Maloney.

"Yes."

The guy turns his back to me, before casually making his way to one of the vehicles closest to the footpath. He leaps into the passenger side and before I see his face again, the door is closed. Why was his uniform much cleaner than most of the others? Were more searchers added?

"Reid." Maloney says.

"Huh."

"You nudged me. What's wrong?"

"I swear everyone I glance at I think is a suspect, that they've taken Morgan."

"What do you mean?"

"That guy who just climbed in to the ute. I swear I knew him."

"Clean coveralls. Light hair ...?"

"Yeah."

"He's one of the local news reporters, Reid. He often helps out like that so he has up-to-date information when reporting to the public."

"Oh. Tell me, Maloney, will you ever be able to find the person who took Morgan?"

"We will. It's our job. We're trained for this."

Nightfall approaches fast. I can no longer see the sun drifting slowly behind the mountains, or the sky colouration merging from blues to oranges and then pinks. It's dark now. I'm standing on the front porch, under the light smoking a cigarette Maloney gave me the moment I asked for one. I've never smoked a day in my life... until now. I needed something, and when I asked for one of these cancer sticks about half an hour ago, it seemed like the best idea. It tastes like absolute shit.

I still can't get a hold of my dad, even though I've tried. I spoke to him at six p.m. which was over an hour ago. I asked about the lawyer, and what's happening with that. The only answer I got was he'd been contacted. My parents spoke to me from the airport where they were awaiting a chance to board any flight that could get them closer to home. So far, there's none departing until tomorrow afternoon that have seats available. From what I understand from the conversation, Cruise and his wife Natalie are not with my parents, instead they are doing some type of tour. Dad said he had no idea where they were, and Cruise still wasn't answering the phone. Dad said they haven't been contactable since Monday. I'm worried about this, but Dad is not. *"They're doing a tour, Reid, one we elected not to accompany them on. We were aware contact would be difficult. Cruise loves all that hiking and shit, and so does Natalie. They could be God knows where."*

I can't help wondering if they too are in trouble. Is Morgan's abduction a payback against something I've done? And if so what? Is this game playing monster trying to achieve a direct attack on my family? Is anyone safe? I don't know what to think.

"Hey, the children are doing fine. I just went over and spoke to your neighbours. Shirley said to tell you not to worry; they've eaten and are watching a movie."

"Thanks," I say, looking at the bottom of the three front stairs where Maloney stands out of uniform in jeans and a white T-shirt. "What movie?"

"Shrek, I believe it was."

"Good. They like that one. Hey, any news from the searchers?"

Maloney shakes his head. "I've heard nothing." He pauses, tilting his head off centre. "Reid. The money."

"Yeah."

"Do you have any idea where it is?"

"Nope. I've said it at least a hundred times. I put it in the safe after I picked it up on Wednesday and I didn't go back into the safe again. Your guess is as good as mine. What I can tell you though is Morgan is the only other person who has access to the safe and nobody else."

"I believe you don't know where it is," Maloney says when he takes the three stairs. "Hang in there, mate." He pats my back before walking through the open front door.

At least someone believes me.

Morgan's parents are inside with Linda and they are talking with a new detective, Detective Lynette Dyson. She arrived about thirty minutes ago when West and Gleaton left. Apparently, they will both return in the morning to do a press conference that has been organised at the house. I'm under strict instructions not to leave the premises for any reason. I'm also not allowed to visit my children right now, nor am I to let anyone apart from immediate family who have been cleared by officers, into the house. I'm a prime suspect. Maloney didn't keep that information from me. In fact, he's answering any questions I have for him when he can. I'm glad he's the one stationed to stay here at the house with me ... well, him and Senior Constable Eric Prospect, the lanky redhead officer who came in with him earlier this morning. He's also one of the officers who conducted the search downstairs and then this evening upstairs. I couldn't care what they look at as long as they find Morgan and soon. Because if they don't, I'll sneak out of here and find her myself. They can't hold me if they don't know where I am. I can leave here without them seeing me. I know there's a way.

Chapter Twenty-Six

The Wolf

Tick tock. Tick tock. The hands of time are moving fast and Morgan will soon be faced with her next challenge. The stupid bitch will fail too.

Red will run to the rusty old car stranded in the middle of a small open paddock. I have no doubt about it. It's the only place over these forty hectares where there isn't a bunch of trees and sheltering bushland to keep a person feeling trapped and lost. I put it there for a reason. It's a shelter to give my Reds a false sense of safety, and I bet they believed they mustn't have been far away from finding help at this point. They're always wrong for thinking this. Psychology 101: Perception. Changing a person's perception of a situation can help to change the situation they're in. It does. But not for the right reasons in my game.

Twelve women have played, and all twelve of them have laid down on the back seat of that piece of shit. I believe Morgan will be no different and I think she's laying across that back seat right now feeling the calmest she has since this game started. Silly bitch. You should never let your guard down.

I'll be heading out there soon, well as soon as I can get away from here without being detected. I can't have people knowing what it is I'm doing and ruin all my fun. Detective West is my marksman. If anyone catches me, it needs to be him.

I sit, drifting deeper into my thoughts, while the mindless chatter around me becomes distant and muffled. I can't stop thinking about how I sent Morgan heading off in the direction of this set-up and how I know she's probably taken the bait by now. I'd be surprised if she hadn't, yet pleased.

If Morgan has any brains, when she reaches the car she will have realised, right before she slipped past the partly open door I left that way for her, that my rusty old broken-down heap of shit, with no wheels, has brand new windscreens and windows. This is the clue. This is the chance for her to stay away. But she'll be blind to the fact like the rest of them. I'm holding onto a glimmer of hope she'll see it for what it is, and prove to me she's smarter than I've given her credit for, but I'm not holding my breath.

Stupid women do stupid things and this how they get killed.

Run away from the car, Morgan, if you want to exit the game here. I laugh, not realising I'm doing so, and quickly stop myself as I turn my eyes down and adjust my expression to one more sombre.

I'm coming for you, Red. I hope you're not too comfortable because you're about to answer my question. Who am I? Your first test is almost complete.

Chapter Twenty-Seven

Morgan

I'm hugging the trunk of a tree that my arms only just fit around. My fingers are laced together and I'm staring in the direction of a car I saw just before sunset. I can no longer see it in the darkness, but I know it's still there because I haven't heard an engine start, or it drive away.

It sits in a small open clearing, far off in the distance, and this strikes me as strange due to the endless amount of bushland surrounding this opening, but it also leaves me wondering how far I've managed to trek today, and if the Wolf's presence in the late afternoon was because he's worried I'm getting close to finding help and getting the hell out of here. I don't think he knows this car is out here, and I believe this will be my only chance of freedom. So, I wait. I stay quiet, and I welcome the cloak of darkness to help me find my way there with the best chance of making the distance. There must be a road on the other side to drive out on. It couldn't have just been dropped in.

The howls of dingoes have me jolting every time they cry out. I know they're getting closer to me because their cries are growing louder. I imagine the other wildlife these bushes contain at night will lead to a deathly attack. I need to get in that car. It's now or never.

I've waited, what I believe to be hours, for this trek and as I wince, using the thick trunk as a support beam, I'm finally standing. My breathing becomes shallow and my mind is clear. I need to focus. Every step forwards I take is tentative. I don't use the torch. I rely on my memory and shift until I'm walking at a forty-five degree angle off to the right. Two large trees block my path. It takes eight paces to get to the first one, and twenty paces to the second. I walked them out earlier as sunset was encroaching. I counted every step in my mind, three times, and by the grace of God, when I put this into practice now, I manage to pass them without a collision. I feel as though I'm hunting. My feet are slowly lifted and placed with precision. I'm doing everything I can to make as little noise as humanly possible. A dingo's howl causes me to jump. I duck low and grit my teeth to shield the fear this causes from exploding out of my mouth. I don't pant.

Instead, I hold my breath. *You can do this, Morgan. Baby steps. There's no rush. You can escape the Wolf.* I'm chanting this in my mind as I find my feet once more. I step carefully, controlling the fear trying to invade my thoughts. I'm in control.

I'm starting to lose hope when my legs burn excessively from the amount of weight I'm applying to each leg at each step. I'm still not able to feel anything with my outstretched hand. I'm reaching for the metal. I'm praying I will touch it soon and then my fingertips halt against something solid. Relief floods my body. It's one explosive rush from my head to my toes as I run my hand over the surface.

What is that?

I scrunch my face at the texture below my fingertips. The surface is rough, almost flaky. Brushing my thumb back and forwards over my fingers, I close my eyes and try to identify the flaky particles stuck to my skin. What is it? Crouching low, I suck back one mouthful of air as a groan rumbles deep in my throat. *I cannot make noise. I need to hold my breath.* I do.

Removing the torch from the backpack I had to go back and retrieve and I've slung across my front proves easy. I swiftly tuck it up inside my blouse to dim its glow. I tilt it upwards to get a better look and my heart drops to my stomach as I gasp loudly. This car has no tyres. This is a fucking trap.

A drawn-out whistle has my heart beating hard in my chest. It grows more eerie the louder and closer it gets. He wants me to hear him coming. He wants me to know he tricked me and I fell for it.

I shut off the torch light and lay flat on my back against the ground, trying desperately to roll underneath the car, but I don't fit, it's far too low. *What the fuck do I do?*

Diving through the open back door I lay as still as I can across the back seat... and I pray.

Chapter Twenty-Eight

Reid

"I'm heading upstairs to take a shower," I say, after I glance at the clock and realise the time's going just as slowly as it has been all night. It's only a quarter past ten, and even though I've been pacing a track from the lounge room to the dining room table for what seems like hours, I learn it's been mere minutes.

Detective Dyson tips her head to the side and eyes me briefly. "That's probably a good idea." Her glossed lips offer me a half smile before she's back focusing on the screen of the large laptop open in front of her. In the short time she's been here, I've figured she's not much of a talker. She's quiet, yet observant. Her hand curls around the back of her neck just below the black bob tucked behind her ears. She hunches her shoulders and squeezes her eyes tightly shut as she rotates her neck in a large circle. Tonight is going to be a long night for everyone.

I pause at the bottom of the staircase and strain to hear Maloney talking. He must be on a call. I can't make out anything except, "He's definitely restless. He hasn't sat down for ages. To be honest sir, he looks like he might throw up." If by he, he is referencing me, then Maloney's not wrong. My stomach is knotted into a million tight pieces of rope balled together. I could vomit at any second from the nausea this is creating.

Dragging my feet up the staircase, has me looking down the dark hallway leading to Morgan's and my bedroom. First, I pass by Brax's room, and then Aleeha's. Both their doors are closed since Ron and Kylee are utilising them for a place to sleep tonight. I wonder if they're doing any sleeping, or if they're blankly staring at the ceiling above them, lost in their own torturous thoughts. My mind won't stop racing. *Where is Morgan? And who the fuck has her?* play on a constant loop.

Clutching the handle of our bedroom door, I take two drawn-out breaths as I pull it down and push forwards. I run my hand over the wall just inside the entrance, and fumble with the light switch. Everything looks exactly how we left it yesterday morning. The bed's unmade, Morgan's cotton pyjamas are thrown over her pillow, her T-shirt still inside out after taking it off and discarding it. The only thing out of place is the towel I'd thrown on the bed after the shower I took earlier today. God, how Morgan hates when I leave my wet towel on the bed. It's one of her biggest pet peeves. I race over to it and swiftly remove it with one flick of my wrist.

The walk to the bathroom has untameable worry growing heavily in my chest. This is how I felt last night when Morgan still hadn't come home. An hour later, the police were inside my house, downstairs, talking with me. Not long after, I raced off in anger to find Morgan, but all I'd uncovered was her SUV.

Twenty-four hours has almost past, and apart from some fucked up calls from a mechanical voice and then one with a British accent, it doesn't appear like anyone has any leads on Morgan's whereabouts. Isn't it if they haven't found someone in the first twenty-four hours, the chance of their survival decreases? Or is it the first forty-eight? I can't be sure. This is a question for Maloney.

Hanging the towel on the rack above Morgan's, I reach into the open shower and turn over the taps before shedding my clothes and stepping in. Lukewarm water runs over my skin as I rest my forehead against the wall behind the shower's spout. The feeling of the soft sprays against my shoulders calms my senses for a moment, but it doesn't last long because Morgan's face displays like a stilled image in my mind. She's more than beautiful — she's angelic.

I roll my head from side to side as my throat constricts and then burns from the sadness I'm trying to rein in. *Where is the money? Why is this happening to us?* I can't figure out the answer to either of these questions.

I don't bother to use the liquid soap to wash myself. I don't do anything but ask myself a million questions that right now nobody has answers to. *This is bullshit.* I reef the taps off, and step out, being mindful to stand on the bathmat I always miss standing on. This also pisses Morgan off. Maybe if I don't make the floor all wet and slippery, and maybe if I don't do all the things she nags at me about, she'll come home.

Morgan's towel is embroidered with her name, pink lettering on white towelling. Taking it into my possession, I still with it rested below my nostrils. It smells clean, freshly washed, and not at all like Morgan. I hate this.

I chuck on a tight-fitted black T-shirt and long cotton pyjama bottoms, and remake the bed, taking extra care to do it neatly like Morgan would have liked me to do more often. *"It's tightly tucked edges ... and the top needs to be turned down for God sake. How hard is this to master, Reid?"* A small crinkle would invade her forehead as she glared at me from her side of the bed. *"The pillows, just stack them neatly."* Morgan's little quirks. Once I thought of these nit-picking things as Type A bullshit, but now I see how it's as important to me in this moment as it was to Morgan every day. *Why did I give her such a hard time about all these tiny unimportant things? If that's how she liked the bedding, I should have just fucking made it that way.* You're a prick, Reid.

I sigh. It's a deep heavy sound, and the result of dread. I'm now dreading I'll never see Morgan perform these little rituals for the rest of my life and that scares me.

The open blind catches my attention and when I move towards it, I stare out of the window into the darkness of the night, feeling dazed, lost and alone.

"Morgan," I whisper.

The glare of the television screen as Maloney flicks through multiple channels annoys me.

"Just pick something already," I groan.

"Mate, I'm trying to find the local news station. I just received a message from Detective West to turn on the television and to have you come sit down."

"What for?"

"There's about to be a breaking news story regarding Morgan's disappearance."

My mouth forms an oversized 'O', even though no sound projects with it.

"There we go. It should be on in a moment." He lays the remote on the glass coffee table and leans back into the navy corner lounge.

I don't get comfortable. Instead I sit on the edge of the seat and wait nervously. My legs jiggle as I push from the balls of my feet. I just can't seem to stop moving.

"Breaking News." Big white letters across a red banner appears on the screen. The tune that accompanies breaking new headlines plays. I swallow excessively as vomit is seduced from my stomach to the back of my tongue. I think I'm going to throw up.

"We interrupt this programming to bring you the latest headlines and breaking news stories throughout Rockhampton, Gladstone, Mackay and the Keppel Bay Region."

A picture of Morgan takes up half of the television screen. Her hair is tied to the side and pinned. Her big browns eyes are wide and filled with joy. Her lips are pulled into a smile. She looks so happy, so content. I notice the soft pink dress she's wearing is the one she wore when Cruise and Natalie got married last year. "How did you get that picture?" I didn't give it to them.

"Linda," Maloney says softly. "She went through your albums and picked it out before she left to go home tonight."

I nod.

"Local Rockhampton woman, Morgan Banks, mother of two, and wife to local architect Reid Banks, has been reported missing. She was last seen leaving her place of work, Tactor Finance and Appraisals, early yesterday evening. Morgan is reported to be around 168 centimetres tall. She has a slim athletic build with long brown hair and brown eyes. It's been reported Morgan was wearing a pink blouse and black business skirt at the time of her disappearance. Police are urging anyone with information to the whereabouts of Morgan Banks, to come forward and call either the Police Link or Crime Stoppers on the numbers displayed at the bottom of your screen. Today, local SES volunteers have searched bushland around the fourth access road between Rockhampton and Yeppoon, but police are yet to report if this search has led to any more information."

Morgan's photograph fades and is replaced with that of the courthouse building.

"In other news, Brendon Carter Johnston will appear in the Rockhampton Magistrates Court tomorrow morning for his alleged involvement in the stabbing of local teenager Christopher Keelage. The family of the victim are expected to be present for his plea entry."

Maloney must mute the volume because the presenter's lips are moving, yet there's no sound.

"You know, I never dreamt in my entire life, I'd be seeing my wife's photo as a missing person. I don't understand why this is happening?"

"Bad things happen to good people all over the world, every day of the week, Reid. We'll find her."

"Alive?" I close my eyes.

"It's the outcome we are hoping for. They really are

doing everything to help your wife."

"I know." I pause. "Do you think it's someone we know?" I say, turning my attention to Maloney.

"I'd say there's a high chance it is, but it could also be someone Morgan's never met before."

"I just need for her to be alive."

"We know. All evidence so far is pointing to the fact that she is Reid."

"He'll call again, right? That bastard who has her?"

"I have no doubt he will."

Chapter Twenty-Nine

Morgan

The whistling stops, and no matter how hard I try to slow my breathing, I can't. Terror is building at such a rapid rate it has me panicking, and with this increased panic, I begin to hyperventilate. The hairs on my neck are standing upright. My palms are slick with moisture. My legs are shaking to a fast tempo and my mind is racing.

Please leave me alone. I can't take anymore.

A beam of light shines straight above me. I follow its path out the front windscreen and this can only mean one thing –– his location is at the rear end of the car.

I take one large breath and hold it. I think of Aleeha

and Brax running around the house -- laughing, fighting, being kids, and I play these images over and over, trying to make my mind believe that's where I am right now, at home, not here with him. *I don't need to be frightened. I don't need to be frightened,* I mouth in a chant. *Fear can only become powerful if I give it my power. Fear can only become powerful if I give it my power.* I mouth these words too. My dad used to say this to me when I had nightmares or I was frightened when young. It's his voice I hear clearly now. It's his hands wrapping around me in protection. My dad will calm me. My dad will save me.

The light disappears. I keep my eyes wide and try to pant small breaths. All that surrounds me is the darkness. Maybe, he doesn't know I'm in here.

The light returns and then disappears quickly. I welcome the darkness once more. Lots of flashing light turns into flickering then vanishes, leaving me blinded in the dark. It's deathly quiet. I dart my eyes up, down, left and right, repeatedly, trying to keep my mind busy.

Tap. Tap. Tap.

I press both hands over my mouth to muzzle the scream lingering at the back of my throat.

Fuck!

Tap. Tap. Tap.

Every small whimper is contained, my hands pressing harder against my lips.

Tap. Tap. Tap.

Don't move Morgan. Don't fucking move.

Each beat of my heart is happening at such an erratic pace, it becomes deafening. I will it to slow down. I beg it to believe there is no threat ... no danger. It hammers even faster and the more my fear takes over, the more my panic consumes my every thought.

I have to run. I need to run back into the bushland. I know if I tell myself I can do this, then I will. And if my horror keeps escalating like I know it will, then it will aid my body in finding a form of hysterical numbness.

Sprint. Don't look back. Keep going. Stop for nothing.

I rise like a mummy returning from the dead. Arms outstretched and slow. I find myself in a trance-like state as I face the open door I entered through. With slight hesitation, I rotate my head as slowly as I rose until I'm looking out of the back windscreen into the thick black of the night.

I squint my eyes shut the moment the light beams into them ... shielding them with my hand simultaneously. The light dulls and after I blink excessively, I see the red letters in what I believe to be lipstick, written there. They are backwards, yet it takes no time to decipher them correctly in my mind.

Who am I?

I move my mouth toward the glass. I blow air against the surface until the heat of my breath creates

a fogged area. With my fingertip, I write,
R E I D.

I see the Wolf standing close, the light turned against his masked face as he shakes his head. His lips are moving and I don't dare look away until he mouths, "Wrong answer."

I drop my head as I slide my bottom over the seating, and before my legs dangle at the opening, he's there.

"Don't hurt me," is all I say as he grabs my shoulders. We struggle. I fight as if I'm in a battle with a hungry wolf who is determined to feed from me. My hands flail. I'm scratching, tugging and slapping him. He's strong. Overpowering.

My hair is looped around his hand as he tugs my head backwards in one pull. The strain on my neck as my chin points to the sky makes it hard to swallow. I don't whimper or cry out because I can't. I can barely breathe. I'm turned in a circle on my arse from his grip, and can no longer see him. With one forceful grunt vibrating from his throat, I find myself pounding hard into the ground.

He's dragging me. I'm kicking my legs, twisting at my waist. I couldn't give a shit if he rips all my hair out due to me flailing about, because at least I'd have a chance to escape if he did. His grip remains tight and he doesn't slow down his caveman style walk; instead he quickens it. By the time he's jogging, my eyes and mind have become fuzzy, and the wounded screams I manage to finally achieve pierce the night air. By the time he is running, I close my eyes and succumb to the pain. I let the fuzziness sweep me away until I feel no more pain, no more fear, nothing ... I submit to the harsh darkness.

Chapter Thirty

Reid

The downlight above Maloney's head creates the illusion of a halo as he stares at the television. He seems relaxed with his arms outstretched on top of the lounge, and his knees spread wide apart from each other. His sneakers start where his blue jeans cut off, and they appear almost brand new when I come to focus on them in the light—stark white, no scuff marks, no tattered laces. I don't know why this seems off-putting to me, but it does.

It's a gentle clearing of his throat that causes me to shoot my eyes upwards. Maloney rotates his head in my direction, from that of the television, and subtly nods before he again turns away. I can't help wondering how Maloney managed to get the job of being my babysitter because that's how this situation seems—like I'm a toddler under constant supervision. All day, and so far, all night, someone's watched my every move. I didn't abduct my wife, and I've never wished harm upon her, not even in my angriest moments. I want Morgan to come home more than anybody. I also want to know where my money is, and why this is happening to our family, and to my wife.

Maloney hasn't said much over the last couple of hours. In fact, he's the quietest he's been since he walked into my home and took up temporary residence here. *Is fatigue getting the better of him as it is me?* My eyes burn, and the headache beating across my eyebrows makes me squeeze my eyes tight together every few minutes to reduce the strain. I should sleep, but I'm too scared, because what if the phone rings and I don't wake to answer it? Will this game-playing son-of-a-bitch kill Morgan like he promised he would if I'm not at his beck and call?

"Reid, are you okay?" Maloney says softly.

"Huh?" I need to get out of my head and away from my thoughts.

"Are you okay?" he says, this time slow and drawn out.

"No," I sigh. "Where's Morgan? Is there any new information?

"We don't know anything yet." He tips his head to the side. "We're doing everything we can." Maloney's go-to phrase. I'm sure I've heard him speak these same words numerous times today.

"It's been over twenty-four hours. I'm worried as fuck, and tired as shit. I bet Morgan is ..." I don't finish speaking because my thoughts flash between differing scenarios.

Morgan's skirt is hiked above her hips. Her knees spread wide. Her knickers rest by her ankles. There's blood streaks down her inner thighs, and when I see the deep purple hand print bruised into her skin I leap to the dirty mattress littering the concrete flooring and use my body as a blanket to cover her exposure.

"No, no, no," I hiss.

There's a miniature train circling a track beside the Ferris wheel. Its horn blows each time it rolls by a fat plastic controller standing at its side. The amusement park is absent of children's laughter, flickering lights and show tunes, until the Ferris Wheel begins to rotate unexpectedly. I tip my chin upwards in search of the children who are now screaming. I smother my mouth with my palms when Morgan's body comes into view. She's tied to the metal structure by her wrists. Dangling so high above the ground.

"Morgan." I blink excessively, trying to halt these visions. I don't want to see Morgan that way. I curl my head into my forearms, muttering, "Leave her alone."

I envision a lake. It's big, with dirty brown water and tree branches hanging over its banks, and there's Morgan, face down, floating in the lake, all the life she had perished.

"Help." It's a weak deliverance of the word from my

lips.

A room, no grander than the area I'm sitting in, is dark. There's a spotlight focused onto a four-poster bed, and as I search for my wife, it's as if the air in my lungs leaves as hers did. She's posed, naked, with her throat slit from ear to ear, and there's so much blood splattered high up the walls that the urge to vomit overcomes me. Morgan's blue in colouration, and cold when I come to brush her cheek with the backs of my fingers.

"Reid." My name sounds as if it's being spoken from a distance. I don't answer.

A dirt road stretches for miles and I'm frantic as I rush down it. I stop when I see a beaten body laid out in the centre. I gasp. The black skirt and heels Morgan last walked out of the house in ... It's her. It's Morgan. I dry-heave at the sight of her trodden body and the view of her skull caved inwards. Red, so much red, creates patterns through the dirt surrounding Morgan, and I jump back in horror when it reaches the tip of my shoe.

"Fuck," I growl.

"What's happening, Reid? Reid, can you hear me?"

I want to vomit. I'm shaking. I can't breathe. "Make it stop." I bolt upright to my feet with my eyes wide and my breath jagged.

"Look at me." His hands grip tightly around my biceps. "I think you're having a panic attack. Just look into my eyes."

I can't because all I see is Morgan. Dead.

Her head is hanging limply between her legs one

moment, and then she's running through uncontrollable flames the next.

A flash of her hanging from a noose slung high from a tree, so high I'd never reach her to remove it, takes over, and I can't seem to make these flickers of film my mind is creating stop.

"Come on, mate. Stay with me." Maloney pauses. "Lynette," he yells.

"Morgan," I cry out, as I brace my body by crossing my arms over my chest.

Fog is filling an alleyway. I'm hesitant, but the need to enter is overpowering. The alleyway suddenly becomes clear, as if someone parts the thick, smoky veil, and there, discarded amongst bags of trash, is my wife's lifeless body.

I cover my mouth. "Fuck." I drool, wiping at my lips. I hold my breath and then let out a gut-wrenching groan.

"Breathe, Reid. Come on now, just breathe."

It's Maloney; I can see his caring eyes searching mine.

"He's hurting her. He's torturing her, raping her." I pant and then moan out my agony as I fold at my mid-section.

"You don't know that. You don't know these things have happened to Morgan or that they will. Come on." Maloney's hand presses against my shoulder as I struggle to draw air into my lungs. "In through your nose, out through your mouth," he instructs calmly.

I do. Three drawn breaths lessens some of the

panic that's hit me like a bus collecting an unobservant pedestrian.

"I've got you," he says. He grips my hands and then tugs me by my arms until my feet drag along the ground. *He's moving me.*

"Sit, Reid," Maloney says.

"Okay." It's a barely audible response.

Maloney is crouched in front of me when I come to eye him. His chin is tilted back slightly and his mouth partly open. "You can't go to those types of places inside your head. Trust me, if you do, there's no coming back from them. Every scenario you play out will consume you, and then you'll be useless to us. You need to stop this so you can be strong for your wife. Falling apart like you're doing will do diddly squat." There's a long pause. "You're stronger than this."

I nod.

"Lynette, can you get him some water please?"

Lynette? Where did she come from? Where is she? I try to locate her, but Maloney obstructs my view.

"Of course, Max." She's courteous.

"Reid, you and I are going outside, aren't we?" Max's tone is laced with concern.

I don't respond.

"We're going to get some fresh air, the two of us. We'll be outside, Detective."

I growl through my teeth as I curl my fists into tight balls and beat them into my thighs. "Morgan," I groan, suppressing the urge to release any further anguish.

The air is still. There's no breeze, not even a hint of

one to come. It's muggy and dry, but even so, I don't want to leave this space. At least I can breathe out here.

Maloney offers a half-hearted wave to Senior Constable Prospect, the lanky redhead who has barely said a single word to me yet. I'm not sure what it is about Prospect, but he seems strange in so many ways. Maybe it's because he doesn't say much, or maybe it's because when I do catch him moving about, he always seems to be scanning his surroundings, like one would when snooping.

Prospect stands a fair distance away from Maloney and myself, out on the lawn, not far from the tyre swing hanging limply from the tree I tied it to not long after Brax was born. I watch as he points with one finger to his ear, and that's when I realise he's taking a call, or maybe he's listening to a message. His lips don't appear to be moving, and I can't hear him speak.

"Hey, don't beat yourself up over losing it in there," Maloney says quietly, his finger outstretched towards the open front door. "It happens to the best of us."

"Yeah," I say, defeated.

Maloney slips his hand into the pocket of his jeans, swiftly removing a pack of cigarettes, and as he does I contemplate what it would be like to put every one of those cancer sticks in my mouth and light them all at once. I know Cruise used to say he smoked because it lessened his stress levels. I wonder if that works for panic, too.

"Would you like one?" The packet is held outwards

not far from my hand.

"I think I'll pass. Those cigarettes taste like shit."

"They do." The corners of his lips rise as he slides the pack right back where he retrieved it from.

"Don't let me stop you from having one though."

"I don't smoke." Maloney's direct in the way he declares this as if it's common knowledge to the world.

I cock my eyebrows. "So why do you have them?"

"We all carry a packet. It's something we learn in the police academy. I guess I smoke, but only when and if I need to. You'd be amazed at how a simple cigarette can get a perp to open up and talk, or a frazzled civilian—"

"Some water." I turn. *Lynette*. Her face mute of emotion. Lynette has such serious features, which become more noticeable as she stands under the patio's light. I'm not sure if it's because of her crow-dark eyes, or if it's because I haven't determined if we're friends or foes at this point, but the unease that comes with being in her company sends shivers like spikes to my spine.

"Thanks." I accept the glass from her and scull the liquid in only a few gulps.

"Would you like more?"

I'm surprised to find her waiting with an outstretched hand; surprised because I've not found her to be patient or caring in the brief encounters we've had.

I shake my head, handing her the glass.

"Okay," she says deadpan.

I don't have a chance to reply with anything further because with a blink of my eyes, Detective Dyson is gone.

Prospect ambles up the front stairs and lingers beside Maloney. I stare him down as he leans into Maloney's side and whispers something, sporting an enigmatic smile. Prospect irks me. What's with this need to whisper?

Maloney inclines his head gravely in response.

"I'm going inside." Prospect eyes me. There's a coldness to the glare he delivers.

"Yep," Maloney mumbles.

"Any news?" I blurt, the moment Prospect disappears.

"No, not yet." Maloney seems distracted in answering, as if he's thinking about something in-depth. Does he have new information he's not willing to share? Is it bad?

"Are you sure? You haven't heard anything from Detective West?"

"No news." He's blunt, and I know he's lying.

The panic that consumed me not so long ago rebuilds. My hands tremble, and I bear down on my teeth as if by doing so I can clamp any remaining hope I have in my heart between them.

"We'll find her." Maloney's soft-spoken.

"You know … Have you …" I can't find the words.

"Ask me anything. I'll answer. No BS. I promise."

"Do you have any children?"

He nods promptly.

"Married?"

He nods again.

"You know when you're in a shopping complex, and you turn your head for only just a moment, and after you do your kid just up and disappears on you?"

He nods once more.

"The feeling of raw panic you experience instantly has your mind conjuring up all the terrible situations that could take place if you don't find your kid immediately. You start yelling their name, and you run, you run flat-strap like it's instinct to do so."

"Yeah. I do."

"You're searching, but every second ticking by is a second you can't change if trouble has found them." I pause, thinking about the times Brax and Aleeha have done this to me in the past. "Then you see a blur of their clothing, or you hear their tiny voice in your haste, and the panic surging your adrenaline leaves you as quickly as it set in. The sirens of danger stop ringing vociferously in your head, and you realise they were safe the entire time. It was a silly toy or bright object which called them away from your side in the first place."

"Mila, my daughter—she's done this to me." Maloney gifts an understanding smile.

"It's the worst feeling."

"It is the worst."

"You walk over to your little brat, and every part of you wants to shake the living shit out of them as you bark how scared you were straight into their innocent face. You need your child to comprehend how dangerous it was that they left your side, but even though this is what you want to do, you don't." I raise my arms linking my fingers behind my head. "Instead, you wrap your arms around their guiltless body and hold them as tightly as you can, thinking, *Thank God you're safe.*"

Maloney's nodding. "That's generally how the aftermath plays out."

"That's what I'm waiting for, Max. I'm waiting for the relief to come so it can drown out the panic swirling inside me. I need these sirens blasting in my head to stop sounding. Right now, I want to run— scream Morgan's name. Let the world flash me by as I search for her."

"I get it. I do."

"If this was your wife?"

"I'd be shit scared. There's no doubt in my mind."

"How old's your daughter?" I'm curious, but also trying to gain a level of friendship with Maloney that might see him open up and give me some information to set my uncertainties at ease.

"She's three."

"I remember my Aleeha being small like that."

"Mila's a good kid." The corner of his lips tug upward until he's contently smiling. "But she's a sassy firecracker like her mamma is."

"Kids are hard work, right?"

"That they are. Thank God I get to leave for work

and take a break from kid-wrangling. I'm not sure how my wife does it all day and night."

"Morgan's an amazing mother."

"So is my Sophia."

There's silence.

"I'll take that smoke now." I sigh. "I need something, anything to try and keep me calm."

Maloney reaches into his pocket, removing the packet for the second time. "After this, Reid, you need to try and get some sleep. Even if it's only twenty minutes, it will help."

I shake my head. "I can't sleep. I don't think I can until I have my wife home safe."

"You can't stay awake forever; your body will eventually shit itself ... Trust me."

"I'll sleep when my wife is home. That's when I'll sleep. Not before."

White water lilies bob up and down in a small pond in front of us. Morgan pauses briefly before taking the microphone to her mouth. "Reid, today you're mine forever, and this makes me the happiest girl to walk the earth. They say when you find the real thing you know, and you don't hesitate to hold it tight in your possession. I knew from the day on those university grounds when I said, 'Hi, I'm Morgan,' that I'd marry you. I truly did." She smiles broadly. "I will love you for all the days of my life. I will hold you in your darkest hours. Honour you in all you accomplish, and laugh with you through every great milestone. Nothing will ever be too much for us to handle, for we will always have each other and will find strength when rough times seek us out." Tears well in her eyes. "Your lips are my home, your hands are my comfort, and your heart guides my future. I'm honoured and privileged today to be your wife. Keep me safe, keep me warm and loved, Reid—that's all I'll ever ask of you, and in return, I'll be by your side no matter what. You're my everything. My Friend. My lover. My now husband. My Reid." Her hands tremble as she grasps the thick gold wedding band between her fingertips. "I, Morgan Amelia Cuttings, take you, Reid Elis Banks, to be ..."

The sound of a door closing causes me to jump. Where am I? Why are doors slamming?

"Reid." It's an unfamiliar voice, and for a moment I'm confused until I find myself standing in a room that brings me the sensation of peace.

I'm looking down on a wooden floor. I'm calm. I know I'm alone, yet waiting for someone.

"Are you ready, baby?" Her hands brush my waistband.

I smile in response.

"You are edible in that suit, Mr Banks."

I turn swiftly and breathe in her vanilla perfume. Morgan's my life. *It's all I can think when my eyes meet hers. "I'm ready to sweep you off your feet and show these clowns how it is we dance, baby."*

Morgan smiles as her big brown eyes fill with mischievous intent. I can read her like a book. I've never felt so close to another person in my life.

"You're my Aphrodite, Morgan. Beauty, pleasure, and procreation draped in a white wedding dress; I'm so glad you said yes."

A sweet giggle slips from her mouth as my arms desperately fold her in, pressing her body taut to mine.

"I love you, Morgan," I whisper against her cheek.

"Reid finally succumbed to sleep. Just leave him there. There's no point waking him." That unfamiliar voice returns, and as I search for the man who has ownership of it, I feel Morgan slipping out of my arms. What's happening?

The room we had our first dance in grows dark and as it does my stomach rolls with worry and the hairs on the back of my neck stand to attention.

"Come away with me," Morgan whispers, and I'm drawn to follow her bright silhouette invading the darkness.

I smell the ocean salt before I see crystal blue water. There's a light breeze rushing over my body as a white curtain sways impeding the ocean view.

"I love it here in Barbados, Reid, and I never want to go home. Can we stay forever?" Morgan lays peacefully in my arms. "I love the sound of ocean waves crashing on the shore. How will I ever sleep when we return home without this sound?"

God, she's beautiful. I don't want to leave her. I don't want to go home. "Hmmm," I moan. "We should stay here forever." I nip gently against her neck. "I love you,

Morgan."

"I love you too." She rolls until she's perched up on her elbows. Her adoring gaze tells me of her love. "I love you so much."

I can't help but pull Morgan down on top of me and hold back the hair falling over her face by cupping my hands to her cheeks. "The honeymoon might be almost over, Morgan, but I can't wait to start my life with you. I promise every day will be just like this."

Her smile is a gift from God. Oh, that smile of hers is a mix of pleasure, peace and heaven.

Ring, ring.

It's a faint sound.

Ring, ring.

It grows louder.

Ring, ring.

"What the fuck is happening?" I rub my eyes, trying to figure out why I hear ringing in our hotel room since we specifically asked for no electronics to be included.

"Here, take it." It's a woman voice.

It's not Morgan's.

"What?" I'm half asleep. Lost.

"Take it. Wait for my signal." A phone is held an inch from my nose. "Reid, get ready to answer the phone. It'll be him."

"Who?"

"Reid. You were asleep. Now you're awake. Your wife is missing. The guy who has her is calling. You need to fucking switch on." Maloney holds my chin in a pistol grip while glaring into my eyes. "Reid, you need to take this call. Morgan's missing. Wake up."

I fell asleep. I was only dreaming. I'm not surrounded by love and happiness.

I'm living a fucking nightmare.

Chapter Thirty-One

Morgan

I'm weightless, and I know I'm being carried because I can feel his chest expanding and then deflating against my cheek. I can also smell the aroma of sweat mixed with something that reminds me of my grandfather's shoe polish. His fingertips are digging into my ribcage and at my thigh, and I desperately want to pry his hands from my skin, but I can't move my arms or open my eyes.

He whistles. It's the same eerie tune I've heard many times now.

Where is he taking me?

"Oh Red, Red, Red, you've had a rough day out there today, haven't you?" He sports a strong British accent.

I want to scream, who are you? But my tongue, like the rest of me, seems paralysed.

"It will all be over soon." He speaks so calmly, and the pressure below my ribcage and digging in at my sides vanish. My body lowers.

At first, I can't place the cold sensation travelling up my legs, over my stomach, then on to my breasts. All I know is I'm suddenly freezing. Inconsistent splashes follow. *Water. I'm wet.*

"Just a few more smudges to wipe away," he says, as my lips begin to sting. "They're busted up pretty bad." His words are laced with contentment. "I know you can hear me now, Red."

My head jerks back, and I hear the thud before the dull ache travels across my skull. I want to scream out, but I'm unable to open my mouth.

"This next bit I will leave up to fate. You will save yourself or you won't. Your life is resting upon your desire to live. You can move, Red; you just have to want it bad enough."

My only response is my heart, pumping hard and fast in my chest.

There's a soft creak followed by the shifting of a latch, and then the sense of someone being close to me is lost. *Am I alone?* Every breath I take is quick and harsh. *Move, Morgan; you need to move.* But I can't. Impending danger awaits me. The threat of death lingers in the air. A neck-prickling fear creeps along my skin.

Water trickles down my cheeks, and without

warning I flinch. *I moved. I can move.* The taste of salt seeping in between my lips alerts me to my flowing tears. I'm crying. My lips twitch as tears continue to race over them, and by the time I take three long breaths to bring myself calm, I have managed to wiggle my fingers.

Move, Morgan! I scream in my mind as I continue battling my conscious state and my limbs, which feel as heavy as stone.

Left. Right. Left. Right. It's only minimal movement, but I rock my head. Urgent warnings sound off in my brain, telling me to stop because I can't see what it is I'm facing. *Why can't I open my eyes?*

I slide. I'm slipping. I try to press my hands down to stop myself, but I can't. *Help me!*

I'm halted abruptly.

Don't breathe, don't breathe, don't breathe. I hear this chant as I struggle against my muscles, which ache intensely. My face becomes as cold and wet as the rest of my body.

My head is underwater.

I flick my eyes wide with ease as if I've been able to do so the entire time. *What is happening to me?* Dirty brown fills my vision and in this brown colouration drifts small clear bubbles, bubbles that resemble those created from expelling air, the air I acknowledge is escaping through my now pressed lips.

I'm fucking drowning. MOVE!

In my mind, I'm thrashing my limbs, but in reality

I'm barely moving at all. I'm running out of oxygen. I know this because my desperation to claim any is frantic.

"Baby girl, Daddy's here. I'm here. You're strong. You can do this, Morgan. Show me. Find the surface." I hear my father's voice as if his lips press against my ear. *"Take my hand."*

I'm reaching, and searching for his grip.

"My hand's higher, Morgan; you need to stretch higher."

I manage to. Curling my fingers, I clutch onto something hard, and with one loud scream bursting through my gaping mouth, I yank myself upwards until I'm left, hung limp, over the side of a stable structure. It's a gaggled gasp that has me coughing, and then my torso jerks as water exits in a vomit from my mouth.

Every breath I take burns as I moan, "Holy fuck." I pant when I spot the concrete floor below, and the need to lift myself out of this water becomes strong … but I'm weak to the point where lifting my limbs seems impossible.

Just keep reaching, I tell myself, as I extend my arms and grunt my sheer desperation, walking my fingers along the flooring below. *You can do this, Morgan.* Pressing my palms downwards brings with it the suspicion I'm being tipped over, and without a second to contemplate what's happening, my body smacks hard into the ground. "Fuck," I wail, coiling myself into a tight ball. *Protection.*

I shiver.

I'm naked.

It's cold.

Soft whimpering grows loud and more forced until my nose becomes blocked and I'm alerted to the fact that I'm the one howling. My wet hair wraps across my face, and in between the gaps it's creating, and through the tears pooled in my eyes, I'm able to locate a wall the colour of silver.

The room. The wolf has brought me back to his prison.

I shuffle on my arse until my spine presses against the wall, and I shift my knees to my chest. I rest my chin on my knees and wrap my arms around my shins.

What the ...?

I brush my fingers across thick threading, threading positioned where my once open gashes were on my shins. Sliding my feet across the concrete has my legs extended, and I gasp when I see the stitches now closing my previous injury. *The wolf stitched me. Why?* Isn't revenge the point of his game and to cause pain and death?

It's then I remember him placing me in the water and washing my lips. I'm urgent in inspecting every inch of my body. I'm terrified when I see the deep purple bruising, cuts, grazes, and rashes covering me. The five words, one through to five, that are tattooed on my inner arm remain, only now there's a strike through *'one'* in black.

Slowly, I bring my knees back to meet my chest and

wrap my hands around each ankle. I whip my head left then right, searching, wondering if the wolf is somewhere in here, hiding, waiting to attack. I stop in a stare when I locate a clawfoot tub, one that not long ago almost claimed my life. Why? Why would he patch me up, clean me? Why did he offer care?

It takes some time to focus on the rest of my surroundings. There's no longer a stretcher, or a table littered with blank papers. The rusty tap that dripped is also gone, as is the drum which had the backpack on its top. The only thing in the room is the tub and a tied garbage bag sitting on the floor right near where the blank projection screen hangs on the far wall.

"Where are you? Go on, show yourself. I know you can see me." I try to yell the words, but they're shaken and hoarse.

Will he appear on the projection screen, armed with vulgar taunts and vacant cold eyes? To my surprise, he doesn't, yet I don't shift my vision from the screen. *Where is he?* I know he'll be watching my every move. I blink and then stare until my eyes burn, and I blink once more. I do this over and over. The screen remains blank. Where is the wolf? Is this my chance to find a way out? Is this my chance to escape? But how? There's still no door. How can there be no door? How does he get me in and out of here?

Chapter Thirty-Two

Reid

Detective Dyson holds her hand across the mouthpiece of the second cordless and hovers her finger above the Accept button. *"Go,"* she mouths.

"It's Reid speaking," I answer, preparing for the worst.

"I think you're missing something more than your wife. Would this be correct?" He still speaks with the same British accent.

Dyson's eyes are wide as she shakes her head in a way that alerts me not to speak.

"Crisp green bills, wrapped in clingwrap … I'm guessing the wrap was your doing?"

"The money," I growl.

"Bingo. Fifty thousand dollars is quite a sum to

keep in a sports bag in your safe. I bet those Bizzies have given you a tough day. You can thank me for that tip-off. Those coppers are nothing more than brainless puppets on strings."

Dyson is rotating her fingers in circles as she mouths, *"Keep him talking."*

"How did you get in? How did you know where the money was? Or that I'd even withdrawn that amount?"

"Taking things you want isn't hard. Do me a favour—tell that bitch detective to hang up the other line or I'll fuck your wife up so bad you won't be able to recognise her when I send her back to you in garbage bags." He's eerily calm.

I swallow hard as my eyes bulge from my head. *This fucker is insane.*

Dyson lays the cordless down on a couch cushion and raises both her hands, palms out, into the air.

"It's been done." My voice rattles.

"Detective Astin West? Now he can listen. Not her. She needs to leave the room. Tell her to leave the room now."

"He wants you to leave the room," I say robotically, gauging Detective Dyson's reaction.

She only shakes her head.

"She can't." I can't believe I just admitted this out loud to the man who has my wife. *Comply with his requests, don't deny them.*

"Well, in that case, let me get your little lady, and I'll kill her while you're listening."

"He'll kill Morgan if you don't." My tone laced with panic.

Detective Dyson's eyes narrow as she mouths, *"I'm going."*

"No. Don't. Detective Dyson is leaving. Don't hurt Morgan." My panic is entwined with these words.

Dyson draws her weapon from the holster wrapped around her waist. She lowers to the floor and crawls the short distance from the lounge room to the entryway.

"She's out of the room. I swear." I look to Maloney who mouths, *"Keep him talking."*

"Say hello to Max for me, will you?"

Can he see us? He must be able to see us. I don't pass on his greeting.

"I would follow my instructions. I have Morgan. I have your money. I even have a collection of your photos and home movies, too ... I'll destroy all of it."

"He says 'hi Max'." I blurt this out fast, my heart pounding as rapidly as Tarzan beats at his chest.

Maloney's eyes narrow into a scowl.

"Good." I can hear the smile in his voice.

The line goes dead.

Slowly I drop the cordless to the ground and bring my hands up, cupping my face. "Motherfuuuuuuucker."

"Shit." I hear Maloney say. "I'm ringing Astin."

Thump, thump, thump, thump, thump.

Urgent feet beat against the staircase. Maloney grabs my arm, yanking me with him behind the couch. "Stay down. Don't make a sound," he whispers.

I watch as Dyson performs an army roll, which sees her back in the lounge area and scrambling behind the small wall that exists before the opening. She kneels with her weapon drawn.

Is he in the house? Fright launches from the bottomless pit of my stomach to the back of my constricted throat.

"What's going on? What's with all the yelling?" It's Ronald shouting.

I exhale with relief.

"Where are you?" Ronald yells.

"Loungeroom," Maloney answers.

Ronald stands in the doorway wearing the same white cotton singlet and loose cotton boxer shorts I saw him in before he retired to bed. His head is tilted to the side as he scratches at the smooth part of his head. "What's happened?"

"Another phone call." I stand so he can see me as clearly as I can see him.

"Is Morgan okay?"

"I don't know." I shake my head because I've no clue if she is or she isn't. Her abductor hasn't let me speak to her. He just makes references.

Ronald throws his arms down and slaps them simultaneously against his outer legs. "I've had enough. I'm going out to search for Morgan. I've barely slept a wink. I can't continue lying around while my baby is out there. My daughter needs me." He turns sharp on his heel.

"Stop, Mr Cuttings. It won't achieve anything."

Dyson reaches out her hand and lowers it to Ronald's shoulder. "Take a seat. I'm calling Detective West."

"Have you pigs found any leads yet, or is this lunatic controlling everything that's happening? Because from where I'm sitting you haven't the faintest idea what you're doing, and you look like a bunch of bloody chooks with your heads cut off." Ronald's once sleepy appearance disappears with his outburst, his limbs now tensed. His biceps are bulging, and his face glows red.

"You're mad about the position you're in. We understand why you are, but this won't help." Maloney, the voice of reason. "Let us do our job."

"A trained monkey could do it better. I'm going to find my daughter, and you'll have to kill me to stop me."

Cuffs swing from Maloney's finger in a brief second. "Do you want to wear these?"

Ronald shakes his head as he stumbles to the couch and flops down with what I can only imagine is helplessness, the same feeling constantly plaguing me.

The clock in the kitchen reads 1:30 a.m., and as I watch the second hand circling the clock face, I listen to the call I took earlier playing through the laptop Dyson was tapping away on not long before Detective West finally showed his face. West has been sitting glued to this piece of equipment as if he's studying the way it starts since he arrived twenty minutes after the call was taken. Six times so far, West has played the call through, and as soon as it finishes he starts it again. Most times he pauses, rewinds, and then replays it to the end. Not this time. A small segment seems to have caught his attention; I gather this because he fast forwards and then rewinds it only after this snippet plays. Why is he doing this?

"Drink?" Ronald says in passing.

"I'm good." I shift in my seat until I meet his sad eyes.

"Kylee still hasn't stopped crying since she came down and went back upstairs before. I don't know what to tell her."

"Tell her Morgan will be okay." I pause, trying to convince myself this is the truth. "We have to believe she will be. We can't give up on her."

"She's a fighter," Ronald says as he walks away from me. There's a long pause before I hear running water. "So, this person took the money?" he shouts from the kitchen.

It's what I've told Ronald multiple times, yet he keeps asking.

"Yep. It's what the psychopath said." I hear my annoyance.

"He's been in this house."

"Yep. It seems so."

"Shit! Who are we dealing with here?" Ronald's annoyance is now apparent.

"A fucking psychopath who when I find him will get

his—"

"Ssssh," West says.

Turning my attention to his scowling face, I drop my shoulders and mouth, *"Sorry."*

"I'm going to take this glass of water up to Kylee, and I'll come back down once I get her settled." Ronald's hand brushes my shoulder in passing.

"Okay," I whisper, trying not to piss West off any further.

"I need quiet." West grunts.

"Understood." Ronald disappears up the stairs.

West plays the call through from the beginning once more. He suddenly jerks his head upright, and the clip stops. "Did you hear that?" West looks to Maloney and then Dyson who sit either side of him.

"What?" Maloney's eyes widen.

West presses at some buttons, and then he replays this segment again. *"I even have a collection of your photos and home movies too."* The clip stops.

"There," West says with satisfaction to his tone. "He's not British. He's Australian. The accent is a disguise. Listen." He replays it again and stops after the word *photos.* "He did well with the accent, but to me, it's an Australian pronunciation of this line, with an emphasis on photos ... now listen to the word *movies.*" He plays the next part. "See."

"Holy shit." Maloney's chin drops.

"It's not a device he's using this time; it's him."

"I didn't hear it until you just pointed it out," Dyson confirms.

"We need to forward this to our vocal technicians in Brisbane to run through it, but I'm sure this is an attempt at disguising himself." West is more than confident. His chest is puffed out, his posture sturdy and towering.

"Excellent, Astin." Dyson smiles.

"Leroy used to do acting before he joined the force. I know he's supposed to be heading off for holidays today, but from memory, I believe he said he's not leaving until later this afternoon ... if you wanted to get him to come listen." Maloney pauses. "We both know the techies in Brisbane are snowed under as always. They won't get to this job straight away." Maloney shifts from foot to foot. "He could help us in the meantime. You know, be sure."

"Leroy?" West hitches one eyebrow, causing the lines around his eyes to crinkle.

"Yeah. Constable Stratt."

"Good call. Max, get him on the phone, and get him here," West says.

"Okay," Maloney stands from the table. He takes long strides towards Morgan's sitting room before he turns down the hallway and is no longer in my sight.

"Why does this even matter?" I say, confused.

"Pardon?" West's grey eyes connect with mine.

"I kept him on the line. You know where he is now. The trace." My shoulders sit by my ears. I'm so tense.

"We don't have a trace yet. Reid, this is a rural town; we don't have this type of technology here. Brisbane needs to set the trace, and we're waiting for it to be put in place. All the red tape to be cut. It can take up to seventy-two hours. However, we can now record the evidence of these calls should we need them in court."

I slam my fist hard into the table. "We don't have seventy-two hours. You heard the freak; you heard what he has, what he said. He's insane. Morgan will be dead by then."

"Reid, the techies have the recording device linked to your phone; we're getting there. These processes take more time when you live in smaller towns like this."

"This is bullshit." The chair I was sitting in crashes to the floor after I launch myself from it. "No! Now! You need to get it done now."

West stares blankly at me. There's no emotion in his eyes. "You have to trust me."

"I don't trust anyone. Someone has been in my house, in my office, and that someone kidnapped my wife. He's playing fucking games with us. He's right, you know. Coppers are nothing but puppets on strings."

Chapter Thirty-Three

Morgan

It takes three attempts to find my feet, but with the aid of a wall, I manage to stand. Swinging my head gingerly from side to side, I scan the room for any way out. I can't see one. Left, right, up, and down—I continue to search for clues, for anything to help me find freedom. There has to be a way out of here. If he can get in, I can get out.

I hobble around the small prison space. I scrape my hands manically along the walls, pressing against each of the silver blocks as I come to them. My hope is that one is not as it appears, and it will lead to a secret door, and my escape. So far, each one is just as it seems—a solid concrete block.

When I come to stand at the silver blocks behind

the clawfoot tub, where my head once laid on what appears to be a wooden chock, I contemplate the possibility of drinking some of the water even though leaves float on top. The colouration is an autumn brown. Plenty of dirt and blood contaminate its purity. My thirst is ravenous, so intense that my need now outweighs the disgust. It's a hesitant approach, but as I come around to the side and bend down, taking the edge of the tub into my grip for support, I'm already relishing the thought of quenching my thirst. Bent over the side, I run the fingers on my right hand through the ice-cold liquid. I need to drink. Cupping my palm, I lower my mouth.

"Do not drink the water, Red." His voice booms.

I jolt, startled.

"Sit." His tone is confident and controlled.

I do. My naked arse rests against the wet and cold concrete. I tuck my legs to the side and cover my exposed breasts with my hands, keeping my eyes turned downwards to my knees.

"You managed to get out. I shouldn't be surprised; you've always been stubborn."

I don't know this British accent, but I do know him from what he's shared. How? How do I know him?

"Did you see the garbage bag I left for you, Red?"

I bob my head, not daring to look up at the projection screen. I don't want to see the man behind the screen.

"Go and get it."

I lean forward and take my weight through my

hands and knees, grimacing from the pain, panting through my teeth to avoid the screams that want to explode from between my lips. Anger burns in me like hot bitumen under naked feet in the middle of summer, and I toss my chin back. I growl when I see him covered by the black mask. I gasp when I look into his dull green eyes. I sob when I notice the thick scar that now invades his upper lip.

He laughs. It's a menacing laugh. "What's wrong, Red? Were you expecting somebody else?" His glare chills me, like a cold fog wrapping itself around my body, seeping through my skin until it latches onto my heart. "I can't exactly make this easy for you now, can I?"

His eyes aren't blue anymore; they're green. Why are they green?

I drop my head. The wolf is playing games. He likes to play games. Am I being faced with a man who likes to play dress-up? Or am I up against more than one wolf? I refuse to believe there is more than one of him torturing me. I refuse to accept that he has an accomplice. Why would two people be so cruel, so malice, and want payback? How could I have pissed off more than one person?

The hairs on the back of my neck have risen. My skin's covered in goosebumps, and my heart is pumping excessively in my chest, the way it does when he's near. The wolf has to be a loner. He's working alone, isn't he?

"You are going to pay for what you've done." It's

what he's said. I lift my head and glare into his dull green eyes. I search them, wondering if this shade is real or an illusion. Is this part of his next trick?

I won't let him fool me again. Yesterday, the wolf had me name Reid as my kidnapper. I believe he wanted to see if I could or would name Reid to be such a monster, and he succeeded, because I did. Another trap, and I fell for it like a mouse chasing baited cheese. He set me up to answer the way I did. The photograph in the cave. The colour blue of his eyes. The perfect shape of his lips. The wolf is wearing many disguises, but which one holds his true identity? I need to figure this out, fast.

"Who am I, Red?"

"An arsehole." It's a rumbled deliverance from my chest.

"Who am I, Red?"

"A monster." I'm mad.

He heckles. "Who am I, Red?"

"A sheep."

"Who am I, Red?"

This time, I pause. I allow all the anger inside me to build until I know I'm expressing every ounce of hate I have for my captor in my eyes. "A dead man."

I don't even blink.

His lips curl upwards, and then he laughs. "Are you ready to play again?"

"I was born ready." Strength is the key to winning. I need to show him my power, and not the vulnerability that leaks from me.

"Well, get the bag and get dressed, because today will be your last."

"Or your last. I can play games too." I'm enraged.

"Now this is a side of you, I've seen before. I didn't think you had it in you anymore."

"Ha." I stare him down without a single clue as to who it is that has me. "And now I know who you are. Would you like to ask me your question again?"

He seems shocked by my disclaimer because his smug smile disappears as his eyes grow wide, so wide I can no longer see his long lashes below his mask.

"Well. Ask me again?"

"You have no idea who I am."

I force a smile.

"Get dressed," he barks, then the projection screen goes blank.

Crawling in the direction of where his image was, I wonder if he's worried there's a possibility I've uncovered his identity as I claimed, or if he called my bluff with ease. I've no idea who the wolf is, but I needed to try something to rattle him. I need time to figure out the wolf, or possibly wolves', identities, even though a small voice in the back of my head keeps whispering, *'Who cares who he is? He's going to kill you regardless of whether you're right or wrong. Just find a way to escape him.'* Can I escape him?

Taking the garbage bag, I drag it along the ground until I reach the corner of the room. I twist slowly, pressing my back against the foundation and close my eyes. One shallow breath is all I manage to take as I proceed to lift the bag.

Ting.

What was that noise? My eyes shoot open.

"Holy shit!" I say under my breath, turning my eyes down. I instantly drop the garbage bag. The wolf fucked up; he must have. I have a weapon, and I'll not hesitate to use it.

Chapter Thirty-Four

The wolf

I pace between the bed and the television, set up not far from its end. Morgan has no fucking clue who I am. Bitch is trying to rile me up, and I won't let her get under my skin. On occasion, I've allowed her to do that ... *fucking whore*. Lines of red lipstick, lipstick owned by Daisy Malone, mark my wall with names. I stalk this list of bitches before placing both my hands on either side. Anger brews inside me. I swing back my leg and let out a primal howl.

Bang!

One powerful kick sees the plaster torn apart, and my foot buried deep in a hole I've created in the fibro.

"Shit," I snarl as I twist at my ankle and rip my foot backwards. I huff when I bend down to retrieve my shoe left behind.

Thirteen useless slags and Morgan is the one I hate the most. She's the devil disguised in angel's clothing. She's the last piece of fruit left to mould in a discarded fruit bowl. Morgan Banks is a storm hell-bent on destroying every single life which comes into her path. I want her dead.

Sitting down on my bed, I keep my eyes planted on my list as I undo the laces of my boot so that I can slip it back on.

~~Daisy Malone~~
~~Cheryl Riddell~~
~~Donna Martin~~
~~Sarah Pilcher~~
~~Christina Monroe~~
~~Elizabeth Shanks~~
~~Lillian Catcher~~
~~Alethia Warren~~
~~Stacey Seymore-Beth~~
~~Octavia Legend~~
~~Anastasia Daughtry~~
~~Katy Hodges~~
Morgan Banks

My trophies. Morgan is the only one I've not finished with yet. Each kill calculated and performed to perfection. Each kill used as practice for this moment, the one I've been waiting for for the last five years. I've never felt as alive as I do when I watch the life drain out of a woman's eyes. It's all in the eyes. The way they open wide due to a shock they've never experienced before. The way they plead. The tears that stain the tender skin surrounding their lashes. Eyes search for help and beg for mercy, but then a glimmer of fight widens the iris' before surrender catches up, shrinking them ... death is finally accepted.

This sequence never leaves me. This final moment washes over my body and brings with it immortality. I'm left feeling strong, so dominant I could lift mountains, create tidal waves, and produce catastrophic storms upon mere mortals. I become a god.

The thirst that grows to the point of unbearable as my game plays out is automatically quenched once these bitches no longer breathe. And after my heartbeat slows, and I catch my breath, I sit quietly in nature, slicing away the fingertips of these women who have brought me pain. I relax to the point I feel weightless ... It's a meditative calm. A woman's touch is all she really owns in her life, and it's the last thing I need to take before I can prepare to hunt all over again.

But even though there are no names left on my list, I know it's not over. I won't be able to stop after I take Morgan's life, like I promised myself I would, because I'm forever hungered for immortality, and I'm forever in need of the hunt.

Morgan no longer appears as the broken doll she did

the last time I locked her in this room. She's still battered, grazed, gashed, cut, and bruised, but now she's cleaned from the elements that hitchhiked on her extremities, and from the dry blood that was staining her skin.

The colour red has always been such a good match against Morgan's pale complexion. It's one she's often worn throughout the years. I watch as she limps around the room in the short underwear and tight white fitted tank top I exchanged her clothing with, and as I do, I exhale my satisfaction. Every single one of my players, bar my first, has worn this uniform to their death. They need to know they're my property, and this is the reason 'Property of The Wolf' is on the breast of each top, written in the colour red.

My game plan is flawless.

The backpack I put together for Morgan is now out of the garbage bag and laying in the middle of the floor. I'm puzzled by this because every other player who has stood where Morgan is now has clutched this bag as if their life depended on it. Not Morgan though.

What is she doing?

Her arse becomes my view as she bends over at the tub. I switch the camera directly to the opposite side of the room to find Morgan slurping from her cupped hand. Her thirst must be extreme to drink such filth. She's the first one of my Reds to do so.

The watch wrapped around my wrist begins to alarm at the pre-set time of 2:45 a.m. It's time for Morgan's next test. Only three players have made it past nightfall on this day, and I hope Morgan can make it a fourth, but I'm not holding out hope; not after inspecting her this morning. She's quite damaged.

She will fall. She will scream. She will have to navigate the dark.

Payback can be such a bitch.

Chapter Thirty-Five

Morgan

The water tastes metallic and earthy as I slurp from my cupped hands—a necessary distraction. I know the wolf is watching me and I need to find somewhere to hide the pair of long-handled surgical scissors I'm trying hard not to stab my lip with as I protect them in my palms against my lips. Where do I put them? How do I get them out of here without him seeing?

The outfit left for me to clothe myself with leaves little room for hiding my find, and trying to get them into the plastic bag, or the backpack will be difficult if his eyes are focused on my actions. He's always watching me. That's what he said. My mind is fuzzy, my heart pumps painfully, and as I stay hunched over the clawfoot tub, I begin to shake.

Rattle, rattle, rattle.

A sound resembling that of a rusty old chain being shaken comes from below. *It's him.* I twist awkwardly and dart across the room to cover floor space, and fast. My beaten body manages to stay upright until I drop to the cold concrete in front of the backpack. The only chance to discard the scissors is now.

I rip open the zipper and dump the scissors inside making sure to scrunch the two pieces of material together in my trembling fist. *Morgan. Calm down. Zip up the bag.* I'm not sure if it's due to my wet hands or the fright shooting through every part of my body, but sealing the bag proves difficult.

Come on, Morgan. Get it together. You can do this.

Clunk.

Screech.

I drop my head and shoulders and use my now damp hair as a shield. *Please do up.* I'm petrified. With my teeth gritted and my determination reaching fever pitch, I hear the zip sliding across its tracks until I listen to it no more.

Thud!

One, two footsteps, and then there's silence.

I jump when pressure applies to the tip of my shoulder.

"What are you doing, Red?" The room fills with the smell of bubble gum, and my stomach instantly rumbles.

He's here, in the room with me. He enters below

the floor, but how? The flooring is concrete. That's impossible.

"Morgan." He pinches me.

I jump. "Nothing," I whimper.

"Time to go. Get up." His British accent is no more; he speaks as he did on the night he took me. My head is yanked back by my hair, and I yelp. "Look at me."

I do, only to be faced with the same green eyes I saw through the projection screen. What does this mean? Why aren't his eyes blue? Where did the accent go? "I don't understand."

"You're not supposed to understand, Red. That's the point." His lips purse. "I thought you knew who I was?"

"I ... I ...I ... do. I know ... know ... who ... I'm n ... no ...not," I stutter.

"Bullshit." He laughs. "Are you ready to kill me now?" He pulls my hair harder.

"Yes." It's barely audible.

"Okay then. Shall we get started? After all, it's your funeral."

I don't want to play. I want to go home, and now I regret putting those darn scissors into the backpack and not keeping them in my hand where I could use them to plunge deep into his stupid neck.

I'm on tiptoes that barely touch the ground. The wolf has lifted me by my arm into the air, like a weightless ragdoll. "Against the wall," he commands.

I want to kick, bite, scratch, punch, and break this man, but I can't. I'm weak in body, and I'm not sure what the fuck my mind is doing. I go between feeling heroic and vulnerable, like a yo-yo.

"I want your hands against the wall, legs spread." He delivers his instructions with an eerie calm. "I'm going to let your arm go now."

He releases his grip immediately, and I fall into a heaped mess on the floor. I couldn't even stay upright.

"Red, I don't have all day. Places to be, people to see, and all that shit. Don't make me throw you up against it."

"I'm trying," I cry out, walking my fingers across the concrete to the backpack still sitting where it fell from my grasp when he ripped me up off the ground. I can't reach it.

"One … two … three … four. If I get to ten, I'll strangle you where you sit."

"I'm moving," I yell arching my back and positioning myself on hands and knees.

"Faster," he snaps.

Every time my kneecaps press against the ground, I yelp. Every time I reach out my hand to move forward once more, I cry. "Arrrrrrrgh. Why? Why?" It's a forced and painful deliverance from my tongue.

"You're waving your arse in the air like a two-bit hooker, and …" He stops speaking.

Whack. My tailbone feels as though it's been shoved through my spinal column, coming to rest like an unused slinky in the back of my neck. My breath catches in my throat, and my stomach convulses until I vomit, the bile landing in my hair splayed out in front of me.

"And I just got you clean. What a waste of time."

"Just kill me." I'm motionless as I moan.

"Dramatics? Now, this is the Morgan I know." I swear if I could see his face, his eyes would be rolling over, judging from his tone. "Get up, you bitch." He yanks me from the ground. I scream as my body smashes hard into the blocks.

"Take my life you fucker," I groan as I'm held in place by his muscled hand at my back.

"You have problems with orders, Red," he says, repositioning my limbs. My arms are now held high above my head, and my legs spread open, kicked apart by his boots. "There. Now you're submitted like I need you to be."

I'm not sure how I manage to stay upright and in position, but I do. Every moan through parted lips spells out my agony and speaks of the horror I'm experiencing at the wolf's hands, which are now roaming my body ... frisking me. All he needs to say is, 'You're under arrest because you've been a really bad girl,' for his actions to make sense. The only time I've ever been in this position was on my hen's night with the stripper Linda hired for the event. I saw a glimpse of the stripper as he arrived, and heard the squeals of the horny women who surrounded him instantly like they were raving in a mosh pit. I had no idea he was coming towards me before my breasts pressed hard against the wall and I was held there, his hot breath on my neck. I smelt the distinct bubble gum flavouring escaping his lips.

Bubble gum. Holy shit. He's the wolf. Cullum Williams is the wolf.

I picture him as he ground against me at my hen's party and cheers filled the room. The cheers of my friends. He spoke. Every alarm rang loud, telling me to run. Goosebumps covered my entire body as I twisted myself out of his grip. My eyes found his. I gasped as the ghost from my past towered over me. I fled to the safety of the amenities.

Cullum Williams was the same fit, muscular prick who also attended my high school with me when I was younger? The same man who once pinned me painfully against a wall in the girl's bathroom at school and ran his hand up my thigh, continuing to trace his fingers under the hem of my skirt until he had me spilling tears. Cullum Williams from Williams Entertainment and Escort Services. I've never allowed myself to forget his name, or the feeling of his callused hands scratching at my skin, or the smell of his bubble gum breath coating my lips, or even the look of delight dancing in his large green eyes when fear shot through me like a cannon, lit and fired.

Holy shit! It's him.

"I'm not sure what you're up to, but I know you well enough to know you're up to something." His hot bubble gum breath rushes across my cheek.

I know who the wolf is.

"Get off me," I scream bucking my head.

"Sleep tight, Red."

I'm dazed and confused. My head bobs from side to side, smacking against something taut, yet not restrictive. Digging my fingers in to gauge what I'm up against doesn't help, so I slap wildly in the hope I can at least figure out what's happening. *Why am I moving?* I try to open my eyes, but they part only halfway. Everything is dark. I can't see. Raising my hands to my face, I feel the strip of thick material where my eyes should be. *What's happening? Where am I?* I drop my hands and realise they fall above my head and not down by my sides like they should. *I'm upside down.* I slap wildly once more.

An eerie whistle dances around me as I continue my wild assault. "Help! Help me!" I whine.

The sound of booming laughter halts the whistling. "Just in time, Red. Welcome back. You know what? I'm getting so accurate with the measurement of these drugs I keep giving you, I even impress myself."

I hear flesh being slapped before I feel the sting racing up my spine.

"Oh fuck," I gripe.

"If your arse wasn't already sore enough, that'll get you there. Now, shut the fuck up, will you, and quit slapping my legs. Put it this way—if you don't hit me, I won't hit you back." His tone is dry.

His legs?

My pulse beats in my head like a drum's solo performance, and it's hitting so loud and fast it's almost deafening. "Stop the noise," I plead.

Suddenly, there's no more bobbing or bouncing. There's only a constant pulse darting between my ears.

"We're here," he proclaims.

Dizziness overcomes me to the point where I believe I've lost my bearings. I've no idea if I'm flipping, falling or being flung around in circles. All I know is I'm out of control.

"How's the blood flowing to that brain of yours?" I hear him sniff. "You've been upside down a while, I bet your spinning around now you're the right way up." He's holding me in an embrace. His chest is pressed to mine. His bubble gum breath skims my lips. His hands are on my back.

"Let me go." *Panic.*

"Sure." He snickers when I fall flat on my arse. "Always so fucking stubborn, Morgan. Maybe you should have worked on this stubbornness of yours over the years."

"You don't know me." I cringe, trying to focus my vision on something that doesn't look black.

"Yeah, I do. Now, up you come."

My arms feel as if they're ripping from their sockets. "Stop, you're hurting me." Silence. "Why? Why are you doing this to me?"

"I told you, it's because you deserve it. Think, Morgan. What could you have done to deserve such treatment?"

"I don't know." It's a frustrated cry. I don't know

what I ever did to Cullum to cause him to bully me as he did back at school, or now. Cullum did many unforgivable things to me, things I never spoke of to a single person, not even Linda, due to the embarrassment it caused.

"You better hold on to this tightly." Something runs up both my arms before I experience three hard pats against my chest. "If you lose the backpack, it's because you didn't hold on tight enough."

"What?" I yell as I feel my body shift in a half circle before I'm nudged from my lower back.

I fall. I'm falling. I'm weightless as I kick my legs. I'm frightened as I wrap my arms around my chest.

I scream out for my life.

Chapter Thirty-Six

Reid

Hours have passed, yet it's still dark outside. I don't think this night will ever end, just as much as I don't believe this nightmare I'm living will conclude with the outcome I'm praying for—Morgan home safe and unhurt.

West tries to discuss the phone tracing situation with me, but I'm not interested. Nothing he says will be able to explain the department's incompetence. I bet I could locate a hacker who could do the job faster than these dipshits who call themselves 'men of the law'. Maybe this is what I need to do—enlist a criminal to help me find a criminal ... a psychopathic one at that. Where would I even start looking? Do I know anyone?

My phone chimes in my hand, snapping me from my thoughts.

John: Hey boy, how're things going over there? Is there any updated news on Morgan?

I wish I could tell John what's happening. But I can't. I don't know how to tell him that the wife-thieving bastard has rung again, and how after taking his call I've come to think Morgan's abductor has eyes on everything we're doing inside this house. *I need proof.* I wish I could tell John that I was starting to put together my theory, a theory which leads me to believe someone working this case is behind Morgan's abduction, somehow ... even someone as high up as West. I can't share any of this with John, because what if I'm wrong? *I need proof.* Could it be West, though? Or his partner Gleaton? Maybe they're both in on this together. Where's that prick Gleaton anyway? Why isn't he here?

I rub my face with my free hand, trying to make sense of my thoughts. Morgan is missing; this is a fact. But where is she? Who has her? Maybe I need a whiteboard where I can pin pictures of those I suspect on display to help wrap my mind around each possibility. I could perform a process of elimination like they do on those cop shows to find her captor. I bet West has a board, and I'll put my equity, hell, my entire livelihood on the fact that my face is pinned as their number-one suspect.

My phone chimes.

Turning my eyes downward, I'm surprised to see a message from Linda. I was expecting it to be another from John.

Linda: Reid, I have information. Are they tracking your incoming and outcoming calls? Your text messages?

Information? What information?

Me: What information?

Linda: Can they see these messages or not? The cops?

I stand slyly and look towards West, Maloney, and Dyson, who are busily working away on differing gadgets at the dining room table. I eye the staircase, deciding it's best to call Linda, but from somewhere I can't be heard by them. A simple twist on my heel has me creeping to the stairs.

"Can I help you with something?" Prospect towers over me from the second step. His red hair is mussed, the corners of his eyes drawn downwards.

"Ummm. Nope. Going to use the bathroom and freshen up." Which direction had Prospect come from? He wasn't on the stairs when I'd scanned them before.

Prospect shimmies to the side and gestures with his hand for me to pass.

"Thank you," I say.

That copper gives me the heebie jeebies. Where

was Prospect when the call came in this morning? Where has he been since? Prospect's like a nightwalker whose footsteps bear no sound. Whose presence is only known when he's right in front of your nose and not before. I need answers, and I need to pin Prospect's face on my suspect board.

Pressing my chin against my collarbone, I try to sneak a peek behind me to see if Prospect's still standing on the step, but I can't see him. I can't see much from this position at all.

Keep walking. Forget about Prospect for now and call Linda.

I don't bump into Ronald or Kylee when I enter the hallway, which has me relieved. I pause by Aleeha's closed door, hovering my hand over the top of her pink-painted name on to the wood, and think of Ronald and the same questions he asks of me every time he enters the room, as I'm about to enter. I'm worried about Ronald. Hell, I'm afraid for all of us. If Ronald doesn't get even the smallest bit of reassuring news soon I fear he'll turn into a bomb and explode shrapnel in every direction he faces. I've no comforting news to deliver to this man because I've no clue how to bring Morgan home. I'm useless. I'm sick of feeling so fucking useless.

Leaning my forehead against the door, I think of Kylee and the weeping mess she appeared earlier. Her slumped posture and sunken eyes told me all her hope is failing. Her closed fist scrunching the material of her shirt over her chest screamed of the ache her heart was undergoing. Her rapid and falling tears were those you know could never fall hard enough to wash away a soul-crushing pain. Kylee's tortured by the loss of her daughter, and she's no help now. Not to me, not to anybody.

"Hang in there. You need to hang in there," I mouth so as not to be heard, but to remind myself that I too need to hang in there.

I reach my destination, the master bedroom, and carefully tiptoe through the small gap the door creates before closing it quietly so as to minimise sound.

My phone chimes.

"Shit!" I whisper, fumbling the phone in my hand, desperate to mute the volume. *Muted.* I need privacy right now.

Linda: Are they tracing your God damn phone, Reid?

I press the phone image besides Linda's name in the open message.

Ring, ring.

"Hi, you've reached Linda. I'm currently out of the office until further notice. Thank you."

She's changed her outgoing message.

My mobile phone vibrates.

Linda: Don't ring me. Just answer my question.

Me: I'm not being tracked, no. What's going on?

Linda: Trust nobody.

Me: What do you know? Where are you? Why did you leave the house so quickly?

Linda: Investigating. I've been seeing someone. He's a cop. He attended Morgan's crime scene and volunteered himself for the searches they've been doing. I have intel.

I'm shocked. Why has Linda kept this from me? Did she tell West or Gleaton about this cop? And by seeing, does she mean romantically, or are they friends?

Me: Seeing? As in dating this cop?

Linda: Yes. For a little while now. Morgan didn't know either. I wanted to keep it on the down-low.

Me: Were you seeing him when we, you know, on the business trip?"

Linda: Yeah, I was. Kinda.

Kinda. How do you *kinda* see someone? Either you are, or you aren't. Why didn't she tell Morgan about him?

Me: Is this cop there with you now?

Linda: Yep.

Me: Ask him about a tall, lanky red-headed cop, last name Prospect, first name Eric.

I sit on the edge of the bed and wait for a reply. The screen flashes.

Linda: Dodgy. His record isn't clean. Eric Prospect has had multiple disciplinary actions in the past. Stay away from him.

My mind is spinning.

Me: What is this boyfriend saying about Morgan? What does he know?

Linda: Reid, what they're telling us is not everything they know. They're keeping things from us.

Shit! I suspected as much.

Knock. Knock. Knock.
"Reid. Are you in there?"
Shit! West.

Me: West is knocking on the bedroom door. I have to go. Come to the house and bring your copper friend with you.

Before I get a chance to discard my phone, it vibrates.

Linda: Delete these messages.

I throw the phone onto the bed and race into the bathroom, pull my T-shirt over my head, and discard it to the floor. A dab of toothpaste coats the bristles on my toothbrush before I shove it in my mouth and seal my lips around it. "Shit!" I mumble, turning the tap on to a dribble, using the water to splash my face. "Coming." It's a muffled call. I breathe a long drawn-out breath through my nose. *Get it together, Reid.*

Attempting my best casual stroll to appear more relaxed, I reach the door and open it a crack. It widens just enough for me to see West and for him to hopefully see the water droplets still sliding down my face, the toothbrush poking out the corner of my mouth, and the fact I'm currently shirtless.

West furrows his brows. "Are you going to be long?"

"No. Just freshening up." I suck back the toothpaste about to dribble from my lip down my chin.

"Okay." The way he looks at me tells me he doesn't believe my little charade. "I'll wait here for you."

I shrug. "If you must."

Am I paranoid? Or can I smell a rat? A rat who's inside my house.

A rat who's responsible for the disappearance of my wife.

Chapter Thirty-Seven

Morgan

Frigid water sucks me under and folds me in. My entry causes a shock that steals my breath and sends my limbs lame. Everything around me is as black as a raven's feather, and I'm not sure if it's just because the blindfold remains in place or if I've sunken so deep, no light can pass through. I must find the surface and then a shoreline.

Swim, Morgan.

I do. With courage.

There's a strong pulling sensation that sucks me down and as it does the blindfold slips from my head. My eyes are wide as I fight the harsh suction. It's so rigorous that my limbs struggle to propel me through the water, but I refuse to give up because I can't drown. I can't die like this. My muscles burn, and no matter how hard I try to push past the pain, I can't. I'm battling a whirlpool much stronger than any rip I've ever been dragged into before, and the more I fight, the more air I lose. I stop fighting and relax my limbs in the same way I would if I found danger in the surf.

Conserve.

Hope.

Pray.

Swim.

It's all I can do.

I'm suddenly weightless as if many hands press me upwards, guiding me to safety. I whip my head below the water, searching for the source of the aid being afforded me, but nobody is with me, and then I'm laid on my back, floating. One harsh suck of air has my lungs inflated, and I don't splutter or cough, which is odd for how close to airless I'd become. Instead, I roll onto my stomach and swim like my life is depending on me doing so. My life is depending on it. I've no idea which way to steer myself; I've no idea where I am, and when I rotate my arms over and over, until it feels like I complete the motion for the millionth time, I find myself raking my fingertips into an earthy surface.

"Oh, lord." I'm trembling when I manage to tow myself from the water. I puff excessively in between each cry I make due to overwhelming despair. I'm weeping like a lost child, fearful and in danger.

Where am I? Why is it pitch black?

Running my hands over my eyes has my eyelashes

folding with the movement. I stare into complete darkness that causes me to shudder. I'm wet, still shivering, and completely scared out of my wits.

Seated on what feels to be a mound of sorts, I tilt my chin upwards and search for light, a familiar object, or a landmark that might aid me in gauging my current position. There's nothing until a half crescent moon pops up out of nowhere. This moon offers a guide. I can't shift my eyes away, not for a second, because what if I lose sight of it? What if it disappears in the same fashion I did ... without warning and entirely unaware? The risk of its loss is far too significant, so I sit fixated on the crescent shape hovering above me.

A loud ear-splitting scream explodes from my mouth as something slithers over my arm and across my waist. I already know it's a snake without having to search for it. Instinctively, I grab the scaly critter from my body with desperation and peg it away from me.

"Shit! Ewww! Yuck!" I leap upwards, squealing.

By far, this is the worst start to one of the wolf's game so far. I slump to the ground, heaped in fatigue. No more tears build, even though I wish I could howl inconsolably to release the stress pent up inside of me. The adrenaline that is now pulsing throughout my body brings with it the wakeup call I need. I can't continue to sit here. I need to move.

I crawl as far as I can either way, but the darkness the night brings makes seeing which way to go impossible, that is until the moon almost transforms into a rising sun, and daylight is only a whisker away.

I must find a way out.

Grey. The colour grey is what I'm met with when I turn in a circle on my bottom. Every direction I look has boulders circling me. There's so many of them they create a vertical cobblestone structure. There's not a tree shooting from the ground in sight, only branches poking out from between the boulders stacked tall. The backpack that was in the wolf's prison with me, however, lays on the ground within arm's reach. I grunt as I outstretch my arm and pull it to my stomach.

As I shift my attention to further along the ground, I tremble when I see many circular white pipes, exposed in parts throughout rich brown dirt, that leads into a pool of calm murky water ... murky water which starts where the soil ends on every side. I flick my eyes across from where I'm sitting, only to gasp at the sight of a huge metal box, taller than I'd stand, wider than I am, with more pipes coming out of it. I don't understand what I'm seeing, but something tells me this is a place the wolf has created as part of his game.

The only way out of here is up. There's not enough room to walk around the water's edge because some parts of the dirt disappear where the rock face enters the ground and the water starts. And I'm not re-entering that pool just to explore the other side.

Round, thick sarsens become my latest challenge,

and although it takes every bit of energy I have, I manage to work up the courage to begin the climb needed to get out of the wolf's trap.

The first time I reach my arms up and grip onto a surface that I think can hold my weight, I fall. The rock is not a rock at all; it's putty in my hands as it crumbles into dust.

Come on, Morgan. Find a path out of here.

I step back and search the structure towering in front of me. Left, right, centre. Left, right, centre. It's like searching through a series of mazes. Each path I choose ends in a place where I could fall to my death, but I keep searching.

I continue my mental process of elimination. Not that path. Or that one. My eyes widen. My shoulders pull back the moment I locate a possible route. It's as clear as day, mapped in my mind when I again reach my arms upwards and take hold of a small smooth surface the boulder creates. Groaning through my gritted teeth, I pull my leg up behind my arm, my trek underway. I can do this.

Each yank of my body becomes more difficult than the last. My muscles burn. My legs shake, and my balance falters. I throw my hand out, gripping the top of a jagged rock and lose my footing. Warm liquid rushes down my inner arm, and I don't have to look to know it's my blood ... the sting from my sweat entering the open wound is knowledge enough.

Fuck!

Darting my eyes to the ground and then upwards,

I realise I've not much farther to go, so I push myself until a final forced growl explodes from my mouth and I launch my body forwards and slide the length of my torso over the edge, scrimmaging with the backpack as it falls off one shoulder and swings around my neck.

"I did it," I puff, falling onto my back, cuddling the backpack tight to my chest. A flood of emotion rockets through me: happiness, relief, fear, sadness ... they all mix into one overwhelming mass, and I'm not sure if I want to scream out my relief, cry until there are no more tears left to cry, or curl up into the foetal position and sleep ...

The need for rest is something I struggle with as my eyelids grow heavy, and my eyes itch with irritation. I'd give my right arm to sleep right now, even just for ten minutes, but I wouldn't give my life to sleep, and if I lie here and do so it will be the end of my life. The wolf has proven time and time again that he is the hunter because that's what wolves do—they hunt. And I'm his bait because that's what lambs are for—they exist as prey. Get up, Morgan, I warn myself.

I do. I find my feet and search the environment around me.

Dry, dense bushland stretches on forever. My heart thrums in my chest. No more bushland. I can't do anymore fucking bushland. Shifting my eyes from left to right, I picture the wolf standing in there somewhere, waiting for me. His evil, hungered glare and his commanding stance already overpower me.

His heart, cold enough to extinguish my soul and erase my existence at a moment of his choosing.

I need to keep focused and stay strong, even if I'm famished and fatigued.

Rustle, rustle.

The sound of a branch moving, even though there's no breeze about to cause a shift, has me slowly peeling back the zip on the bag hanging at my front. I've no idea what's inside the backpack apart from the scissors I slipped in there. What if he searched the bag when I was no longer conscious? What if they aren't in there anymore? Please let them be in here.

I frantically move my hand as I try to keep the remainder of my body still. Oh my God, where are the scissors?

Chapter Thirty-Eight

The Wolf

When I get the chance to return to where I discarded Morgan, she'll either be floating face down in the water, bloated, with no life filling the vessel that once homed her devious soul. Or she'll have escaped and will be nowhere I can see. I'm hoping for the latter. I'm enjoying this game far too much for it to end here.

Entering the hidden compartment beside my cabin in the woods, I'm confident my cadaver, and victim number twelve, will have thawed. It doesn't take a forensic scientist to learn how long the process will take or what temperature to store a body at. Or even how to succeed in defrosting and preserving a fresher corpse. Any imbecile can research this shit on the

Internet. Any dumbarse can put it into practice.

I've been keeping Katy on ice for three days, and thawing her slowly for two. She has another purpose for me, more than my kill, more than my revenge. She's a prop in an experiment I want to unleash. An extra cast member in my grand finale. Punishment will be gained against those who've robbed me, and Katy is the perfect diversion in my Game of Life with Morgan.

A smooth-cut tree stump rests by Katy's blackened feet. I lower my body until I relax on the log, and slide my eyes up and down her naked spread legs. She's more beautiful in death than she ever was in life. I admire every gash tainted to her flesh and the blotches of black covering her skin from where her blood pooled at her death. My artistry is outstanding. I'm in awe.

Breaking my kill sequencing brought initial anxiety. After all, I had perfected a polished murder, which fulfilled all my desires. I like to watch bodies deteriorate. They never follow the same path because so many factors come into play. Environment, weather, injuries sustained before and during death, and also the attacks from wildlife in the area at the time. But now, I realise I didn't have a reason to worry about my after-death rituals. Red number twelve may not be decomposing in the bush, supplying the smells of rotting flesh I crave, and acting as compost to my vast graveyard ... but she's whole. As intact as the day I saved her from herself and crossed her name from my list of bitches. And I like it.

I've never envisioned this situation in dream or imagination. And this has me asking a question of myself. Do I freeze Morgan? Do I want to admire her in the same light I am Katy right now? Days after her flame's burned out? Days after I've gotten my release?

I think I'd like to view Morgan this way.

What feels like hours only equates to a total of forty-five minutes. That's how long I spend looking at Katy laid out on the wooden floor of the hidden compartment alongside the cabin. I'd like to stay with her longer, so I can bask in my achievements, but a long drive awaits me, and an unfinished game must still be completed.

The alarm on my watch sounds, alerting me to the fact that I have a life to lead outside of my game and my need to kill. I must maintain a balancing act. Keep all my balls in the air and make appearances.

How fast time flies when you're having fun.

Red will have to wait until I get back. One quick public display is all it will take to keep my cover intact and allow me to hunt again. Who knows, I might find my next victim. That would be rewarding.

When a killer walks among society, do you think you could pick him out of the crowd?

Chapter Thirty-Nine

Reid

Three hours. That's how long it is until I'll be sitting in front of cameras and completing a press conference from my loungeroom, pleading to those responsible for the disappearance of Morgan to let her come home. A lump forms in the back of my throat, causing me to swallow excessively in an attempt to dislodge it. *A press conference isn't going to work, so what's the point of this?*

Running my finger around the rim of the empty glass has my mind bogged down. How? Why? Where? When? I go over every memory I have from the moment Morgan left me that morning until now. How the fuck did this happen? Why is this happening to us? Where is she? When will I hold her again? Will I get to hold her again?

"Reid, honey. How are you doing?" Her hand rests on my shoulder, her tone low and nurturing.

"Kylee." I shift in my seat until her eyes find mine.

"I'm sorry." Her hand brushes my hair. "I know I've not been here for you ... I ... well, I've ... It's a shock, you know?"

I bob my head.

"I'm here now. We're going to get through this; I promise we will." Kylee's eyes gleam with tears. Her chin quivers, but she smiles. A mother's false smile. I've seen Morgan do this when concern is plaguing her, yet reassurance is necessary for the children.

"There's nothing to worry about. Mumma's here. I promise you everything will be okay."

Morgan's voice. I miss the sound of her voice.

"Morgan," I call out. Her words are as clear as if she were standing beside me.

Kylee wraps her arms around my head and pulls me against her shirt. "I know. Shhh. I know."

I don't allow myself to shed a tear even though I want to rid myself of bucket loads. I don't grant my panic a chance to consume me because it's a pointless act. I've been there and done those things already. Last night, Maloney walked me through it; he got me to breathe again when it felt impossible to do so. *Stay in control, Reid.*

I squeeze my eyelids together tightly and pray for relief. I pray I won't play horrible images in my head like a nightmare on repeat.

"Reid, it's going to be okay. It will all be okay. I promise." Kylee repeats this over and over. Her grip is tight. Her words echoing through her chest. Her heartbeat races in between them.

"Are you ready?" Ronald's deep voice has Kylee pulling away. She runs her hand over the top of my head once more and then brushes my cheek with her fingertips.

"We're family, Reid. Nobody gets left behind. We will find her." And there's that smile again. That fake-as-fuck smile. The one which shows she doesn't believe this to be true; she just wills it to be.

"*I know,*" I mouth these words because sound doesn't press them out.

"We're going to see our grandbabies. Detective West said we can now, and John and Shirley are waiting. The kids are awake."

Shit! John. I forgot to message him.

"I didn't reply to John's—"

"It's okay. We've filled him in. He understands," Ronald says this calmly.

What happened upstairs in Aleeha's bedroom to make them so focused and in control of the situation? Did they just need time to digest and process their shock?

"Hug them for me. Tell the kids I ..." My throat strains, causing me to clear it. "Tell Brax and Aleeha—"

"We will." Kylee's eyes are soft, yet circled by black rings. Her hair is brushed, and her clothes are changed. She's exhausted. Broken. Hurting. But living. One minute at a time. One hour at a time. One day at a time.

It's how we will do this.

It's how we will bring Morgan home.

"You're doing all you can, Reid. Don't doubt yourself. Don't think of the what ifs. Instead, turn to the right now, okay? Picture Morgan walking through the front door and she will."

I nod.

"We'll be back soon."

"Okay." It's all I manage to reply.

Detective Dyson has a glint of pity in her eyes as she bobs her head just once in my direction. She has a computer bag slung from her shoulder and a set of car keys hanging from her finger. Lynette doesn't say a word, nor does she glance back after she steps through the threshold of our home. Will I see her again? Or is her involvement now complete?

Gleaton is wearing jeans and a collared navy shirt when he arrives in a rush, entering the moment Dyson exits. "Reid." He nods as he lays a folder on the kitchen counter I'm standing not far from.

I offer a half-hearted wave in response.

"One hour. I'll be back in one hour. Constable Stratt is en route to the house; don't let him leave before I get back." West marches past Gleaton, leaving only those words behind in his haste. Prospect is hot on

West's heels.

I don't have a chance to speak or ask questions before West is a flash of denim now gone. Why do I feel like I'm standing still, but the world is blurring and spinning around me?

"What's going on?" I need answers.

Silence. Complete silence. Not even the hand on the clock recording the seconds can be heard.

"We're doing our job. We're going to find your wife." Gleaton stands close to me when he finally answers. The smell of burning woodfire fills my nose. His cologne is strong. His expression is relaxed. His eyes are bright; he's bushy-tailed. *Did he sleep?*

"Max." I hear Gleaton say as he strolls towards the lounge room.

"He's asleep on the chair."

"Good. Max will need it. He's stationed with you until the end." Gleaton peeks at a thick gold watch secured to his wrist, and then to the mobile phone cupped in his hand. "Coffee, Reid?"

"Nope." The thought of food or drink turns my stomach. Why is Max with me until the end? And when will this end?

"Can I see my children? I miss them." Surely, I'm free to come and go as I please now I've been cleared.

"Sure, but if I were you, I'd keep time away to short intervals given the threats our caller has made and the fact he seems unstable. Twenty minutes, maybe?"

I'm shocked.

"Take your mobile phone, okay?"

I jump forward. I'm not sure why—maybe because I never expected Gleaton to say yes. "Really?" Did I just hear him right?

Gleaton nods when he says, "Twenty minutes, okay?"

"What if another call comes in?"

The corner of his lips lifts upwards. "The trace is in place. All calls will record immediately, and when they come through the landline, we can divert them to your mobile. A short visit is fine; your kids need to see their dad."

My mouth drops wide as a glimpse of relief sears through my veins. "When did that happen? You said it could take longer?"

"West just sent confirmation."

"Thank God."

The grass cushions my feet, making it seem as if I'm hopping between clusters of clouds. I'm weightless. I don't knock. I don't speak. I fling the door open and run until I see the lounge area.

"Daddy, Daddy."

My sweet Aleeha's voice is music to my ears. She leaps from a bean bag chair and bounds toward me. Her face is filled with happiness at first glance, but as she closes in her sadness is obvious.

"Is Mummy home?" she questions as I kneel, and she collides with my chest. I hug her with every bit of strength my arms have.

"No, sweetheart, not yet. Soon," I whisper against her cheek.

"I want Mummy. Can we go and get her from ..." She pauses. "Daddy, where is my mummy?" Her beautiful eyes search mine.

"Grandma and Grandad are here. That's exciting, right?" My question is delivered with the hope of a needed distraction.

Her bottom lip sinks. "I want Mummy."

"I know you do. Soon, baby girl. Soon." The skin on her arms is soft as I rub my hands up and down them. Her cheeks look stained from what I assume is dried tears, and her cheeks are reddened.

"Can Brax and me, can we come home now, Daddy?" Her voice is sweet, as sweet as the familiar strawberry smell of her detangling hairspray filling the room. *She must have taken it with her.*

I sigh. I wish they could.

"Brax is outside with his grandad. They're passing and kicking the football." Shirley is standing behind Aleeha when I look up. Her hair rollers are still in, even though she's dressed in one of her flowery day dresses.

"Is he okay?"

"No. Brax isn't up for talking, but he's hanging in there."

I nod.

"Come here, muffin." Lifting Aleeha to my hip has contentment holding my heart. Her little chin tucks around my neck. Her long drawn-out breaths provide warmth to my skin. "Let's go see Brax."

Aleeha nods against me.

Standing on the back porch, I spot Brax in his bright yellow football jersey immediately. His right leg swings back and connects with the ball. The loud thump that accompanies his kick causes me to smile. "Brax," I call. He doesn't look in my direction or acknowledge I'm standing there. My smile disappears as I sigh.

Kylee sits on a lawn chair with her eyes turned upwards. A flying football sails in the direction of Ronald. It's a peaceful and serene morning. For me, though, hell hovers. It hangs like a storm about to smother the earth with strikes of electricity.

"Brax, Dad's here." Kylee stands from the chair.

"Brax," I call. He doesn't follow my voice to find me. Instead, he keeps his head turned away.

Aleeha drops from my hip to her feet, nestling close against my side. I keep my arm wrapped around her as if she might get swallowed whole if I don't.

"Mate. I'm here." I try again to gain Brax's attention.

I don't. He catches the football Ronald kicked high, then drags his feet in the opposite direction to me until he stands to face the farthest fence.

"Give him time." John's deep voice comes from behind me. "He'll be okay." I feel his hand on my shoulder.

"Yeah." I sigh.

"Daddy, I missed you last night," Aleeha whispers.

"I missed you, too. Soon we'll all be home together,

just the four of us, how it should be." I crouch so I can press my lips to her delicate cheek, leaving a tender kiss. I can only imagine what this must be like for them as children.

"Daddy?"

"Yes." I watch as Aleeha's narrow eyes widen.

"Shirley let us have choc-chip pancakes for breakfast." A cheeky grin washes over her lightly freckled face.

"You're fortunate," I reply, searching for Brax. He's back to where he was before I showed up and interrupted his game with my presence. Brax is angry and he wants to show me how much by his actions. I just wish he'd talk to me.

"I added the chips into the pancake mixture. I ate a handful of them. Shirley said it's okay to eat chocolate for breakfast because you're allowed to do that when you're staying at someone's house and not at home. You're allowed to, aren't you, Dad?"

I wish he'd talk to me.

"Aren't you, Dad?"

"Sorry. What did you say?" I turn my attention back to Aleeha.

"Shirley said it's okay to eat a handful of chocolate chips for breakfast because you're allowed to do that when you're staying at someone's house and not at home. You're allowed to, aren't you, Dad?" Her head drops toward the ground, so I take my finger and gently lift her chin so our eyes connect.

"Of course you're allowed to, and when Mummy

gets home, we can make these wonderful choc-chip pancakes for her. She'll love them." I get closer to her face until our noses touch. "Guess what?"

"What?" she says, quietly.

"I think it'll be okay for you to eat two handfuls of choc chips for breakfast."

Her smile beams and a glimmer of happiness fills her expression. "Okay, Daddy."

"Aleeha," Kylee calls out to her.

"Yes, Grandma?"

"Can you come here, sweetheart? I want to show Grandad just how tall you are beside me now."

And just like that, Aleeha leaves my side.

Sitting on the porch has me scanning the clean-cut backyard. The gardens are in full bloom. The freshly painted rustic green gazebo, the one I helped John do a few weeks ago, looks as good as it did the day we painted it. I wish I could go back to three weeks ago and see what I see now. Morgan and I were having troubles, and if we'd just taken some time away together, we could have found a way to work it out. Maybe she wouldn't have stayed back at work. Perhaps she wouldn't have been taken.

"Reid, can we talk?"

I crook my neck to be met by Shirley's kind eyes.

"Sure."

"Inside will be best."

"Okay."

John passes the both of us on the way in, a mug extended from his hand. "Coffee for Ronald," he says in passing.

"We'll be outside soon," Shirley says to John, even though he's no longer in view.

As Shirley sits at the small square table situated just off the kitchen, I take a moment to scan the room. Everything is still the same as it was the last time I was here. Figurines, photographs, and knick-knacks fill the shelving on the wall. The large gold-framed wedding picture of John and Shirley some thirty years ago hangs on the wall.

"Reid, what are the police doing over there? This situation is getting too much now. Do they know anything?"

I sigh as I take a seat across from Shirley and drop my head.

Vibration. There are lots of vibrations against my leg.

I forgot to turn my phone's volume back on.

"Hang on." I reach into my pocket, retrieving my mobile.

Private Number flashes across the screen.

"Oh shit. Shirley, say nothing. It could be …" I can't even say it out loud, mainly because I'm fearful, and because Shirley's expression fills with worry.

"Hello." I hold my breath.

"You're not where you're supposed to be."

"I am."

"No. You're not."

"Please. Don't hurt Morgan. I'm going home now."

"Smoke and mirrors. Illusion. What can be seen is

never unseen, but what you don't see is the clue. Do you even know what's under your nose, Reid? Am I visible? Or am I not?"

"I don't understand." My blood whizz's through my head before it constricts my heart.

"The day my hand shakes yours, and it will, just know that it hurt Morgan. Tarnished her and marked her. That it was the last to ever touch her skin. Not yours. Mine. My hands will be responsible for extinguishing her soul and I will walk beside you one day. Until then, enjoy the nightmares."

The line goes dead.

"Oh fuck. Shirley, I have to go."

Chapter Forty

Morgan

It may only be a small blade, but it's sharp. I hold the scissors as a weapon in my clenched fist, shifting left, then circling entirely to my right. *Where are you?*

One step, two steps, three steps. I keep my eyes focused on the movement I hear coming from in front of me. Four steps, five steps, six steps.

"Fuck!" I scream as I barrel over a sharp object protruding from the earth. The burn at my shins is enough to tell me the sutures binding my skin together are no more. Blood trickles over my feet. I groan, falling on to my bottom and eye a cut tree stump misplaced in a sea of towering trees. *You came so far, Morgan.*

I did. I've been walking, running, sneaking, and jumping at every noise I've heard for what I believe to be hours. And now my legs sting, burn, and ache all at once, until they don't. I'm numb. I try to stand. I fall. I try to pull myself up once more, only to find my arse meeting turf.

"No. No. No." Why is this happening? If I can't walk, I'm sitting prey. Please God, let me walk.

A beam of light, the colours of red, yellow, pink, indigo and blue, forms an arch before my eyes. It hangs in limbo in mid-air. I follow the rainbow downwards until I see the scissors still wrapped tightly in my grip. I still have a weapon. I have a chance.

I'm shaking when I inspect my reopened wounds. They're deep, and I'm not sure what I'm seeing … blood, so much blood.

There's no longer a bandage inside the backpack. There's nothing except an empty canister and a compass. *The tank top I'm wearing. I can use some of the material.*

Every cut I make is close to my stomach, and I flinch, worried I'm going to plough this sharp utensil through my guts. The constant dizziness I'm experiencing, whether from blood loss or starvation, is making this task hard. *Concentrate, Morgan. You don't need to inflict your own wounds.*

"I know," I scold myself.

Take the fucking shirt off.

"Of course," I murmur dropping the scissors to the ground and slowly pulling the top the Wolf had left for me over my head.

The material is not hacked or jagged; it's a neat cut that travels from back to front. When I make the last snip, a band of material falls away. A snip on either seam gives me two lengths.

It's a growl more than a groan that bursts from my lips as I tie each length around my shins. The white turns red almost immediately.

You can do this, Morgan. Encouragement is all I have left. I'm feeling broken, so fucking broken.

Elbow, wrist, pull, scan my environment. Elbow, wrist, push, scan. Elbow, wrist, push, scan. Any ground I crawl over is good because I need shelter from the scorching sun, and an aid to assist me with walking. Sitting on my arse, feeling sore and sorry for myself, will result in my death, and death is not an option for me.

It must take more than a hundred turns of my scratched-up arms against the rough terrain to find the perfect-sized fallen branch to use as a walking stick, but I locate it. Sun dances behind the trees as different-shaped shadows form. My eyes burn as a blinding light saturates them with a bright beam. My head lifts from the dirt, and I'm squinting, everything in front of me blurred.

Where is the light? It has to be the wolf.

I contemplate an attempt at running when fright

leeches onto my heart, but something in my brain overrides my current fear and encourages me to move towards the light and not away from it. I find my feet and hobble, putting as much weight on my arms and the stick now acting as my cane. Every baby step is a victory. Every stumble without falling is my encouragement. The beam of light I previously saw grows fierce and broader in size, causing me to place my free hand on my brow, trying to shield my scrunched eyes. Where is the light coming from?

Music.

Soft music plays. Smooth, piano music. Sweet, gentle, and caressing. I shift my head left, right, up, down—I can't see anything. The music grows louder, and when it does, I realise it's coming from one direction. It's coming from the same direction the beam of light is, so I shuffle, following the sound. The more ground I cover, the more the beat vibrates through my chest. It's a female voice singing, the words are indecipherable, but I hear her.

I know this song. I can't place how or who is singing it, but I know this song.

The music stops playing. It just stops, and all I hear is every quick breath I inhale. I take a step. Both my knees crack violently. Pain shoots up my thighs and into my spine. *Walk it out, Morgan. Push through your grief.*

I do. I take another step, and with that step, the music again starts to play—the same piano music.

The ground below me is brown, burnt leaf upon brown, charred leaf, which is forgiving under my feet—soft and cushioning. The smell, however, is mouldy and rotten.

The music stops. Then starts. I concentrate on the words as I continue to shuffle gingerly forward. Does this mean something? Is the wolf trying to give me another clue? Or is this a trap?

With every hobble I make, memories flood my mind. Memories of Reid and I, meeting on the university grounds, me in my red dress. Reid would refer to me as the lady in red from that day and many years after. Red—it's what the wolf also calls me. This can't be coincidental. So, can the wolf still be Cullum Williams? Or is this tied to Reid in some way? How could the man I love be so evil though? *Confusion.*

"Birdy," I mouth. The Artist. "People Help the People," by Birdy. It's the song. Relief has my shoulders dropping. I knew I knew this song. I once played it over and over for weeks. I was drawn to it, her raw heart-filled words. Aleeha was around two and Brax four. The kids would be sound asleep, and I'd play it on repeat.

"Melodramatic ... this song is so dark, Morgan," Reid would say, yet he'd sit watching me, as I cleaned the kitchen and sang.

I tip my chin back and close my eyes, picturing the kitchen in our newly built house, which now holds years of memories. I see me singing and swaying my hips like I was on centre-stage in a packed auditorium, Reid never taking his gaze from me. He'd explore me like it was the first time he'd ever seen me. Our love— it was intense in a way. We couldn't breathe without being loved by each other. Like the world would cave in on itself if we couldn't feel each other's presence.

We lost that. We let it slide through our fingers. I want it back. I want my life back. My husband. My children. Reid can't be responsible for this. He can't be.

I still, crying out with every bit of pressure I can force through my vocal cords. "I want to go home. Let me go home."

Is anybody coming for me. I scream in the hope that someone, anyone, will hear me. Maybe just this one time, someone will. If I could hear the music, maybe someone else could hear it too.

"I don't want to play your game," I scream, my pitch so high from my bottled anger that it could shatter every piece of glass residing on this Earth. My throat stings from the pain of its force. The taste of blood coats my tongue.

It's a deflated feeling. Twelve others have been where I am, and none of them has won the wolf's wild, twisted game. Not one. Why do I think I have a chance? My survival skills are less than limited. Hell, I can't even keep my husband happy or be there for my children when they need me.

I sink to the ground, and for one moment I pray it

will swallow me whole and put me out of my God damn misery.

Do I sit here and wait for him to come finish me off? Or follow the music to what will only be another test, or trap, or some bullshit I've no control over?

Will I walk to my death?

Chapter Forty-One

Reid

Detective West folds down the lapel on my suit jacket, brushing over the material before snatching his hand back. The lines around his eyes appear more profound than they did the day I met him, and the grey colouration even more haunting. West looks fatigued, and I wonder if I look just as bad as he does.

"Reid, you need to forget about the call. Put it out of your mind for now. They're ready for you in the loungeroom. Remember, just speak from your heart. Plead for the safe return of Morgan, and remember this is going out to every home in the country. A live broadcast. Any slip-ups could see us going backwards. Are you sure you can do this?"

I nod.

"I'll be sitting right beside you. Hold your chin up and look right into the lens. Pour your heart out. Say something to Morgan, and if you think you can cry, do it. Compassion is everything in these situations."

Cry. I can't cry. I'm angry, blood-boiling angry. How did that fucker know I'd left the house? Gleaton—he's involved. He must be. Do I voice this concern to West? Or is West also playing a part? I trust no one.

"Reid, are you listening?"

"Hmm." Is how I respond, wrapped up in thought.

"Focus on what is happening now. You're going live on television. Pleading for the safe return of Morgan."

"I know," I snap annoyed.

"Okay."

"How did he know?" I say quietly.

"Know what? Who?"

"The call. How did Morgan's abductor know I'd left the house? Is it—"

"We've searched every room since, and there are no bugs to be found. We're not sure, but we will find out."

"Gleaton said—"

"Reid, we can discuss this later."

Maloney stands at the entrance to Morgan's library. "Gregory Stiles is here. I just saw him step out of a car. Would you like me to usher him into the lounge area?"

West swivels on his heel. "No. We'll meet him at the door and offer introductions." West nods, in a way that indicates Maloney should disappear, and he does.

"You can do this." West pats my upper arm.

I can do this.

Walking beside West makes me feel like a soldier marching in line. I stop when he does, and shift my position until we are stilled, shoulder to shoulder as West opens the door and we stand in the doorway. Gregory has short blond hair. Wide shoulders. A groomed light stubble covers his chin as he closes in. He smiles. It's only a half-hearted smile, but it's directed at me.

"Detective West." Gregory jumps up the steps to the veranda. His arm stretches out as he takes a long stride towards us. "Wish we were meeting again under more pleasant circumstances." His fingers part, his hand still awaits that of West's, who finally obliges, taking his offer of a handshake.

"It's good to see you, Greg. And I agree, we need to stop meeting in circumstances like these." Professionalism at its finest. They release their grip and put distance between each other.

"The boys are set. I'm ready when you are." Greg's posture is strong. His tone is controlled.

"Now is fine," West says.

"Good. Mr Banks." He turns his attention to me. "I'm Gregory Stiles, a reporter from Channel Sixty-One. I'm so sorry to hear about your wife. We will do all we can to help bring her home." His arm outstretches again, this time an invitation to me. I nod as his firm grip squeezes against my knuckles.

"I know who you are. I've seen you on the

television," I mumble.

"Of course." And there's that half-hearted smile again.

"I also saw you on my lawn with the searchers." I cock my eyebrows in question.

"Yes." Greg's voice is not as deep as I thought it would be for a man of his size. "It's important to be connected with stories you report on."

"Oh, okay," I say. Greg seems genuinely concerned and caring.

I turn and stride towards the living area and become surprised by the hand now resting on my upper back, guiding me. There's a soothing comfort to Greg's touch, and the way he strides half a step behind me, offering me the lead. This gives me a sense of control, something I've not felt over the last couple of days.

"Reid, just remember to breathe and take your time. We have all the time in the world, and I can only imagine you will need to pace yourself so you can say what it is you want. Please do not cuss; we won't be able to censor it while the broadcast is live. Just be genuine, and I'll do the rest. I will keep my involvement to a minimum. It's your floor. Let your heart speak."

"Okay." It's a soft deliverance.

It's mid-morning, and I'm sitting on the couch beside Kylee, who is next to Ronald, in our loungeroom.

When did they arrive?

It's all I think as I look away from the bright lights in front of me, the lights emitting so much heat I can feel sweat beads forming at my hairline. Maybe this jacket wasn't such a good idea. West said it was. The feeling of suffocation is mixing with the nerves circling in my stomach. Maybe I can't do this. I puff out my cheeks, slide my hand up and down my jeans leg. What am I going to say?

Greg takes a seat in a chair placed across from me just as West passes beside him and then sits on the opposite side of me on the couch. We're packed in like a can of sardines, and this causes my temperature to rise further. I'm suffocating even more.

When I glance to my left, I see an older man, early to mid-sixties, with a grey beard, wearing a Broncos baseball cap. He's standing just off to the side of a large camera on a stand. I instantly think about how much this sight would piss Morgan off. Morgan loathes hat-wearing inside buildings; it's something she has never allowed. Should I ask him to remove it?

"Reid." Greg's tone is soft, controlled, yet calm when he speaks my name. I shift my attention to him. "Two minutes and we'll be live. Do you need anything?"

I do. To get the fuck off this couch. But I say nothing and shake my head.

The cameraman standing behind Greg is short and stocky. He'd be at least the same height as Morgan. He's so young, maybe all of eighteen, and as his head disappears behind another large camera on a stand, I want nothing more than to yell, *"GET OUT! Everyone get out of my house."* I can't breathe.

"He's not been mic'd." Gregory's statement is one of frustration, yet he doesn't say it with even a hint of disappointment. He's a professional, and it's obvious he's been doing this job for a long time.

"Sorry, Greg." The bearded baseball-hat-wearing man says before he moves through a narrow gap in front of me and pins a microphone to the lapel of the jacket West fussed with earlier.

"It's okay, Reid." Kylee's hand cups my upper arm, and when I rotate my head, I spy the tissue poking out between her fingers. Tilting my chin back, I search Kylee's expression, and view her glazed eyes. She's already about to cry. How will I cope with her crying beside me?

"You can do this, son." Ronald's words are barely audible, and when I look to the jacket he's wearing, the black coat that is almost identical in style to mine, I see the small red rose pin attached under his microphone. Morgan has always loved roses. Maybe I should have done something like he has.

"Okay, we're ready," Greg says after he assists in running the wire of the microphone up under my shirt and helps tuck the pack at the back of my pants. He offers me a look of sorrow I've only ever seen people express when offering condolences. Why do I feel like I'm about to attend Morgan's funeral?

My eye begins to twitch as my nerves increase.

Kylee shudders beside me, as one would if someone was treading over their grave ... We're a mess, and we're about to be seen by everyone in the country. My guess is, appearing a mess will be expected.

"Today I'm in the Banks household with Reid Banks, who is a local and upstanding member of our small community. He's joined by Detective Astin West of the Rockhampton CIB, and missing local wife and mother, Morgan Banks, parents', Ronald and Kylee Cuttings, also join us. Thank you for allowing me into your home, Mr Banks."

I nod in response.

"The shock of Morgan's disappearance is one we believe will be felt throughout our community, and we're asking anyone who has information to come forward and assist the police. Mr Banks has prepared a short statement he wishes to deliver ... Mr Banks."

"Thank you, Greg." My voice wavers. "I'm Reid Banks, and I'm the husband of Morgan Banks. On Thursday night, Morgan, my wife, did not return home from work, although she was en route to our home at the time.

"It's been over thirty-six hours since she's been missing, and our families are losing hope that Morgan will be found safe and returned to us. Morgan and I are parents to two beautiful children, who are both missing their mum and just want her to come home." I stop and take a deep breath. My throat goes instantly dry, and my mouth follows suit. I close my eyes to compose myself and take quick breaths before reopening them. Looking straight down the barrel of the giant video camera situated behind the reporter's head, I swallow again, trying to bring moisture to my lips, but it doesn't work. *Say something, Reid.*

"My Morgan is of a slim build, with chestnut brown hair and dark brown eyes. Morgan's 170 centimetres tall and was wearing a pale pink business blouse and a black business skirt when she left to attend work on Thursday morning, the morning of the day she disappeared. We know a man stopped to help Morgan change a flat tyre on her journey home that evening. Police are investigating his whereabouts. If you were the Good Samaritan"—I stumble over the last two words— "please contact the police and give them any information you can. Morgan is a loving mother to our two children, Brax and Aleeha. She is also a loving and caring wife. Her safe return is our only focus, and until we find her we will not rest." I stop speaking, and I look into the lens and speak to my wife from my heart, just as West said I should do. "Morgan, honey, if you can see this, please know I love you, we all love you, and I'm doing absolutely everything I can to find you. I'll never give up. *I PROMISE.*" I emphasise the word "promise" as I hear Kylee sobbing beside me. "Please help us find Morgan. She's our world, and without her, we're nothing. I need my wife to come home; give her back to us. Please, if you've taken her, just let her come home." My voice cracks, on the word "home". Tears well in my eyes.

"Bring her home," Kylee sobs.

"Give me back my daughter," Ronald follows.

"Detective West, what information can you offer the community, and what leads are you and the police force pursuing at this time?"

"Thank you, Gregory. As Mr Banks has said, Morgan is a Caucasian woman, About 170 centimetres tall. With brown hair and brown eyes. She was wearing a pale pink top and a business skirt at the time of her disappearance. We are asking the community to help identify the man who stopped to help Mrs Morgan Banks change a flat tyre on the night of her disappearance, before she was involved in a minor collision close to her home. Morgan's SUV, number plate B.A.N.K.S 0.2, was recovered on the evening of her disappearance, and we are asking any witnesses who may have seen the collision to come forth also. At this time, we are following many leads and remain positive that we will locate Morgan safe. We need the community's help. Please, if you have any information call Crime Stoppers."

"That number for Crime Stoppers is now flashing across the bottom of your television screens. Detective West, have there been any demands for a ransom or calls made to the police in connection with Morgan's disappearance?"

"We would prefer not to comment on that at this time. But what I can say is that Mr Reid Banks, along with family members, are not suspects in Morgan's disappearance. They have no involvement and are desperate to have Morgan home. They are cooperating in all matters related to Morgan's disappearance."

"Thank you. Again, if you have any information, please call the Rockhampton police or Crime Stoppers."

Every bit of me hopes someone watching can tell us where Morgan is, and I also hope that psychopathic prick is watching and knows that I'm coming for him. I'll get my revenge, even if it takes until the final seconds of my life to do so. As Greg's shoulders slump, and the red lights on the camera behind him disappear, I realise I'm scowling.

I'm going to kill the bastard who took Morgan with my bare hands; I just need to find him.

Chapter Forty-Two

Morgan

A mirror!

No doubt it's a trap, and visions of the wolf slitting my throat as I watch my murder in the reflection causes my teeth to bear down as I shiver.

Moving closer, another gleam of light blinds me. This process repeats until I'm flush in front of the mirror. *A mirror. Why?*

It's an oval, rustic antique-looking—sterling-silver mirror, and there's writing scrawled on the glass in bright red lipstick.

Morgan, the game is almost over. Look at your reflection; you're disgusting.
I've left a present for you on the back of this

mirror, Red.
I'm coming for you.
Who am I?

It becomes hard to swallow. Tears will drown me if I let them fall again. I can't melt into a puddle of pity like I allowed myself to do before. I need to keep my emotions under control. Visions of Reid and the kids far from my mind. *Focus. Focus on what I can do to help myself now, not what I'll lose if I don't.*

I'm hesitant at the thought of looking behind the mirror. My breathing is rapid. I discard the stick acting as my cane. What is waiting for me behind this mirror resting in the middle of bushland like a prop from a movie set?

I inhale three breaths and hold onto the frame as I shift my position. I gasp, strangling my mouth with my hands, sucking back my need to scream out. I'm haunted. A large photograph. It's a collage of photos numbered, one through to thirteen. Under each number is a corresponding picture of a woman who has died brutally and disgustingly. The music playing only intensifies the horror these images supply. My mouth falls open, and I dry-heave until my stomach stops rolling over itself. I don't want to look again, but I force myself to view each one. Any information is important. Do I know any of these women? I soon realise I don't, not even one from what I can make out from these photographs.

Each visual is worse than the last; my stomach

clenches as my heart pounds with a sense of urgency. All I can identify is that each of these women lies lifeless in bushland, and each of these photographs has freshly bloomed roses scattered around the corpse. I start with the first picture and count the roses; there are thirteen. I move to the second and count the stems; also thirteen. I don't stop until I get to number thirteen, which also has thirteen roses laid out on a white background. There are two words written in the centre of the white background.

Red, RUN!

I spin in a circle … searching. I can sense his presence. Goosebumps coat my skin from my wrists to my ankles.

But there's nobody here. It's just me, this mirror, and twelve ghosts who once lived. Twelve spirits who have a horrific story of their own to share, but no voice to do so. I need to be their voice. I need to survive for them, too.

The music stops. My heart thuds one intense beat and then races. I'm not running. I'm still. Fearful. Broken. Hurt. Lost.

"You just couldn't be what you were supposed to be, Morgan." His voice plays from the boom box on the ground in front of me, the same one that's been playing the song. "These bitches weren't what they were supposed to be either." There's a long pause. "This is what happens to thieves, traitors, and whores … they get their punishment."

I scrunch my fists together and raise them in front

of my face.

"I knew you wouldn't run, but I wish you had. You're going to wish you did, too."

"Fuuuuuck!" I scream as I'm pulled down like the earth is swallowing me whole from below my feet. I'm falling.

Wrapped in a blanket of darkness, my body bounces from side to side. I roll before I'm upright once more. I reach out my arms like Jesus on the cross and dig my nails into what feels like compacted soil.

"Oh God, oh God," I cry out. "Ouuuuch." I cry harder as I feel my nails peel away from my flesh. I flip over myself. I flip again … *thud*.

I can't breathe. I can't breathe.

There's a halo of light in the distance. A blurry tattered curtain sways with a gusting wind that rushes through the ripped material and brings a coolness to my limbs. At first, it's pleasant, welcomed. Then it freezes cold and burns. It's burning me. I try to move from its path, but I can't even lift my head. I'm a lump of lead, one too heavy to carry or shift. I feel trapped in my own body with my mind racing, ordering a million commands, my body unable to follow a single one.

"Help." It's a weak deliverance of the word, spoken so quietly even I barely hear myself.

"Morgan. Morgan." The call of my name sounds laced with worry. "Baby, you're not alone. I'm here. I'm with you."

"Reid." I can smell his cologne. I can feel his fingertip tracing a line down my cheek.

"Yes. I'm here." He's cradling my head.

There's warmth, so much warmth fighting away the cold I'm experiencing, and the sound of my heart beating is loud but slow. I relax into him.

"You can't give up. Promise me you won't give up."

I cry, beads of liquid tickle my lips.

"Don't cry, Morgan. Please don't cry." Soft pillows press to my forehead. "I've got you. Don't cry."

"Reid." I flick my eyes upwards in their sockets, almost rolling them into the back of my head. One painful thump accompanies this action.

"Close your eyes. Take a moment. Rest. You need rest."

"Reid," I cry out once more.

"Morgan. Sleep. You need your strength." My fingers are stretched wide, and then I feel his fingers slipped between mine. "I'll stay with you. I'll guard you while you sleep. Nothing will happen. You trust me, don't you?"

"Yes," I breathe as I allow my eyelids to fall closed, and I listen to every slow drawn-out breath he takes.

"I'm waiting for you, Morgan. I'm searching for you. We're doing everything we can to find you. I won't let you down, baby. Please don't give up on me."

"I won't," I mumble as I feel my shoulders drop and my limbs lighten. I'm no longer lead. I'm free … floating … at rest.

"Morgan. Wake up. You need to wake up now." It's a panicked request. Reid's breathing is rapid. His hands are rough. They pull me and shake me.

"Reid?"

I bolt upright. I'm panting, searching ... It's so dark. *Where the hell am I?*

Chapter Forty-Three

Reid

The mattress of our bed takes my weight. I sit staring out the bedroom window, thoughts running through my head as I eye the well-manicured grass of the neighbouring property across from us. What must our neighbours think of all of this? They're probably concerned.

"Morgan. Where are you?" I say as if she could answer. She can't. Was she anywhere near a television to see the interview? Does she know we're searching for her? Does she know how much I love her? I fucked up when I kissed Linda, I did, and I fucked my marriage. If I'd not been so cowardly, and I'd just opened up and been honest with Morgan ... explained the innocence of the situation, I believe over time

Morgan would have forgiven me. I made a mistake—a drunken mistake. *You're gutless, Reid.*

I hear the en-suite door slide open. I jerk my neck and fling my body around to face that direction. "John," I say. I'm surprised I had no idea he was in there.

"Reid, how are you holding up?" He's wearing his denim coveralls, the ones he dresses in when I help him with maintenance.

"Why? What? John."

He places the small toolbox he has in his hand on the carpet in front of him. "I was using the bathroom before, while you were doing the interview. The downstairs loo door was locked. I noticed the tap over your basin was running, and I thought if you did try to catch a few winks the dripping noise would piss you off. You need to sleep, son."

"I can't sleep." I drop my head, and keep my eyes fixed on the jacket I'd discarded on the floor when I came up here.

"For Morgan. You need to sleep for Morgan."

"The bastard who stole Morgan called twice this morning."

There's silence until the mattress sinks lower below my arse. I don't need to look to know John is now sitting beside me.

"What did he say?" His tone is tender.

I sigh, squeezing my eyes tightly together. "A bunch of crap."

"Yeah."

"The phone was successfully tapped, West tells me. The tech team routed it to come through my mobile too."

"That's smart, right?"

"Yeah," I breathe. "They haven't got a trace from what I know. I don't think he stayed on the line long enough." I pause. "But that fucker knew I wasn't at home when the call came in at your house. How did he know I was at yours?"

"Have those useless coppers looked for bugs?"

"It's all clear, they say. No bugs. So how did this man know?"

"I don't know, maybe…"

"Maybe it's one of the coppers."

John doesn't answer.

"You're thinking it, too, aren't you, John?"

"I'm not sure what I'm thinking. I can't understand why anyone would do this to Morgan. She's sweet, kind, a great mum—"

"She is. It's revenge. But revenge for what?"

"I don't know, Reid."

"Me either."

"How about you try and eat something? I can make you a sandwich or even just a cup of coffee. I'd ask Shirley to fetch it for you, but she's with the kids next door."

"I'm not hungry."

"Something, Reid. Eat something." His hand squeezes my bicep. "Come on. Let's go back downstairs. We'll eat together."

"Just a coffee," I say, my stomach so raw that it causes acid to burn a path to my throat just thinking about food.

"Coffee it is." His weight becomes absent. "Come on."

Lifting my head, I witness his dirty aged hand held out awaiting mine. It's I who should be assisting him. After all, he's more than double my age.

"Coffee," I mumble, pressing my hands into my thighs and using the weight of my arms to push myself up.

Side by side, we take the stairs. John's holding the toolbox he used to fix the leaking tap. I wasn't aware it had been leaking.

"Where the hell have you been, Stratt?" It's West's voice I hear, but I don't see either of them.

"I made it, didn't I? I was leaving for my holiday when Max called. I had to change my flights."

"I've been trying to call you."

"I've had no missed calls."

"I thought you were driving."

"I am. Once I fly into Melbourne. Why are you so interested in my arrangements, anyway?"

I round the corner, and there stands West talking to a man in navy board shorts and a T-shirt. I believe it's Constable Stratt, who attended my call on the night of Morgan's disappearance. Maloney's standing to the left of them. He seems to be listening to the situation, more so than being involved in it. They don't see us, or if they do, they don't pay any attention to our presence.

"What's with this recording?" Stratt seems irritated. He's shifting from foot to foot. His posture is stiff, rigid.

"We've had the sound techs go over it already in Brisbane, and they've sent confirmation. Our perp was trying to disguise his voice with a Pom accent."

"So you don't need me now?"

"No, this morning I bloody did. You said you were coming straight in."

"I told you—"

"Yeah. Mate, we have a fucking woman missing. You could have saved me time if you'd come as you said." West's tone is laced with disappointment and frustration.

"Astin, I'm sorry, okay? I had to get shit sorted, and I arrived as quickly as I could."

I cough, causing both of them to search for me.

"Reid, I'm sorry I didn't see you there," Stratt says. His green eyes are vacant, lacking any actual sort of apology on contact.

"You're dismissed. Enjoy your vacation." West doesn't even address me. Instead, he turns his back in my direction. I'm not sure if this is because he's embarrassed I witnessed them disagreeing, or if it's because he's blatantly being rude.

"Alright. Sure." Stratt's tone is clipped when he rolls his eyes in front of me, and I'm left wondering why they're arguing in the first place. There's overt hostility between these two, and you can feel the tension in the room.

"Max, I need the shitter. Where is it?" Stratt seeks Maloney's assistance.

"Come with me, and I'll show you."

Stratt nods, flaring his nostrils before they both take to the hallway.

John seems puzzled when he comes into my line of sight. When he shrugs, I find myself shrugging, too.

"I'm going to put your toolbox in the office, and then we'll have that coffee?"

"Sure."

I take refuge on the veranda, swinging on the love seat that banged excessively against the wall on the night of the storm … the night Morgan never came home. For the last few hours, Detective West has been in a pissy mood, biting everyone's heads off and snapping orders. Detective Gleaton's copped the brunt of it. Maloney, on the other hand, has steered clear of him, and spent most of his time talking to me about life, his family, and how he became a cop. If I didn't know better, I'd think we were great mates, but we're not; we've only known each other for a such a short period of time. Talking to Max, though, is easy; I could see how under different circumstances we would be great mates.

Max is leaning against the railing, patting at his pocket. He's changed since Stratt left. He's now wearing a grey T-shirt and knee-length black cargo pants. I guess he too had to freshen up. I'm still in the jeans and the white polo T-shirt I wore under my jacket when interviewed earlier.

"Smoke?" Maloney says when he retrieves the packet from his pocket.

"Why the hell not?" I say, knowing it will make my stomach queasy, but lessen my tension. I spark the lighter and draw back hard, coughing not once, but twice. Maloney doesn't partake, but I get the feeling he wants to right now. He's jittery, and jittery doesn't suit him.

"So, what was that disagreement before?" I'm curious as I hand the lighter back to him.

A ghost of a smile touches his lips when he reaches out his hand and takes it.

"We don't have to—"

"Cops being cops, mate, nothing more. Everyone's highly strung at the moment."

"Morgan?"

"Yeah, they're getting close to some pretty good leads. It's the waiting game. Nobody likes the waiting game."

"Why are West and Gleaton here and not out doing investigative stuff?" This has crossed my mind numerous times today.

"Good question. I've asked myself the same. But then again, I'm not a detective, and I know almost the entire force is out there searching and collecting information." Maloney is twirling the lighter between his middle and pointer finger.

"Something isn't sitting well with me," I confess after taking another draw and bringing nicotine to my once clean lungs.

"What's that?"

"I'm trying to figure out how this prick knew that Gleaton had allowed me to leave the house and go next door to John and Shirley's. Gleaton says the property has been checked, and there are no bugs, so how did he know? And if he knew there was a tap on the line, why would he call?"

There's a long pause, and I'm not sure if Maloney is thinking of a way to divert the conversation, or if he's deciding what he will share with me. I wait.

"I've wondered this too." Our eyes connect. "That call came in, what, all of twenty minutes after the tap was in place and the landline routed to ring through your mobile phone?"

I nod. "Which means Gleaton, yourself, John, Shirley, my father and mother-in-law knew I wasn't here."

"And you."

"Obviously, I knew where I was at the time. Why would I do that? I didn't take Morgan. I'm not responsible."

"I believe you, but I'm confident none of the people you've mentioned are involved either. Think about it. West and Gleaton have both been here when the calls have come in. I've been here with you the entire time. John and Shirley are next door in the neighbouring property, tending to your children's needs, and your in-laws have been beside themselves since they arrived. I think someone is watching this house, but I suspect it's nobody who's here." He pauses. "And as for the phone tap, if he knows it's in place, which I suspect he does, he's pretty fucking brazen in calling. It takes a bit of time to get a location, but not much. He cut that call short, before we got a location ... this tells me that he understands how they work."

"That red-headed cop, though ... he's ..."

"Eric."

"Yeah."

"He left with West and had no idea you went next door. Don't think I haven't had a thought once or twice that it could be an inside job. I've done the maths, and it doesn't add up. It can't be."

"But what if—"

"Reid, you're barking up the wrong tree. You're suspecting everybody, and you should be, but I'm eliminating everybody because that's my job."

"Yeah." I take a drag of the cigarette; now so small it barely peeks between my fingers.

"You want another one?" Maloney's eyes turn towards my hand.

"Nope. They taste like shit." Just as I flick the butt over the side of the veranda, I spot Linda's car pulling up to the curb. "Linda," I murmur.

A tall, broad man with blond hair and five o'clock shadow, quite muscular, walks beside her down the path. He's not holding Linda's hand, but he's close enough to her that the bottom of the flowy dress she's wearing blows against his leg. This must be the copper boyfriend she texted me about earlier. What took her so long in getting here? What further information does this man have?

"Dodger, fancy seeing you here. How's light-duty going?" Maloney recognises him immediately, and before I even blink, Maloney has taken to the path and is shaking his hand.

"You know. Being shot in the arse isn't as bad as desk duty." Dodger laughs. So does Maloney.

I stand from the swing and wait at the top of the stairs. Linda walks in front, Maloney and Dodger following behind, muttering among themselves.

"Where were you?" I mouth to Linda.

Linda just nods and continues to walk right past me.

"Hi, mate. Dusty McQuill. Everyone calls me Dodger though. Linda's told me a lot about you and your wife." He holds out his hand. I hesitate to take it in mine.

"So, what are you doing here?" Maloney says as Dusty steps back from the top step to the middle one, letting go of my hand.

"Unofficial business." He points to the casual attire he's wearing—denim knee-length shorts and a surf-branded T-shirt that reads *Surf Tide.* "Max, this is my latest squeeze, Linda." He shifts his pointer finger towards Linda. Dusty's so relaxed and causal in both body language and the way he's socialising; it gives the impression we're at a staff Christmas party, about to have a few drinks and dinner.

The front door flies open, and when I twist on my heel, I see West holding a piece of white photographic paper out in front of him. It's a big piece, A4-sized.

"Reid, fingerprints have come back from Morgan's vehicle. They found a print on the busted tyre inside Morgan's boot. Do you know a Winston Sampson?"

I think hard and mutter his name, "Winston Sampson? No. I've never heard of him."

Linda steps forward quickly and begins to pace.

"Linda, do you know a Winston Sampson? Has Morgan ever mentioned that name to you? Is he a client of the firm?" I'm firing questions at her, but she continues to pace in what I believe is deep thought. Then she stops and turns in my direction. Her face drains of all colour as if she's seen a ghost.

"Linda!" I snap, concerned.

"Not a Winston Sampson, but a Falcon Sampson." As the words slide from her tongue, my body tingles, and I feel the colour from my own face drain away.

"Falcon Sampson is Morgan's ex-boyfriend," I follow.

West's eyes narrow. "When did Morgan date this Falcon?" His brows crease.

"Right before we hooked up in the first year of university. Morgan broke it off with Falcon after we met, I'm pretty sure. I've never met her ex. To be honest, I've never even seen a picture of him or the two of them together. Morgan seemed to have no reminders of past boyfriends in her stuff when we moved in together, but I didn't have any reminders of past girlfriends either. They were high school sweethearts, I believe." I look towards Linda for confirmation.

"Yes, that's true, they were. Dated from year nine until around the time Morgan met Reid." She pauses. "So, what's that? Five years or so?"

"Give or take," I say.

"We've had a witness who came forward. He claims to have seen the man we believe to be Winston on the highway helping Morgan. When the prints came back and the photograph we have on file matched the description our witness gave, we suspected we'd found the man who helped Morgan in the storm. Have a look at this photo, you two, and tell me if you recognise him."

"Sure." Linda makes the short distance, standing close to me.

West hands me the photograph, and I hold it out in front of both of us. "It can't be?" I'm shocked.

"Do you recognise him, Reid?" West says.

"I know him." I pass the photograph to Linda and run my hands through my uncombed hair. "This man is not named Winston, though," I declare. "It's Vactrim, from Handy Car Wash and Mechanics. Vactrim details our vehicles."

"Reid, this is Winston Sampson, and this is the photograph taken by the Department of Transport, the one on his driver's licence." West places his hand firmly on his hip and furrows his eyebrows. He's confused. Hell, I'm confused.

"Well, either he has an identical twin brother who looks just like him or he's masquerading as two people."

"Reid, are you sure?" West's voice is quiet.

"One hundred per cent. I talk with Vactrim at the end of every month when I get both the cars detailed. I take Morgan's in on the first day of the last week of each month. And I do mine in the same week, but on the last day of the month. It's him."

"Morgan talks to him as well?" West's tone is hushed.

I shake my head in slow motion. "No. She doesn't. She never takes the cars in to be cleaned. Only I do." I stop, taking a moment to really think about whether there has ever been a time when I've asked Morgan to do it in my place. There hasn't. "I don't believe Morgan has ever met him. I take care of all the servicing and cleaning arrangements with our vehicles."

"Do you know him, Linda?" West asks.

"No." It's a prompt reply, but as I turn towards Linda, I can see the word *liar* written all over her face. Linda's flushed and glowing red.

Why did Linda just lie?

Chapter Forty-Four

Morgan

The space is too small to stand, so I hunch and hobble through tunnel after tunnel until they shrink, and I'm forced to continue in a crawl. Spots of sunlight appear through cracks in the structure around me, sunlight I've not seen until now. The farther I venture, the more holes appear, which means more light gains entry and I have fresh air to breathe. *I must be going in the right direction.*

Every muscle aches. There's a high-pitched wheeze that follows each breath I take, and even though my jaw shoots sharp pains into my head from how hard I'm clenching my teeth together, I don't cry out or scream. I stay silent and keep trekking.

The ground below my knees falls away like sand

being pulled out to sea by harsh waves, but it can't be sand because I see a dark colouration ... soil. I'm underground, as I suspected. How did the earth give way as it did? *The wolf.*

My head rams into a wall. I've reached a dead end. There are no more tunnels to take to the left of me, or the right when I swivel my head. I've nowhere to go. I don't want to go back the way I came; I'm far too exhausted.

"Help," I plead.

A sound reminiscent of an air-conditioning vent whistling has me almost crawling over the top of myself. I stretch my arms and use my toes to push forwards. I need to know where it's coming from because there's no air-conditioner I can see around me. This must be a man-made tunnel. The tunnels are too perfectly dug, and placed, to be something nature created.

As I trek towards the distinctive whistling I see a circular space I missed initially. A stiff breeze rushes through it. I'll never fit through this hole. I'd be surprised if a teenager could climb through the space.

One, two, three times I nudge my head gently against a protruding rock located right beside the gap I want to squeeze through. I'm frustrated, breathless and tired. A long huff comes with me curling my body into a tight ball. *Try. Just try.* I do.

First, I push the backpack to my front and then throw it through the hole. I hear it land almost immediately, so I know whatever I'm climbing into doesn't have a significant fall on the other side. I could look—there's enough room for me to peek my head through—but the idea of seeing what's below causes anxiety to crawl through my veins. *What if it's a pit of spikes? Fuck!* I take a deep breath and poke my head through, looking down. I see the silhouette of the pack on the ground. I don't see anything sharp, just what appears to be leaves and dirt.

Wasting no time, I tilt my head sideways and scrunch my shoulder to my ear, managing to pass both through the circumference, however my other shoulder jams. *I'm stuck.* I shuffle, pull, and rock my body. *I'm still stuck.* I repeat this action multiple times until I scream, curse, and manage to pop through the other side, falling backwards and landing with a huff.

"I did it," I breathe before relaxing my limbs and looking above me at a high roof made from compacted dirt. It takes a while until I find the energy to manoeuvre myself into a seated position.

"What is that?" I gasp. A single red rose grows in the centre of what I quickly glimpse to be an ample open space. A spotlight illuminates its beauty … aimed to its position in the ground like a spotlight for a stage act. Does this rose mean something? Could it be connected to the thirteen roses in those pictures?

My legs shake, and when I find my feet, I shuffle towards the rose, focused only on its petals. The wolf has created a game for me to play, and I know this rose has to be a part of it. I'm petrified of this rose, the possible symbolism it may have. I'm trembling, and

I'm not sure if it's because I'm cold or if it's because I'm frightened. *Calm yourself, Morgan. Try and find calm.*

"Fears," I breathe. "Are." I slide my right foot across bark and leaves beneath my sole. "Stories." I slide my left foot in the same fashion. "We." I close my eyes briefly. "Tell." I drag my right foot once more. "Ourselves."

This is not real; it's only a story. *There's nothing to fear anymore, Morgan, because stories aren't real, they're fictional, and what is happening to you is fictional.*

I still. I flick my eyes in as many directions as I can without moving my head.

"No, no, no," I scream, then wrap my hands around my lips and smother any further screams with my palms. My eyes bulge. My heart pumps dangerously fast. I can't take my sight from it. I can't look away from the skull.

"No," I murmur into my palms, flicking my eyes in every direction possible once more. Bones, so many bones, ones I believe are of human origin. Why are there so many of them littering the ground?

Oh, fuck!

I'm in his graveyard.

Chapter Forty-Five

Reid

"You lied," Linda and I both say simultaneously, standing behind the mango tree in my backyard.

"I didn't lie." I didn't. Linda did.

"Reid, you did. Vactrim! Who the hell is even named Vactrim anyways? What are you hiding?"

"I'm not hiding anything. It's you who has something to hide. Linda, that's Vactrim from the fucking place I get my cars detailed."

"It can't be." Linda shakes her head.

"You said no when West asked you if you knew the man in that picture, and since then you've been distracted and trying to avoid that Dusty, Dodger, whatever-his-name-is fellow ... What's going on? Why are you lying?"

"To protect you." Her face strains as she keeps her voice to a soft projection. "The man in that picture is Winston Sampson, Falcon Sampson's brother, just like the detective said it was. He may be older and more substantial than he was when I was in high school, and I know I only ever met him a few times since he was away with military training, but I swear it's him." Linda's face scrunches, and she flares her nostrils. "Why did you ... What are you ..." She stops. "Reid, Falcon and Winston looked a lot alike. Both had wavy blond hair, and those piercing blue eyes you saw? Well, Falcon had them too. Like you and Cruise. You both have bright blue eyes, and you two have very similar characteristics."

"No, we don't," I scoff. It's preposterous Linda even thinks we do. Cruise is a fucking actor for God's sake, admired throughout the country for his good looks and charm. I'm the brother who doesn't even come close in the attraction department.

"Reid, you and your brother are very alike. You might not see it, but it's true."

"So this leads us to what? Can this guy be two people?

"I don't know. Possibly. I guess. No. How?"

"Why didn't you just tell West that you knew who he was when he asked you? Why didn't you confirm it was him just like West was saying?"

She slaps my chest. "Obviously I thought you were trying to hide something and I didn't know what it was, and I don't trust these cops and ... I just want

Morgan to be found and for her to come home."

"Linda, Morgan has been fucking missing for nearly forty-eight hours. I don't give a shit if it looks like I'm hiding something. You need to tell the cops everything you know. I want Morgan back, today, right now."

"I don't trust these cops, Reid, and even though I know you didn't have anything to do with it, you've already been set up once. Dusty said the guy who took Morgan also took the money from your safe, and from the beginning, you've been made to appear as the prime subject."

"All husbands are the prime subjects. You've watched enough of those bloody cop shows with Morgan to know that." I'm mad at Linda for not being honest right from the get-go with West.

"How would Falcon or Winston even know where you live, let alone know the combination of your safe?"

"How would the cops know the combination to my safe? I presume whoever it is used illegal means to do so. Plus, Vactrim knows our address. It would be on my file at the car dealership. If they're the same person, then they'd know."

"Morgan hadn't seen Falcon since a few weeks after she met you." Linda's finger extends, and she pokes it into the air in front of me. "Why would he care what you two were doing anyway? Why would he care this long after the fact? He's probably married with kids and living in the 'burbs somewhere."

"Maybe I pissed Vactrim, or fucking Winston, or

whatever his name is off. You said her ex was infatuated with her … borderline obsessive, I think is the term you used the very few times his name was brought up." I wrap my hand around Linda's finger and lower it to her side before letting go.

"He was a horny kid, but he understood they'd grown apart, that it was over. The last I heard about him was that he'd moved on, and so had Morgan with you."

"Morgan never—"

"It just fizzled out. That's what I understand regarding how it concluded."

"Fizzled out?"

"It's what she said months before she even started university … that it had lost its spark and she was slowly putting distance between them, and then they split. And that's exactly what she did."

"Why didn't you tell this to the cops?"

"I was protecting you."

"Or yourself."

Linda shifts from foot to foot; she's growing uncomfortable. "Pfft. Pull your head in. I've nothing to protect myself from. Morgan meeting you the week before they split was nothing but a coincidence."

"Linda, you need to tell West and Gleaton everything you know. They'll go digging around searching for shit, and you have information. They'll figure it out with or without you. They'll also know you lied through your teeth."

"Fine," she huffs.

"Maybe this Good Samaritan brother of his isn't such an upstanding person after all."

"My only question is, if Winston stopped to fix her tyre, and Dusty said they parted ways after the job was done..."

I'm not sure where Linda is going with this.

"Well, from your account ..." Linda continues before she stops speaking and taps a finger to her chin. "Does this mean Winston followed Morgan after they parted ways and then rammed her car?" Linda pauses. "The car that stopped on the side of the road that night was a small sedan from the police reports. The car that hit Morgan inside the estate was bigger, with a wider tyre track."

"How the fuck do you know all of this stuff?"

"I have a cop on the inside, remember?" She rolls her eyes.

"I need you to tell me everything," I bark.

"The searchers found something at the site where Morgan's car was."

"What?" My voice heightens on the word.

Linda's eyes grow wide. She drops her head and mutters, "Reid, we have eyes on us. Astin is coming our way."

I don't shift my head to look over my shoulder because I can already tell Linda's freaked out by how fast her shoulders launched upwards.

"Cry," I whisper.

"Why?"

"It will seem like I'm comforting you."

And just as quickly as the words leave my lips, Linda bursts into tears like any Hollywood actress could. "Why haven't they found her? I can't do this anymore. Why haven't they found her?" she yells through her tears.

Slipping on sweatpants and a cotton T-shirt, I discard my sopping wet towel in the wash basket and replay the conversation between West and Linda over and over in my mind. Linda came clean after West interrupted us, and she gave him all the information she had on the photograph and the person she believed it to be, Winston Sampson. The man identified as the one who stopped and helped Morgan. The same man whose fingerprints were on the tyre in Morgan's boot. I stood by my statement, that the man in the picture West supplied was Vactrim, the detailer at the company we use to service and clean our cars. Even though Linda and technology seem to dispute my claim, I know I'm right, and soon Detective Astin West will know I'm right, too, because he put out a call immediately for Detective Dyson to find Vactrim.

After West made the call, he took down notes as if it was an Olympic sport, and Gleaton recorded their further conversation with Linda on his phone. I listened carefully, hoping Linda would reveal information she hadn't shared with me. She didn't. It was the same story. She'd only met him a few times. He had distinctive blue eyes, as did his brother, and the relationship between Falcon and Morgan fizzled out long before Morgan and I began dating, even though they split only a week prior. The split went well, from Linda's account of what Morgan had shared with her, and later, Morgan and I would relocate and get on with our lives.

But could Winston or Morgan's ex-boyfriend, Falcon, or the both of them be involved? It makes no sense as to why, but then again, Morgan had been very coy about revisiting her past with me for our entire marriage. We were so young and barely had a history to mention in retrospect, but is that because she knew one day her ex would kidnap her. If so, why?

As soon as Linda and Dusty left, so did West and Gleaton. Maloney remained to hold down the fort, as he pretty much has since the start of this nightmare. John also stayed, I guess to offer me company, while Kylee, Ronald, and Shirley tended to the kids next door. The coffee John made earlier didn't sit well after only the first few sips, and the sandwich he put together remains untouched. I can't stomach food. I can't stomach another moment without knowing where Morgan is.

My phone chimes. I take three long strides to reach the bedside cupboard and retrieve it from the charger. Running my finger up the screen reveals a message.

Natalie: I've just reached Rockhampton airport, and I'm climbing into a cab. I'm on my way. I'm so sorry, Reid. I'll be there as soon as I can.

Relief. I feel nothing but relief that my brother and my sister-in-law are here in Rockhampton. *About fucking time.* I still haven't heard from Dad or Mum, but this gives me hope they are either with Natalie or not far behind.

"Reid. Baby. Reid." The distinctive sweet-sounding voice of my mother is music to my ears. The following sound, feet pounding down the hallway, causes me to rush to the bedroom door, swinging it wide.

"Mum," I call.

"Oh my God, baby, I'm so sorry. I just saw John downstairs and he said they still haven't found Morgan." Mum's arms wrap around my waist, and her head tucks against my chest as she sobs.

"Mum, don't cry," I say softly.

"Why haven't they found her?"

"I don't know."

Leading Mum to the edge of the bed, I help her to sit. Taking the box of tissues from Morgan's beside cupboard, I hand it to her. She dabs her eyes before I even have a chance to say anything.

"Have you slept, Mum? You look exhausted," I say, looking at the black bags circling her tear-stained blue eyes.

"A little. Getting a flight home was disastrous, and your father was delaying us with trying to find Cruise and Natalie. We've had no luck. You?"

"No, not until just before. Natalie texted; they are

on their way from the airport in a cab."

"Oh, thank God," Mum cries out. A mother's worry, love, and need to help her children is always present. I can see it in my mother's eyes as I admire her. I've seen this same look in Morgan's eyes. "Take me through everything from the beginning?"

"Where's Dad? Maybe we should discuss this with him present. It will save having the same conversation twice."

"He's downstairs with John and a man named Max. He said he's a police officer." I nod to confirm this is correct. Mum dabs her eyes with a fresh tissue she pulls from the box, the old tissue I see discarded by her feet. She holds out her arms, waiting for me to hold onto them. I do. Mum smells just like she always has—freshly washed. "We should wait until Cruise and Natalie get here, too."

"Sounds good." I relax just for a short moment.

I'm not sure how long I sit with my mother, exchanging hugs, but it seems to be a while. She takes my hand, and I brush the brown locks falling against her face behind her ear and say, "Let's head downstairs, Mum. It's been a long day, and we have a long night ahead. Maybe when Detective West and Gleaton return they'll have some news as to what tonight and tomorrow will bring." I stand, holding out my hand for her to take.

"Are they good men?" she asks, placing her hand in mine.

I don't answer because I'm not sure. If I wasn't so

suspicious of every one of the police currently handling Morgan's case, then maybe I'd say they are.

When we make the bottom step, I hear West talking. He's returned.

"Any news?" I spit the moment he comes into my view.

"We have some new leads, yes." He's nodding. I think he might even be smiling, or is he smirking? I can't be sure.

"Son." Dad's voice is raspy, as if he's sick with a cold. I can tell because his ordinarily wide nostrils are inflamed and glowing red, and his light blue eyes are dull.

"Are you sick, Dad?"

"Just a cold, mate. Nothing a scotch won't fix." Dad and his medical scotch advice. Scotch fixes everything in his books. "Come here." He holds out one arm.

I don't hesitate to stride towards him. His arm is just as hairy and long as I remember. His Cowboys jersey hangs well past the band at the top of his cargo shorts. When Dad wraps his hand around my back and places it on my opposite shoulder, I get a sense that all will be okay now. Dad's a strong man, a man who was once a major in the army. He's worked the land, and he's survived a car crash that was pretty much unable to be survived. My dad is the toughest of the tough; he's my hero.

Knock, knock, knock.

There's a loud knocking coming from the front door. Detective Gleaton, who's standing about a metre from the handle, makes the opening.

"I'm Natalie Banks." I hear her say.

"Come in." Gleaton steps to the side.

"Oh my God! Poor Morgan." Natalie drops a small overnight bag to the floor and rushes to me. *Where's all her luggage?* It's a strangling hug she delivers.

"Hey Nat, where's Cruise? Is he bringing in your luggage?"

Natalie shifts until she's holding onto my hands. "Huh? He's not here?" she says in question.

"I'm sorry, he's not where?" Why does she think he's here?

"Cruise is already here with you guys?"

"No." I shake my head.

"Shit!" She curses quietly under her breath.

"Natalie." Mum's voice shakes.

"He's supposed to be here. We fought, it was a big one, and he stormed off. He never arrived back at the hotel, and the next day he didn't show up. I managed to track him back home to Australia. The credit card showed he purchased a flight."

"When was this?" West says from behind us.

"It was Tuesday gone."

"When did you arrive in Australia?" West asks.

"Six a.m. this morning." Natalie turns her body side-on. "I stayed in our hotel to gather myself before heading back home to Australia. When I got back, I went to our apartment in the city, thinking Cruise would be there ... I thought he'd be sulking, like he tends to do, and even though he hadn't and still hasn't returned any of my calls, I'd expected to him to be at our apartment. He wasn't, and neither was his luggage."

"So, none of you know where Cruise is?" West's eyes connect with mine.

I shake my head.

"How did you know to come here, Natalie?" I know the tone West uses; it's the same one he used when interrogating me after Morgan first went missing, then again when the money wasn't in my safe.

"Our neighbour, Cali. She rang the doorbell and told me to turn on the television; she must have seen me arrive home. As soon as I saw you on the news, Reid, I booked the flights to get here. Melbourne to Brisbane, Brisbane to Rockhampton."

"So ... so ... is Cruise missing too?" Mum's as pale as a ghost when I flick my attention to her.

"I don't know." Natalie is holding her thumbnail between her teeth.

Ring, ring, ring.

West points to the handset on the kitchen bench before making the short distance to the laptop. He nods once.

"Hello," I say on answering.

"Well, Reid, didn't you play the part of a scared and sad husband well on television this morning? Boohoo. Pfft! I didn't buy a minute of it," he says, eerily calm and minus a British accent and a mechanical machine. He doesn't appear to be disguising his voice anymore. "We all know Morgan wasn't treating you right, don't we?"

I hiss at him without thought. "What the hell would you know about my family and my wife? You know nothing—you've got this all wrong. I love her, and she loves me, always has and always will. I know who you are, arsehole, and Morgan didn't love you, so why would you have wanted her to stay?"

"Morgan promised to love and she didn't, so for that, she'll pay. You were never any better." He snaps.

The line goes dead.

And right there, in a nutshell, we have the answer. I eye Gleaton, who's shaking his head. "No trace. He didn't stay on the line long enough."

I twist my neck and look into Detective West's dark-ringed ash grey eyes. "It's him you heard, right? It's her ex, Falcon; you've got proof now, so go find him."

"Reid, it didn't prove anything. It only showed us that the person who's taken Morgan seems to know you both well. But regardless, we have officers hunting down Falcon and his brother as people of interest." He pauses, placing one hand on his hip. "Reid, where do you think your brother might be? Does he have any property he wouldn't want others to know about except maybe you?"

What is he getting at here? Cruise? Not a chance. Cruise has no reason to hurt Morgan or me. It's not my brother.

Ring, ring, ring.

I grasp the handset. I take a short breath. I don't get

a chance to say anything before a high-pitched scream barrels through the line, and It's so piercing it causes pain to shoot through my ear. I hold the phone at a distance. West rips the headset plugged into the laptop from his ears as I stare at him with fear leaching into my heart.

The screaming stops. I bring the handset close to my cheek.

"She's a dead bitch now." His words are laced with poison.

The line goes dead.

Chapter Forty-Six

Morgan

There's red paint on a blackboard on the opposite side of the rose. How I made it this far, how I walked over the skeletal remains, I'll never know, but I did. Every step I took had me crying for those who lay here. Every breath I took shook. I just knew I needed to continue so I could go home. I can't be buried here with them. Nobody will ever find me. Nobody will ever take these women back to their families if I don't get out.

WHO AM I, RED?

His ultimate question, and the first line on this board, is written in capital lettering. I trace my fingertips over the painted lettering; it's dry. Is this paint, or is this blood? I cringe at the thought and snatch my hand back. I try not to think about it being anything other than paint. I work so hard, but my mind screams. *You've touched their blood. Run away from the blood.*

I stumble backwards, trying to escape my own panic. This man is beyond sick in the head. He's my worst nightmare, and he has me trapped in his graveyard. Is this where the game ends? Is this where he kills me?

A light flickers, just as a fluorescent does when first turned on. *Who turned on a light?* The lettering appears larger, thicker, sharper than before the light shone upon it.

WHO AM I, RED?

The glow is beaming down from above the words, and that's when I see a long tube fixed to the top of the board. I fall to my bottom and slide my arse backwards before cowering, waiting for his return.

"Please, please, please. Let me go." It's an automatic begging.

There's no answer.

"Please, Cullum. I know it's you." Do I though? Was this even a well-thought-out assumption. He smelt like bubble gum. He frisked me the same way Cullum did on my hen's night before I fled. It can't be anyone else. "Cullum, please," I cry.

There's no answer. No whistling. No nothing. *Where is he?*

Time passes, and I believe I've searched as much as I can. I've looked for a way out, a door, anything, but there was nothing to be found. I'm not sure how much time continues to pass, but it feels like an eternity, and as I sit cowering, waiting like an animal ready for slaughter, I whimper.

"How does he get in?" I mumble under my breath. There is no way the wolf could ever fit through the hole I managed to. He's much too broad-shouldered and far too tall, so how does he get into his graveyard? There needs to be another way in and out.

The skin on my hands is raw, bleeding, and even though they shake I don't stop scratching the compacted dirt walls with my nails and the scissors as I resume my search. I couldn't just sit there. I had to try again. I'm not sure how much time I have until the wolf comes, but I'm going to do what I can to get the fuck out of here before he arrives and overpowers me. At this point in the game, only a fool would think they'd be able to challenge him physically. All I have as my armour is my mind and this one pair of surgical scissors. I need to work out how he gets in.

Rattle, rattle, rattle.

It's a chain, and it's coming from underneath the hole I climbed through after taking the maze of tunnels he forced me into. Fuck. He's here. My mind races with the same pace as my thrumming heart. I wasn't quick enough. I wasn't smart enough to figure this out earlier.

I run towards the sound. I fall. I get back up. I

hobble. I trip. I get back up. I run until I can reach my arms out and touch the wall beside where I heard the noise coming from. Can I slip out as he comes in? It's my only hope.

Pressing my body flush against the dirt wall, I hold my breath and bite down on my lip to muffle the cries I can feel being summoned to my tongue. The dirt folds inwards and then opens like a door. I hold the scissors in my clenched tight fist by the side of my face, ready to strike if I need to. I don't make a sound.

He whistles his eerie tune, and although I jolt from the fear creeping through me, I still don't make a sound.

"Red, I'm home. Did you miss me?"

I bite down harder on my lip. The wolf's back is quickly in my view. There's a black T-shirt covering his muscular frame. His head slowly shifts from left to right, and in this one split second, I realise he's not aware I'm behind him yet. With the door still open wide enough for me to escape through, I hold the scissors in my now trembling hand and launch myself forwards.

"Fuuuuuuccck!" He makes a loud yelp after I swing my arm wildly and then continue to plunge my weapon into every bit of his flesh I can. I'm frenzied. I need to escape. The smell of metal coats the fine hairs in my nostrils, and as the smell grows stronger I scream, a high-pitched sound, releasing all my anguish with the noise. I no longer feel the handle of the scissors when I try to pull them back. My hand is slippery, sticky ... It's coated with his blood.

I dip down and scoop an item from the ground that catches my eye as it falls from the wolf's possession. I run. I run like the wind, and I don't look back, not once after I make it through the door. I don't dare to even risk searching for him. And although I don't hear him following me, I've learnt not to expect to. The wolf makes no sound when he moves because he's a ghost.

I can't stop running. I need to find a place to hide. Do I have a chance at freedom?

Home. It's a place I'd run to even if I had no skin left on the soles of my feet to protect my flesh. I won't stop trying to go home to my family. I won't stop running, regardless of my pain.

Chapter Forty-Seven

The wolf

That fucking bitch. That fucking piece of shit. I'll find her, and when I do, there will be no second chance. Morgan Banks is a dead bitch the moment I can wrap my hands around her neck. Fuck the game, and fuck her.

Reaching my hand over my shoulder, I run my fingers down my soaking shirt until I locate the object she attacked me with poking out of my skin.

"Whore," I groan as I rip my hand and the object upwards. There's too much blood to see exactly what it is, so I spit into my palm and use my glove to wipe it down. *Surgical scissors. Fucking surgical scissors. How the fuck did she get them?*

Every step I take into the surrounding bushland

makes me angrier. I made a mistake, and I never make mistakes. I underestimated Morgan, and this is probably an even bigger fuck-up than the scissors were. She's always been smart, but I'd never have thought she'd have this type of determination in her. I never thought she'd actually try to kill me. I smile. *Impressive.*

Where is she? She won't have traipsed too far with the injuries she has.

Darkness.

Quiet.

Patience.

Invisibility.

Training ... these are my weapons. I'll find Morgan in the dark of the night. I just need to let her come to me, which she will. She'll run in circles. Her sense of direction has always been poor, and her ability to stay hushed when she's frightened is not one of her finer qualities.

The howls of dingoes fill the air, and it's my favourite sound. Their need for a kill is predatory. They want fresh meat, and so do I. The direction of their cries is the direction I take. Morgan is bleeding. They'll smell her, and I will too, as soon as I get close enough.

Come to me, Morgan. Find your death.

I close my eyes and sniff wildly, picturing Morgan laying beneath me with my hands squeezed around her neck, her eyes wide, her breath laboured until she doesn't breathe at all. I search for the look of horror that will permanently fix her expression until her acceptance of death arrives. I want to watch the life drain from her, and after I've succeeded, I will remove her fingertips, her touch erased. She never earned the right to touch another or hold another. She deserved nothing she was given.

Crack. Crunch. Rustle.

"Silly bitch." The smile lifting my lips speaks of my satisfaction.

There you are, Red. Darkness can't keep you hidden.

Chapter Forty-Eight

Reid

I'm still in shock. Mum, Dad, Natalie, John, Kylee, and Ronald are all here, and Shirley waits back at the house with the children even after John called to tell her what had transpired.

Maloney stands near the front door, looking toward West who's only a metre away typing something into his phone. Maloney appears stressed. His stance seems rigid, his eyes narrowed, his chest rising and falling quickly. What's going on? Do they know she's dead, or are they worried he's killing her right now, like I am?

Maloney reaches into his pocket and retrieves his phone, and as he stares at the screen, his free hand reaches for the portable radio attached to his belt. He fiddles his fingers on its side.

"Dispatch, this is RK-681. We have a body. Female. Caucasian. Brunette. We need all units in the area of Yeppen Lagoon to respond. I think we've found our missing person."

My balls launch into the back of my throat. I leap from my chair and barrel towards West. I've no idea what I plan to do when I reach him, but punching him in his mouth seems like a fucking good idea. West said Morgan was still alive. He said it was just an act, an empty threat, something to scare me with. It fucking scared me.

West lied.

"RK-681, this is dispatch. We are dispatching CBI, and forensics are already en route. Please hold your position and secure the area."

"Max, turn your radio off," West snaps as he glares in his direction.

"Yes, sir. I tried." Maloney is quick to answer.

I see red. I want West to tell me this isn't happening; that it's a mistake.

I lunge towards him.

"Reid. Stop," West commands with both palms raised and facing outwards.

"Morgan. Is it fucking Morgan?" I scream.

"Let me go to the scene. I need to inspect this for myself."

"Is it Morgan?" A tortured sound releases from

within me. My heart rate increases to the point where I don't think it will ever beat at a slower pace again. Heat surges through my veins as every thump of my pulse echoes in my ears. "Astin, is it Morgan? You know something; I know you do."

He stares into my eyes, and I know I don't want to hear what he will say. I don't break contact though, and prepare for the worst.

"Reid, I've been receiving messages from the officers who have located this body." He pauses. "The outfit she's wearing is the same one Morgan had on the day she disappeared." He breaks eye contact and drops his head.

He killed my fucking wife.

Morgan is gone.

I can't breathe.

My knees hit the floor before my hands do, and my back arches as I curl into myself. "No. No. No!" I scream. "Noooooooo!" I suck back a needy mouthful of air. "He killed her. He killed my wife."

I won't survive this. The kids won't survive this. He took everything from me just as he promised.

Morgan is dead.

Chapter Forty-Nine

Reid

I dip my head and lower my body until I'm sliding across the back seat of the car. The belt meets the buckle, and I jolt from the sound.

My heart shatters all over again. I'm never going to be the same man I was before.

The car door opens on the opposite side to me, and Maloney sits and then shuffles in his seat. My stomach rolls in a vicious circle causing acid to burn the back of my throat.

They've found Morgan. There's no life in front of us. No more memories left to create. No more "I'm sorrys" to be exchanged. *Morgan's dead.*

"We're leaving now. Are you ready, Reid?" Maloney's tone is tender. His eyes filled with pity.

Make it stop. Make it stop, my mind pleads as I turn my head in a shake and drop my vision to the seat below.

I'm not ready to see my wife. I'm not ready to say goodbye. I'm not ready for eyes that speak of sorrow and pity to be my future.

Maloney clears his throat at the precise moment I hear car doors opening.

"It's almost time. We're just waiting on Detective West to finish these phone calls," Maloney says softly.

I don't look at him.

The streets I've not travelled on for days await. It wasn't supposed to end like this. Our love wasn't supposed to end at all. I didn't even get a chance to tell Morgan I loved her with all my heart, and that I was sorry for letting her down. "I'm sorry for pushing you out of my life, Morgan," I say under my breath.

"Reid," Maloney says.

"What?" Our eyes briefly connect until I rotate my head towards the laminated glass window in front of me. It fogs with the heavy breaths I take.

I didn't hold true to the promises I made Morgan. I wasn't the man I vowed to be for her, the man who'd catch her if she fell. I wasn't the man I promised myself I'd be either.

How do I go on from here? How do I live with my guilt? How do I raise our children right? How do I live without Morgan?

"We're about to leave, Reid," Maloney mumbles.

Maloney. *My rock.* I want to laugh at the realisation

that this man, a stranger I met two days ago, is the person I requested to be with me as I take this final journey.

When I see Morgan, Maloney will see me fall. I will fall at the sight of Morgan. I will never get up again.

"Reid, Detective West is climbing into the car now," Maloney commentates.

"Do not let the press get wind of this yet. We have to see if Reid can give us an identification." West stops abruptly. "No! It's not protocol, but sometimes rules are meant to be broken." He stops speaking. "Because if it's not, then we still have time," he continues. "If we don't do this, we're waiting for dental records. Do you want to risk that?" West's tone is harsh. "Good. Hold tight. I'm taking her parents as well, in case he can't do it. I'll call you as soon as we do or don't, okay?" He pauses. "Bye."

I rotate my head mechanically and catch West lowering his phone to the console.

The click of the key twisting in the ignition makes me jump. The engine firing has me swallowing hard. I close my eyes.

Dear God,

Can you please work a miracle? Because I need a second chance to be with my wife. Grant me one more chance, and I promise I won't mess it up.

Amen.

Slow—that's how the car moves. It's like we're in a

funeral procession as we follow a red undercover vehicle that rolled up to the house earlier this morning. Gleaton is at its wheel. His mission: to escort Morgan's parents on the drive.

My heart sinks low into my belly when I picture the devastation that would have been painted on Ronald and Kylee's face's after that fucking call came in. I blink to clear my vision—to help silence the ear-piercing screams that accompany it. It doesn't work, and panic leeches my heart, strangling my blood flow, causing an unbearable ache to reside. The need to run has me bouncing my knees. My stomach rolls again, this time in a tsunami fashion, and my heart thumps so hard in my chest I will for it to stop beating altogether. *I can't do this.*

Maloney's hand presses to my thigh. "Reid. Breathe."

I inhale slowly. *I have to do this.*

Roundabout.

Red light.

Roundabout.

Bridge.

Roundabout.

Red light.

Then a white and red sign reading *Rockhampton Base Hospital* comes into view. We drive down a hidden path, one I never knew existed.

The car comes to an abrupt halt. I shudder as if someone is walking over my grave, and I instantly twist my head in search of Maloney's eyes to seek comfort, only to view the back of his head.

The car door beside me opens. I expect an aged face and a black/grey moustache; instead, it's a youthful pale complexion and red hair filling my vision. *Prospect.* Why is he here? When did he arrive? And who with?

I climb out of the vehicle. Prospect moves a few steps back to give me room.

"Mr Banks." Prospect offers me the same look of pity Maloney did. I look away to see West striding in my direction.

The crunch of hiking boots on gravel has me turning my eyes downward, towards West's feet. He's not wearing hiking boots, yet the sound is loud as if he was. *Is he stomping?*

"This way," West says in passing.

I turn, but I walk through fog … I'm in a daydream. My body is weightless, and I feel as though my soul is no longer housed inside me. *I'm Lost.*

Ronald, Kylee, and Gleaton await us, stationed outside clear automatic doors. I take two steps past them. I don't say a word as the doors part.

Kylee reaches for my hand, linking her fingers with mine. I shake her away. I need to take this walk uncomforted. I don't want social niceties. I don't *deserve* them.

"Eric, keep any reporters at bay. Text me if they show up. You need to man this door," West says, matter-of-factly.

My bones freeze as I step inside. *It's so cold.* Chilled

air laps my skin as a strong smell of bleach fills my nose.

The noise of leather shoes tapping across polished flooring comes from West and Maloney who now walk half a metre in front of me. I can't stand the sound. I want to turn back. I want to run away.

A blue door on the right reads *Morgue One*. Briefly, I pause to stare at the silver lettering. Is this where Morgan's lifeless body lies?

"Reid, Honey," Kylee speaks softly. I feel her hand squeeze my shoulder from behind. Again, I shake her away. *You don't deserve comfort,* I remind myself.

The last few steps are the hardest I take. They're hesitant and my legs quiver, even when I come to a dead stop, positioned between West and Gleaton.

I stare through a clear petition which takes up the upper quadrant of a hand-smudged white wall. The room behind this window appears empty. Blue and grey marble flooring shines under stark white lights. There's a door located at the opposite wall, to the left, and I focus on the silver doorknob.

"They're going to bring her in now. Are you ready?"

I flick my head to my left, following the direction of West's words to find him bobbing his head.

There's a firm grip applied to my right shoulder. I whip my head to my right. Maloney doesn't look at me, even though the pressure of his grip increases. Instead, he stands tall, with his eyes forward. I don't shake him away. I need his grasp because fear is ripping through my body and I just need to feel something, anything.

I fixate on the silver doorknob once more, and as I do, I shudder. *This is it.* My heart kicks up another gear, and the pain in my chest leaves me breathless. My palms become sweaty. My breathing labours. The doorknob twists. My heart skips a beat before pumping even harder. I close my eyes.

The smell of the paper Morgan buys in a roll for the children to draw on fills my senses. *Butcher paper.* Why does it smell like butcher paper here, when on entry it smelt like cleaning chemicals? *This makes no sense.*

I flick open my eyelids to find a white sheet hanging over the top of a mound. A man wearing thick black glasses, with protruding lenses, stands with his hands limply dangling in front of him. He nods. I'm not sure why, but after he nods he lifts his arm and peels back the white sheet. He folds the material over itself, stopping above her breasts, not exposing anything more than her head, neck, and upper chest.

Brown hair—that's all I recognise. The face is swollen and bruised beyond recognition. *She's unidentifiable.*

I hear a gasp, then another, followed by sobbing coming from the opposite side of West. *Who's crying?* I search for the source, taking my eyes away from the body laid out in front of me.

Kylee has her hands splayed out on the panel with her forehead pressed against them. "No, no. What did they do to her?"

A deep, winded cry comes after she speaks. Ronald lays his head on the top of Kylee's and cries; a sound I've never heard in all the time I've known him.

"Reid." West's grey eyes infringe my vision. "Is this Morgan?"

"How the fuck can I tell? Her face. Her face is ..." I dry heave, folding at my mid-section. I pant. I pant fear, anger, and sorrow into my palms cupped around my mouth.

Small circles rub against my back. "Does Morgan have any markings we may be able to identify her by?" Maloney says calmly.

I slowly pull myself upright. Maloney's hand falls away. I seek his comfort, the calm that comes from the way he speaks, and then I nod.

"Where? What?" he says.

"A pink heart-shaped birthmark where her bra sits across her back." I don't have to think about any other. Morgan's birthmark is unique.

"Okay." His tone soft.

"Irwin, please check her back for a heart-shaped birthmark. Pink in colour. Located where her bra strap would sit." I'm not sure how the man in the room can even hear West say this, and I don't look to find out if he does. I keep my eyes fixed on Maloney's while trapping my breath behind my lips.

"The window has gone black," Maloney says. "He'll be repositioning her with privacy." He pauses. "When the glass becomes clear again, I'll tell you, and you'll need to look, okay?" His eyes are sympathising, yet broad.

I nod.

"Reid, you can do this," Maloney encourages.

I swallow hard.

"Keep breathing, mate."

I gulp a needy breath.

"We can see the room now. Irwin's pushing the table closer to the window. I'll tell you when we're ready."

I nod.

There's silence around me, even though inside my head it's loud.

"We're ready." Maloney breaks eye contact when he rotates his head.

I follow suit. Purple, green, yellow, and black are the colours of the bruises that splotch her back. Patches of white skin shine in comparison, standing out between the discolouration. I search for her birthmark, the place it should be.

It's not there. Only white skin.

There's just pale milky skin.

It can't be Morgan. It isn't Morgan.

"It's not there." Pure shock. "It's not Morgan. It's not Morgan," I cry out as I slide my hands down the transparent panel and slump to the floor.

I weep. I weep for the woman who lies on the table unidentified. For her family and whatever it is she's endured at this sick psychopathic man's hands. Her death is related to Morgan's disappearance. As West said, she was wearing Morgan's clothing.

Has her kidnapper killed before?
Is he a serial killer?
Are there more women to be found?
What has he done to Morgan?

Chapter Fifty

The Wolf

I can navigate the bush that surrounds me in any weather or light. I'd know it with my eyes closed, like the back of my hand—I know this bushland. There are forty hectares I've spent years walking, yet I worry. I worry that Morgan might find her way off my land, infringing on another's.

The closest neighbouring house to mine is another one hundred hectares away, yet their land is much, much closer. There's no way Morgan could have made it to their home during the night on foot even with the healthiest of bodies. She's a walking corpse—a fucking walking corpse that managed to ambush me.

"Fuck," I groan.

If I don't find her today, there's a possibility she'll

stumble her way out of here, and if she does, I'll go on a massacre. I'll kill any fucker who gets in my way until I've found her. My fury will be unleashed. I'll take more lives than I planned to. I'll do anything to see that bitch dead. I was never going to let her live—I just wanted to give her a chance to figure out the game. *She's royally fucked up my fucking game.*

Leaves rustle above me, stealing my attention. I tilt my head back. The sun has me squinting my eyes as I search for the source. A grey fur-covered claw reaches out scooping a handful of eucalyptus leaves from the old gum tree in front of me. It's not Red. It's a fucking koala.

Where the fuck is Red?

She should have run her circle and collided with my chest by now. She should have been in those bushes last night, too, only she wasn't—a fucking possum was, though. That glowing-eyed critter copped the full brunt of my rage as it flew off the end of my boot. I wish it had been Morgan's face connecting with my swinging leg, then I wouldn't be out here walking these grounds like I am.

Each foot I place in front of the other has me thinking about the wildlife that hunts these parts alongside me. The wildlife always hungry for blood, just like I am.

Have they ripped her to pieces? Have the dingoes, foxes, and wild pigs taken the pleasure I want for myself?

I growl, "Fucking hope not."

Morgan's life is mine for the taking, not theirs.

Grey stones fill my vision. A massive rock wall, too high to scale, has me huffing. I'm going to need my equipment to find her. I'm probably going to need to borrow some of Winston's high-tech shit as well. It won't take long for the day to become night.

Thank fuck Winston is out of town hunting, which means I have full access to his gear without any questions asked. Winston is a nosey bastard, but given his past, and what he once did for a living, it makes sense he's suspicious. You don't roll with the mafia and not think every person is out to get you.

Four hours, give or take a few minutes, is how long it usually takes for me to reach Winston's shack and get back. Add in the time it'll take to retrieve the stuff I need ... "Shit, Morgan, you've messed with the wrong fucker today."

I breathe. I close my eyes. I calculate the amount of time that's passed in comparison to the condition Morgan's in, and the time I'll need ... I'll be cutting it close to how near to freedom she could get.

Disappointment rushes through my veins, and with a harrumph expelling from my pressed lips, my temper rises. I whip around and stomp heavily towards my cabin. I think about the fucking holes ripped through my shirt and torn through my skin. That bitch left those there. Morgan has taken so much from me, and I just want this game over.

Calm yourself.

Don't lose control.

You will find her.

I will find her.

A good hunter knows how to keep his patience and wait for his target to find him. I'm letting all my training go down the shitter because of one woman. Hell is not where I need to allow myself to travel right now. Instead, I need to sort the memories of my previous Reds and draw on those accomplishments.

Don't let your emotions erase your composure. You are more manly than this.

I take three long drawn-out breaths and search for someone to extinguish my brewing anger. Red Number Three was one of my favourite captures and kills to date, and I replay our meeting—her wrongdoing—and her capture, over and over in my mind. It's like a show on television playing before my eyes, and it eases the growing tension invading my muscles as I navigate the bushland home. Donna Martin will keep me rational and focused.

"Hi, I'm Donna." She grips her bottom lip between her glowing white teeth as she leans against the mahogany bar. *"Can I buy you a drink?"*

Her breasts heave, and as her ample cleavage demands my attention, spilling out of her tight hot pink dress, I realise she has figured out who I am. Her wide star-struck eyes and lightly flushed cheeks are a dead giveaway.

This bitch likes powerful men. Even in another town, I'm recognisable. I shouldn't be surprised. "Sure. A martini, shaken, not stirred."

She bats her eyelashes, then squeezes her muscular thighs together. Her teeth pinch her bottom lip between them. She knows what she wants and how to get it. And If she wants a movie-worthy fuck, I'll give her one. I'll play James Bond, and she can play the slut I bed and leave behind in my wake.

Women only want to be taken by men with money and power. They want jewels and the beautiful things in life. They need the promise of being financially taken care of. They don't want to be loved by a heart or worshipped by a tender touch. Women don't want love; women never seek true love.

It's a giggle, a flirty fucking giggle that has me focusing on her sapphire blue eyes. "Okay, James." She walks her long, pink-painted nails up the sleeve of my black business jacket. They're the same pink as her stained lips.

"Thank you, Red." I name her appropriately for her behaviour.

Her eyes grow even more prominent. "Oh, Red? I like it. It matches my hair."

"I knew you would." Fucking tramp.

"Bartender. One martini, shaken and not stirred." She pauses. "Make it two." She brushes her long flowing red locks over one shoulder and again grips her lip between her teeth, only this time she lets it slowly escape, really fucking slowly.

My dick jumps in my pants. I may hate women's souls, but I sure like to bed them and make them surrender to my dominance.

In the next hour, she'll submit. She'll let me do whatever it is I want. I'm going to do things to her she never dreamt she'd allow any man to do.

I laugh outwardly.

Her head whips to me. Her hair falls in a bounce down her back. "What's so funny, James?"

"Nothing." *I offer a toothy, yet playful smile.*

"Oh, you're a naughty boy, aren't you, James?" *She's a seductive piece of work.*

"Would you like to find out?"

Her pale cheeks blush a pretty pink. "Smooth talker." *She cocks an eyebrow and skims her nails up and down my jacket.*

I laugh before leaning into her. I breathe against her neck and skim my lips along her earlobe. "I can make you wet by whispering how fucking delicious I know your pussy will be in your ear."

She swallows hard. She pants.

I slide my hand over her soft hair and down her back until I stop at her arse. Her breath catches in her throat, and the sound makes my dick jump in my trousers once more.

"I-I-I ... well," *she stutters.*

"I think you should go play with the little boys, love. You can't handle what I've got." *I take her hand, which is hanging limply by the side of the bar, and move it until it's pressed against my erect cock.*

She takes a short breath, then her blue eyes gleam. She reins in her surprised expression. She bites her bottom lip, rolls her eyes, and whispers, "You'd be *surprised by what I could do with that." Her hand becomes tight around my shaft.*

Red is confident. I like it.

"Bartender, put those drinks on my room." I wink before turning my attention back to the large busted redhead in front of me. "After you." I grin.

Her lips stretch wide. Her eyes close halfway. She's drunk on adrenaline. She turns on her thin peg heels. Her hips sway from side to side. Long legs travel on forever until the dress covers the way they join at her arse. Red peeks back over her shoulder and offers me a sweet giggle.

A fierce groan echoes in my throat.

I fuck Donna Martin every which way I can. For hours. No orifice becomes off limits, and no hard slap on her arse or pull of her hair seems too much for her. She takes me roughly. She submits. I own every bit of her until my erection goes limp and I can't plough myself into her sloppy pussy anymore.

"Oh, James." She stands from the bed and bats her long black eyelashes. "Is that all you have in you?" Cum trickles between her thighs. "I thought you were one of the big boys. It seems you're all cock and no stamina."

I grit my teeth so hard my jaw spasms. I leap from the mattress and reach out until I roll my hand into her hair. I wrap her locks around my palm multiple times. Her neck lengthens and then extends backwards as I pull. "Red, I will fuck you until you bleed. Shut your mouth." Her body goes stiff. "I want your blood oozing down my cock. I want your insides mangled so nobody can ever touch you again." I pause to add new fear. "Do you want me to rip you apart? Because that's all I can offer your sloppy date now."

She trembles against me. "Wh-what? N-n-n-no. Too ... too far." Her lips pull down, and her eyes leak tears. "Please, let ...let ...me ...go."

"Don't bait me. Don't fucking bait me again," I snap.

"Sorry," she cries.

I release her with a hard shove, and as she stumbles backwards, I swing my arm and strike her across the cheek with the back of my hand.

She screams out. "Please. No!" she cries harder. "I'll take my money, and I'll go. I'll go."

Money? What fucking money?

There's a moment of quiet when she wipes the blood away from her lips. "I don't play these types of games, James. I'm just here to get laid and get paid."

Games? What games? Paid to get laid? What the fuck?

I deliver a fierce stare.

"Look, mister, please. I'm just doing this to pay my bills and my university fees. I-I don't go that far though. No money could make me let you do anything like that. Rape fantasies are not my thing."

"You're a whore?" I bellow.

"I'm a call girl. I'm not a whore. I don't have a choice. I need an education and a better life for myself."

I'm livid, and as I pace back and forth, growling like a beast that has a thorn wedged in the pad of its foot, the need to strangle the life from her stupid fucking neck grows.

"Hey, what we just did is further than I've ever gone before, but—"

I stomp my foot.

She stops speaking. Her skin turns a shade of grey.

"No. You get not a cent." I offer a murderous stare.

"Please. One thousand dollars and I'll be gone." She's trembling.

"Are you deaf?"

She shakes her head.

We're going to play games. We're going to play my game if this cunt doesn't leave this hotel room right now. How will she like playing The Game of fucking Life with me?

"Get your clothes on," I bark.

"I thought you knew. I thought you—"

I launch myself across the room, wrapping my arm around her neck, smothering her lips with my opposite hand. "I had no idea you were a fucking prostitute. Get dressed and get out," I snarl from deep within my throat, pushing her away.

She scrambles to pick up her clothes, and as tears roll in a line down her face, streaking her heavy make-up, I find myself unable to look at her a minute longer.

I march angrily into the bathroom, slamming the door behind me. The walls shake from the force.

The mirror above the sink catches my reflection. I gaze into my narrow eyes, see my flared nostrils and pressed lips.

I want her blood to spill on the floor. I want it now.

Click!

The sound of the latch has me reefing open the bathroom door. She's leaving.

"You've got to be shitting me," I yell.

Her body stiffens. She drops the wallet, my wallet, the one she's holding in her hand. She doesn't turn to look at me. Instead, she runs with her high heels hanging from her fingers.

"I'm sorry," she calls back. The panic in her tone is exhilarating.

I leap forward. I want to chase, capture, but I don't. I stop dead in my tracks.

That bitch has a death wish, and it's a wish I'm going to deliver. The hunt will be worth every moment. Her death will be the best revenge. "You're a dead bitch, Red," I murmur.

For three weeks, I stalk my prey. I case her school, her workplace, and follow her regular clients who are nothing but sleazy vermin who should cease to exist. Red's daily schedule becomes burned into my memory. She makes it easy, and I'm like a greyhound picking up her trashy scent wherever she trots.

The security at her rundown one-bedroom apartment is pathetic. Why do women think that a cheap Home Depot lock is all they need to keep out a determined predator?

Dumb bitches.

I wait in a dark corner of her bedroom, the floor littered with clothing and high heels. She treats her stuff like trash. She is trash. A sharp needle containing a sleeping agent hangs between my fingers. Red will sleep well—until I can get her over state lines and into my territory, that is. Then, the fun begins. The lock turns over. Screech. Bang. Clip, clop. Clip. Clop. She's walking right towards me. She has no idea what's about to happen. She won't escape. My heart gallops. I smile. She's finally mine.

Donna Martin: university student. Daughter. Sister. Hooker. She never saw what was coming, and the moment I stuck that prick into the soft skin of her neck, she fell limp in my arms. The rush of pure adrenaline I craved filled me completely. I exhale a satisfied moan.

Oh, how much fun we went on to have. Donna was feisty to the end. She was no Morgan though.

Morgan! Where the fuck is that bitch?

Chapter Fifty-One

Morgan

Stuck between a rock and a hard place isn't just a saying I've used often, but it's where I am now. I'm trembling; I'm shaking so badly that the mobile phone threatens to dislodge from my grip.

Sheer luck. The wolf's phone falling from his possession in my attack was nothing but sheer luck. I managed to grab it off the ground straight after I plunged those scissors into his shoulder. Now, if only the phone would work. I bang my finger against the digits alight on the screen, trying to call for help.

Fear is still coursing through my veins and exploding sharp nails into my chest. I wince for what feels like the hundredth time. I need to contain this fear, but I can't, because I can still see the wolf as I did not too long ago when his back, the holes in his T-shirt at the shoulder, was right in front of me. I stared at him through the small peephole created in this boulder—the boulder nuzzled close to the rock wall I'm tucked tightly behind. He was too close for comfort, and I was scared he'd find me. That he'd see my eye peeping through the hole. I worried he'd smell my blood and the stench of BO I can sniff on myself. I feared he'd never leave without me gripped tightly in his hands. He didn't see me. He didn't appear to smell me. He didn't capture me. But I still tremble uncontrollably. It's a violent shuddering, and as my skin becomes slick with moisture and sweat rolls down my arms, taking my focus, I'm left to wonder why my body is betraying me even though I've not been moving for ages.

Why can't I stop shaking?

Tensing my jaw, I try to stop the chattering of my teeth. I'm not cold, yet my teeth bang together as if I am. The heat that rips through the bushland is unbearable, and it gives the illusion that my body is folded up inside an oven set past two hundred degrees. Panting doesn't alleviate the heat. Nothing does.

My head spins. Everything is whirling in circles.

What's happening?

I pull my legs tighter to my chest and try to catch my breath, even though the heated air filling my lungs makes me feel as though I'm suffocating.

Blurry vision has me blinking with haste as I fight

an overwhelming terror that enters me like an electric shock. I look at the screen of the phone I'm holding an inch from my nose.

"Please get a service bar. Please!" It's barely audible, but I'm begging. I try to focus on the keys. I press my finger against numerals. I'm not sure which numbers they are, but I hope they will lead to someone. I stifle my need to cry and tell myself to focus.

There's no reception here. The phone's not working. It hasn't, not once, even on the way to this tight spot. I need to move. It's only a matter of time before he finds me. But how? My body is royally fucked up.

My vision goes black when my eyes momentarily roll over in my head. I can't seem to gain control of myself. I can't seem to concentrate at all. The shaking I'm experiencing, the chattering of my teeth, the sweat dripping from my skin—it only increases.

"What the fuck?" I pull my shoulders up until they sit under my ears, and scrunch my face tight.

Why am I suddenly so itchy?

I rub at the tattoo on my inner arm, and as I do, the itch spreads from my hand to my elbow, then to my shoulder. It travels across my chest and down the opposite side of me. It feels like an army of bugs creeps under my skin, and no scratching can relieve it.

As I slide my feet back and forth against the dirt, anger builds in my gut. It creeps up into my chest and then explodes from my mouth in a primal roar.

I want to hurt. I need to kill.

I squeeze my eyes closed tighter and curl my hands into fists. Each beat of my fists against my forehead, out of frustration, has me crying. "I need my pills. I need a fucking fix."

Oh fuck, I'm detoxing.

He's given me no drugs; my body needs the chemicals it's reliant on to settle. *Morgan, what have you done to yourself? Look what you've fucking done.*

 Using my teeth, I begin to gnaw against the skin on my bicep, then my hand, and then the inner side of my arm … anything to scratch this itch. It doesn't work. Instead, it only worsens.

The spinning I experience grows wilder and causes the anger bubbling away inside me, to skyrocket.

Move, Morgan. Get up and run. Use this pain, hatred, and rage to find a way to call for help.

I do. I find my feet, and I amble towards a splotch of grey that's so blurry I can't even make out what it is.

What if it's the wolf? What if you're running straight to him, Morgan? Go back. Go back, my mind screams.

Which way is back? I can't see. Everything is hurtling around me at full speed. Why did I even try to run at all?

I hear an eerie whistle invade the dry air.

Oh, fuck. Is it him?

My eyelashes flutter open. I roll my head against

leaves. "Oh, God," I moan.

Where am I? Where's the wolf?

I sit upright and then shuffle backwards on my arse as I simultaneously try to gauge my surroundings.

Left. Right. I'm searching for clues. *Rock walls.* I tilt my chin back. The blistering sun sears my face, and I blink, crazed, as it burns my irises. I drop my head. Leaves fill my vision. Dried, yet springy at the touch.

The phone. Where's the phone? I slide my hands across dirt and leaves in a panic. I'm frantic to discover the only device that can bring in a cavalry to save me.

Sunrays gleam against a shiny black item about half a metre from me. I moan as I press weight against my feet to stand. I can't. I throw my body backwards until my head bumps the ground. Side to side, I swing my arms and legs until I roll onto my stomach. Front to back, over and over, I move. I feel a lump press against my spine.

"Oh, thank God." It's barely audible.

I tuck my arm under myself and retrieve what I can now see is the phone I was searching for. I shift my eyes to the screen. It's not cracked, and there's still power. The battery bar reads twenty-eight percent. Two thin bars fill the service section.

My eyes grow wide. My heart accelerates. I press my finger against the digits I can now see clearly. *000.*

"Fire, police or ambulance," the automated voice says.

My need to cry grows strong. It may only be an

automated voice, but it's the first I've heard apart from the wolf's in days.

"All units." My voice trembles.

Ring, ring, ring.

"What is your emergency?" His voice is soft, tender.

I sob. "Morgan Banks. I'm Morgan Banks. Help me. Help!"

"Morgan, what is your emergency?"

The line goes dead.

Noooooooo. The word screams in my head, but I don't dare shout it aloud.

I punch in ten numbers, ten numbers that can bring me help. Ten numbers that will lead to someone who knows I'm not where I'm supposed to be.

"Reid, pick up. *Pick up the goddamn phone.*"

Chapter Fifty-Two

Reid

The sun is bright. I dip my chin so I'm looking towards the gravel. My legs and arms warm to the point I rub one hand over my wrist to alleviate the burn.

Kylee reaches out her arms, wrapping them around my waist. We stand in an embrace beside West's car in the hospital car park, as sweat drips from my brow.

"It wasn't our girl. It wasn't our girl," Kylee cries against my chest.

I stroke my hand over the top of her hair repeatedly. Pain constricts the flow of blood to my heart as images of the woman who West said wore my wife's clothing plays on a loop. *If that's what he did to her, then what has he done to Morgan?*

Ring, ring, ring.

A vibration tingles against my thigh. The sound coming from my pants is enough for me to force myself from Kylee's embrace. I fumble the phone inside my pocket and then bring it to my ear.

"Where's my fucking wife?" I scream down the line before he even has a chance to say a word.

"Reid, help me." Her voice is soft, yet croaky.

"Morgan!" I screech.

"Help me," she cries.

West marches toward me.

"Baby, where are you? Tell me where you are?" I plead.

Kylee clutches my free arm. "Mumma's here," she yells.

"I'm here," Ronald hollers.

"Mum. Dad," Morgan cries harder.

"Morgan, where are you?" I shout. I don't mean to yell, but I'm scared, I'm so bloody scared.

"Trees." She puffs. "Bushland. Lots of bushland."

"Bushland." My throat stings from the tears filling my eyes.

West snatches the phone from my grip. "Morgan, I'm Detective Astin West. We're trying to find you. We need your help. Do not hang up." He pauses. "Good girl," he says. "How are you? What condition?" He stops speaking, and it feels like an eternity until he says, "How bad?"

He pauses. "Okay. We can get you help, but you

need to help me find you. What can you see?" He's listening intently. "A rock wall ... Good work. Okay, what else?" He pauses again. "Your children are fine. They're fine, I promise." He stops speaking. "Morgan." There's a long pause. "Morgan, Morgan." He waits. "Morgan! Morgan, can you hear me?" His tone oozes desperation. "Morgan, answer me if you can hear me." He stomps his foot to the ground. "Shit." He drops his arm and then his head.

"No," I spit.

West stretches out his arm toward Gleaton, still holding my phone. "Roland, call the techies now. See if that line is the line we're tracing. Tell them if it's not to try and track the GPS on the number that Morgan just called from. I'll text it to you from Reid's phone. Meet me back at the house."

"On it." He nods.

"Prospect. Maloney. You two hit the road and do a sweep of the house before we get there."

"Yes, sir," Maloney says with a military response.

"Reid, Kylee, and Ronald, you'll ride with me. Let's go."

Ring, ring, ring.

West stops mid-stride. "Hello," he says hesitantly. "Morgan. You've got bad service. The battery is dying. Okay, you're doing a good job, but I need more information from you. What can you tell me about the people who have you? Is it one person or two or more?"

I'm stiff as a board. My fingers seize in a claw and

my jaw tenses, shooting pain through my temples.

"Okay. Good job. Have you somewhere to hide?" He begins to pace. "Go there. Stay there. Don't come out. We're doing everything to find you. Save the last of the battery so you can turn the GPS on, and we will try to track your position. I need you to make sure the GPS is turned on. Do you know where to look?" He stops dead in his tracks. "Yes, yes, that's right." West tilts his chin upwards, looking at the sky. I'm not sure why. Is it something Morgan said?

"Okay, Morgan. Hang on." He jogs straight toward me and presses the phone against my cheek.

"I love you," Morgan says, weakly.

"I love you, Morgan. I love you so much. I promise we'll find you, baby—just hang on for me. Fight for us! Morgan, I'm sorry. I'm so sorry."

She's sobbing. "Bye, my love."

The line goes dead.

Chapter Fifty-Three

The Wolf

Nothing is going as planned. The long stretch of road does nothing to decrease the searing anger hell-bent on keeping me livid. I close my eyes, blinded to possible oncoming traffic, and ask myself if I need to get Winston's night-vision headgear, or if I can find Morgan before sunset with what I've got. Time is of the essence.

My work phone chimes. I flick open my eyes and reach down to the console. *Private number* flashes across the screen.

"Hello."

"What phone have you lost?" It's a worried tone.

"None," I reply, as smooth as butter.

"Sure of that?"

"Yes."

"Bullshit. Morgan has a phone, you fucktard, and she's made contact with her husband."

"What?" I think hard. "Oh, shit! My emergency phone was in my pocket." I reef the steering wheel in one hard pull and drive to the side of the road. The tyres of my ute go sliding through dirt until I reach a dead stop. "My emergency phone," I repeat, patting down my pockets. *It's not there.* "That fucking bitch."

"Do you have this under control or do you need a plane ticket out of here?"

"I'll sort it."

"What's on that phone? Is it the one you've been calling Reid on, or ..."

"It's the one I take out to the bush with me. There's nothing on it." I pause. "Oh shit, there is."

"Will she figure it out?"

"She'll come close."

"How did she—"

"Stabbed me in the fucking back with scissors."

"Shit." A tense growl follows.

I hear voices.

"I have to go."

The line goes dead.

"Fuuuuuuuuck," I roar, but then I stop. I close my eyes. I think. I can track the GPS. My lips tug into a smile. It looks like this may turn out to be the best outcome under the circumstances I've found myself embroiled in.

"I'm coming for you, Red," I breathe, yanking the

steering wheel and completing a U-turn.

I need to find Morgan, now.

"There's a wolf in the dark, in the dark,
Turn around, don't be blind, you can find him.
There's a house in the dark, in the dark,
There's a light on the hill ... STOP! Look behind you.
Never stop running. Never stop searching. Or the
wolf will destroy you."

My mother's voice is singing the song of "The Wolf" in my mind—the song she sang to us each morning from the age I turned five. It's a tune created to teach us to run if we were scared as evil is always behind you.

I laugh, a bellowing laugh. I never run. I never get scared. I was the wolf in the making, and my mother was blind to the monster she herself had created.

Hooooonk! Hoooonk!

A glimpse of a white cattle truck catches the corner of my eye.

I rip the steering wheel in a hard left, bouncing over the rough terrain on the side of the road. *Holy shit. I didn't see it coming.* I raise my hand in an offer of apology to the driver of the small cattle truck that continues past me.

Where the hell did he come from? Better still, what the fuck is he doing out here?

The wheels of the ute spin as I regain my position

on the road. I drive for more than ten kilometres with every possible thought plaguing me—that is, until I replay the call I took over in my head. I need to sort this, and fast. A hard left-hand turn has me on the final long stretch of road that will take me home. I take a breath and look for something to occupy my mind. Donna Martin. Red Number Three. Now that's entertainment. I need the rush of endorphins. I need to watch her demise.

Every time she kicks inside the boot, I turn the music up a few clicks louder to drown her out. It takes an hour before she stops. They always give up in the end. They're all guns blazing to start with, then dead on their arse in such a short period.

I laugh, amused.

When I see the Waltux sign in the distance, I slow my sedan, preparing to take the off-ramp. I merge left without any issues and cruise along a narrow street until I pull up in front of the petrol pumps. The orange needle on my gauge sits at a quarter full when I climb out of the car. Best I don't risk running out of petrol before I see another fuel station. I take the nozzle from its holder.

Donna doesn't make a sound as the fuel guzzles into the tank, but even if she did squeak or squawk it wouldn't faze me. People are either too stupid to butt their noses in the business of others, or they believe any cock-a-bullshit story you tell them.

I hit the central locking button on the key tag,

securing the car, and head into the small shop on site. I grab a snack and drink, and not one person in the building shows even the slightest awareness that they know what I'm harbouring—a woman who needs to be punished lies inside my boot. I snicker at the thought.

I mosey on back to my vehicle, prepared to commence the rest of my journey home.

A man wearing a fluorescent orange jacket approaches reluctantly and holds his hand up in a stop sign pose. He pauses when he reaches the bonnet. "I'm lost." The man's eyes scan a device he has cupped in his hand.

"Oh." I step towards him.

"I'm trying to get to Mackay, but I'm not sure which turn-off I need to take." He points to a map enlarged on the screen when I reach him.

"This one, mate." I smile, pointing at the screen.

His lips curl upwards. "Do I know you?" His eyebrows dip downward, and I'm not sure if it's because he's trying to place me or if it is due to the harsh reflective rays bouncing off the bonnet. His eyes bounce back to mine. He stares. I guess he was thinking.

"Not sure, mate." I offer a toothy grin.

"Thanks for your help." He pats my shoulder and turns on his heel.

A high-pitched squeal has me whipping my head in the direction of the boot. I quickly rebound my vision to the man who had turned his back to me only moments ago.

"Mate." The stranger twists on his thongs and eyes

me with an air of concern.

"Yeah." A look of guilt will raise questions. A soft smile will erase suspicion. I smile.

"Did you hear that?"

"Yeah, mate, I did." I nod, and then look out to the vacant bushland beside the station. "I'm not sure where it came from though, are you?"

"No idea," he says as he offers a half-hearted wave and turns his back to me once more.

Casually, I lift the handle and slip into the driver's chair. I take my time putting my drink into the cup holder and my food onto the passenger seat before I turn the ignition. My knee cracks when I press my foot hard to the pedal and speed off, as chilled as a cucumber.

"Nobody will help you, Red," I shout the moment I reach the one hundred-kilometre speed limit.

I can still remember the bold green scenery that flashed by me as I relaxed back in my seat and cranked out AC/DC songs like it was yesterday. If only I could go back and live each capture and kill over and over again. I sigh before drifting back into my memories.

Her legs wobble when I lift her by her arms. I wrap her hands in duct tape. I push her until she falls to the ground with an almighty rip-roaring scream.

The heat of the sun causes her pale freckled shoulders to pink as they take the brunt of the sun's rays. Her head hangs downward, as I directed. I place my boot in the middle of her back, adjust my mask, then apply pressure, just a little to begin with, then more until her back makes cracking sounds and she groans out her agony.

"My knees." She pants through loud sobs. "My knees are slicing open, stop."

"This is just the beginning."

My dick jumps inside my pants as I picture Donna there, submitted before me. I press down the indicator and take a left turn. "Oh, the memories."

"Please. Please let me go."

"Okay Red, you're free to go. Let me just cut that tape off." I toy with her.

"Really?" Her voice quivers.

"No, you dumb bitch." I run my fingertips up her thigh, stopping at the bottom of her Daisy Dukes, breathing deeply into her ear.

She sucks in a harsh mouthful of air. "Please. No."

"I'm bored with you, little lamb," I whisper against her cheek.

She whines in response, which pisses me off.

"We're going to play a game. Do you like games, Red?"

She shakes her head and howls out, "No."

I slide my foot to the back of her head and use it to push her nose into the rocks. "I will ask you again. Do you like to play games, Red?"

"No," she screams.

I drop to the ground just out of her arm's reach. *Everything I've been waiting for is in motion. Excitement whirls through my gut and shoots up into my chest. The need to hunt proliferates and sends adrenaline to my limbs.*

How far will she get?

How far can I push her?

After all, I'm still perfecting my skills, and there's so much more I want to try … to learn.

"You'll be needing this," I say, handing her the bag I'd prepared earlier. "Now remember, I'm always watching. Follow the path leading into the bushland, and you'll find the first piece of your puzzle."

I whistle as I tread away and climb back into the car.

I drive, leaving her stranded there, only I don't go too far— just far enough that she can't see me, but I can see her through the pair of binoculars I have to my eyes.

Donna retrieves the backpack as I sit, idling. She pinches it between her fingertips, her hands still bound in front of her. She never opens the bag. Instead, she stands and runs right into the bushland.

I cock my head and rub my chin. My last Red didn't start this way. Instead, she'd sat on the ground for ages, crying non-stop.

"Hmmm," I murmur.

Broad daylight was a gift for Donna. Red Number Two, Cheryl Riddell, had been dumped in the pitch black of night. I needed to experiment. I wanted to test out the difference of a daylight beginning over a night-time one, and it appeared a woman was less fearless of bushland under the harsh light of the sun. It's just a matter of waiting to see the difference in how long they can play and how quickly they die.

I park the ute in front of my place and slam the car door hard on exit. *Morgan is fucking with my entire schedule.* I stomp into my cabin and head straight to the bedroom. When I reach the police scanner, I roll the dial between my fingertips until it can't shift upwards any further. There's a lot of chatter, but none of it is about the body I left for the coppers or Morgan Banks.

"Well, that's disappointing," I snarl.

I plonk onto the stool in front of the computer set up in the far corner of the room. Shifting the mouse gets the screen opened. Each finger hitting the keyboard has me one step closer to regaining my player. I type in the codes needed to run the GPS scan on the phone Morgan robbed from me; this is how I'll find her. It'll take a few hours, but soon she'll be a sitting duck in a vast landscape.

Don't close your eyes, Red, don't even blink. I'm coming for you, and when I reach you, I'll grind your fucking bones to dust.

Morgan's death will be more painful than she'd ever dreamt it could be. When she's extinguished, I'll package her skin and flesh and send them to her family piece by fucking piece.

Chapter Fifty-Four

Reid

On the way home, not a word is exchanged. I think the shock realisation that Morgan is still alive bounces through each one of our hearts.

Ronald rides shotgun, while Kylee sits beside me in the back seat of West's car. Her hand places on top of mine. I don't shake her away. Instead, I welcome the warmth her touch provides.

Morgan's not only alive, but she's found a way to call for help.

I wrestle with feelings of despair, and ones that yell for me to rally a search party of my own, one I can lead through bush, over hills, to the devil himself, until I've found my wife.

I can't search for Morgan myself; I know this. I also

know I need to find a way to trust West, Gleaton, and the rest of the police force. I still can't.

I don't trust any of them.

The porch is littered with bodies when West pulls his car in behind Maloney's vehicle that's sat dormant on the curb since the morning he turned up to the house.

Why Maloney? Why did he attend the emergency call I made on the night Morgan went missing? Why did he come back after we parted ways? Why is he staying with me?

I shake my head. Stop it, I reprimand myself.

Linda is the first to run down the path, followed by Mum, Dad, John, and Natalie. Tears rush from Linda's eyes as she closes in. Her arms are outstretched as she collides with my chest. "Morgan's alive. She's alive," Linda sobs against my neck. "How did she sound? When she called you, how did she sound, Reid?"

My eyes narrow. I grip Linda's upper arms firmly and pull her from me until she's standing at arm's length.

"What? How did you know Morgan had called?" I study Linda's swollen bloodshot eyes, waiting for an answer, for a lie she might tell. My nails dig into her skin, and I can feel her flesh sinking below them. *I don't trust anybody.*

"Ronald sent a text through to John. We all know." Linda stiffens like a board. Her irises expand. "Reid," she says, barely audible.

"Sorry." I snatch my hands from her skin. "I

shouldn't have grabbed you like that. I'm sorry."

"It's okay." Linda rubs her upper arm with her opposite hand. "It's okay," she sobs.

"Morgan." My voice cracks. "She sounded depleted of all energy. Her voice was gruff—she said goodbye."

"Goodbye!" Linda screeches.

I nod.

"No, she can't." Linda's mouth falls wide. "No!" she snaps, smacking her lips together.

"Inside." West's tone is short and direct as he passes us by. "Get inside. I have to run through some things with you all. We need to debrief, and then I need to get the hell out of here and do my job. Morgan's on her last legs. We don't have time."

As a pack, we enter through the doorway.

Maloney and Prospect eye us from the table. Bottles of water rest in its centre, like the two officers sitting there knew this would be the next step.

My head spins as my eyes connect with Maloney's. Did he case the place like West said to do? Did he check on my kids? Unease settles into my stomach as I look to the copper who's been with me this entire time. *Could Maloney be behind Morgan's disappearance? How could he be though? He's not left my side.*

I clear my throat. "Max, do the kids have any idea of what's transpired this morning?"

Maloney shakes his head. "No, they have no clue." His eyes study mine. There's a long pause. "I checked on your children and Shirley as soon as I got here, and they're okay. She's keeping them well occupied."

I nod, feeling a subtle sense of relief. The fewer people I have to worry about right now, the better it is for me.

"Sit," West says, hunched over the table. His palms are flat against the surface, his knuckles a ghost white between the patches of red. "I need you all to listen. I will not be updating anyone from here on out. This is what we know."

He shifts his attention to the clock hung on the wall, and then rebounds his sight back to me. "The clock is ticking, and Detective Gleaton and I need to get back to the station because we have multiple tactical crime squads, coming in from Brisbane. They will land within the next thirty minutes."

"A team?" I pull out a seat and drop down.

"Yes. Specialist search-and-capture teams. We'll have the bodies to find Morgan; we just need a rough location."

Mum sits beside me, her hand tightly grasping mine. A dull ache radiates through my fingers from the pressure of her grip.

Dad places his hand on my upper shoulder as he pulls out the seat beside me and sits. I don't have to look to know it's my dad there because I can hear every rattled breath he's taking. *Support.*

Scanning my eyes down the line across from me, I see Linda, John, Maloney, and Prospect. *Where's Natalie?* I tilt my head forwards, only to find Natalie chewing on her fingernail, sitting beside Dad.

West stands upright and then moves to the chair at the head of the table. He doesn't sit. Instead, he holds onto the backrest.

"Morgan has made contact. She has a mobile that has a low battery. We're tracking the GPS. The moment that phone dies we can no longer track her location. We know this is our best chance of pinpointing exactly where she is."

"Did she tell you anything that gives you an idea where to look?" Kylee dabs a tissue against her cheek.

"That isn't information you need to know. What you do need to know is that your daughter is alive, and contact was made. She's doing her best to help us."

"Okay." Kylee's voice is soft.

"Detective Dyson has been able to confirm that Vactrim and Winston are the same people. We are in the process of locating him too," West continues.

"It's Falcon. He has her." I glare at West.

He shakes his head. "He can't."

I narrow my eyes and clench my jaw. "Bullshit."

"Falcon Sampson is deceased. He's been dead for the last six years."

My chin falls open, exposing my teeth.

"What?" Linda's shocked expression matches my own.

Disbelief, anger, and confusion flood me like an angry sea, crashing hard into the shore. My hands curl into fists and my need to punch someone, anyone, grows to the point where I leap from the chair.

"Sit down," West barks.

I do.

"I received a call from our coroner this morning before we went to the hospital. He went on an extensive search of the death records for Falcon. It was quicker for him to do it than to wait for Births, Deaths and Marriages. At first, it seemed to be a maze of dead ends, but he located them."

I look into West's eyes. They are drooped and glassy.

"Reid." He pauses, letting his head drop as he pinches the breach of his nose. "Falcon committed suicide. He left a note that records show had Morgan's name in it. We don't have that note, and our system doesn't seem to contain a copy of that note either. But the Coroner's report specifically discusses a letter retrieved and reviewed in finalising Falcon's cause of death. Morgan's name, along with others, was listed in his findings."

My mouth gapes open, as do my eyes.

"Falcon's mother possessed the original copy of Falcon's letter. It was handed back to her when the investigation was closed. She has since passed away, so we believe his brother will have it now."

"Vactrim," I say.

"The one and the same," West replies.

"Okay." My voice shakes.

"We also need to find your brother."

"My brother wouldn't—"

"Your brother hasn't been located. He's a ghost in

the wind at this point. Cruise has made no contact with anyone from the television network he's employed by, with Natalie, you, or your parents. Nobody knows where he is. He landed back in Australia, and from the airport he seems to have disappeared. Let us do our job, and Reid, stay with Maloney."

"Okay." *Do I even have a choice?*

"I'll keep trying to get a hold of him," Natalie says quietly, softly.

West nods in Natalie's direction before saying, "Let's go, Eric."

There's a clearing of a throat that has me swivelling my arse until my head twists towards the front door. The same tall, broad shouldered, muscular man who turned up at the house with Linda yesterday now stands in the doorway holding a parcel.

"Dusty." Linda runs straight to him.

"Hey, babe. I came as soon as I could," he says, catching Linda by the waist. He tucks her close to him. "Morgan rang. That's wonderful news to get, babe."

Dusty knows Morgan rang too?

"You might want to check this out. A delivery guy just handed me this package. It's addressed to Reid and there's no return address on the back. I checked. The driver is out on the street in his van, waiting. I said you might have questions." Dusty reveals a white post satchel from behind his back.

West walks towards him.

"Could be something, right?" He holds the parcel

out. West takes a step back.

"No. You put it on the table. The fewer hands touching this without gloves on the better. If it's from Morgan's abductor, we might get a print from the packaging."

"Sure," Dusty says before he takes long strides and places the satchel on the table.

"Max, can you get me a knife?" West flicks his eyes from the package to Maloney.

"Yes." Maloney's response is immediate, and as fast as he's gone, he returns, holding a steak knife. "Do you want me to open it?" His eyebrows raise.

"No. Put the knife on the table. I will. I'll need gloves. I don't want to risk any evidence being unnecessarily tainted at this point. They're in my car." West doesn't walk towards the front door to go to his car. Instead, he stalks the package. "Someone get me some gloves," he snaps as Prospect appears from behind him holding a pair of cream latex gloves. *How does he do that?*

"Thanks." West slides them on, pinging the band at his wrist before he picks up the knife and gently slices the blade along the top of the bag.

"What's in there?" Mum's voice shakes as much as my hands do.

West doesn't reply.

West places a small cardboard box on the table. "Evidence bag," he mumbles.

Prospect appears again, holding a clear bag with the word *evidence* written on its front.

"Thank you." West slides the postal satchel inside, then Prospect seals the top.

Taking up the knife once more, West slices between the two folds taped together at the top of the box. He shifts his head until it blocks my view.

"Three evidence bags," he says, closing the folds back together.

"What is it?" My heart thrums in my chest.

"A wedding ring." West doesn't look at me when he says this.

"Morgan's?"

"You can tell me in a minute, once I've bagged it." West turns his back to me.

I don't see what he puts into two of the bags, but in the last one he places the small box that had contained the ring.

West's arm stretches out. A bag dangles from his fingertips, and I snatch it from his grip within a second.

A thin gold band is resting at the bottom. I turn the ring on its side and look for the dent and scratch I know to be there, a dent and scratch caused by a plastic racket in a tetherball game we had set-up in our backyard last year. I close my eyes and watch the final parts of my hope flutter away like ducks heading south for the winter. "It's hers."

"What's in the other bag?" John croaks.

"A thin ticket of paper." Prospect eyes me even though it wasn't me who asked.

"What does it say?" John holds out his trembling

hand, like he wants Prospect to pass the item to him.

"Death. Now we part," West answers.

"What does that mean?" Kylee cries.

The room falls silent.

Does this mean her captor has found Morgan before the police could?

My world shatters around me, only this time I know there won't be a second chance. If this fucker has found my wife and killed her, then I'll hunt him like a rabid dog and tear him limb from limb, even if it takes me the rest of my life.

Morgan, I will avenge your death.

Chapter Fifty-Five

Morgan

Goodbye. It's the last thing I said to my husband, and as I sit tucked up between the rock and the boulder I ventured away from earlier, I can't help wondering if that was the last time I'll ever get to say goodbye to Reid.

The fear lacing his tone was palpable. The few words he'd spoken screamed his torture. I want to take his pain away as much as I want to diminish my own. A tear springs to my eye, then rolls down my cheek. I jet my tongue out of the corner of my mouth and catch it. I'm so thirsty that this single tear is better than no liquid at all.

My mouth is bone dry. My tongue is rough like

sandpaper. My lips sting and bleed. I'd give anything for a drink.

A powerful and painful growl vibrates in my stomach, telling me I've not eaten for days. I don't feel hungry at all. Instead, I feel sick.

Bugs wiggle below the surface of my skin. I know they're not there, even though my mind tries to convince me they are. I can visualise them moving in rows. I scratch at my skin. I bite at my wrists. I gnaw on my fingers.

I'm inside my own living hell.

My sight changes between hazy, spotty, and clear, and with these variations, my mind changes too. One minute I'm coming up with extravagant plans of escape, and the next I'm focused on the percentage marker that indicates how much battery power is left on the phone, willing it not to drain.

Darkness often threatens to sweep me away to a place where I'm unable to think, feel, or be aware. I fight it, but soon enough, I know I'll fail. It's only a matter of time.

The need to sleep is causing my gritty eyes to sting, and keeping them from closing becomes more difficult each time a rush of tiredness whizzes around my brain. I'm too scared to rest, so I continue fighting to stay awake, but after what feels like the hundredth time, I'm not strong enough to make it through the brain-numbing sensation. With the last flutter of my eyelids, I moan. "Shit."

I'm walking down the long hallway separating each office space from the other. When I reach the end of the corridor, I'll enter my door. Each step I take gets quicker as excitement bubbles deep down in my gut, but I'm not sure why I'm feeling so damn excited.

The corridor suddenly fills with blinding light; it's so powerful that I shield my eyes and tuck my chin to my chest.

"Hello," I whisper, unsure of what's happening.

There's no answer.

"Hey, gorgeous." Linda twirls her finger into her red hair as she smacks gum loudly and smiles in my direction. The light has disappeared, and I'm now sitting at my desk at work. I feel irritable. Stressed. Overwhelmed.

"What's wrong?" Linda tilts her head to the side.

"So busy," I moan.

"Tell me about it. It's been a crazy week all around. I wish I never came back from Canberra now. How are you holding up?"

"I'm pissed about the entire situation, to be honest. I knew that we were going to sink into hot water with George Anderson's account, yet I still took part."

"Union Sully said death threats came in today."

I nod. "It was a major blunder, and I'm not sure how the company will fix this."

"Don't even worry about it. You played such a small part that it will have no bearing on you."

"Hmmm," I groan.

"Maybe we should both go to Canberra until the heat dies down."

"About that." I twist my chair until my shoulders are square in front of Linda. "Do you think Reid is acting weird?"

Linda shrugs. "I haven't seen him since I got back."

"Was he acting weird in Canberra?"

"Wouldn't know. I only saw him briefly. We had a drink. I told him about the boring-as-fuck conference I sat through, and he told me about the riveting one he'd enjoyed."

"That sounds about right with you two."

"Things got worse with him and you? Is he still being short-tempered? An arsehole?"

"Yep." I roll my eyes. A horrible itch circles my wrist. I scratch at it manically.

"You look pale. You're sweating, but you're shaking, and scratching. Why is your office so cold? How high have you cranked the air?"

"I am?" I run my trembling hand across my brow, and it's damp. "I hadn't realised. Maybe this major fuck-up is messing with my head even more than I realised. Or it could be hormones." I know why it's happening. I need more of my pain pills. I need a fix. I need the drugs that are controlling my life.

This seems to be something I'm experiencing more and more as the weeks pass. I need to stop taking all these pills. I don't even have pain. I'm not suffering from anxiety, and opiates? What the hell am I thinking?

Snap, snap.

I look to Linda, who snaps her fingers once more. "Earth to Morgan."

"Huh?"

"You just spaced out."

"I did."

She bobs her head. "Maybe you're coming down with something?"

"Yeah, that's probably it."

"I better run." Linda's lips stretch across her face before she turns on her heel, and I watch her clear the doorway and shuffle past the window.

"Thank fuck she's gone."

My bag is tucked under the drawers at my desk. I lean down and search for its strap and then reef it onto my lap. The long zipper peels back with ease, and without looking at the labels on the little orange bottles, I clutch two. Using my teeth to pry open the lids has me pouring pills into my cupped palms. I throw my head back, drop six tablets into my mouth, and chase them down with the bottle of water I retrieve from my desk.

Get a grip, Morgan.

"Conference room now." I only see a flash of Brett when he says this.

Before I even stand, the room fills with the same blinding light I experienced before, only this time the light fades to complete darkness. I run, my hands in mid-air, trying to locate my desk. Nothing.

"Hello?" I call with a rattle to my voice.

There's no answer.

Thump. Thump. Thump. Each beat of my heart is so loud it echoes around my head. "Hello?"

"Red, do you want to play my game?" There's an eerie laugh. "You need to be punished. What did you do, Morgan?"

"Nothing." I walk, trying and navigate the pitch black with my outstretched arms.

"You will pay for what you've done." His voice is familiar, deep.

There's whistling.

I step forward and press all my weight on my front foot as I think to run, but before I get the chance, my ankle is ripped out from under me and I face plant the ground with a loud huff expelling from my chest.

"You're the thirteenth bitch to play my game."

"What game?" It's barely audible.

"The Game of Life."

Pressure is applied to my neck. My face heats as I struggle to claim any air.

"Who are you?" I choke as my eyes become saucers.

"I'm your worst nightmare."

Booming laughter.

My eyes shoot open. My arms wrap around something hard.

I heave. I cough. I gasp.

"Help." It's a weak deliverance.

Every breath I take becomes slower and steadier. The colours, grey, green, brown, and blue, all blur together into a giant mass until eventually they even out and I see trees, leaves, the sky, and then a rock wall.

It was a dream. I slept.

Oh fuck. Is the wolf close?

Chapter Fifty-Six

Reid

"Reid, son, you need to calm down." Dad clamps my balled hand in front of my face. "This doesn't mean anything. The lunatic is messing with you, just like he's been doing the entire time. He's playing a game. It's what you've told me." Dad pauses. His blue eyes are wide and staring into mine. "You spoke to Morgan; you know she's still alive. Don't let this wedding ring façade mess with your head."

I nod, grinding my back teeth together, and huff, frantic.

"Your father is right." Gleaton takes Dad's place in holding my fist. "We are going to find her. Just relax."

I breath slower, more drawn out.

"You've done everything we've asked of you. Now,

do one more thing for us. Stay here with Max and your family and let us bring your wife home. Don't try and call her; we need to preserve the battery. We will call you as soon as we know anything."

My eyes sting. Tears threaten to pour from them as my throat burns from anger, sadness, and despair.

"Okay," I mouth.

Gleaton pushes against my hand until it's lowered to my thigh. His eyes are glazed, and heavy bags swell below them. "You'll know as soon as we have her."

I bob my head.

"Wait here."

I nod.

When Gleaton disappears from my view, I drop my shoulders in defeat. My legs feel like jelly, and my stomach burns a trail of acid to the back of my tongue—my tongue, that feels like leather inside my desert dry mouth. I'm thirsty, really fucking thirsty. I also need a moment to breathe, to be alone, so I bypass my father and the bottles of water on the table and head to the kitchen.

Shuffling my feet, I walk to the kitchen cupboard and retrieve a glass. I need to trust the police. I have to believe none of the officers working my wife's case could be responsible for her abduction.

I hold the glass under the tap. I turn the faucet on and fill it to half full. If I don't find a way to see that the police are on my side, I fear I'm going to combust.

Every heavy gulp of water pains me as it travels down my throat, but I finish each drop before placing the glass into the kitchen sink.

I need to let go of my desire to run and fight, and let the law take up the fight for me.

Each step I take is sluggish, and before long, Dad's hand presses against the middle of my back as he guides me towards Mum who stands beside the lounge.

"Reid." She speaks softly, and when she links her fingertips with mine, I no longer feel the presence of Dad's touch or guidance.

"Sit down, love." Mum doesn't unlink our hold. Instead, she lowers with me. "We're all here. Morgan's coming home. It's only a matter of time now."

There are so many things I want to say ... so why can't I say any of them? *Why can't I vocalise my worries?* Things like: What if Morgan's found but not repairable? What if the things she's experienced have broken her heart and darkened her soul for the remainder of her life? What if all her future holds now is gut-wrenching, mind-torturing agony? I saw that corpse in the morgue, and it doesn't take a genius to figure out the lady endured more than any human body should ever be capable of receiving. Morgan's fighting—it's been nearly three full days, and she was still able to make a call and talk. That must mean something. But how does Morgan go on to survive after she's escaped the monster who's taken her?

"Reid, look at me." Mum's voice is distant, but loud enough to have me zoning in from my thoughts to watch her lips move as she says, "One step at a time."

"I know," I murmur, making eye contact.

"Every minute counts. Be brave. You're strong. I bred both my boys to be fighters. You boys are wolves." She pauses. "Reid, you need to sleep. You need to get some rest."

I swallow hard. "Where's Cruise?"

Mum's eyes fold closed. Her head drops. "I wish I knew."

"Mum, what if Cruise did do this?"

"He didn't take Morgan." Mum's voice is stern and her eyes are fierce when she comes to look at me. "He wouldn't hurt Morgan. He loves you. He loves her. He loves the kids. Maybe he's just gone walkabout again."

"We all know what he was working on, and why you four took off overseas like you did. It wasn't a pre-planned vacation, it was an escape. Why isn't anyone discussing this?"

"It's not relevant. That's a show. This is real life," Mum huffs.

"Mum. Mum, listen to yourself. Cruise was playing a character who abducted a woman in a brutal way. He holds her for ransom, and hides her in the fucking bush. You don't think that maybe, just maybe, Cruise snapped and the line between fiction and reality disappeared?"

"It was too much for him. He couldn't handle the crap they were putting his character through. He wasn't dealing with it. That's why we had to get him out of the country. They took a break from filming so he could regroup and come back ready to finish."

"And now he's nowhere to be found and my wife is missing. Maybe we're too scared to see what's right under our noses."

"He didn't do it. He didn't."

The sound of sobbing has me twisting my neck. Natalie's hair creates a shield around her face. All I see is the top of her head as it hangs low. I catch sight of the droplets of water dripping to the ground below.

Kylee's feet slap against the flooring, and she wraps her arms around Natalie's shoulder's.

Every single one of us suffers. If Cruise has done this, then he meant for it to break us all. Is he capable of murder though?

"He didn't do it." Mum's eyes plead with me, but I can't tell her no because he's not here.

"If he didn't do it, then where is —"

"He didn't do it." Dad's tone is commanding. He stands in the doorway, every set of eyes in the room on him. "Reid, you need to sleep. Grandparents, our job is next door, with our grandchildren. Natalie, you're coming with us." He pauses. "John." He stops. He doesn't offer further instruction. "Linda, you look like crap. You need rest also."

"I'll take her home and bring her back later," Dusty says, his arm wrapped around Linda's waist.

"Okay." Dad's tone softens. "Max, is this the plan?"

"Yes." Max stands by the television with his hands on his hips. He tries to hide his grin by squeezing his lips into a fine line.

"Sleep, son." Dad smacks my shoulder, causing a

sting to rush across my back. "Sleep."

"John." I don't say another word, I just look at him.

"I'll be here. I'll sit and talk with Max. Clean yourself up and get some shut-eye. Morgan will need you soon, okay?"

The corner of my lips arch. *Morgan will need me.*

Every step I take up the staircase has my muscles burning. I feel as if I've run a marathon twice over. My stomach growls and groans from hunger, and even though it hurts I still can't fathom the idea of eating anything.

When I reach the bedroom door, I pause. It's only for a moment, but it's long enough to hear the sudden slamming of another door behind me.

I twist on my heel and glare down the corridor. "Morgan," I whisper.

Silently, one foot in front of the other, I approach the children's bedrooms. Aleeha's is where I stop.

I place my hand on the handle and push it wide open. "What are you doing in here?"

My finger is pointed in Dusty's direction as he bends over Aleeha's bed.

"Reid." He flings his body towards me. His hand whips outwards, and in his grasp there's a purple pony. "Linda asked me to get this."

"Why?" I snap, stepping towards him.

"John said she wanted it, and your folks are going next door."

A blowing curtain steels my attention. Aleeha's window is open.

Was it open earlier? When was the last time I came in here? I can remember Shirley holding Aleeha on her bed; that was the last time I was here in her room. Maybe Kylee and Ronald opened it? Or was it Dusty?

"The window." I point in its direction.

Dusty crooks his neck and looks behind him.

"Did you open it?"

"Yes," he says, facing me once more.

"Why?"

"The room had a bad ..." He stops speaking. "The room needed some airing. I couldn't hold it in."

"You farted?"

He nods. "Mate, I just came to get the pony as instructed."

"Hon, have you —"

I swivel on my heel. Linda's eyes are wide. Her lips are pulled tight.

"You tell him to get this toy?"

"No, John did. What's going on here?" Her eyebrows furrow.

"I'll explain downstairs." Dusty walks towards me, turning sideways to slip through the gap between me and the doorframe. "I let one rip in there. I opened the window to let some fresh air in and the door slammed. Reid got a fright, I think."

Dusty passes Disco Bash, Aleeha's pony, to Linda.

"Reid." Linda steps towards me. "It's okay." She runs her free hand down my arm. "I'll see that Aleeha gets Disco Bash."

I close my eyes and cup my hands to my forehead. "Just go," I huff.

I want to be the one taking my daughter's toy to her. Giving her the comfort she seeks. Not any-fucking-body else.

"I'll ring you. Remember what Dusty said. Keep your eyes on the cops."

"Why is that again, exactly?" I drop my arms until my hands dangle at my sides.

Dusty looks to his left, then his right. "Because there's a lot they —"

"Linda, have you got the pony?" John calls. I can hear the sound of his feet hitting each stair.

"Got it," Linda yells.

When John's head pops into view, his eyes narrow. "Reid, what are you still doing up? Go and get some sleep, for the love of all things that are holy."

I shift my eyes to Dusty, then to Linda, then back to John.

"Okay, I will. Linda, are you staying?"

"I'll be back later." She frowns. "You need sleep."

"It's what you all keep telling me." I take a step back. The tension in the hallway is thick, and I'm pretty sure all of it's coming from me. *Who the fuck is this Dusty fellow? And why the fuck did he come here?*

I take four steps in the direction of my room before I press my chin to my shoulder and look behind me.

Linda's eyes await mine. *"It's okay,"* she mouths.

Nothing is okay.

A wall of humidity slaps my face when I enter the bedroom. It's stifling, but I shouldn't be too surprised. It's as hot as Hades outside today. I locate the remote in the holster on the wall and press the button to turn on the air-conditioner. If I'm going to get a wink of sleep in here, I'm going to need it to be cooler.

I need to pee. I drag my feet to the bathroom. I lift the seat and press my hand to the wall above the unit. As I listen to the stream of piss pounding the water below, I remember the drip from the tap John fixed. Forcing the last trickles out, I shake, pull up the front of my pants, and turn sharply to look for even the slightest drip coming from the spigot—not a droplet escapes. John did a good job. He's always right there when I need him, helping, getting jobs done. We're a good team, him and I, and the fact that he's downstairs manning the fort right now brings me some peace.

Maybe I can sleep. God knows I need it.

My eyes sting. Rough sand particles seem to rub behind my eyelids every time I blink. I open my mouth and yawn. Fuck I'm tired.

I think I should shower, and when I shove my nose to my armpit and sniff, it's clear I need to—I reek. But I don't take a shower. Instead, I rip my T-shirt over my head and walk to the drawer.

Grabbing a tight fitted black T-shirt and a pair of basketball shorts, I change, discarding my pants on the carpet. I stand by the window and stare down at the street below. I'm dazed, spent, and lost.

Do they know where Morgan is now? I can't call

her, but will she try to call me again?

"Where's my phone?" I murmur. "What?"

My jaw drops. My mouth hangs wide. A flash of brown hair catches my eye. A woman sprints toward the driveway. I step closer to the window. *Morgan?*

She disappears. I glue my eyes to the footpath, awaiting her return.

Is my mind playing games with me?

"Morgan!" I yell as another flash of brown hair fills my vision. I see her. It must be Morgan.

I turn and run down the hallway until I hit the top of the staircase and almost trip the entire way down. My feet smack against two of the steps in my dash to the bottom. I burst through the front door, and as my soles pound against the ground my heart races.

I can hear Maloney calling after me. He catches me quickly. There's pressure being applied to my shoulder, pulling me to a dead stop. My eyes move, crazed, as I search frantically for Morgan.

Nobody is out here. Where did she go?

"Where did Morgan go?" I'm panting.

"Reid, what are you doing?"

I try to answer Maloney, but I'm breathless. I hunch over, my heart still racing as my legs throb.

Questions, lots of questions are fired at me, but I can't focus on any of them because I'm a million miles away, unable to understand where Morgan went.

Maloney claps his hands, and my eye catches his firearm, inches from my side. I want to grab that gun out of the holster and continue to run with it aimed and ready to fire. Morgan has to be here—does that mean her captor is too?

"Reid, where are you going?"

"John." I see him standing beside Maloney. I straighten.

"It's—it's ..." I stumble, placing my hands on top of my head. I can't talk.

"Take your time. Just catch your breath," John instructs.

I do. *In then out. In then out.*

"Morgan. I thought I saw Morgan." I fold at my midsection. I'm puffed, depleted of energy. I press my hands hard into my legs above my knees, trying to stem the muscle burn ripping through my hamstrings. Maloney's revolver catches my sight again. I stare, lost, as I picture myself removing his gun and running away with it.

"Where? Reid, where did you see her?" I can hear the panic in John's voice.

I stand upright again, looking at Maloney and then John. "Just there." I point in the direction of the footpath.

"Nobody is out here, Reid," Maloney says calmly.

I shake my head. "I saw her. It had to be Morgan."

Maloney's eyes fill with sorrow as he taps his hand against my shoulder. "Come on. Let's try and get you some rest." He sighs.

"I fucking saw her."

"Reid—"

"Shit, what's that?" John's pitch is high.

"What?" Maloney swivels his head.

"There." John points to our mailbox.

A pink bow holds a clump of long brown hair. It hangs out of the front of the mail slot.

"I'm calling West. Don't touch it." Maloney reaches into his pocket.

I saw Morgan. Did she put it there?

Is she even missing at all?

Chapter Fifty-Seven

Morgan

Vibrations fill my palm. It takes me a while to figure out I'm sitting on the ground, holding the phone in my hand.

There's a message on the screen. It's blurry, yet I can make it out.

Unknown Number: *Morgan, It's Detective West. If you need to call, call this number. Only this number. Check for any names, contacts, and photographs on the phone you have. We need any details that can tell us about the person responsible for your disappearance. Then preserve the remainder of the battery. We're coming for you.*

I should be more excited. Butterflies should be

dancing in my belly and happiness should be exploding through my chest at the mere thought that a search party is coming. However, butterflies don't dance, neither does happiness explode. Instead, misery, hopelessness, and surrender cause a dull ache to rip through my heart and flow through my blood.

They'll never find me here.

There's just too much land to search.

There's not a road, a person, or help anywhere. I'm probably on some vast reserve tucked far, far away from civilisation.

I try to reply.

I hover my finger over the keys, but I'm unable to put the letters together to form any words.

I'm not going to make it out of here. I'm never going home. I'm going to die here—it's all I can think. The mental battle I've been experiencing for what seems like hours doesn't appear like it will let up anytime soon.

Morgan, you need to concentrate. You need to send something back—anything.

I try to focus on the letters to create even one simple word, "yes", in response. I can't.

I feel as if I'm walking neck-deep in a muddy river, my wet clothes dragging me down. It's a heavy, pulling feeling, and as I try to fight it, I experience sharp pinches all over my flesh. It hurts like hell, and as I squirm and wince, it robs me of my breath. *Winded.*

Violins play in the distance, scratching away,

increasing in speed. They're out of sync, and I scrunch my eyes closed. The sound is so nauseating.

My head hangs limp. The back of my hands flop against the earth, and when I manage to open my eyes, and the screeching strings are no longer making a racket, I see the phone on the ground a few inches in front of me.

The shivering I've been experiencing becomes a distant memory. I'm not even able to hold my head up on my shoulders or slide my fingers through the dirt. I moan out, "Nooooo." Dense black fills my vision. The darkness comes to me, and all I can do is cry until I can't hear myself crying at all.

My head is cushioned, my body relaxed, and as I stretch my arms above my skull and curl my toes, I yawn. I need more sleep than I got, but then again, I always feel this way lately.

I'm unable to think straight. I'm worn out, exhausted, and it's all because of the man standing inside the canvas I'm now focused on. The one hung on our bedroom wall.

I love him, I don't doubt that, but am I still in love with Reid? It's been weeks of bickering and disagreements. Everything I do is wrong, and everything he does is erroneous. We clash, our tempers colliding in the most epic of ways, and then I feel an awful sadness wash over me, so I walk away. I brush him off. I avoid him.

Things will get better. We'll get through this. Everyone goes through tough times in their marriages; that's what I keep telling myself.

Up until recently, we hadn't had any problems worth worrying about at all. We were solid. We had such a profound love. We were soul mates.

I follow the perfect ironed crease in his suit pant leg down to the shiny shoes he wears in this photograph, the one taken on our wedding day. We're struggling—there's no doubt about that. We both want to wear the pants in the household—have the power—be dominant. It's not working out for us. We're not working. We can't own our mistakes and admit our faults.

Are we truly as broken as I think?

I roll over in bed to find Reid's not there. I'm not surprised there's no comfort to be found in his embrace. I'm so done with the bullshit that is my life right now.

I don't shower, there's no time, but I make myself up and choose a soft pale pink blouse to accompany a tight black pencil skirt.

I'm mad when I venture downstairs and find Reid in the kitchen, and I'm furious by the time I kiss the kids goodbye and walk out the door.

I don't look back when I leave the house, but I have a feeling I should have as I climb into my SUV.

Turning the key in the ignition has my stomach tied in knots. I feel lost, off … something is very out of place. My entire life is upside down and topsy-turvy.

The garage door rises, and I reverse down the drive.

A black mask. A black long-sleeve T-shirt ... fill my revision mirror. I slam on the brakes. I'm huffing. I'm shaking.

"Wake up, you dumb bitch. You can't change the past." His perfect blue eyes shine before he throws his head back and laughs. "Are you ready to play my game, Red?"

My eyes spring open. I'm standing between two thick brown tree trunks. There's a mobile phone in my hands, and I'm holding it out in front of me like one would hold a weapon. I pant between long sobs.

"Get away from me," I scream. "Get away."

Chapter Fifty-Eight

Reid

West doesn't come for the lock of hair, Prospect does. And when I ask him continuously if they've found Morgan, if she's rung again, if there's anything he can tell me, he just narrows his eyes and flares his nostrils like a bull about to charge his horns through my torso.

Prospect has had it in for me from the beginning, but why?

He holds a clear evidence bag, and when Maloney drops the length of hair inside, Prospect seals it quickly and marches away.

"You didn't see Morgan, Reid," Prospect shouts with his back to me.

"Fuck you," I roar. *Prick.*

I'm not sure if I did see Morgan or not, either, but someone was lurking out on our street, and that someone was a female. You can't mistake a woman's silhouette.

"What is up his arse, seriously?" I cross my arms in front of my chest.

"Eric's a serious fellow, but good at his job. He'll be wanting to get back to the station; don't worry about him. He's cool." Maloney says that, but still watches his people in the same way I do. I can tell by the knowing nod that follows and the way his eyes remain focused. Always searching, and analysing … He suspects everyone, just like me.

"He hasn't called the landline," I blurt out.

"Who?"

"The prick who has Morgan. There have been no more calls. Why?"

"Don't know." Maloney pistol grips his chin.

Maybe nobody else has realised we've had no more taunting calls, or perhaps they have but had hoped I wouldn't.

"Let's sit outside for a bit. You want a smoke?" Maloney shifts from foot to foot. I nod.

Maloney leans against the rail as I sit on the swing on the patio. He reaches into his pocket, retrieving the packet of cigarettes and the lighter. This time, he removes two cigarettes before placing the pack back where he removed it from. "Do you mind if I join you?"

"Not at all." I offer a half-hearted smile.

The sweet, sweet taste of nicotine enters my lungs with more ease than it has previously. I don't cough or splutter. Instead, I enjoy the rush of chemicals exploding in my brain.

Maloney stares past me. He's in a daydream. I can tell by the way his head tilts to the side and the blank stare he delivers.

There's a period of silence.

"My daughter, Mila." He stops speaking, takes a deep breath, and sighs.

"Yeah," I encourage him to continue.

"When she was two, she got sick." Maloney looks into my eyes. "She'd been playing outside under the hose for about thirty minutes in the morning, and her mamma had put only a few centimetres of water into one of those shell pools. You know the ones?"

"Yeah." I nod.

"She was all giggles and squeals. I'd come off the night shift. I was so fucked. A long night, a lot of drunk drivers to haul in, and way too much paperwork."

I relax back into the swing.

"I watched Mila as she played. I watched as my wife created another memory for her. Sometimes, just admiring them is enough to wash away all the bad shit I see in my job." Maloney crosses one of his feet in front of the other. "I towelled Mila off. Took her inside the house and put a new nappy and T-shirt on her. We sat together at the table eating watermelon. I still remember the streams of pink juice running down the front of her white top. I haven't always been the smartest when it comes to messy toddlers and clothes." He stifles a laugh.

"They make a mess," I say, before taking a long draw from the cancer stick poking out between my fingers.

"They sure do." Maloney sucks hard from the butt of his smoke, before flicking ash over the railing. "I went for a lie-down after that, and I was so deeply asleep that when my wife screamed for help, I didn't hear her at first. It was the beating on my chest and her screaming by my face that jolted me awake."

"Shit." I cringe. Where's this going?

"Mila was limp in her arms. She was on fire to the touch, and her entire body was covered in this nasty-arse rash. I couldn't even explain it if I tried. Blotchy, red and fierce."

I cock an eyebrow.

"It truly looked like someone had beat her." Maloney takes another draw of his cigarette and slowly exhales. "I didn't know what had happened, but I took her tiny, limp body and held the inferno that she was against my chest."

I take in a mouthful of hot air before I flick my butt over the railing past Maloney.

"You should put those out before you flick 'em. It's fire season, you know." Maloney smirks.

"What happened?"

"We took a ride in the ambulance, sirens blaring, to the hospital. They whisked Mila away from us as soon as they rolled her and the bed through the emergency doors. I just stood holding my wife as she trembled against my chest. I wanted to take all her worry and fear from her, you know, but I couldn't because I was experiencing the same fucking fear myself. Big strong copper I was, hey?"

"Puddle of mess on the floor instead?"

"Yep." Maloney rolls the small butt between his fingers until the cherry pops out and onto the ground. He shifts his foot until he covers the burning cherry with the sole of his shoe. "The next time we saw Mila, she was in the ICU. Tubes and shit were coming out of every part of her body. A large machine was doing all her breathing because she couldn't. Her organs had shut down, one by one, they told us. They prepared us for the worst."

"She wouldn't be coming ..." My voice breaks. I clear my throat.

"Home? No. They said they weren't sure what was happening, or why it was happening to her. They thought it was likely to be either leukaemia that had gone undiagnosed or some terrible bacteria that had invaded her body. I was in shock."

"I couldn't even imagine."

"Five days I sat by my baby's bed. I couldn't leave her. I created her with the love of my life. She was my only child. Mila did improve slightly over a few hours, but remained critical."

"Shit," I breathe.

"We learnt she had a parasite in her body; it's this deadly thing that lives in tap water. That fucking thing had gone to her brain. I worried she'd never grow up to be all we wanted for her. I kept asking myself, what if she could never say Daddy again? It broke my heart."

My gut churns before it sinks low.

"And then on the sixth day, we had the priest come to the ICU and read her last rites. We were prepared for the worst, but we never let ourselves truly believe that Mila would leave us." Maloney pauses. "Then, about an hour later, Mila magically started to breathe on her own." Maloney tilts his chin and looks to the sky, to the heavens above. "By that night, she'd opened her eyes and was trying to rip out her breathing tube. It was a true miracle, Reid. Mila's proof they happen."

Maloney smiles. "And you'd never believe the first word out of her mouth was Daddy." Silent tears stream down his face. "I never gave up on her. I knew she had my fighter's blood inside her and her mamma's positive spirit. My little girl came back to us. She was my perfect little girl after a few months of rehabilitation."

"Why are you sharing this with me?" I wipe my brow—it's dripping with sweat.

"Because I can sympathise with all the emotions

inside you. Because we're becoming fast friends."

"Is this why you're the one left to babysit me? Because you best understand my situation?"

Maloney chuckles. "Mate, I don't have to be here. You could have kicked us all out on the first day. We can't invade your home."

My lips pull tight. *What the fuck?*

"But I want to be here for you. You've done all you can to help us in finding Morgan." Maloney pauses. "I know you worry that there may be someone on the force who knows more about how Morgan came to be where she is—hell, I've had my own doubts—but I think you're barking up the wrong tree. I think the kidnapper is someone Morgan knows well, or someone who's known her well."

"I thought it would be her ex, you know? But he's dead."

"His brother though—do you think he's involved?"

"Winston helped her that night. That's what you guys have told me. He knew where she was. Have you found Winston, or Vactrim, or whatever-the-fuck-he-calls-himself yet?"

"Not that I know of. All I know is he goes deep into the bush and spends days out in nature with no way of being contacted. Morgan said she was in bushland, and I'm just putting two and two together. Major alarm bells are ringing for all of us."

"But they are looking for him, yeah?"

"Sure are. He's our prime suspect. We're also

looking for your brother."

"I can't believe that Cruise would—" I can't even say it.

"I think we've found our man in Winston, but we also need to locate Cruise so we know that he's safe. Is this normal behaviour for Cruise? Disappearing? I know he's some soap actor, high profile and all that shit, but does he disappear like this?"

"Three times," I mumble, sitting further upright.

"Really?"

"Yep. When the world gets too much for him, Cruise goes on what Dad tells everyone is a walkabout."

"Walkabout?"

"Cruise finds somewhere to hide out, where nobody can find him, and drinks himself fucking stupid. The last time, probably two years ago, he ended up having his stomach pumped because of alcohol poisoning. Mum and Dad tried to get him to seek professional help after that episode, but he refused."

"Substance abuse problem?" Maloney cocks his eyebrows.

"Yeah. I guess. Cruise has a mind that's so creative that at times, it gets the better of him and he can't seem to find a balance between what's real and what's not."

"I see. Has Cruise ever seen a shrink about shit like this?"

"Ha. Yeah, no. Not Cruise. He doesn't believe in shrinks and their healing powers. He believes in hitting the bottle until he drowns out the noise inside his brain and he finds his equilibrium once more."

"Good to know." Maloney stretches his arms above his head.

"Sore? Tired?"

"Yeah." He arches his eyebrows. "You could say that."

"Cruise was playing this character at work. It got to him. That's why he and Mum, Dad, and Natalie went overseas. The network issued a break in filming because Cruise was going off the rails. I remember talking to him about it on the phone. He was so down, and short tempered. You heard me talking to mum earlier."

"Yeah. I did."

"Cruise has always been this harmless fellow. He never gets into fights—he gets along with everyone." I grin. "Cruise is the quintessential loveable teddy bear, with an amiable face and down-to-earth attitude, you know?"

"Yeah. But all men get into biff barges."

"Not Cruise, unless it's with me. He can get rough and tumble with me, but I'm his little brother so that's been a lifetime thing." I smirk. "I've always given back as good as I've gotten."

"This Natalie. His wife?"

"She's the best thing that ever happened to him.

However, two of the three times Cruise has gone walkabout have been due to feuding with her and working long, much too long hours at work."

Maloney nods as he removes the cigarette packet from his pocket, retrieving another two fags. "Another?"

"Sure."

The flash of the flame coming from the lighter in front of my face tells me I need to make sure that this stops once Morgan's found. Stress or not; these cigarettes kill.

"Do you think it was Morgan who put that lock of hair into the mailbox slot?" Maloney's eyes narrow.

"I think it was a woman, but I'm not sure if it was Morgan. I think I wanted it to be really bad though."

"Why don't you think it's her now?"

"Because she would have wanted to see the children. She loves her kids."

"Do you think you could have been seeing things and nobody was there at all?"

"I'm so fucking tired, it's possible." I pause. "Why don't you go home to your family? You said it yourself—you don't even need to be here. I bet you aren't getting paid for this."

He laughs. "I'm getting paid. No, I'll see this out to the end."

"Mila would be missing you."

"Yeah, she would be, but I have a duty, and that is to serve and protect above all else. My little girl will understand, as will my wife." Maloney takes a draw from his cigarette, blowing small Os with the smoke on his exhale.

"Have you at least spoken to them?"

"I have. Many times."

"Shit. I never even noticed."

"Most times we don't even notice the things that are right under our noses."

And as the words leave his lips, I wonder if Morgan's kidnapper is right where we can see him, but too close to see.

Chapter Fifty-Nine

Morgan

I rotate in circles. I'm in bushland with no idea how I came to be here. I've bare feet, and I'm stripped down to a pair of boy-legged knickers and a singlet.

Bruises, cuts, bites, and grazes mark my entire body, and the numbers one through to five, are inked inside my inner arm, with a line crossed through "one".

Two large gashes gape across my shins, and my feet are a filthy black.

I'm holding a mobile phone, a phone that's not mine. I stumble forward, then rock backwards. *How did I get here?*

As I manoeuvre in a circle, pain rips through my

brain and beats behind my eyebrows making me dip my head and brace it between my palms. *Why do I hurt so bad?*

Heat scorches my skin, skin I can tell has already burned. Blisters rise on the tops of my legs. I seek shade, and as I shuffle, I wobble as I would after way too many glasses of wine. *Have I been drinking?*

I press my back up against a smooth palm tree trunk that shelters me with its leaves. I look at the screen of the phone I have clasped in my fist as if my life depends on me doing so. It's blank. I swipe my finger over it and the screen lights. I open the contacts. There are none to be found. I move to the gallery and see nothing apart from a document icon. I press download and stare in wait. An arrow pointing downwards travels in a repetitive pattern. I continue to wait. The screen goes white before the document opens.

Dear Morgan,

I received your letter, and I'm sorry you feel this way. I know things have been hard for me, and I wish I weren't such a burden on all the people I care deeply for, but I am. I know you need space to live the life you've made for yourself with Reid, and after this letter, you won't hear from me again.

There's so much pain buried deep inside me … it's a living hell from which I can't seem to escape. No matter how many times I tell myself it's only a nightmare, and if I try hard enough I'll wake up, I don't. Morgan, I never wake up, no matter how much I beg.

There's so much I wish I could destroy inside my mind. There's an evil that lurks inside me, and it's one I struggle to contain. There are so many things I wish were different for me, one of those things being you. I guess you were the glue that was holding all my broken pieces together, but over time you couldn't stick with me anymore. I understand why, I do. I'm sorry I couldn't be all you deserved.

You mean well—I know it's why you've continued to write to me for so long. At first, it was a relief after you moved away. I missed you intensely. I pined for you like a child who'd lost his very first puppy. That probably sounds psychotic, right? But from the very beginning, when I met you, I knew you were someone special. I also knew you'd always stay true to your word. You have for as long as you can, and I thank you for doing so.

I was in love with you, Morgan. It wasn't lusting, or puppy love, like you said. It was a deep, all-consuming, heart-stopping love, but for you, it wasn't those things. In the end, you couldn't fall as hard for me as I had for you, and that's always been my fault.

I tried to hide my darkness. Keep its venom secured away in an airtight jar, but it wasn't bullet-proof, and bit by bit that jar got shot to shit, and parts of me, I didn't want you to know existed, escaped. It tarnished what we had. Neither you nor I are responsible.

As the days keep passing, I've realised that time itself cannot heal my wounds because my wounds grow deeper with each ticking minute. I want to be at peace. I want to find my order, and I've figured out how I can.

I need to say goodbye to you, Morgan.

I need to let you go.

I'm letting you go, my rose.

Please continue to blossom like the perfect flower you are. Remember that twelve long-stemmed roses will never be enough for a beauty like you. You will always be one more, one more perfectly cut bud, better than all the other women who walk this damned earth. It's the reason why I always gave you thirteen of them, instead of the traditional dozen.

Before I let you go, promise me you'll always remember that in your eyes the sun rises, in your smile it sets, and that your grace and beauty are so deep down beyond your skin it means you were angel-sent. I'd rather fly with angels than stay wrapped up in my nightmare.

Morgan, a soldier goes to war and fights for the freedom of his country. I will instead go to war with myself and fight for only yours.

I'm giving you my final gift, Morgan.

Your freedom.

I never deserved you, but I was blessed to have you.

Sleep tight, Red. I will love you from beyond my grave.

Forever yours, Falcon x

"Falcon." I remember this letter, but it's not a blue-inked handwritten letter like I know it to be. This is a photocopy, a photographed version. Why do I have only this on my phone?

Suddenly, it's like a shooting star explodes into vibrant fireworks before me. Pinks, blues, purples, greens—they fill my vision. As these colours blur, then form into the brightest rainbow I've ever laid eyes on, my life flashes behind my closed eyes, one clip after the other. It plays out quickly, so quickly that when I see myself running, fighting—when I look at blue eyes that change to green—when I hear the eerie whistle that means danger—I remember. I remember where I am, how I came to be here, and what I'm fighting so hard for.

I cry so forcefully my shoulders shake.

Four hearts beat for me—my own, my husband's, my son's and my daughter's. I need to survive, and now I have a chance because I know who has me— Falcon Sampson. The man whom I couldn't love like I wished I could. A man who'd shown me a darkness I never wanted to see. A man who'd frightened me, but not in a way that had me fearing for my life; he made me fear for his. I guess I'd been wrong; I guess my life was always on the line.

Thirteen long-stemmed roses filled the pictures behind the mirror. The song that played from the small boom box was one that reminded me of home with Reid and the kids, but was also one I'd shared with Falcon right before this letter came. That song spoke of his kind, yet tortured soul.

They were my hints. Falcon has been telling me who he was all along.

The blue eyes, then the green, the change of voice—it was all a disguise. Falcon had always been a true master of disguise throughout high school.

I sob harder.

If Falcon's shyness were not so overwhelming for him, then the stage would have been his oyster, and he would have found the bright lights and fame that the universe owed him. The dark side of Falcon, though, would never have allowed him to pursue such a life.

Now, he wants my life.

I wipe my eyes with my free hand and flick them down to the phone as it vibrates.

Unknown Number: *Morgan. Let me know you're okay.*

I'm not okay; I'm not okay at all.

I read the previous message.

Unknown Number: *Morgan, It's Detective West. If you need to call, call this number. Only this number. Check for any names, contacts, and photographs on the phone you have. We need any details that can tell us about the person responsible for your disappearance. Then preserve the remainder of the* *battery. We're coming for you.*

I bash my finger against the keys in response.

Me: *It's Falcon Sampson. He has me. His mother owns a property out past Corbet's Landing. I've never been there, but Falcon told me she did. It must be where I am. I'm somewhere in acres upon acres of bushland around Corbet's Landing.*

My finger shakes as I press down and hit send.

I watch, waiting for the word "sent" to display. It's taking forever. I look at the service bar. There's not even one, and the battery only reads six percent.

I walk frantically. I walk in every direction, holding the phone up high, out to one side, then to the other … I'm trying to get enough service to push the message through. One bar appears. I stop dead in my tracks.

The screen goes black.

"*Fuck,*" I cry.

I've no idea if Detective West got my message before the phone went flat, and I've no other way to get help.

I drop the phone and run. I run so fast that my once weak legs hold my weight.

Bang!

I can hear myself blood-curdling scream as I shrink to the ground. My head lays to the side. Black boots infringe upon my vision.

"Who am I, Red?" His voice is thick, and one I knew I recognised from the very beginning.

"Falcon Sampson, what have you done?" I

whimper.

He laughs. It's the most psychotic laugh I've ever heard, and even though the hairs stand to attention on the back of my neck and my heart leaps into my mouth, I try to get up.

"Wrong, wrong, wrong, wrong. Wrong, wrong, wrong, wrong." He sings this to the same tune as church bells.

"I know it's you. I saw the letter on your phone." I sit on my arse, looking up at the black mask covering his face. "No, I saw your letter on your phone." A shotgun dangles from his shoulder.

Before I have a chance to look away he moves the shotgun, pointing it right at my chest.

"You're wrong, Morgan."

Every thought I have jumbles into a twisted knot. "No. No, I'm not." I shake my head at the same rate as my legs tremble.

He takes two steps toward me. I see him do it, but I don't hear a sound. "Get on your knees."

"No," I shout. "I figured it out. I know it's you. Take off your mask."

He laughs. Spittle lands on my cheek.

"I know it's you."

"Get on your knees, or I'll make you."

Slowly, I twist. The cracking sounds my knees make when I apply pressure to them cause pain that has me sucking air through my clenched teeth.

"Put your hands behind your head."

"You can't do this to me, Falcon."

The gun's barrel will be against my head. I could be killed execution-style. My stomach turns and my heart thrums so hard that pain shoots into my chest.

He moves as quick as lightning and before I can blink, I'm laid flat on my back as he straddles my waist. His gloved hand hovers above my throat.

"This is your end, you bitch." His fingers curl around my neck. He squeezes.

I can't breathe.

"I don't want to play this game with you anymore, Red." He smirks.

My eyes are bulging from their sockets, threatening to pop clear out of my head.

"Show me." I manage to spit out with the last breath I have.

He removes one hand, using the other to keep pressure against my windpipe, and tucks his fingers under the bottom of his mask. Slowly, he begins to peel it away.

Frantically, I suck air into my lungs. I groan as I place my hand on my head where a massive egg protrudes. My eyes flutter open, and as I jump upwards and slide backwards, I realise that I'm alone. I hold my neck and cough repeatedly.

What just happened?

There's a thick tree trunk straight in front of my line of sight. *Did I run into a tree? Did I knock myself clean, cold out?*

I think I did.

Chapter Sixty

The Wolf

I watch the circle on my laptop go around and around. Searching, pinpointing, locating. My lips curl upwards. Morgan might have outsmarted me in a moment of overconfidence, but she's just a worm waiting to be picked off by a vulture now.

The need to take Morgan's life with my bare hands has all but diminished. All I want is for air to stop entering her lungs and for her heart to stop beating. I can't believe I fucked this up. I can't believe I'd been so stupid as to leave scissors out for her to find. I huff, thinking about how many times I've played out Morgan taking her last breath in my mind. Now I'll miss that moment. But I have a new plan, and I can't wait for her to burn.

"Ashes to ashes, dust to dust, burn in hell, Red, because I've had enough."

The circle keeps turning. Hours have passed, but I know it's close. I see that my revenge is just around the corner.

Ding.

The noise coming from the computer speaker is music to my ears.

I watch the screen, and there she is—a solid red dot on a map about three kilometres from the major road at the back end of my property. She's made some ground. I'm surprised.

I know these location points can change quickly, and the target can move out of range before any ground is made, but with the weather about to turn in a few hours, I take no time in charging through the back door and grabbing the jerry can full of fuel.

The heat of the midday sun causes my black clothing to heat up; I don't mind, though. I quite enjoy the humidity summer brings, and the fact that a storm is on the horizon and will approach fast. The birds chirp high in the vibrant blue sky, and as I load the jerry can onto the quad bike and tie it down, sweat dripping from my eyebrows over my eyes, I take solace in the fact that the heavy predicted rains will somewhat extinguish the blazing inferno I'm about to create. If the storm passes us by though, I'll have no choice but to flee and never come back. Well, until it's safe to do so.

Flames are about to rise—hellish red flames.

Morgan should appreciate this gesture, since it resembles the exact place she'll be going once she's dead. Hell, she'll be Lucifer's problem after all of this. I know he'll do a much more thorough job of breaking her down than I did. The thought brings me comfort as I turn the key and the quad bike roars to life.

I head in the direction of Red, my soon-to-be-dead player, and as I do, I howl the sound of the wolf. The sound of my impending victory.

I zigzag between trees and hop mounds in my haste to get to Morgan, and even though I'm not going to be able to stick around for the grand finale due to the rapid speed of the blaze about to take place, I know that when I get back, her charred remains will be waiting. It'll be worth every minute of the game we've played together. Even though this time the game didn't go quite as planned, the memories will still cause electricity to sear through my chest and bring me the sensation of exhilaration I seek.

I've not chargrilled a Red yet, so the experience has me curious.

I stop my bike right where the GPS said she'd be. My heart leaps. I'm not surprised she's not standing here—it's a given that these things are off at least a small radius in any direction, and that she's had time to move.

I unhook the jerry can from the back and lay it across my lap, positioning myself so that when I ride, the fuel will spill.

The atmosphere is power-driven. The smell of the

petrol has adrenaline bulging my muscles. I feel each one twitch under my clothing when I twist the throttle and listen to the engine roar. I drive. I feel each glug of petrol exit the jerry can on my lap. The sight of it splattering to the ground below makes me drive faster. I'm circling one deliberate lap. "Here, mousey, mousey," I laugh.

The stale air mixed with petrol keeps a smile plastered on my face, and as I pull to the left, I think back to Red Number Three and the moment I took her life. She fought so hard, but she never made it out of my underground cemetery, not as Morgan did.

"Please, please. Don't. Don't!" Donna's on her knees, *her hands held in prayer, begging for her life.*

I don't care to hear it, so I take my boot from the ground and hover it in the air.

"Please. Please let me go."

"Who am I?" I say.

"I don't know. I don't know who you are."

"Wrong answer."

Crunch.

The sound of her jaw shattering from the impact of my swinging foot has me cracking my neck, followed by my fingers.

Blood sprays out from her mouth, and as she screams an ear-piercing scream from deep within her chest, I position myself on top of her, applying every bit of weight I have to her stomach.

Her eyes bulge before her chin points upwards and

she struggles to draw air.

"Lights out, Red." I smirk as I squeeze my hands around her neck and gaze into her shocked eyes.

Blood pools in the whites of her eyes, and I can't help but think how stunning it looks around her blue irises. "You tried to rob me. You didn't disclose you were a hooker and fucked around in my business. You wronged me, and you will pay."

She tries to speak. She can't.

"Save your energy, Red. I want this to last as long as it possibly can."

Her lips change to the same colour as her eyes, and in this one moment, Donna is the most beautiful woman I've ever seen. So much destruction covers her skin.

All the colour drains from her pale face before blood rushes to replace it with red. Her fingers are scratching at my gloves. She's trying desperately to pry me off her, but she can't because she's weak.

I laugh. I laugh so hard, spittle lands on her face.

She gurgles. I focus and watch as all the fear leaves her expression, and a peaceful acceptance takes its place.

"You can't hurt anyone anymore. I'll be sure to watch you rot."

One final gurgle takes place, and then her hands drop away.

She's gone.

The quad skids and for a split second, I lose control. "Stay focused," I murmur.

I arrive back where I started, and when I pull off my gloves and hold the matches in my hand, I begin to whistle.

There's something magical about the way the earth can light up with the strike of a single match, and as the dead leaves burn rapidly, I drive away. Each twist of my head over my shoulder shows me the flames rising, and this pleases me. *Burn, baby, burn.*

If only I could stay around to see it engulf Morgan in the blaze of glory I know it will be.

Chapter Sixty-One

Morgan

I walk for what feels like hours; it's more likely to have only been minutes because the passing of time eludes me.

I jump, panic, stop dead in my tracks, cower, fall, scream, run, and collapse, and I pant excessively when I can no longer move a muscle, and I'm laid out on the ground.

A terrifying darkness whisks me away, stealing my breath and sealing my eyes shut. I can't escape it, so I don't even try. Instead, I wait for the light, and when it comes, I'm instantly comforted. I'm drawn by it; homed by its glow. Its warmth wraps me up safely like a hand-knitted blanket. I never want to leave the light or the memories that play out while I'm in it, so I hold on to every moment.

And then it's gone. The blanket is ripped away from me, as is the light. A force, much stronger than any I've ever experienced, tugs my limbs in different directions. I can't see this force, or even touch it. It just exists.

The walls tumble down, and then I'm running barefoot through the bushland. My heartbeat pounds in my ears, and I cry, but I don't dare stop running. My life is in danger because I'm being hunted like prey, and all I have left is this chance to escape. I know who's chasing me now. I know it's Falcon. It took me knocking myself out to put all the pieces together, and a dream to remember what once was.

I pass a tree, then another, but my limbs grow weak quickly, so I'm left to walk once more. Time moves like this in a loop, and I don't know how much has been erased. I wish I still had the phone. I wish it wasn't a piece of trash now littering the bush like I am. Why couldn't the battery have lasted longer? Why? I could tell the detective where I believe I am now, and who has me. *Falcon Sampson.* I look to the solid blue sky above and try to make a judgement on what I see, only nothing has changed from before. *So, does that mean time hasn't moved at all?* I walk sluggishly, my shoulders hunched, my head drooping, and before long I collapse, hitting the ground with an almighty thump that knocks the wind from my lungs. I catch my breath, then cry. I smother the noise I make with my hands, telling myself to be quiet because he moves like the wind, and I can't hear his footsteps … He could be right behind me.

A fierce breeze whips up wildly, and instantly cools my skin. I roll onto my back and watch as sizeable black storm clouds invade the stunning blue sky, drifting in from my right.

It's going to rain. I'm going to be relieved of my thirst, and the humidity that's draining the vessel that homes my soul.

Excitement fills my veins just as electricity flashes above me in the sky.

But then the air smells and tastes like heat. It's dry and sharp with the distinct acrid flavour that comes with the smell of burning wood. The dark storm clouds above glow a bright orange as black snow floats down like flurries onto my face.

"No, no, no," I cry. *That's ash. The bush is on fire. BANG.*

The sound, although distant, vibrates through my chest, and I launch to my feet, whipping my head left, then right. I'm searching for the direction of the crackling and popping that intertwine with the claps of thunder. Each sound creates a musical symphony to fill the bushland I'm trapped in, and as it does I run again.

I need it to rain now.

"Rain! Oh my God, rain!" I scream.

A blanket of orange and red silk catches the corner of my eye. It's racing towards me from the left-hand side. It's a magnificent yet terrifying beast of flames I fear will engulf me before I get a chance to find safety.

Fire is never a gentle master, and it's not something any human or animal can outrun, but I don't stop trying as I will the storm to release its fury before these flames swallow me whole.

"Rain!" I scream again.

The coolness I felt only moments ago is replaced by a heat so intense it feels as though my skin is melting away from my flesh. A grey ash cloud billows over the top of me. I blink excessively to ease the instant scorch to my eyeballs, but it's pointless because now I can barely see. A thick front of smoke drifts and traps me.

Every breath I take scalds my airway, and as I splutter and cough, I panic.

What do I do? I don't know what to do.

I throw my arms into the air and drop to my knees. The agony that rips through me is nothing compared to my inability to take a breath due to the suffocating pain wrapping around my lungs.

Holy shit. I'm going to burn to death.

I cough. I splutter. I wrap my arm over my mouth and nose for protection.

"Help me." There's no sound.

Boosh, boosh, boosh, boosh, boosh.

I fall as the sound rings out like gunshots from behind me. I find my feet and aimlessly amble forward. A massive roar of thunder shakes the sky, causing me to jolt ...

And then I feel it. Liquid slides down my arms.

One foot in front of the other. I have no idea where

I'm walking to, but I just keep taking step after step. The hard pounding of heavy rain stings my skin. I'd know this feeling anywhere, and although I can't see the droplets, I can feel them.

This is my only chance to survive.

I don't look back. I don't dare give my mind the chance to spy how close the flames of this fire lick at my heels. I just keep moving.

Four hearts are all that matter in my life. Three of those hearts wait for me to come home, the other one thrums intensely, trying not to stop. I can't give up now. I have no choice but to outrun this fire. I need to outrun the wolf.

Chapter Sixty-Two

Reid

It's late afternoon, and thunder cracks as rain buckets from the sky. It's been pissing down for hours. I'm restless. I pace the floors, and I'm sure if I keep going this way I'll burn a permanent track in my wake. My stomach churns, and my heart thumps viciously. Nothing can bring me calm. Nothing can take away this overwhelming fear pumping through my blood. Cruise is still nowhere to be found, and with every minute that passes I think more and more that he, my brother, is responsible for the disappearance of my wife. He has been given all the tools to carry this out. His fucking role as Frank Turvay, a once friendly face on the Bay, now turned serial killer, seeking revenge against those who loved him. I can't shake the feeling that this is what's been right under my nose the entire time. Has Cruise snapped? And if so, why Morgan? Cruise had the hots for her, he made sure I knew it the moment he met her, but he never acted on it. Or did he?

West, Gleaton, and Dyson have not made a peep regarding Morgan's condition, safety, or if they've located her yet. Why haven't they called? What are they keeping from me? Where are they?

The stress of the day is doing me in. Morgan. Where is she? Is she coming back? Why is no one calling? It's been too long. Panic steamrolls through me. I need this to end now. Morgan needs to be in my arms, not in some bushland, not fighting for her life. I can't help her. I'm useless, pathetic, and tortured.

I can feel Morgan slipping away from me. She's fading, just as the day will soon enough. Another night without Morgan awaits me. We have no time left.

"What's happening?" I yell the moment Maloney walks from the direction of the kitchen right into my view. "What do you know?"

Maloney shakes his head. His lips are pressed hard together. His chest rises and falls slowly.

He's calm. Why is he so fucking calm?

"Come on, son." Dad places his hand on my shoulder, and as I flick him away, I glare at Maloney with red-hot flames burning around my irises. I'm so fucking mad I know that if Maloney doesn't say something, anything, I will drill his thick body through the wall, gun or not.

"That prick knows something, Dad." I glare at Maloney. "Go on—deny you do. Lie to me. Lie to my face."

My feet slap on the floor as I march until I'm standing nose-to-nose with Maloney. I want him to look into my eyes and tell me he doesn't have any new information so that I can knock his fucking lights out.

"Reid, they have a location, but it's broad. They'll have to search it all."

"It's pissing down rain. How can they help her?"

"It may not be raining where she is."

My eyes widen to saucers. I stop breathing. My head spins. I'm going to faint.

I stumble backwards. The room whooshes around me, and as I reach out my arms to grab onto the blurry shadow of Maloney in front of me, I fall.

"I've got you," Dad says, and I can hear his sobs. Is he crying? My dad never cries. Never.

His hot breath rushes against my neck. His arms strangle my chest. "I'll never let you fall, Reid. Not on my watch. They know where Morgan is. Reid, they're bringing her home."

"Morgan," I whisper. It's barely audible.

I sit on the ground with my head tucked between my legs. I'm trying to suck air into my lungs in small quick breaths, yet nothing seems to be filling them. Hyperventilation.

"Sssh. Sssh. Sssh. Come now. Come on, just breathe, love. Just breathe. Mamma's here." Mum hugs my head.

I hear tortured howls. They rumble and roar around me. I want to look to where the sound is coming from, but I can't—I can't move. I'm howling. I've lost all control. My mind has finally broken. I've lost my marbles.

My legs wobble as Mum helps me to stand. The room spins around me until the back of Dad's head comes into view. I can't do this anymore. Where's my wife?

The sound of the door hitting the wall has me reaching out my hands. Thick arms push through Dad and John who stand in front of me. "Get out of my way," he roars. "Reid, Reid."

I'd know his voice anywhere. It's the voice of the man who shares the same blood as me, whose job it is to protect me, to show me the way in life, to be my guiding light. My two-faced wife-stealing brother.

"I'm so sorry. I'm so sorry." A soaked light blue shirt with a pocket half torn off takes my vision. The colour of crimson marks his collar. Cruise's nose is swollen and bruised, and his left eye blackened. There's a cut to his cheek. "Brother, I only just found out."

I press off my heels and launch myself at Cruise. I curl my arms around his neck and fold my legs around his waist to bring him down to the floor. I'll mess his face up more than it already is.

We hit the ground the moment Cruise's wet feet slip out from under him. I land on top of his chest, but he flips me underneath him before I have time to blink. Finding a strength I've never had, leads me to grunts and groans that see me back on top of Cruise and hunched over his face, straddling his waist.

Cruise gives up fighting. Cruise never gives up.

"Get off me." He reels in pain. "What are you doing?"

"Where's my Morgan? Where did you put her?" I strangle his collar. My knuckles turn a shade of white. "Tell me where she is!"

"Break it up." Maloney's voice booms. "Get off him."

"No! Not until he tells me where Morgan is." I slip my hands around his neck and press down, applying pressure that will cut off his airway.

"Reid. STOP!" Mum screams.

"He didn't do it, Reid. He's not responsible," Dad shouts in my ear.

My ear pops, and a dull ache has me scrunching my eyes shut.

"Get off your fucking brother." Dad applies pressure to my back as his fingers try to pry mine off Cruise.

"No! Get off, Dad." I try to jerk away from him, but he's much stronger.

I'm being dragged by my collar, my grip torn away, and I fight. I fight as if my life depends on it. Every pounding of my heels on the floor, every thrash of my torso, means I can go back to strangling the fucking life out of my brother.

I'm defeated the moment I feel my arms yanked behind my back.

Click, click. Click, click.

I hear the handcuffs secured before I even feel the pressure against my ulnas.

"Don't make me arrest you for assault." Maloney towers over me as I sit puffing.

A bead of sweat drips from his eyebrow and falls onto my cheek. I thrash my head. "Pig."

"You want to play it this way? Do you think that's a wise decision?"

"I think you have these cuffs on the wrong man. That's what I think."

Maloney grabs his radio from his holster. "Dispatch, RK-242."

"Yes, RK-242, go ahead."

"Constable Maloney here. We have located Cruise Banks. I need a unit to the home of Reid Banks, where our suspect currently is. It's about the missing person case of Morgan Banks."

"Requested unit is on its way."

Cruise sits across from me. His hands are pressed against his neck, his body slumped over itself. His knuckles are grazed. They're fucking grazed.

"What have you done?" I yell, glaring in his direction.

"Nothing, you dumb fuck. I've done nothing." He bolts upright.

"Reid, shut your God damn mouth. You're helping no one." Dad shoots me a death stare.

"Always on his side. You've always been on his side. Why? Because he's some bigshot bloody actor? I'm the disappointment, aren't I, Dad? Go on, admit it."

Dad lays his head into his palms. He roars. I sit upright.

"You boys both make me proud. You're my legacy. I'm proud of you both." Dad drops his hands and points his finger at me. "Don't!"

I huff loudly.

No sooner do Dad's eyes disconnect, then he's crouched in front of Cruise.

"Where the ever-loving fuck have you been?" His voice is stern, yet controlled.

"Wagga."

"Wagga. Why the fuck were you in Wagga?"

"Escaping the world. Natalie said she wanted a divorce. I lost it, Dad. I lost it."

"So you ran away. Are you telling me you hopped a plane to escape the issues, problems you're having with your wife?"

There's no reply.

"You smell like a brewery. Are you drunk?"

"No. Hungover as shit."

"How did you get here?"

"Drove. Metho lent me his ute."

"You've been with Metho this entire time?"

"Yes." Cruise coughs.

"You drove drunk?"

"I drove. That's all that matters."

"Why are you so banged up, boy?"

"Bar fight." He punches the words out abruptly.

"You look like you got your arse handed to you."

"I did."

He doesn't even talk himself up. That's unlike Cruise.

"We've been calling you nonstop. Natalie has been beside herself with worry."

"She wouldn't care if I lived or died. Ouch!" Cruise yelps.

I catch a glimpse of his face as his head bobs to the side after Dad clips him around the ear.

"Don't be a fool. You probably did something to piss your woman off, and she probably said more than she meant to, but Natalie loves you, always has and always will. When she finds out you're here ..." Dad pauses. "You're going to be a dead man. She thought you'd been taken too."

"Morgan." Cruise has agony in his tone.

"Still missing."

"I'm sorry, Dad. I'm sorry I didn't know."

"How did you find out?"

"Metho saw it on the television at the TAB. He raced back to tell me."

"Why haven't you answered your phone?"

There's a long pause.

"Because I don't know where it is. I lost it after I passed out in some bushes off Metho's property."

"Don't you ever do this —"

"I know, Dad."

Dad wraps his hand around the back of Cruise's head and rests his forehead against his. "You had me worried. Sick with worry."

"I'm sorry."

"You need to be here now for your brother. Get upstairs, get out of those filthy stinking clothes, and pull your shit together."

"No." Maloney steps towards Dad. "Right now, Cruise is under investigation and those clothes, and his body, are evidence."

"I didn't take my sister-in-law. You have to believe me." Tears drip from Cruise's eyes when Dad sits to the right of him.

"It's not a matter of believing you, mate. It's a matter for the law to decide."

"You're kidding?" Dad huffs as he stands.

Maloney shakes his head. "Not a matter for anyone to decide, bar the detectives."

"But he just told you where he was and what's happened since?"

"Look at his jeans. They're muddy and grass-stained. His face is a mess. His shirt is bloodied." Maloney's finger points to Cruise.

"And that makes him look guilty." Dad smacks his

hand to his forehead. "My son didn't do this. Max, he didn't do it. And he has an alibi, with a witness."

"Then you'll have no problems, will you?"

Maloney walks around Dad and stands beside Cruise. "Are you coming willingly down to the station?"

"Yes." It's barely audible.

"Good."

"I'm calling a lawyer," Dad says.

"Good decision," Maloney says.

"I never thought I'd have to call a lawyer for both my sons for the same fucking reason. I hope he doesn't have to show, because he costs a fortune." Dad holds his mobile phone beside his ear. "I'm not sure what the hell your mother and I ever did to raise boys who couldn't keep their bloody wives satisfied and messed up their entire bloody lives in such an epic fashion."

"Dad," Cruise and I snap simultaneously.

"What? It's true, ain't it?"

We both know better than to reply.

My brother is led away by two coppers I've not seen before, while Maloney undoes the handcuffs he slapped on my wrists.

Cruise's head hangs low. His shoulders are hunched, and when Dad taps his shoulder he cries out in pain.

"I'll be right behind you, son."

Cruise doesn't reply.

"Does Natalie know?" I don't know why I care, but I do.

"Yes. Natalie's out by the car, waiting. I think Cruise will have more to worry about with her than he does with the police." Mum rubs her thumb across my cheek. "I'm going to go with your brother."

"I figured," I scoff.

"Do you honestly think he's done this?"

I drop my head. "Nope."

"I didn't think so."

"I'm mad though, Mum."

"I know. I know you are. We all are. I'll be right back."

And just like that, my parents abandon me, leaving me without my wife or my family for support.

"Morgan's on the news," Kylee screams.

Maloney's shoulder catches mine in our haste to get to the television. I snarl but keep running.

Three backs create a shield in front of the television. John, Ronald, and Kylee stand so close it's impossible to see.

"Move," I yell.

They don't.

Clutching my shoulder with my hand, I push myself beside Kylee and stare at the picture of my wife filling the screen. Her brown eyes are soft and gazing straight into mine.

"Local Rockhampton woman Morgan Banks is still

missing after another long day of searching by the police and SES volunteers. Hope for her safe recovery is dwindling for this small community, and the family are co-operating and offering any information they can to assist the Rockhampton police."

The image changes from that of Morgan to a video of a stretcher with a blue tarp covering it. It's held upright by men dressed in white coveralls as they carry the stretcher up a small embankment.

"The body of an unidentified female was found at Yeppen Lagoon early this morning. However, it's not believed to be the body of missing mother and wife Morgan Banks."

The video clip changes from the stretcher to that of Detective West, striding towards the front doors of the police station.

"Can you tell us if you've found any leads concerning Morgan's disappearance?" Gregory, the news reporter who interviewed me, is holding out a microphone.

"We're doing all we can, and we hope to return Morgan to her family safely."

"The body this morning, can —"

"No comment at this time." West strides through automatic doors that part and then close behind him.

"Morgan Banks is still missing, but as you just heard, the police are holding onto hope that they will be able to return Morgan home safely soon," Gregory's blue eyes look straight through me.

"Nothing. We still have nothing." I shake my head.

"They're doing all they can," Kylee says quietly.

"It's not enough. Turn it off." I twist on my heel and stomp towards the kitchen.

Maloney is on the phone when I make the kitchen table.

He must spot me, because he turns and walks towards Morgan's sitting room.

I wait, glaring at Maloney's back. I press my neck forward, trying to understand what he says. I can't hear anything.

Maloney turns in slow motion. His hand drops to his side, still holding the phone in his grip.

"Max." My voice shakes.

He steps towards me. "They've deployed two tactical teams to search. It's a big area, Reid. All you can do now is pray."

"Two teams." My voice heightens. "Where?"

"I can't tell you. I'm sorry."

"Where?" My voice raises.

"Reid, come on. They have men on the ground; it's all I've got for you."

"Why isn't everyone out searching?"

Maloney scratches his forehead. He's hesitating. Why?

"Conditions aren't great. It's almost sunset. They'll have every officer out, come morning."

"Not good enough," I bark.

Maloney throws his hands in the air and then

shrugs. What the fuck is that supposed to mean?

"We'll bring her home." Maloney's head bobs.

"And what if they don't? What if he's already—" I can't even say it.

"Pray, Reid. All you can do is pray."

Tonight will be the longest night of my life. The storm that started all this seems to play out again, and when the swing on the veranda smacks into the foundation of the house, I look to Maloney and feel like I'm starting this nightmare all over again.

Waiting, wondering, wishing, and fighting—fighting to find my wife.

Chapter Sixty-Three

Reid

I sit watching the hands on the clock rotate slowly, so slowly it appears they don't move at all. 3:40 a.m., and still no word. Not a whisper. Nothing.

Shaky breaths part my lips. My jaw clenches tight at the same time as my hands. My stomach rolls like a tidal wave, then knots into a tight ball. Why haven't we heard anything? Is no news good news?

He places his hands on the breakfast bar. His platinum wedding ring flashes past my vision, catching my attention. I can see the grazes on his knuckles and hear every unsteady breath he takes, but I don't look up and meet Cruise's gaze. Instead, I turn my eyes back to those slowly rotating hands barely circling the clock.

He clears his throat, but says nothing. I know he wants me to look at him, but I won't. *I can't.*

Since Cruise's return three hours ago, we've kept distance between each other. I'm mad, in pain, and on the verge of an internal death, one that will obliviate any chance of me coming out of this the same person I once was. I have no fight left. I'm not even sure what is left to fight for. I know my brother didn't take Morgan—the police have cleared him—but I hadn't realised how much I needed Cruise to be here by my side in the most difficult moment of my life. He wasn't here. Now that he is, I want him to leave.

It remains quiet in the house, apart from each breath Cruise takes and the ticking sound from the clock.

The storm whipped, beat, and thrashed the earth until just after midnight. It was loud, violent, and powerful, worse than the weather the night Morgan disappeared, and I can't help thinking that if she was out there in that, I doubt she'd have survived. What shelter did she have, if any?

I thought the storm would never stop, even though I pleaded for it to, for Morgan's sake, for ours, for the officers who were out searching for her.

Eventually, it did, just as abruptly as it arrived. An eerie calm has since replaced those furious howls of wind, and no matter how hard I try to shake an overwhelming sense of doom, I can't.

"Reid," Cruise whispers. "Everyone's asleep."

I don't give him my attention or answer. Instead, I keep my eyes fixated on the clock.

"I'm so sorry, brother. If I had known, I would have been here in a heartbeat."

It's too late for apologies.

"Talk to me. Please."

I close my eyes and try to pretend he's not even standing there. I just want Cruise to disappear and go back to his mate's place, far, far away from me.

"Talk to me."

"Nothing to say," I murmur.

"But there is. I'm here." He pauses. "I'm here for you. Let me help you."

"Find Morgan. Bring her home," I punch out. "That's the only help I want."

"I will. Tell me how, and I'll bring her home."

Mechanically, I rotate my head. "If I knew, wouldn't you think I'd have taken care of it myself already."

He blinks. His lips part. His Adam's apple bobs in his throat, forcing his mouth to close. "I'd never hurt Morgan. You know that, right?" Cruise speaks softly. His eyes are pleading when they connect with mine.

I nod.

"Together, you and me, we can work this puzzle out. I know we can."

"You stink really bad." He does, like a mix of stale ale, rotten eggs, and the unique, pungent odour of papaya. I want to dry heave with each inhale.

"Yeah. I fucked up, okay? I need to pull my head in and get my shit together."

"You need a shower first."

He grins. "That bad, hey?"

"Worse than having my head stuffed inside a horse's arse." I pinch my nose.

"Can I borrow some of your clothes?"

I nod.

"Mum, Dad, Natalie, and Max are asleep in the lounge room. Ronald and Kylee are upstairs in the kid's rooms. John's gone home, and Linda left, too."

I'd not been paying attention to what had been happening around me. I had little clue as to the movements of others, and I really didn't care to know now.

"I'll use your bathroom then, so I don't wake anyone?"

I nod.

"Give me ten minutes and I'll be back."

"Coffee?" I'm not sure why I offer him social niceties, but I do. Maybe it's because I know he won't leave, and if shit hits the fan today, I'll need Cruise to comfort Mum and Dad when I won't be able to.

"Please." He reaches out his hand and taps my arm just like he's done in moments of comfort throughout my youth. "We'll find her. Me and you, brother."

My lip quivers. Cruise means what he says. The determination laced in his tone is strong, but I know we won't find Morgan. Too much time has passed.

A massive storm punished most of Queensland, and Max hasn't been able to contact Detective West or Gleaton for hours. The game is over. And now I sit here and watch the hands on this clock take away every dream I'd thought possible for my future.

I wait for the call to tell me my wife has not been found alive.

Chapter Sixty-Four

The Wolf

There's nothing like the sound of rain pelting against a tin roof, and as I lie in bed listening to it lighten, I think about Morgan burnt beyond recognition.

Everything's finally gone to plan. The fire spread quickly, much quicker than I'd anticipated, but the storm eventually prevented it from blazing out of control. I couldn't get close enough to find Morgan's body before the sun went down, so now I'm left to wait until the sun rises to claim my latest prize. My thirteenth victim. *My Red.* My excitement is so palpable that I can't sleep.

The glare from the television catches my attention. I reach across the quilt, retrieve the remote from beside my head and turn up the volume. Even though Morgan's gone, I'll always have my memories of the game we played, and those videos of her looking lost, defeated, and pained whilst imprisoned inside my Red Room.

I smile as on the screen, she writes in the notepad. I didn't think she'd write the letters, scrawl her final messages. I haven't read them, and I won't. Anything Morgan had to say is of no interest to me. She's a ghost. A tortured hellion. A dead bitch.

As her hands shake, my lips stretch wider. I really can't wait to deliver her final thoughts to Reid and those brat kids. My word is my bond. I'll give him the fucking letters along with a handshake.

I rewind the film. I relax my head back into the pillow and take a long inhale.

Photographs shoot across the projection screen. Morgan's filthy, covered in mud with blood dried on her skin. She stares at the screen as picture upon picture layer on top of each other. The panic and terror in her eyes, the way her chest rises and falls rapidly—it's everything I'd hoped it would be. The pulse in her neck thumps, but she doesn't turn her head away. Her eyes remain glued to the life she once had playing out before her.

The screen goes black. Morgan's legs buckle when she stands, causing her to launch out her arms. She stumbles forward until her body hangs off the edge of the table. Morgan wobbles, stretched up on her tiptoes, until she manages to push her heels down and finally balances. She rummages with desperation through the mess I left on the table for her, snarling, and it pleases me.

Whack.

A notebook and pen fall to the concrete flooring. Morgan's big brown eyes grow wide. Her chin quivers. A moment of realisation fills her expression, one I'll have the pleasure of watching over and over on repeat. "They're blank, aren't they, Red?" I snicker, and affect a feminine voice. *"Oh, what does this mean? Why are all the pages absent of writing? Why did he do this?"*

I laugh.

Slowly, her body lowers until she sits slumped on the concrete. Her head hangs low. She's disappointed.

"Oh, poor Red." I continue to laugh.

Beep. Beep. Beep.

On the video, the timer sounds, the one I hung to the wall in my Red Room. Even now, my heart gallops with glee.

Morgan gasps. Once again, panic stretches her eyes open excessively. This moment is one I'll treasure long after I bury her in my graveyard.

Her head turns in a whip, and she stares, spotting the red numbers of the timer.

I lift my arms above my head and stretch, only to wince at the sting radiating through my shoulder where that dumb bitch stabbed me. How the fuck did she get those scissors? It had to have been after I stitched her leg wounds.

I kick off the blankets and rock until I'm in a seated position. I need that footage.

Ring, ring, ring.

Reaching out my arm, I grab my mobile phone from the pillow beside me.

"Yeah?" I say in answer.

"Is it done?"

"Yep."

There's silence.

"Are you happy?" he says.

"Very. Very fucking happy."

"Good."

"What are you doing with Morgan's body?"

"I'll have to see what condition she's in, and then I'll decide."

"What?" His voice is hushed, but strained. "You've collected her, haven't you?"

"Couldn't get close enough, that fire took off like a wild bitch. The storm only just calmed down now. I went out again a few hours ago, but couldn't see shit. I'll go get her in the morning. Well, if there's anything left of her, that is." I can't stop the grin that follows.

"The coppers are searching. I have no doubt they're out your way."

"I'm not worried."

"Well, I am." There's a nervous tone laced in his words.

"Calm down. I've got it sorted."

"Once you find her body, get your shit out of the fucking cabin and burn it to the ground. I don't want this coming back—"

"It won't. Calm ya tits. What? Does she know?"

"No. She has no clue."

"Reid?"

"No."

"Nothing to worry about."

"Burn the fucking cabin down or I will. It can't come back to me."

"But I've done so much work out here to get my game—"

"You got what you wanted. I supported you. Now it's done. No more hunting. No more killing. Your revenge is complete. The game is over."

I laugh. "Oh, this is just the beginning. I'll head home for a little while. I'll get out of Queensland, for your sake, but I'll be back."

"That wasn't the deal."

I scoff. "We don't have a deal, and I suggest you get on board or I'll take someone's life away from you."

"Listen here—"

I hang up.

Screw him. Screw everybody. I have a pang of hunger that needs quenching. I'm not about to give up the chase, the hunt, for anyone.

Not even him.

Chapter Sixty-Five

Morgan

Crackle, pop.

Although the sound is distant, I'm aware that the fire still burns in spots.

I try to tip my chin forward in an attempt to lift my head from the ground. I must work out how close the flames are, but I can't. I have nothing left in the tank.

Rain beats down heavily against my skin, and as I scrunch my eyes closed, I cry. Everything hurts. Breathing, moving, thinking … it all hurts so much. I want nothing more than to sleep.

The overwhelming burning sensation that ripped through my upper right thigh, has all but disappeared. There's pain, but the intensity is gone. Maybe I didn't get burnt after all.

I try to shift my hand from the top of my stomach to my leg, so I can touch and explore the area where the most agonising pain I've ever felt existed, but it, too, is as heavy as lead and won't budge.

I can't move.

So, I cry. All I can do is cry.

I shiver.

I take laboured breaths.

I cough.

I cry even more.

It's a vicious cycle I fear will never end, not until I take my last breath.

I will die here, in these ruins, alone.

Chapter Sixty-Six

Detective West

The automatic doors part and, as Detective Gleaton steps in front of me, I take a final drag from my cigarette and flick it behind me as I enter the police station.

"Coffee?" Roland says, passing me the disposable cup. "It's hot." He warns before I have a chance to knock it back.

"Is everyone in place? Has Lynette been in contact?" I ask, reaching his side.

"Yes. And yes, Lynette has. The two SERT teams from Brisbane that were on the ground searching throughout the night have retrieved nothing, and have now resumed their instructed positions for our search. That storm has made seeing anything hard,

Lynette said."

"Warrant?"

"I've got the warrant." Roland pats at his jeans pocket.

"Good. Let's get this show on the road. We need to drive out there before daylight. Morgan must be located this morning."

As I enter the project room, each officer's eyes turn to me. The chatter I could hear from the hallway ceases.

Eric hands me an A4 photograph when I reach him. "Morning." He stands at attention.

I don't respond as I sidestep him, then pass, heading to the podium.

Holding the picture up by my ear, I swivel until my shoulders are squared to the many bodies of the officers filling the room. "This is our target. Winston Sampson, also known as Vactrim Blight. He's using an alias for his employment. However, all his DMV records, deeds, and insurance are under his birth name of Winston Sampson."

I stop speaking as Roland comes to stand beside me. "Departure in twenty-five minutes," he whispers for my ears only.

I nod. "Winston's brother, Falcon Sampson, deceased, is the motive for Morgan's kidnapping. Our evidence is clear and precise. His death, nearly six years ago, relates to this abduction."

"Winston is currently out of town hunting, as per his employer's statement. We are yet to locate his whereabouts. What we do know is he's due to resume his job this coming Thursday," Roland says, reaching for a folder on the lectern beside him.

"Winston was once a part of the Melbourne mafia. We believe he no longer has any ties with the organisation and his alias is for protection from this underground crime syndicate. He's also ex-military, so he's considered dangerous." I look to Roland as his lips part.

"We have a warrant to search land and property belonging to Winston at Corbet's Landing, along with any vehicles that may be on-site. Two teams are in position and currently surround the cabin. We've had eyes on the ground since yesterday. There's no movement at his home from our intel, but if Winston is on-site, you are to negotiate a surrender without a kill, unless you're in immediate danger," Roland instructs, turning his eyes to mine. "Our main priority here is locating Morgan Banks alive."

"And this is what we've learnt from Morgan and the GPS PING in place. She's in bushland, land at Corbet's Landing. The GPS has narrowed this vast landscape down to a radius of one hundred hectares. We're looking specifically for a large rock wall that has a huge boulder on at least one side. During the last contact I made with Morgan, she informed me this was where she was hiding. However, that was more than eighteen hours ago now, and due to the weather, she most likely repositioned. We'll have four teams in total moving through this scrub. Two that are already in position, and the two teams we'll form here this morning." I scan my eyes over the many stern faces. "Your mission: to tackle each direction of this land mass, and continue inwards until we've covered all ground."

Gleaton steps forward. "You all know the team you're assigned to. Let's gear up and meet out back."

"Let's get this done. Four teams. Blue and red are our two teams. Yellow and green are the two teams squatting in wait. You'll respond to these colour codes only for radio contact. Turn your radio station off the main dispatch channel and switch to station ninety-one." I pause, looking at the many nodding heads. "Move out."

Eager feet march down the ramp and towards the police vehicles.

"You all know where you need to go. Remember, team blue, you'll be searching the house, vehicles, and the other two teams, currently lying in wait, searching the surrounding property. Team red, you'll stop on the way out and come in through the bush, make sure to approach with caution. After this task is complete, we'll break into our four teams and cover the PING location from the GPS. No stone, rock, or fucking blade of grass gets left unchecked. We find Morgan. This ends today," I shout.

"Yes, sir," they reply in unison.

I slide into my car just as Roland does, and without a minute to fasten my seatbelt, I shift the car into gear and pull out in front of all other vehicles. Roland leans forward, flicking the switch that controls the siren, and as the noise wails into the dead of the night, I press my foot flat on the accelerator.

I will find Morgan. I will bring her home.

She will be alive.

Chapter Sixty-Seven

Reid

Over an hour has passed and still no word. I can't fucking breathe.

"Your coffee's gone cold." Cruise presses his lips into a hard line.

"Can't stomach anything." I sigh.

"That's the sixth cup I've made you since I came downstairs. I think I'll just tip this down the sink and give up on the coffee-making."

I shrug. "Yeah."

My yellow surf tee, the one Cruise now wears, tapers at the back when he carries the mug into the kitchen. There's no doubt he's more muscular than I am, the T-shirt at least one size too small. His waist narrows like my own, yet the boardshorts he's borrowed suction to his larger thighs. Linda's right—Cruise and I do look very much alike, apart from this slight size difference, and there's no mistaking us for siblings. I guess it's only natural. Siblings do often look alike ...

Wait.

What if Winston isn't Winston?

What if his brother Falcon has been masquerading as him this whole time?

My mind races. Cruise and I could pull off a stunt like that if we ever needed to. Linda said Winston and Falcon had many similarities, and the two resembled each other. It would give him motivation.

And if my theory was right, it meant he'd killed before—likely his own flesh and blood.

Wait, what am I thinking? I'm jumping to conclusions.

What if Morgan was dead.

Did any of it matter?

Water dripping from the tap onto the metal sink gives me the urge to pee, so I pull myself up from the stool and make a beeline for the hallway leading to the downstairs toilet.

Tap, tap, tap.

I back pedal at the soft sound of tapping coming from the back door.

The automatic porch light is on.

I hesitate in my approach and shuffle until I see her.

Grey hair wraps around curlers. Thin-framed

glasses sit on the bridge of her nose. A purple shawl hangs from her shoulders. *Shirley*. Oh shit. Are the kids okay?

I fling the door open and rush towards her as she stands on the back patio. "Shirley, are the kids okay? What's wrong? Where's John?"

Her finger is pressed against her lips. "Shhh." She looks frightened. Her finger trembles against her mouth. "Inside."

It's all she says.

I take her hand, helping her in from the dark.

"Who's here? Are they awake?" Shirley's eyes move in every direction.

"Cruise is awake. He's the only one apart from me. Shirley, what's wrong?" My heartrate accelerates, and my hands are instantly clammy.

Shirley steps away from me.

"Tell me what's wrong."

"Oh, Reid." Her lips quiver as tears leak from her eyes.

"Shirley."

"John ... he ... There was ... Reid." She drops her head.

It takes every ounce of strength I have to stop myself from marching the small gap between us and clutching her arms. I want to shake Shirley. I'm so frightened I want to shake whatever it is she's trying to tell me out of her mouth.

"You need to get the detectives here. I know where Morgan is."

I stumble. I stumble backwards. My legs weaken until I almost fall on my knees. I clutch the material of my T-shirt between my strained fingers, over top of my heart. *Morgan.* Shirley knows where Morgan is.

"Please," I beg her to put me out of my misery right here, right now.

"You need to tell the police. I'm sorry." Shirley shakes her head as she wraps her hands around herself in what I believe is protection.

"How? Where? How do you ..." I can't spit out what I need to say because I'm in shock, so much shock.

"I heard John on the phone, Reid. Oh my God, what has he done? I don't know what he's done."

I puff out my chest when anger rips through my body like a cyclone reaching land. "Tell me everything," I snap. My temper is clutched behind my teeth, barely trapped, about to break like a thin thread held above a flame.

"She's dead." Shirley's tears fall rapidly as her shoulders shake. "I heard John say Morgan's name when he was on the phone. I heard him ask about where her body would go. Reid, I don't know who he was talking to, but he told whoever it was to burn down the cabin because he couldn't be traced back to Morgan's abduction." Shirley whimpers as she uses the back of her trembling hands to wipe her tears away. "He said, if you don't do it I will. Reid, John knew who had Morgan and where she was the whole time. I heard him. I heard him." Her voice rises.

Every pound of my heart has me panting. *The kids.*

Holy shit! I'm seething—seeing red. I want to march across the grass between our two properties so I can grab that backstabbing prick John, and throw him up against the wall. I'll beat him within an inch of his life to get the information needed to get to Morgan. I must also keep our children safe.

My fingers fold inwards until my fists squeeze so tightly they shake.

"She's at Corbet's Landing. She's at the cabin you've been to with John when you helped him build that extra carport we needed."

"Where are my kids?"

"I promise they're fine. They're sound asleep. John doesn't know I heard him. I promise you, he doesn't know."

"John." I spit his name from my tongue like venom that's invaded my mouth.

"He's asleep," she cries. "I waited until he went to sleep."

"What's going on? Shirley, why are you crying? Reid. Brother. Oh no. What's happened?" I didn't hear Cruise's approach, but when I glance to my right, there he is. "Don't do anything stupid, brother. Relax. Just relax."

I give Cruise a murderous glare. The light from the patio brings some light into the open area.

"Shirley, go home. Climb into bed and do nothing."

"I can't," she sobs softly.

"Climb into your bed and pretend to be asleep. You need to act as if everything's normal." I'm still glaring at Cruise. I don't shift my eyes from his. I need Cruise, more than I've ever needed him in my life, and he's here, beside me, about to be the only person I can count on to do the right thing—to go find my wife.

Chapter Sixty-Eight

Detective West

A convoy of flashing lights fills my rear-vision mirror. I don't say a word, and neither does Roland. I'm focused on the white lines dotted along the bitumen in front of me.

Before long, I'm indicating to turn onto the main highway, and as trees flash by in a blur under the shine of our headlights, I'm thankful for the cloak of darkness we travel within. The roads are empty, and we're gaining momentum without disruption.

I rotate my head to the right, completing a shoulder check as we speed towards double lanes. A tug on the steering wheel has the lane change complete.

An hour and a half—that's how long we race along the bitumen before radio silence is no more.

"This is team red. We're taking our allocated turn-off. We'll be in contact once we achieve our positions."

"Team yellow. We're maintaining visual on the cabin. No movement. We're awaiting instruction to approach."

"Sirens off," I say, twisting my neck in another shoulder check to my left. I coast over the white lines dotting the centre of the road and hold my position in the left lane.

Another ten kilometres pass.

"Team green. We have visual on a white off-roader approaching the cabin. A white four-by is approaching the property."

"Shit," Roland mutters.

"Hold your position. Do not approach," I command.

"Team green, holding our positions."

"Team yellow, holding our positions."

"Team red, heading into the bushland now."

I flick my eyes to Roland.

"Looks like Winston might have returned," he says.

I take a deep breath, staring down the white lines. "We just have to get there."

"Team green, we have a male, approximately one hundred and ninety centimetres tall, exiting the vehicle."

"Get eyes on him. Give me a positive identification." I'm calm. Focused. I hope this is Winston.

Minutes pass.

"Team yellow. We have visual. White male, match is positive to the description given and photograph supplied for our prime suspect."

"Hold your position. Do not approach," I say.

"Team yellow, holding our positions."

"Team green, holding our positions."

I take another deep breath. "We'll come in on foot. I repeat, we will come in on foot. Expect a fifteen-minute delay on our expected ETA. I want to take this prick down myself. Nobody approach."

"Team green, your instruction has been received."

"Team yellow, your instruction has been received."

"Team red. We're now approaching through bushland on foot."

"Slow and steady. No sudden moves, team red," I instruct.

"Team red, your instruction has been received. We're slowing our pace."

Another ten kilometres pass before I shift the indicator to the left and slow until I've come to a dead stop on the shoulder of the highway. The vehicles trailing me follow suit, parking in a straight line behind my car like well-placed dominos. The headlights dim until they disappear completely, then beams of light from torches replace them.

"Hold your positions. This is team blue. We're now approaching on foot. Hold your positions." I speak softly.

"Team yellow, holding our positions."

"Team green, holding our positions."

"Team red, still approaching with caution."

Opening the car door, I leap out. I take the strap at

the bottom of my bulletproof vest and reef the Velcro back, pulling it tighter around my lower stomach until it becomes firm. I fasten the belt back into place.

I twist on my heel and face the twenty officers who form team blue. They're geared up and watching me, eyes alert.

"Ready?" I look to Gleaton, who nods in response. "Turn off your torches. Move out," I yell loud enough for the team to hear, but not loud enough that my voice will project too far.

We're shielded by the cover of darkness.

My firearm is gripped in my hand as I walk down a dirt track off the highway.

Gleaton holds the radio to his mouth. "Team blue now approaching. I repeat, team blue now approaching."

"Team yellow, holding our position."

"Team green, holding our position."

"Team red. Shit. We have a problem."

"Fuck," I growl before taking my radio from my holster and holding it by my mouth. "Team red, what's the problem?" I hold my tension between my teeth.

"We've hit a lake. Boss, this wasn't on the map."

"Team red, hold your position. Do not cross the water."

"Team red, holding our position." There's a pause. "Sorry. Astin."

"Halt all radio contact. We're going in," I say quietly.

"Team red, radio contact disabled."

"Team yellow, radio contact disabled."

"Team green, radio contact disabled."

I slip the portable back into my holster and catch a glimpse of Roland as I turn my gaze to the high grass in front of us. His eyes roam our surroundings. His weapon is held out in front of him, and I do the same. He's ready to fire. I'm ready to fire. We take no chances.

We move one foot in front of the other. I keep my eyes forward. I don't blink. We're going to take down Winston Sampson, and then we're going to bring Morgan home.

To serve and protect above all else. I took an oath.

I will protect Morgan.

Chapter Sixty-Nine

Reid

Shirley did what I asked after some further convincing, and when I look towards Cruise after she walks out the back door, he drops his chin low to his chest.

"Do you trust me?" I take a sharp inhale, hopeful Cruise will see that what we need to do far outweighs any possible need for him to go running through the house and alerting Max as to what's unfolded. Cruise might play the hero on screen, but in reality, he's far more analytical, and law abiding.

He nods.

"You said you'd help me bring Morgan home. Help me, brother."

He doesn't answer.

"John. John knew. He ..." I stop speaking as I try to control my racing thoughts and bury the betrayal from a man I'd considered to be a second father to me. "If John can do this to us, then the police can't be trusted either. Hell, I know someone on the force is involved. Dusty, that guy Linda's seeing, he told me not to trust the police. He had intel, Cruise. Those pigs haven't told us all they know, just bits and pieces. They can't help us. Max is the only one I trust, but he's only one officer, and he's not even high ranking. Do you see what I'm saying?"

Cruise doesn't reply. He doesn't even bat an eyelid. He just stares.

"I'm going to get Morgan, and you're coming with me."

Cruise's lips part, but I give him no time to speak.

"You need to get the biggest butcher's knife from the kitchen, and grab Ronald's car keys. They're next to my wallet on the bench. Cruise, do it quietly. I know where the cabin is. I know where to go."

He shakes his head.

"You will get the knife and the keys." My tone is strained. "I'm going to write a message for Max and tape it to the back of the front door."

"Reid, no. Let the police handle this. The kids, they —"

"They will be safe. I know they will be okay."

"No. They're not. Morgan would want you to go to them."

"Morgan needs me. Max will get the kids out safely.

Trust me. Cruise, please be here for me."

"I am," he mumbles.

I reach out my hand, placing it on his arm. "This is my wife, and I know if Natalie was out there you'd —"

"I'd move hell and high water to get to her."

I grind my teeth together as I nod.

"Okay." He places his hand on top of mine. "Okay, I'll help you."

I release a long exhale. Tears well in my eyes just as I see tears brim in Cruise's. "You get the knife and car keys, and I'll write the note."

I sneak towards the office. Slowly, I turn the handle and push open the door. Flicking the light switch on, I rush towards my desk. I pull out the printer tray and remove an A4 sheet of paper before grabbing a pen.

Max,

John is involved in Morgan's disappearance. Get my kids out of that fucking house and keep them safe. You're the only person I trust.

Now, I need you to trust me. Shirley is not involved. She didn't know. I know where Morgan is, she's in a cabin John owns at Corbet's Landing. I'm bringing my wife home.

Reid.

I pull four long strands of tape from the tape dispenser on the desk and stick them to my finger. I turn off the light and hurry down the hallway until I've reached the closed front door where Cruise stands, holding a long carving knife in his hand as he shifts from foot to foot.

"Are you sure this is the right thing to do?" he whispers.

I nod.

"Okay."

I tape the note a little higher than my line of sight knowing that the moment I start Ronald's four-wheel drive, and blow the horn, Max will wake and realise I'm gone. He's been a light sleeper every time his eyes have closed since he's been here. I predict he'll bolt to the front door to chase us, and hopefully, he'll see the note. It's what I need to believe will happen.

I flick my hand towards Cruise, indicating it's time for us to leave. Cruise's Adam's apple bounces in his throat in response.

I swallow hard as I quickly spy the clock hung on the kitchen wall. 4:50 a.m. I know I'm not thinking clearly, but this is what my instinct is screaming for me to do. I need to run. Run until I find Morgan. She needs me. She's not dead. Shirley mustn't have heard John right.

"Give me the knife," I whisper the moment I gently close the front door to the house. "Get into the car. I've got this."

I stop. I take a deep breath, then draw my hand back with the knife held tightly in my grip. "I'm sorry, Max," I say as I plunge the blade into the back tyre of his police car.

Hissssssss, hisssssss.

I slash all four tyres in minutes. I run towards the open driver's door of Ronald's car. There's no turning back now.

I need to know if Morgan is alive, and this is the only way. Now I just have to hope the screeching tyres, and the long blow of the horn, are enough to have Max jumping out of the lounge, or even the complete neighbourhood rising. I need someone to see that note—to safeguard my children.

Chapter Seventy

Morgan

My eyelids flutter open before they close again. I'm drifting in and out of consciousness. I can no longer feel the rain. Has it stopped or am I just numb to the sensation? I can't decide so I force my eyes to open before turning them left, then right. I can hear every shallow breath I take, but not the rain.

I made it through the storm. Now I just need to get up.

Get up, Morgan. Get up, my mind screams.

I moan. But I can't manage to move.

"Help." There's no sound.

Get up, Morgan.

I can't.

My eyelids flutter and then, as they close, I moan

once more.

"Mummy, mummy, where are you?" Aleeha's sweet voice calls me, and as a ray of light fills the staircase, the staircase inside my dream house, I smile. I'm home. I won. I found my way back to my family.

"I'm coming, baby." It's my voice. It's intense, but relaxed.

Each step I climb has my heart galloping with excitement. I've missed my daughter. I've missed her so much.

My hand is on Aleeha's bedroom door handle. I can feel a pulse in my fingertips as I push the door open.

Aleeha sits on the ground. Her blue eyes shoot to mine as she gifts me the same smile she does first thing every morning. "Mummy," she screeches, leaping from the carpet beneath her. "You're home. Brax, Brax, Mummy's home. She's home."

An aura of peace fills her room at the same time as warmth hugs my heart. Aleeha bounds into my arms and as I embrace her tight against my body, I whimper. Her hair smells like strawberries. I've missed the smell of her detangling spray. "I missed you, baby girl."

Her head nestles into the space between my neck and my shoulder. I fought so hard for this moment. I never gave up. I couldn't. I'm a mother, and mothers do everything it takes to find their way home to their children. They never say die until they have exhausted every possibility.

"Mum. Oh, Mummy." The call of my name comes

from behind me. Brax's voice is music to my ears.

I jolt forward with the impact applied to my back. I didn't get the chance to see Brax approach. Instead, I feel his long arms squeeze around my tummy so tight that I cry out my relief. "My babies. Oh, my babies." Slowly, I kneel until I'm on the floor.

Two heads snuggle into me. Four arms wrap me up in a cocoon. Two hearts beat strongly against my chest.

"I thought I was never going to see you again, Mum," Brax sobs.

"Of course, you were. Don't be silly, buddy. You know I'd never leave you two behind." I mess his hair before kissing the top of his head.

I hold my son and daughter for what feels like an eternity, too scared to let them go, and too happy to allow this moment to end.

"Morgan. Morgan..."

My head shoots upright. The voice of the man I've loved for many moons is calling for me.

"Reid." My heart skips a beat.

"Baby. Baby..." There's desperation in his tone.

Stomp, stomp, stomp, stomp.

His feet hit the wood of the staircase. I twist my head over my shoulder and wait. My chin quivers when he comes into view.

Blue eyes, much too beautiful not to be admired whenever in sight, connect with mine. My husband races towards me. He's more handsome than I remembered. When he falls to his knees behind the children, the meadowsweet, woodruff smell of his cologne has me inhaling deeply.

"I love you." His voice cracks as he folds his arms around the children and me, and I don't know how they all manage to fit laid against me, but they do. Six arms are now wrapped around my body, and three hearts beat against my chest.

"I knew you'd come back. I knew it." Reid tilts his head until his eyes gaze into mine. "Welcome home."

His lips edge towards my own, and as they do, I close my eyes. His lips are as soft as pillows when they press to mine. They're just as I remember them. He kisses me wildly, igniting a fire in my soul.

Fire.

Danger.

Bushland.

The wolf.

I need to run.

Run, Morgan. Get up.

My lips are left naked. *Instant panic.* My eyes spring open. Reid's crying.

"I'm here. Don't cry." I'm trembling.

"Morgan. Please. Fight. Don't leave us." Reid's arms reach for me as I feel a strong pull rip me away from him.

I blink.

The warmth and security that calmed me and protected me disappears as fast as my children do.

Chapter Seventy-One

Detective West

A small wooden cabin comes into view. A soft patio light provides a visual of the front door and an old rusted table at its side.

"We're going in," Roland whispers through the radio. There's no reply. Radio silence is maintained by all units as requested.

I point to the right, then to myself, then to the SERT team before circling my finger in the air. Each officer moves in the exact direction they should without me speaking a single word. I nod to Roland, who shifts to my blind spot to cover any threat, while the five remaining officers flank us.

One step in front of the other. Our feet make no

sound. We're trained to hunt predators and to deliver the element of surprise.

Three stairs leading to the patio, and a distance of about one metre stands between me and the front door. I flick my head to my right, place two fingers to my eyes, then point to three separate officers. Their mission: to stay at the bottom of the stairs with their rifles aimed at the door. They are my eyes on the ground, and they won't hesitate to shoot if necessary. They waste no time in following my unspoken command.

One, two, three steps I take, with Roland right behind me, still covering any threat. I lift my leg and launch it straight into the wood. The door bursts open.

"What the fuck?" he yells. A tall, broad man wearing camouflage throws his arms high into the air. He shakes his head as I aim my revolver directly at his chest.

"Winston Sampson?" I'm calm.

"Yes."

"Detective Astin West from Rockhampton CBI. Do you have a weapon on your person?"

"Yes."

"Please disarm yourself. Slowly."

Only one of his arms lowers past his hair that appears to be clumped with mud, before continuing by his blue eyes that shine under bright lighting. He stops when he reaches his waist. "I'm going to put my hand behind my back to get my pistol."

"Don't do anything stupid."

His hand disappears until it slowly reappears by his hip, holding a black Glock.

"Put it on the ground, slowly," I instruct.

Winston gingerly bends his knees, leaving one hand placed behind his head, sliding the gun across the floorboards before resuming his upright position.

"Do you have any more weapons on your person?" My voice rises a fraction.

"No."

"Step back," I demand.

He does.

"Search him." I relax my grip on my weapon and some of the tension in my shoulders as Roland marches towards our suspect.

"Turn around," Roland commands. "Hands behind your head, legs spread."

"What is this about?" Winston says as he stands with his fingers linked behind his head and widens his stance.

Neither of us reply.

I don't take my eyes from the pat-down taking place. Instead, I remain alert for any possible threats that might come my partner's way. Roland completes his examination upon reaching Winston's muddy boots.

"I have rights. Am I under arrest? What have I done?"

Neither of us answer.

Roland rises, nodding in my direction. "He's clear."

It's what I was waiting for him to say. Winston isn't harbouring anything else harmful inside his clothing.

I lower my gun and place it back in the holster, knowing I'm protected by the two highly trained SERT officers at my back. They won't lower their rifles. Instead, they'll keep them aimed at Winston's chest, ready to deliver a bullet if needed.

"Do you know Morgan Banks?" I stand stoically. I'm in command, and if this thing blows up, it's all on my head. After all, it's not normal practice for a country town detective to lead a tactical crime team in the first place. I'm just fortunate that Eli, who controls all special emergency, was in my unit when I used to run my own SERT team years ago.

"No. I don't."

"Are you sure?"

"I don't know her." Winston's hands remain pressed against the back of his skull. His legs are still parted from the search.

"She's a local woman who's gone missing. She's also a wife of a client whose car you detail."

"I don't know her." His lips are pursed.

"I don't believe you. Morgan's also the ex-girlfriend of your brother Falcon Sampson."

His eyes widen. "Morgan. As in, Falcon's high school girlfriend, Morgan? Morgan?"

"Yes," I say.

"I know her then." He exhales. "I haven't seen her for a very long time though, not since Falcon finished school. She's missing?"

"Since Thursday night. Where were you Thursday night between the hours of five and eight?"

He lifts his chin slightly and turns his eyes to look towards the ceiling. He stays in this position for almost a minute before he returns his attention back to me. "Thursday was the night we got that storm. It's what had me delayed in going hunting." He pauses. "I was at work. I left work late, and then I came home. I would have been driving home in that timeframe."

"You didn't stop on your way to get petrol or meet up with anyone?" He's lying, but I need to give him a chance to rearrange his thoughts before I slap on the cuffs and get his arse hauled down to the station.

He shakes his head. "No. No, not Thursday night." His eyes narrow when he stops speaking. "Actually, yes, I did. I stopped to help some lady fix a tyre ... an SUV, it was."

"Morgan's tyre?"

His lips part. His eyes bulge. "Nah. Mate, you've got this wrong. That was Morgan?"

"Yes."

"I had no clue. Shit, it's been more than ten years since I've seen her. Fuck! Hang on. No, no, no, you ain't pinning this shit on me." He's immediately agitated. He drops his arms to his sides. "Mate. No. I didn't take that woman." He points to my chest. "I've been out fucking Whoop Whoop since early Friday morning. Search my shit. I had nothing to do with any lady going missing, let alone someone who dated my brother. I've got nothing to hide."

"Winston Sampson, this is a warrant to search your house, land, and vehicles." Roland holds the warrant out in front of him, and Winston takes it gently from his pinched fingers.

"Search away." Winston's shoulders slump as Roland retrieves the handcuffs from his belt.

"Come on. You don't need to cuff me. By now you must know who I used to be and what I used to do. There's no need for the cuffs. I'm not going to bolt. I'll tell you what you want to know. Search. I've got nothing to hide."

"Ex-military, and a runner for the mafia," I prod.

He drops his head. "I'm not proud of my past. Look, I live out here away from society and keep to myself. I-I … That life is well and truly behind me."

"Vactrim Blight?" I keep my statements short and to the point, letting him talk, giving him a moment to slip up.

He lifts his head and grins. "Yeah. That's me. It's easier than people finding out who I used to be, you know. Even though my work for the underworld wasn't disclosed, people still find ways to figure out who Winston Sampson was. Bloody mafia groupies hunt you down, even aeons later."

I shake my head towards Roland, who instantly slaps the handcuffs around his wrists.

"Come on. Seriously?" Winston sighs.

"Groupies?" I continue my questioning.

He nods. "Women who want to marry you. Men who want to be you. Take your pick."

The radio is in my hand. "Team red, begin searching from the lake outwards. Team yellow and green, begin your search in surrounding property. Team blue, search the vehicles and house."

There's a moment of silence.

"Team red, understood.

"Team green, beginning search.

"Team yellow, beginning search.

"Team blue, coming in."

"Shit." Winston cocks his eyebrows. "I knew you'd have me well and truly surrounded." He shakes his head. "I come back early because Luna radios me to tell me there's been a fire, possibly near my land, and I'm confronted with this bullshit. Fuck my life," he mutters.

"Fire?" My shoulders stiffen.

"Punk kids do it all the time. Come into the bush and start spot fires that get out of hand. You guys should be thanking us. We put most of them out ourselves, as quick as they start. Someone has to stop a massive bushfire."

"Whose Luna?"

"A hermit that lives a few properties over. She's been livin' out here longer than the lot of us. She knows this bush like the back of her hand. Every nook and cranny."

"Where did she say this fire was?"

"You tell me. That's what I was about to do—check it out. Luna said there was a fire. That's it."

I place the radio to my mouth. "Team red, you need

to look for an area where a fire has been burning or is still burning. Any smoke you see, head in that direction. Morgan might have lit it for us to find her."

"Shit," Winston exhales. "Poor Morgan. You think she's out there in the bush somewhere?"

I look Winston up and down but don't answer. "I have questions."

"You let me have a smoke out on the veranda, and I'll tell ya whatever ya want to know."

I swing my arm outwards. "After you."

Winston sits on the rusted chair beside the table. Rubbing his wrists now absent from the handcuffs I removed, with a lit cigarette hanging from his bottom lip.

I bring the lighter to the end of my own cigarette, cupping my hand to contain the flame. I keep my eyes fixed on Winston, watching his every move. "Falcon—"

"God rest his soul." He interrupts.

"Your brother took his own life?" I place the lighter on the table and take a long draw from my smoke.

"Yes. Falcon was a such a troubled, lost, loner boy, but nobody should be trapped inside themselves like he was. Driven to make it all stop in the end."

"So you saw it coming?"

"Nope, I didn't. But I probably wasn't around enough to notice. Not a day goes by that I don't wish I'd been home more to take care of him." He takes a long draw from his smoke. "Ten-year age gap didn't help. I was in training for the army, and he was in Melbourne. I always knew he was troubled—hell, so did Mum, but he seemed happy enough with his best mate by his side and Morgan on his arm."

"Best friend?"

"Thick as thieves they were, him and Logan."

"Logan?"

"Logan Raffety. It was Falcon, Morgan, and Logan against the world back then. They went everywhere together. Did everything together. Then when Morgan went off to university, and they busted up, he still had Logan."

"Do you see Logan? Is he from around here?"

He shakes his head. "Nah. He's still back home in Melbourne where we all grew up. He's a police officer actually, so he won't be hard for you pigs—I mean, cops, to find."

I shift my eyes to Roland who is leaning against a single rail, writing into his notepad. He nods to indicate he'll arrange someone to look into Logan Raffety.

"Do you have the copy of the note Falcon left before his death?"

Winston ashes his cigarette. "Nah, I don't. I put it in the coffin with Mum, and it burned with her. Falcon's death broke mum's heart. She kept that note on her dresser, never far from her side, every day after the coppers returned it. She couldn't stand the thought of him hanging himself as he did. She was the one who found him."

"Your mother's death entitled you to ownership of the land and cabin.""

"Yeah, it did. She had dementia, you know. You'd think she'd have forgotten Falcon and the circumstances of his death, like she'd forgotten everything else, but she didn't. It was the only memory she clung on to. It tortured mum. It's one of the reasons I came here—to take care of her. I decided to stay after she was gone. Live a quiet existence." He closes his eyes momentarily. "Mum died here in this cabin. She loved the wilderness. She was happy, happy in this home, right to the end."

"Was Morgan's name in the suicide note, like our records indicate?"

"I wouldn't know. I never read it. Couldn't bring myself to try and understand a single word. I harboured a lot of guilt over his passing. Do you think Morgan going missing has something to do with Falcon taking his life, his death?"

"It was our strongest lead. You were our strongest lead."

He flicks his wrist. "Nah. Nope. It had nothing to do with me. And anybody who knew Falcon would never wish harm upon Morgan. Not me, not a soul. There'd be no one harbouring any ill wishes toward her because of his death. Falcon was mentally disturbed." He places his finger to his temple and taps. "He had problems up in his head, extensive problems. He was wired wrong, I think, and for a long time he never shared what he was going through with his family, just his best mate. Lucky for us, Logan kept giving us updates about how he was travelling."

"They were that close?"

Winston nods. "Morgan didn't cause Falcon's death. Falcon did. He took his life. If anything, Morgan probably gave us more time with him than we would have had otherwise. He was much happier and stable when she was around." He pauses, then takes a long inhale. "I'm not gonna lie, even with her around, there still was this lonely, confused, and tortured boy inside him."

I drop the butt of my smoke to the wooden slats of the veranda and stomp until the cherry no longer burns.

"So are you taking me to the station, or are you going to let me see where this fire might be?"

"We'll take care of the fire. You need to give us a statement."

"Fine." Winston spits on his fingers and extinguishes his smoke between them. "Let me get my wallet and shit."

"Sure."

We conduct a one-hour search, and the house turns up nothing. My stomach drops. This isn't our guy. He doesn't even have a bloody television.

I feel like I'm back at square one. I've no idea who has Morgan, but I do know she's out here somewhere.

The sun is peeking out from behind the mountains and a blanket of light fans across the once-dark landscape. Daybreak is only moments away.

"Pull out," I call to the blue team. "We're going inland to search. Morgan's out here." At least we'll have light.

As quickly as I instruct them on our next move, we're heading for the cars. Here's hoping we're not too late.

"Astin, we have a big problem." My partner cups my arm and yanks me, causing me to stumble over my feet.

"What the fuck are you doing?" I'm shocked. Roland has never handled me in such a way.

"Listen," he barks through his teeth. "Shit has gone down. Reid is MIA in his father-in-law's four-wheel-drive. He has a passenger on board—his brother. John—you know the neighbour? He's just been placed under arrest and has been hauled down to the station. Shirley, his wife, is assisting with the investigation, and she's also down at the station. Lynette is holding the fort. Reid and Morgan's parents are caring for the children back at the Banks home, and we have four uniformed officers on-site with them. Max has a unit with him, and they're coming in our direction."

"When?" My body stiffens. My heart beats hard in my chest.

"This all went down about an hour ago. Look." He holds out his mobile phone. I start reading the messages.

"That's the address Reid's going to?" I snap as I point to the screen.

"Yes. The neighbours own that fucking cabin. Astin, this property didn't show up in our title search." He pauses, then shakes his head. "Shirley has advised that John has been communicating with the abductor. She overheard him having a phone conversation about it."

"Who is the abductor?"

"Shirley didn't know, and John hasn't said. They're grilling him down at the station, but he's giving nothing up."

"Fuck," I hiss. "So now we have two fucking civilians about to enter the field. Are they armed?"

Roland shakes his head. "We don't think so."

"Do they have a fucking death wish?"

I grasp my portable radio. "All teams, all teams, we have located the property where Morgan could be. We have two civilians, Reid and Cruise Banks en route to the cabin at sixty-seven Lane Road, Corbet's Landing. Team red, you're the closest. Get your arses there and make sure those two don't get themselves killed. This is a state of emergency. Everybody, move out."

Urgency overcomes us, and as I climb into the car, I already know that this won't end well, and someone's going to get killed. The question is, how many body bags are we going to need by the time it's all said and done? I can only hope we're in line for a miracle.

What the hell is Reid thinking? And how did he give Max the slip?

"Roland, get Max on the phone, now."

The sirens blare. Red and blue light the sky. We have three lives to protect.

This just made my job so much harder than it already was. Why didn't Reid trust that I'd bring her home?

Chapter Seventy-Two

Morgan

I'm frantic when a chill pricks my skin. I search with desperation. Where's my family? *Don't go. Don't leave me.*

My body feels as if it's floating. I lift.

"Help. Help me." There's no sound.

The distinct smell of petrol fills my nose. My eyes open only a crack and I see a flash of what looks to be a hand. Whose hand is that?

My bottom impacts with a hard surface.

Thump thump, ba boom, ba bump, lub-dub.

There is a heart beating calmly against my ear.

VooRRRR, vooRRR, vooRRR.

An engine revving has my head rolling.

The revving stops, replaced by an idle.

"How the fuck are you still alive? Now, this just pisses me off." There's so much anger, so much hatred in his tone.

The hairs on the back of my neck stand on end and a sense of doom rushes through my veins.

"Are you ready for the end?"

The wolf has found me. I'm the thirteenth victim in his fucked-up game, and I couldn't escape him. I tried so hard to get help, but I didn't do enough. I'm at the mercy of the wolf, and I've no energy left to fight.

I was his prey. He'd hunted me relentlessly, and now I'll be disposed of with all those other women who couldn't get away.

Chapter Seventy-Three

Reid

We've been driving for more than an hour. The adrenaline that was pumping through my body when I sped away from the house has settled somewhat. I no longer feel like I can lift trucks off toddlers, but I still feel like I can take down an armed murderer with only my bare hands.

Cruise hasn't spoken a word since we left the house, and neither have I, but each time I glimpse to the side of his head, I witness his jaw clench and see the strain popping the vein at his temple. There is no doubt that tension pulses rapidly through his blood.

One hundred and fifty-five—that's how fast the speedo tells me I'm travelling. I press my foot down slightly and watch the orange arrow shift to one hundred and seventy. We're on a straight road, and there's no traffic. However, that will change as soon as the sky grows even brighter. The thick black night we'd departed in has all but gone. Morning is now upon us, and that means traffic will soon be here, too.

"We don't have a weapon. We aren't even wearing shoes," Cruise says matter-of-factly, entirely out of the blue.

"We have a knife." I shrug.

He huffs.

"It's a weapon."

"A knife won't do shit. Why the fuck didn't we get shoes?"

I shrug again.

"Do you even have a plan?"

"To get Morgan."

Cruise drops his head and cradles it in his palms. "I'm calling the cops. We need their help."

"Sure, go ahead. Did you bring your phone?" I'm smug. I hear it in my tone.

He lifts his head, and when his eyes meet mine there's anger swirling in them. "No."

"Detective West has mine. Trust me, brother, we've got this. At least it's no longer dark."

"You're not thinking clearly. Reid, what if John hurt the kids?"

"Max would've heard us take off the moment we pulled this beast away from the footpath. I held that horn down the entire stretch of street, there's no way he didn't hear that. Shit, you know Mum would have if he didn't. She's the lightest sleeper we know." I nod, confirming my own thoughts. "Max would've seen the note. He'll get help. I trust him."

"And what if none of that has happened?"

"Shirley wouldn't let John hurt the kids. She loves them."

"John apparently loved your family, too."

My heart instantly aches. How could John betray us? Betray Morgan? He was a father and grandfather figure to our family. A pillar of strength. We'd built a foundation for our families on pure honesty and good morals. He was like blood. I thought our bond was unbreakable.

My hands grip the steering wheel as I think about John taking the call Shirley described. Did he set out to befriend us knowing that it would lead to this? Would he actually go as far as hurting our children?

"This is bullshit," I growl. "Shirley wouldn't let him hurt the kids. No. She wouldn't." *Who am I trying to convince? Cruise or myself?* My stomach drops with sudden and intense worry.

"How do you know Shirley isn't in on this as well? Right now, we could be driving straight into a trap, this could be a bloody set-up."

"Morgan is all that matters," I bark, hearing insanity entwined in my words.

Maybe I'm not doing the right thing. No—my instinct tells me this is what I have to do. Morgan doesn't have any time left. Max will have the kids. The coppers will already know we're on our way out to the cabin, and they will be in pursuit too.

But what if none of that's happened? What if Max or mum didn't wake and the kids are in danger? What if he hasn't told the cops the new location where they need to search for Morgan? Are we racing straight into a trap? Did I even think this through?

My mind jumbles with so many thoughts that I snarl out my frustration, and rip my hands from the steering wheel only to bang them back down again. "You said you'd help me, and if you're not going to, then you can get the fuck out of the car." I lift my foot from the accelerator and we instantly slow.

"I'll help you." Cruise sounds defeated in his response. "But Reid, brother, I want to protect you, too."

"I don't need protecting. Morgan does."

My foot hits the gas again.

Minutes pass. We're flying as we were before, and I still can't get my mind to settle. I'm trapped, walking a tightrope between right and wrong. Have I made a calculated decision, or have I let emotion cloud my ability to do so?

Wind suddenly blows my hair and causes me to blink excessively. "What are you doing?" I eye Cruise, wondering why in the world he's lowered the window.

"I needed fresh air."

"The air-conditioning is on."

"I need fresh air." He turns his head away from me.

A red car is coming, followed by a black one. I shift

my eyes to the rear-vision mirror only to see a white utility off in the distance. We're no longer alone on these streets, and soon we're going to be surrounded by traffic.

I press my foot harder against the accelerator and hope I can get to the cabin before the traffic boxes me in.

I need to get to Morgan before the police do, because I don't plan on leaving there without Morgan in my arms, safe and warm, or without the fucker who took her dead.

Chapter Seventy-Four

Morgan

I'm running so fast I feel as though I'm travelling at the speed of light, my legs don't tangle, or trip me over. How I'm able to run this fast and stay upright, after fighting for my freedom —prying myself from the strong hold of the wolf and throwing my body off the speeding quad bike—I can't fathom, yet I am.

I'm not where I once was. There's no destruction or burnt land around me. Instead, I'm in thick, green overgrown plants with another chance at liberty. I'm running for my life, for my family's future. I don't stop. I can't stop.

I've escaped him *again*, but I know he won't give up, even though I no longer hear an engine running like I could only moments ago.

Ahead, there's a beam of light that reminds me of sun rays bouncing off metal. I turn away from it, worried it's radiating from the quad bike, and that the wolf is sitting there waiting for me to run straight into his arms.

You can do this, Morgan. I tell myself as each foot pounds hard against the damp earth. My body feels ghostly as it ducks, weaves, and moves through trees that stand tall and protective. The farther I travel, the lighter my frame becomes.

Maybe I'm dead?

Did I die when I hurled myself from the wolf's hold and bounced along the ground? Or did that not happen? Is it possible I never regained consciousness in the first place to escape him?

These thoughts plague me, yet they don't deter me. I continue to run.

A breeze whips at my face, causing me to squeeze my eyes closed to the point where I can't see. I zag to my left, then circle until the breeze stings at my back instead. The beam of light I previously saw returns and I turn away from it once more.

I don't know which way to run.

I whimper.

Tears rush down my cheeks when a sharp pain sends hot spears down my spine. It squeezes my lungs like a vice, and I struggle to catch my breath. I drop onto my hands and knees and I scream, but there's no sound. I pant. *I'm alive.* And this agony now ripping through me is all the proof I need of my existence.

Please let me breathe. My stomach sucks in under my ribcage. Each gasp I take rattles. I can barely stand the pain. I'm going to pass out again.

I can't. Fight, Morgan. I open my mouth wide and tilt my chin back, so my airway expands. I pant, I pant rapidly, willing oxygen to find me as I seek it. It doesn't. Silent tears drip from my chin as I fight to survive …

And then, as quickly as the pain knocked the air from my lungs, it's gone.

I take one big breath, then another, then I splutter and cough until I don't, and I've caught my breath.

Slowly, I roll my shoulders back. I'm taking all my weight on my knees. They burn, they burn fiercely, so I drop back down and crawl until I manage to stumble to my feet. I amble forward, then shuffle … I achieve a jog … and I run. I don't dare look back. I don't dare slow down. I move as fast as my legs can take me.

Bang!

A gunshot rings out.

He will find me.

I can't fight him.

I'm running out of time.

"Let me go home. I've answered the puzzle, Falcon. It's you!" I cry with despair, my abductor hot on my heels, his presence easy to sense even though I can't hear his footsteps or feel him breathing down my neck.

"Morgan, oh Morgan. Where are you?" His eerie tone could freeze the healthiest of beating hearts, and upon hearing him, I scream, yet I don't stop moving.

I don't want to die.

Swerving to my right, then to my left gives me the sense I'm running in circles. I jump at the sight of a shadow, then dig my feet into the ground. I halt, turn and run back the way I came. *Keep it together, Morgan. Do or die.* Loud and forceful breaths part my lips.

"You know I love a good cat-and-mouse chase, Red." The anger he once harboured is gone. He's calm, much too calm, considering I'd smashed the back of my skull into his face so he'd release the strong grip he held me in, and I could throw myself off his damn quad bike.

A silhouette appears in the distance. I turn and run back the way I'd come.

"Oh, this is going to be so much fun for me, Red. Did you think you could hide and get away with it? Did you think you could win?"

I stifle my need to scream.

"What did you think of the fire show? I can't believe you survived that fucker." His awful and sadistic laugh booms, and I cringe before changing my direction to the opposite way from which his voice travels.

He's close, too close, and his heckling only motivates me to move faster.

"I spy, with my little eye, a little mouse that's about to die." He taunts.

I jerk my head until I peer over my shoulder. I can't see him, and as leaves whip my legs and arms, I turn my eyes forward and try to go faster. Hot spikes prick my neck and travel down my spine. I hiss through my teeth and throw my head back to fight the pain. A million ants march inside me, pinching my internal organs. I groan and stumble over my feet, but I don't fall. I keep going.

Thump, thump, thump. A pounding throb bashes inside my skull and leaves behind a hellish ache. My feet tangle when I bring my hand to my brow, but I don't let it knock me down. I keep running, until the bushland echoes with my deafening scream. My eyes are wide. My feet are cemented to the spot. My heart pounds to a techno beat.

He wears a black ski mask, long black pants, and a long-sleeved T-shirt. A rifle is hanging from his hand, and a large hunting knife is slipped through his belt, secured in a leather holster. I can't freeze now.

He smiles, steps forward, then lunges his arms in my direction.

"No! No!" I yell. "Noooooo!" I shriek as I shift to my right and bolt between a row of thick tree trunks that catch the corner of my eye.

A small hill fills my vision. A familiar sound has my neck extended and my head bouncing from side to side. The noise grows closer and louder. I've been dreaming of running engines or a loud honking horn. I can hear both.

The highway.

I can't see any road, but I desperately try to imagine what it will look like as I track with a faster pace toward the noise that is plainly traffic.

"Morgan, oh Morgan. Can you feel the rush? Isn't this wonderful?" he heckles from behind me.

Hoooonk. Hoooonk.

Do I hear cars? Or is my mind playing tricks on me? Is this a part of the game? My body shakes with periodic tremors.

Don't stop. Run. Don't look back. It's the only option I have. If what I hear isn't real, then I will die today. If it is, I might have a chance to survive.

"This is the best part, Red. Hunting you, and I'm sad this will be our last time. Aren't you?"

I whip my head over my shoulder to gauge how close the wolf is. I screech as my legs jumble and I crash down. The sound of scattering birds from high above has me scurrying on my hands and knees, crawling like a dog, trying to find my feet.

I'm so tired. I don't want to run. I don't get a choice.

Death is lurking behind me. Freedom could be in front of me. I roar as I pull myself up until I'm standing.

"Boo."

I gasp when I see him standing right in front of me.

His lips spread into a broad smile. His blue eyes gaze into mine. "Give up, Red."

"Please, just let me go." My voice rattles. I know he has no intention of letting me escape. Every clue, every test, everything I've endured tells me this has all been part of a game intended to claim my life. It's what he came here to do, and when I'm gone, he'll win. "Please, Falcon, I never meant to hurt you. Don't punish me for this. Why now? Why now?" I cry out, as the sound of cars becomes even more readily heard.

"It's time to go to sleep, Red."

"No," I cry.

He reaches out his gloved hand in the way a parent would to a scared child.

I shake my head.

He laughs.

"Please, let me go," I beg.

Bang! Bang! Bang!

Three loud gunshots ring out in the distance, and when Falcon turns, rotating his body to look behind him, he mutters, "Fucking hunters."

I swing away from his hand and take off.

There's a small clearing in front of a steep incline. Oh, God. I can't make it up this. I moan before I see a glimpse of the freeway over its top. A red car passes by.

"Oh my God," I whimper as my mind screams at me to climb the fucking incline. With every bit of strength and energy I can muster, I press forward. I run like my life depends on me doing so, because it does. My life comes down to this climb.

He whistles. I can hear it coming from behind me. It's almost as clear as the cars whizzing by. I cry. I cry so hard my shoulders shake with the force. I slip. I lose my footing. I reach out my arms to help stop myself from falling, and I scrunch my hands into the dry earth to gain traction.

Morgan, you're there. Climb, for the love of God ...

climb.

My fingers dig into the natural flora, gripping handfuls of dirt, scratching, pulling to regain a grip. My torso hunches and my toes curl as I push down hard with my legs. The road is so close the tyres passing by are sending the smell of rubber and asphalt up my nose.

I scream with every bit of air I can force behind the noise. "Help! Help me! Help!"

My bare feet keep sliding, and I clamber on, finding traction where I can.

"Here, mousey, mousey." He lets me hear his footsteps. He wants me to know he's here.

Please, no. Please.

"No ... no ... no." My voice quakes with fear as my heart thumps wildly in my chest. "Let me go." Tears fall as my panic builds to the highest level I've ever experienced. "Please."

His fingers snatch my ankle, then he applies pressure. I scramble and kick to free myself, but it's not working.

I scream a primal scream as I fight, terrified and desperate. "Let me go, Falcon."

He snatches my other ankle. He tightens his grip around both. His fingers dig into what feels like my bones. I buck my body in response to the agony I'm experiencing, then reach down with my hands, trying to rip his fingers from my legs, but he holds on firmly.

I'm sobbing as he drags me like a rag doll back down the incline and away from the road, the road I'd worked so desperately to reach. His actions seem effortless. His breath isn't even laboured. He's much too strong for me. This game is over. It ends now. He wins.

"HELP! Somebody, help me," I cry in a last attempt to summon a saviour.

His lips are stretched into a smile when I look up at his mask. His eyes have no mercy. "It's over, Red. It's over."

I don't relax. I continue to buck and scream in the hope that someone, anyone, will hear me.

The sound of the leaves separating and being destroyed beneath me as he drags my body across the ground will be the last sound I hear. He offers no mercy for my ankles as his fingers continue to dig into my raw skin. He whistles his eerie tune, and although I'm bucking my body and twisting against him with everything I've got, it's pointless because he remains in control.

He drops my legs, and even though my mind shouts at me to get up and run I'm unable to move. The sky, a brilliant blue, is so clear I can't see a single cloud. I stare, keeping my eyes attached to the vision, and as I do I decide that no matter how painful things become, or how frightened I am as I die, I will think of this sky and remember how my life was once as vibrant as it is.

I heave each breath with rising panic. Tears drip from the corners of my eyes as I let my exhaustion finally take over and accept that this is what it is—a game I can't win no matter how hard I try. I want more than anything to be stronger, to try harder, but I've conceded the fact that this will be the end of my life.

His masked face invades my view as he stands above me. My chest rises and then falls with force. I try not to whimper out loud, but it proves impossible and a wounded sound projects from my parted lips. Blue eyes that should belong to an angel, become too much to look at, so I don't. Instead, I close my eyes and block him from my vision.

"Look at me."

I focus on each frantic breath I take.

"Red, look at me now." He raises his voice.

"No." It's barely audible.

"Look at me, or I'll pry your eyes open and rip your eyeballs from your head."

I cry.

"Now," he snaps.

I flutter my eyelids open to be faced with irises that are large and gleaming with satisfaction. He's disguised so much of himself, but this enjoyment, the one causing his eyes to smile down at me, this is as plain as day to see.

"Well, Morgan, here we are." He leans farther over me. "The hunt for you has been more exciting than I could have hoped for. You did better than I expected. I feel pride for unlocking some fight in you." He takes a deep breath. "But as always, you had to go and fuck everything up."

I hate this man, a man I once lusted for, more than

anything. The one I cared to write to for years after we parted ways. If I could find the strength to lift my leg right now, I'd kick him in his balls and then rip his fucking head off with my bare hands.

"How did you like my game, Morgan? Was it fun?" His words are filled with derision.

I say nothing, and concentrate on the few final breaths that will part from my lips.

"Oh, no. The cat got your tongue again?"

The sound of cars racing by drowns out my breathing. "I hate you," I manage to sob.

"And I fucking loathe you." A bellowing laugh follows as he digs the butt of his rifle into the ground and uses it as an aid to lower himself until he's straddling my waist, his weight cutting the blood supply to my legs. *Is he hurt?*

"You're a monster." It's a hushed whisper.

His eyes narrow. "Well, that's true." There's an unexpected anger in his tone. "This is your last chance to leave here alive. Are you ready to answer my final question?"

He holds the rifle an inch from my nose.

My breath launches into my throat. "Yes." It's barely audible.

"Who am I, Red?"

My lips quiver. "Falcon Sampson," I whisper, sniffing back tears.

He removes his weight from my waist until he's pulled himself upright and *towers* above me with his rifle aimed between my eyes. "Wrong answer,

Morgan," he finally says when I regather my sight.

How can that be?

"You're lying." My voice shakes.

"Morgan, Morgan, Morgan. How stupid are you really? How the fuck could I be Falcon? You tell me."

Confusion rushes through my mind like a jet in pursuit of invasion. "It's you."

"You know shit, Morgan. Shut your stupid mouth," he spits, pressing the barrel of the rifle hard into my forehead.

Every muscle in my body tenses as I become too scared to breathe.

"Falcon is dead, and if you ever cared for him you would have known that."

"Please stop," I yell with my hands wrapping around the end of his gun.

"You killed him, Morgan."

"I didn't. You have the wrong person. I didn't even know he died. I've never taken a life."

"Oh yes, you have. You destroy lives. You killed him, and now you'll pay and suffer just like he had to." The rifle that could blast my life away with one pull of its trigger is yanked from my grip and shifted from my head. He lifts one leg and presses his boot lightly onto my chest. "Who am I, Morgan?"

"I don't know," I cry.

He shoves his foot down harder against my sternum, which threatens to crumble under the weight. "You were supposed to remember your wrongs, but you fucked up my game. You fucked up my life. You fucked up everything." He pauses. "If you had let me put you through all the tests I had set up for you, then you would know now that you deserve it. You'd be wanting me to kill you, begging me to."

"Please, let me go," I pant, winded. The need to fire words of hatred fills me, but I can't speak because the pressure of his boot against my chest increases to the point where air doesn't seem to be able to enter my throat.

"Who am I, Morgan?" he asks again, but I have no idea who the hell he is. He lifts his foot from my chest only to stomp it down beside my head, causing me to jolt. He nestles the rifle under his armpit. "Will this give you the answer?"

He uses his free hand to reach down to the bottom of the mask he wears. Slowly, he peels it back. Blond stubble covers his chin, and when the mask finally parts from his head I see his thick blond locks.

I swallow a loud gulp.

"Well." His lips stretch across his face.

"The ... the ... you're ... I never... I've never done anything to you."

"Are you sure?" His straight white teeth become more visible as his smile grows. "Who am I?"

"You're from the news." I'm confused. I don't know this man other than through my television set.

"Am I though?" His thick, light eyebrows dip inwards.

I cry.

"I mean, that's one of my jobs. But this will make

you see." He slides his hand down his side until he reaches the bottom of his shirt. With one hand, he jerks the material from his body.

I gasp.

Inked skin. Blues, greens, yellows, and oranges all sit inside the black lines of a large tattooed jester taking up the right-hand side of his chest. I know the cheeky smile on its face, and the hook-shaped keloid scar above the jester's hat. That scar was caused in an accident from a boat's propeller. Finally, I have my answer.

Life is just a circus. The words are written under the tattoo. I shriek in horror and screw my eyes tightly shut to try delete the image.

"Who am I?" he speaks softly.

"Logan!" I croak out. I want to say more, but I choke on my own tongue.

"Logan Raffety the Third, to be precise," he chortles. "Known to all in this bullshit town, and all over, in fact, as Gregory Stiles from Channel Sixty-One."

"Why? Why are you doing this, Logan? Why are your eyes blue and not brown? Why do you look like this?"

"For you. I came to get payback." He lowers himself down until he kneels with either leg on each side of my torso.

"I didn't do—"

"I watched you break Falcon. I was left with the pathetic man he became after you walked away. He showed you who he really was, and you ran for the fucking hills. You're a whore. A worthless bitch, like all women are," he snaps. "You destroyed him. Those fucking letters—why couldn't you have let him be? No, you wanted your cake and to eat it too, didn't you?" Spittle lands on my cheek.

"After you forced Falcon to kill himself, my life was never the same. Nothing was the same. He was my best friend. The three of us were inseparable until you decided to move on, to go to university then dump us for that dumb fuck husband of yours. I tried to save Falcon, but I couldn't do it alone. I couldn't save him." He leans into me. "Drugs became my escape. Everyone I loved disowned me because of who I had become as a result of your actions .... It's all your fault, Morgan. You. You're responsible for everything. Those twelve other women who broke hearts, who took men for granted, stole from them, used them, just like you did to Falcon—their deaths are on your head."

I can't stop shaking.

"You're evil, Morgan."

"You were my friend," I manage to whisper.

"Pfft! Friends, yes, once, but you left and never looked back. He showed you. He gave you all of him." His eyes narrow. "And you walked away. That's not what a friend does. Where were you when he died? Where? Not back home. Not at his funeral. Nowhere."

"I-I didn't know. I swear." I'm petrified.

"You never should have left him."

"Falcon wouldn't want you to do this to me," I

plead, hoping he'll realise this to be true.

"He would, Morgan. He couldn't do it himself, but I have more balls than that broken-down man you left behind. Instead of taking my life, I've taken the lives of the people who were really responsible—bitches like you." His anger booms into an evil rage.

"Please, please! I didn't know. Don't kill me, Logan. I don't deserve to die."

He throws the gun onto the ground. Blue eyes, eyes that look just as Falcon's did, stare into mine. "You do deserve it, Red. Shut up!" A small vein protrudes from his forehead. "You had to be number thirteen. You know, as a tribute for my fallen friend." His nose crinkles as he smiles. "Justice is about to be served."

The sound of wailing sirens fills the air.

"Help!" I scream. "Help me."

He smothers my mouth with his hand. "You treat everybody you meet like shit. You treated your husband like shit, too. He's better off without you." He has angry eyes and a devilish frown to match. "I've been watching you, Morgan. You and your family. I've seen everything that goes on in your house. I've heard it all and seen everything."

"You hear that, Logan?" The sirens grow louder, more urgent. "You can kill me, but the police will know it's you," I mutter against his palm.

He shakes his head. "You really are stupid. Aren't you? They're not coming for me. They, too, have been playing a game, and their clues lead right to Winston. You remember him, don't you? Falcon's brother. He's about to spend the rest of his life in prison for not protecting his brother. I didn't forget him when it came to my punishment. I was more family to Falcon than his own flesh and blood." He removes his hand from my lips. I take a needy breath.

"They'll figure it out," I say breathless.

He laughs. "I was a fucking cop, Morgan, before you destroyed my life and I had to do all this to my face. Before I had to move from Melbourne to this shithole. I know what I'm doing, you dumb bitch. People are stupid. Your husband, for example." A wicked grin is all I see. "That dickhead has left your children with my uncle. You really made this so easy for me, moving in next door to them. Uncle John knows what you've done, what you stole from me. He knows who's to blame for my fall from grace. He didn't abandon me, because he loves me."

My eyes are bug wide. Vomit seduces the back of my throat. Time stands still. *Aleeha. Brax. They're in danger.*

"Oh, don't worry that ugly little face of yours. I probably won't hurt them. After all, they didn't do anything wrong—it's not their fault they were birthed by you."

My tears begin to stream at thoughts of John, my friend, someone who was like a father to me, who'd known all along that this would be my fate.

"You're insane, Logan. Reid will find you. He'll figure it out. Mark my words, you'll see your end."

Logan's hand reaches for mine, and before I can

snatch it away he clutches my middle finger. "Don't say his name."

Crack!

"Fuuuuuuck!" I wail. "Oh fuck!" I suck air through my teeth as a fierce throb creeps up my arm.

"Time to die, Red."

Don't let him do this. Fight, God damn it! Morgan, fight. Your babies are in danger.

I scream. I don't stop screaming.

Chapter Seventy-Five

Reid

The grass stands waist-high. Trees surround us in every direction. Cruise is a metre in front of me, and all I keep thinking is he's taking me on a wild goose chase and we're wasting our time.

Before we stopped the car and took to the bushland, we were not far from the turn-off that would have led us to the cabin. I shouldn't have followed Cruise down here. I don't believe he heard anyone crying for help at all. Maybe this is a ploy to give the police more time to get to Morgan instead of me. After all, Cruise hasn't stopped pointing out how under-prepared we are to be entering such an environment with no idea of what we're walking into.

"Just listen," he says for the third time.

I do, but I hear nothing.

Cruise walks forward. The sun beats down on my brow. It's so hot in here, it's like the pit of hell. I stay still, contemplating leaving Cruise behind and racing back to the car now idling on the shoulder of the highway above us.

"Come on." His arm flicks in the air, indicating that he wants me to follow.

"I don't hear anything," I snap.

"I heard screaming. I swear, I heard it."

I glimpse a flicker of light, but then it's gone. My eyes narrow as I explore the area from which it had beamed. I can't see anything apart from tree after tree.

This is pointless.

A woman's high-pitched scream beats against my eardrums. I search for Cruise, and run, as he does. Hot air fills my lungs, cramping them. I push through the pain and a heat-filled airway and continue to race in the direction of the screaming we just heard.

I stop when I hear the voice of a male coming from the direction we're heading. Cruise stops also. We squat, side-by-side in the long grass and listen.

I can't understand what's being said. I jump to my feet and take off only to be crash-tackled to the ground. My mouth is covered. My body is pinned.

Cruise places his finger to his lips with one hand while he continues to cover my mouth with the other.

"We are unarmed," he whispers against my cheek.

I don't give a shit that we're unarmed. I don't give

a shit if I die, as long as Morgan doesn't, and Cruise is here to make sure that doesn't happen.

I bite his hand. He shows his teeth as he traps the bark I know he wants to let out behind them.

"For me. Do this for me," I mouth.

Cruise nods.

"If it's Morgan on the other side of this hill, you save her, you hear me? Get her out of here and don't look back," I say in a strained whisper.

Cruise nods. "I'll save her. Promise."

"Get off me."

"We move slowly, okay? Until we can get a visual."

"Okay."

We both stalk in approach. I have no idea what we're about to face when we climb over the huge overgrown hill in front of us, but if Morgan is on the other side, together, we can save her.

Chapter Seventy-Six

Morgan

I spit into Logan's face. He stands abruptly, hovering above me and wiping the saliva from his cheek.

"Fuck you," I sneer, kicking my leg upright into his groin. His face reddens as he crumbles. I roll out of the way of his falling limbs.

Run, Morgan. NOW!

I pull my protesting body upright and begin stumbling back toward the incline, my legs pumping, pounding hard against the earth.

"Help! Somebody please. Help!" I scream.

It takes mere seconds until my head is flung backwards. A clump of my hair tugged hard. My body follows. He drags me down. I try to twist away. He readjusts his grip and pulls my splayed and aching body along the ground. A huffed sound expels from my lips. I lie there, gasping, when he again straddles my waist.

"No. Fuck you, Morgan." He smiles, with his hands grasping either side of my lengthened neck, before he applies pressure to my throat. "You will die like Falcon. He hung himself, you bitch, and you'll face the same strangling death."

His hands tighten, choking me. I can feel the blood pooling in my face as I desperately scratch at his arms. Colours dance in front of my eyes as my vision is obscured, all bar his eyes. I can't breathe. I'm dying.

"Morgan. Nooooooo!" The roar of my name pounds in my head before the crazed eyes that bore down at me disappear. Strong hands remain firm, pressing harder into my neck. My head spins, then fogs. Black. Everything turns black.

I gasp frantically. I scratch at my neck. My mouth is wide. *Get off me. Get off me.*

"Run, Morgan. Run." Pure urgency comes with these words.

I can't run. I'm trying to get Logan off me, but soon I realise he's no longer on me at all. I roll onto my side until I flip onto my stomach. My cheek digs into the ground. I draw one loud, gurgling breath before darkness swallows me.

I hear scuffling, but I can't open my eyes.

"You need to run, Morgan. Get Morgan. Get Morgan." *Reid.*

Thump!

I flick my eyelids open. Two blurred objects roll in my direction.

"Move, Morgan! Go!" More words are yelled at me. "Get Morgan. Get her out of here."

I cry hearing the voice of my husband yelling.

"Reid." I make no sound.

Relief washes over me before it's replaced with a gut-wrenching panic. Is my husband now in the hands of the wolf?

Chapter Seventy-Seven

Reid

"Cruise, get Morgan out of here." I'm desperate as I'm pulled under the shirtless man who I saw strangling my wife.

"I can't leave you," Cruise yells.

Fuck!

Blue eyes, light blond stubble, and hair—it's Greg, the reporter who came into our home and conducted an interview about the disappearance of Morgan.

"You fucking prick." I swing my fist only to wince from the pain shooting up my side.

He spits in my face before he jerks away from me. I jump to my feet, clutching again at my side, just in time to see his fist connect with Cruise's jaw.

"I'm going to kill you." I throw myself at Greg who

towers over Cruise with his chest puffed out. My head turns as wide as the arm swinging towards it, but I manage to duck quickly as I suck air in through my teeth.

Bang! Bang!

Two loud gunshots fill the air. I still.

So does he.

"Get on the ground and put your motherfucking hands behind your back." Cruise's tone is not laced with fear. Instead, it's full of control and confidence.

I look in his direction, briefly, just long enough to see the rifle he has pointed into the sky. "Do it now."

Where did he get a rifle from?

Sirens sound, and as they do, white flashes of anger make me growl like a tiger about to devour his prey. I whip my head and watch as Greg lowers himself until he's perched on his knees.

"Holy shit, Reid, you're bleeding. You're bleeding."

"Get Morgan out of here. Leave this to me," I yell.

"No. Brother, you're bleeding from your stomach."

I turn my eyes downwards. There's a slash in my T-shirt. Blood covers the material surrounding it. I look to the ground. There's a knife with blood staining its blade. *The fucker cut me.*

"We walk out of here together." Cruise is stoic in the way he says this.

I take two steps towards Greg, whose eyes connect with mine. I grind my teeth as I swing my leg backwards and then kick it straight into his jaw. He falls onto his back from the force. I pant as another rip-roaring pain splits my side. "He leaves in a body bag."

"No," Cruise barks. "I have a gun to protect us, and the cops are coming."

I hover over Greg. Blood drips from his lip. He launches himself upright, so I drop onto my knees until my weight presses against his chest, knowing full well Cruise won't shoot me. I mimic the position I found this pig in when I came racing towards him and he was on top of my wife.

I shift my eyes to Morgan who lies on her stomach, with one side of her bloated, bloodied face dug into the earth. Her eyes are sealed shut. Her hair is matted and singed. She's not moving, or speaking, or reacting. A tear rolls from the corner of my eye and skirts my cheek.

This bastard is leaving here in a body bag.

Greg swings his fist, but I pull my head back in time. Without thought I wrap my fingers around either side of his thick neck.

"Reid. Let him go. Get off him."

I can hear Cruise's panic. However, I feel none. I'm completely void of thought or sensation.

A blast of gunfire sounds. I don't even jolt.

With all my might, I drive my weight against Greg's airway. His eyes bulge from the immediate pressure. His face quickly fills with blood and becomes the shade of a ripened cherry. I glare at him through animalistic eyes. I want his last breath. I want him to pay for what he's done.

"Reid. Get off him." This time it's not my brother who demands this of me, it's Constable Max Maloney.

I don't search for him. I don't shift my position either. Instead, I keep my eyes glued to the man who has tortured and maimed my wife. Morgan's beaten and bruised, lying lifeless on the ground not far from me, and the sight of her has me picturing a woman I met laid out on a table inside the Rockhampton morgue. This man is a murderer. A torturer. A villain. He's worthless and shouldn't get the privilege of life. I must take his life to save others. To get justice.

"Get on the ground, Reid, and place your hands behind your head. Do it now." Maloney's wasting his breath. I'm not leaving here alive, not if Greg does.

"RK-147, we need all units. All units." *Dusty.* I recognise his voice immediately. "We've found Morgan Banks. We need all units."

An anger I've never known swirls in the pit of my stomach, forcing itself into my heart before exploding through my lips in a tortured sound.

He gargles. He's trying to pry my fingers from his throat, but I keep forcing my weight down until I no longer feel Greg's chest rising beneath my legs.

"Cruise, drop the rifle. Reid, get off him, and get on the ground or I'll shoot," Max shouts.

Another gargling sound exits Greg's throat, and then his body falls limp beneath me.

Pride warms my skin, and as I slowly release my grip, I breathe. It strikes me like a harsh spark of electricity that I can't remember taking a single breath while I strangled the devil now lying motionless.

"Reid. Get on the ground and put your hands behind your head." Maloney is shouting so loudly it beats across my brow.

I hear his instruction and lift my body until I reposition myself, kneeling on the ground beside Greg. He doesn't move. His chest doesn't rise.

I killed him. He's dead. And I feel calm.

I place one hand, two hands to the back of my head, linking my fingers, and I breathe like a weight I've been carrying for days, one too heavy to carry in the first place, has been lifted from my shoulders.

"What have you done?" The worry in Max's tone doesn't extinguish the pride that fills my core. An eye for an eye. He had to pay. I made him pay. I've no guilt, no remorse burdening me. I'm free.

Heavy footsteps approach from behind. I don't look in that direction. Instead, I shift my eyes to my wife lying unmoving on the ground. I defended my family and got revenge for Morgan, and for the woman who laid in that morgue, unrecognisable. I'm not a sinner. I'm a saviour. I did the right thing.

A weak cough has my eyes widening.

"Morgan, open your eyes." Cruise kneels down behind her. He gently brushes her cheek with the back of his hand.

She coughs again.

My heart sprints. My head whirls. *Morgan's alive.*

"She's breathing." Cruise isn't facing me when he

says this. He's looking past me. Why isn't he looking at me?

My heart launches into the back of my throat. My body trembles. Tears flood my face. "Morgan."

"Try not to touch her, Cruise. The ambulance is en route."

Dusty steps into view. He's dressed in full police uniform as he crouches down beside Morgan and places two fingers against her neck. He's quick to snatch them back when a blood-piercing scream escapes her throat. The noise she makes has my body shuddering.

"Don't. You're scaring her," I bark, panicked.

Again, Dusty moves his hand to touch her neck.

"Leave her alone." I drop my arms and crawl towards her.

"Put your hands behind your head." Maloney's pissed. "I will shoot you."

I halt.

"Reid." It's barely audible, but I hear Morgan call my name.

I crook my neck and search for Maloney behind me. *"Please,"* I mouth.

He shakes his head. His pistol is aimed right at me. "Lay on the ground."

Morgan coughs once more, and then she cries. It's a cry filled with pain, fear, and desperation. I want to hold her. I'm helpless.

"Reid, please, just do what he says. I've got her. I'm right here. I won't leave her, brother."

Silent tears rush from my eyes as I lie until my chest and my cheek press against the ground. I keep my head turned towards Morgan's face. Her eyes are closed. Her lips are peeled, cut and swollen. Blood covers her skin.

"I'm here, baby," I speak softly so as not to startle her. *What have I done?* Sliding my hand through the leaves, I wince, but continue to extend it as far as I can. I'm still quite a way from being able to touch Morgan.

"Reid Banks, you're under arrest. Put your hands behind your back."

"No," I mumble, keeping my arm right where it is. "Sorry, Max. I can't."

Morgan's eyes shoot open. They're no longer the chestnut I once admired. They're washed of colour, a horrible honey with grey hues.

"I won't leave you again. I promise. I love you." My lips quiver. My heart thuds.

She doesn't say a word. She just stares as tears fill her eyes.

"He can't hurt you anymore."

Morgan closes her eyes.

"You're safe. I'm right here. I'm not going anywhere."

Her eyes spring open again, and the look she delivers me speaks of a thousand horrific tales. I want to erase Morgan's memory so she never has to remember a moment of what she's endured.

"The kids are fine. They're safe." I have no idea if this is true, but if Maloney's here, then they must be.

He wouldn't have left them in harm's way. Not after the stories he's shared with me about his own daughter. Leaving my children would go against all Max was trained to do, would go against the oath he took when becoming an officer of the law.

"The ambulance is coming, Morgan," Dusty says.

She squeezes her eyes closed and scrunches her face before trembling.

"You're fucking scaring her." Anger rips through my core. "Get away from her."

"I agree." Cruise's tone quivers. "You are scaring her."

"Back off," Max orders. "Call dispatch and find out how far the ambulance is from arrival. Also, get them to pass on our coordinates to Detective West. We need back-up. I have them covered."

Dusty backs away slowly until I can no longer see him.

"Let me go to her." I hold my breath, hoping for a little salvation from Max.

"You can't touch her. Everything on her body is evidence, Reid. Hell, you're fucking evidence now."

"She's a human being who's hurt. Don't make her hurt alone."

"Fuck," he curses.

"Please," I beg as I watch Cruise stroke Morgan's cheek with the back of his hand.

"It's Cruise, Morgan. I'm right behind you."

She opens her eyes.

"Max." I raise my voice, and Morgan jumps.

"Okay. Just try not to touch her too much." I see the conflict in Max's expression.

Inch by inch, I slide my body across the leaves. I trap my need to groan behind my teeth. An intense sting slices my stomach over and over.

I stop when our faces sit just a few centimetres from each other. "Hey, baby." I lift my hand and take the place of my brother, stroking her cheek. "Help is on the way. You can rest now. You're safe."

Her eyelashes flicker before her eyes close.

Chapter Seventy-Eight

Morgan

I'm swallowed by darkness, but I fight. I fight to keep my eyes open, and when I'm met with tears streaming down my husband's cheeks, I know I've won again.

In my mind, I'm speaking. I'm yelling. I'm telling him I hurt so bad I can't stand it a minute longer. But I can't manage to get those words to travel from my brain and connect with my lips.

His fingers brush against my skin, back and forth, back and forth. I can feel Reid's touch, but I can't respond. I'm not able to move a single muscle in my body. I've no control. I'm as heavy as lead.

"You're safe, Morgan. Help is coming. I'm here." There's so much fear in Reid's words, and although I know I'm not alone in this bushland, I don't believe I'm really safe.

I jolt when the dirt below me suddenly feels as if it's falling away. I reach out my arm and grab onto Reid to stop myself from falling, or so I think. My arm hasn't moved at all and I remain paralysed.

Panic rockets through each of my nerve endings. The ground continues to tug away. I'm falling, and there's nothing I can do to stop it.

Is Reid falling too? Help! Help!

My heart races. My stomach sinks and then I hear one intense beat of my heart in my head. I take a breath. I listen for my heartbeat. I can't hear it beating. I can't feel it beating either.

Reid fades away, and then he disappears altogether. A white light fills the space he took in front of me. I'm no longer in pain or consumed with fear. I'm as light as a feather.

And finally, a sensation of peace washes over me.

I'm free.

Chapter Seventy–Nine

Reid

Maloney keeps Morgan's chin pointed upwards and her nose pinched. Cruise cups one hand on top of the other and commences pounding on Morgan's chest.

"One. Two. Three. Four. Five. Six. Seven. Eight. Nine. Ten. Eleven. Twelve. Thirteen. Fourteen. Fifteen. Sixteen. Seventeen. Eighteen. Nineteen. Twenty. Twenty-one. Twenty-two. Twenty-three. Twenty-four. Twenty-five. Twenty-six. Twenty-seven. Twenty-eight. Twenty-nine. Thirty." Cruise is huffing when he straightens.

Maloney closes his mouth around Morgan's and breathes. I watch as her chest rises and then falls.

"One. Two. Three. Four. Five. Six. Seven. Eight. Nine. Ten. Eleven. Twelve. Thirteen. Fourteen. Fifteen. Sixteen. Seventeen. Eighteen. Nineteen. Twenty. Twenty-one. Twenty-two. Twenty-three. Twenty-four. Twenty-five. Twenty-six. Twenty-seven. Twenty-eight. Twenty-nine. Thirty." Cruise counts for the seventh time. He's sweating and puffing excessively.

Maloney again places his mouth over Morgan's and breathes for her. "Come on, Morgan," he roars.

I watch her chest rise and then fall.

Cruise places his ear to Morgan's chest. "No heartbeat." He repositions his hands. "One. Two. Three. Four. Five. Six. Seven. Eight. Nine. Ten. Eleven. Twelve. Thirteen. Fourteen. Fifteen. Sixteen. Seventeen. Eighteen. Nineteen. Twenty." Cruise stops counting, but he doesn't stop compressing Morgan's chest. "Thirty." He falls back on his heels.

Maloney leans in, closes his mouth over Morgan's, and again delivers his breath to her.

"Fucking breathe. Breathe, Morgan." I'm desperate. I can't take it a minute more. Why has her heart stopped beating? Why isn't she breathing?

Sirens wail. The roar of motorbikes has me shooting my vision towards the bushland. Men wearing black police vests race towards us.

"Help is here," I shout.

Within the blink of an eye, officers, and then paramedics appear. Morgan's still not breathing, but at least now we have help.

Don't let go, Morgan. Fight. You're almost home.

Chapter Eighty

Reid

"It's just a flesh wound. You'll need to have these stitches removed in ten days." The curly-haired doctor, old enough to be my grandfather, says.

"How's my wife?" I'm pleading with him to give me an answer because my aggressive barks at Detective West don't seem to be working.

He smooths a dressing over the place my stomach once bled. "I'll leave you to it."

The doctor gives his attention to Detective West and Gleaton, who stand beside him.

Fucking dick. Why won't anybody tell me anything apart from my children are safe and my family are here?

I tense my muscles and as I do, the metal of the handcuffs rattles against the bars of the hospital bed I'm secured to.

"Are you going to cooperate?" West glares at me as if I'm scum. The smell of stale nicotine and coffee on his breath makes me want to shove my fist down his throat. If only I could escape these binds.

"Are you going to tell me how my wife is?" I snap.

"Answer our questions."

"Answer mine."

The hospital bed I'm in isn't even surrounded by walls. Instead, it's surrounded by blue curtains that are pulled closed.

"Reid, we need your statement."

I'll give you a statement. My foot straight up your arse. Who in the hell arrests a man whose wife is dying in front of their eyes? That's what I'd like to know. Not only was I ripped away from Morgan when the men in black arrived, I was thrown in the back of an ambulance without her, wearing a pair of handcuffs.

"You've taken a life. You've been arrested for manslaughter. This is serious. I told you to trust me. You didn't. Now, help me, help you."

"Trust you. Pfft. If it wasn't for me getting to Morgan she would never have been found. You want to help me? Then tell me how my wife is. Tell me if she's alive. I just want to know if she's alive. Please." I look into West's grey eyes hoping this time he'll tell me what I want to hear: that they'd restarted her heart, and she's okay.

"Logan Raffety. Did you know he was a nephew of John's?"

"Logan Raffety." What the fuck does John's apparent nephew have to do with the price of eggs in China? Never met the man. Didn't even know he existed.

"He's responsible for Morgan's kidnapping and subsequent …" West doesn't continue.

"The fucking news reporter did it. I should know. I strangled …" I don't say another word.

"Gregory Stiles and Logan Raffety are the same man. Now, did you know John's nephew Logan or not?"

"Nope. Didn't know he had a nephew."

"We need your statement, Reid. I have to follow procedure."

"And I need you to tell me if my wife is alive. Just tell me," I roar, trying to sit up, the restraints cutting into my wrists and pulling me back down against the bed.

"She's in resus."

"Is her heart beating?"

"I don't know."

"Get me a lawyer."

I close my eyes and picture Morgan's chest rising. I listen for the sound of her heart beating and try hard to believe it's not unmoving as it was the last time I saw her. Morgan's a fighter, and now all I can do is hope that she had just enough strength left inside of her to find a way to live.

Chapter Eighty-One

Reid

Six months later

I sit stretched out on a deck chair sunk into the lush white sand on the island of Barbados. I think of Morgan, our honeymoon spent in a place we both never wanted to leave, and I wish we never did.

I watch in silence as the waves crash hard against the shore, and our two beautiful children run in and out of the ocean's force, tumbling and squealing as they resurface.

Six months has changed many things, but I still have a long way to go. As the sun glistens over the clear waters, I tense as I'm pulled back to those torturous days of hell my wife endured at the hands of a complete psychopath. These thoughts refuse to leave me, as well as the memory of the man who smothered everything we created for our family. His bulbous eyes still haunt me when I sleep. It's on constant replay in my mind—that moment when the flame that was alight inside him was extinguished by my hands. Even though in the eyes of the law I'm free of all guilt, and my actions have been deemed to be those of a man performing self-defence, I'm still haunted by my decision to end his life. Clarity is a beautiful thing. Any person who says taking a life can come without punishment is a liar. I'll be forever punished. I'm not God. I had no right. An eye for an eye was not the correct decision in the end. I hope one day, I find forgiveness for myself.

"Daddy, Daddy, are you watching?" Aleeha shouts, a smile lifting her cheeks.

"Yes, sweetheart, I saw you. How clever," I say as she completes another cartwheel along the soft sand right in front of me.

"Did you just see that flip, Dad?" Brax's chest puffs out with his pride. His somersault was perfect.

"I did, buddy. Loving your work." I smile, pleased by the resilience my children have shown despite being so young.

The sun beats against my skin, causing a line of pink to form below the bottom of my boardshorts. It's beautiful here and so far, being in this country has supplied me with a relaxation I've not felt since before

Morgan was stolen from me.

"What are you thinking about, handsome?" she whispers. Her lips full, her sweet voice causing my heart to beat faster.

"Just about you, beautiful."

She giggles. Beams of light fan behind her hair forming a perfect angelic glow. When she shifts into the shadow of a well-placed umbrella, I'm greeted with a seductive smile and fluttering eyelashes. "Did you miss me?" She sports the cutest pout when she crawls up my legs in her hot pink tankini, before straddling my waist.

"Only every second you've been gone, Morgan." I wrap my arms tightly around her waist, pulling her head onto my chest.

"Let's stay here forever," she says softly.

We lie there, entwined in each other's embrace as I twist strands of her brown locks around my fingers. "Whatever you desire." Anywhere she wants to live is fine by me, because if we're together then we're home.

Morgan's the bravest woman I know. I can never imagine the full extent of what those days in that hellhole were like for her. I can only assume from the marks on her body and the domino effect it's had on her mental health since. Morgan barely speaks of her time in captivity, the fact that she died for a period, or even her ongoing recovery. Instead, she saves those conversations for the many doctors and counsellors trained to help her get through the coming months and years.

With me, Morgan converses about the things she wishes for in her future—in our family's future. I know she suffers greatly, even though when she's awake she curtains her true emotions behind thoughts of new beginnings.

Each night when I climb into bed beside her, stroking her hair until she's asleep, I stare at the ceiling playing Russian Roulette with my own torment, waiting for the moment to come when I'll need to save Morgan all over again. Only now, I must save her from the kicks, punches, and screams that accompany her fight with our bedsheets. Or on Morgan's worst nights, I'll be forced to take chase after she leaps from the mattress and runs for a life she forgets she doesn't need to run to save anymore. Morgan's never awake when she does these things, and after I have her settled in my arms she relaxes. The following morning brings not a memory of the night prior for my wife, but for me? Well, I never forget one single nightmare.

"Are you getting hungry? I know I am." A soft kiss tickles my pec.

"I could eat."

"Okay. I'll go and get the kids. They're back in the water."

"No. I'll get them. You relax."

She perches herself on her elbows, her chestnut eyes gazing into mine. "I want to go and get them every chance I have for the rest of my life."

Morgan presses forward and I graze my lips over hers before she devours my mouth with love, so much love.

"Be right back." She hops to her feet and jogs down the beach. Morgan may be scarred, and still embroiled in an internal nightmare, but she's beautiful just as she's always been, inside and out.

All I'll ever need to feel whole is Morgan, and the knowledge that her heart continues to beat, that her blood runs freely through her veins, and her soul remains tucked deep within her, protected from all evil.

Morgan is perfection. Mine forever. I'll never stop fighting for her, with her, or to have her. I learnt the hard way to never go to bed angry because tomorrow just might not come. I'll spend every day for the remainder of my life showing Morgan love in its purest form, making her feel the definition of the word beauty. I will help her heal over the coming years.

I saved her once, and I'll save her each and every day for the rest of my life.

Chapter Eighty-Two

Morgan

I survived, I endured, and I won.

Now I need to find a way to rebuild my life, even though scars remain thick on my shins and scattered all over my body. And then there are the tattoos on the inner side of my arm that I keep covered for the moment; until I can bring myself to look at them without trembling or bursting into tears.

The wolf's still with me, permanently inked on my skin, and forever playing games with my mind. Even though he died, I don't think I'll ever be completely free again—free from Logan, free from the fight. The doctors tell me often that in time I'll forget certain things, but I don't think I'll ever be able to escape the visions plaguing me. *How do you forget something like this? How can you not be forever changed?*

For now, I spend my days embracing this new version of myself: scars, panic attacks, anxiety, and all. I know I'll continue to get stronger, more confident, and less jumpy and fearful. If I could survive days in a dense, hot, terrifying bushland with a maniac, and then survive being clinically dead, I guess I can brave this aftermath, too.

Today, I'm in the one place on earth that feels pure and giving, that cleanses my soul and washes some of my torment away. This is a place our family needs to spend time to make the big decisions on where our future will begin. I want it to be in Barbados, far away from Australia, and far away from Reid's parents' place in Melbourne where we have been staying.

We never did go home to the house we'd spent years making for ourselves, the one next door to an elderly couple whom we'd loved like our own family. There was no point returning to a tarnished neighbourhood that only represented betrayal, pain, and heartache.

John tried to take everything from us in the most underhanded way, and Shirley? Well, she broke my heart when she stood by John, and continued to throughout his trial, regardless of what he'd done to me, to our family.

Twenty years to life imprisonment, with the chance of parole after fifteen served, was John's punishment. Shirley? I've no idea where she ended up and I couldn't care. I hope wherever she is that she's living uncomfortably and filled with regret. I still don't believe she was as innocent as she claimed. And regardless of what Reid and the detectives have said, I believe Shirley knew where I was and who had me just as John did. I also think Shirley's guilt got the better of her or she feared the possibility of spending the remainder of her life behind bars. Why else would she have come to Reid in the early morning only to later stand by her husband's side in the aftermath. We'll never truly know the entire truth, but I hope Shirley is somewhere praying for her sins.

"Mummy. Mummy. Come spin with me." My sweet Aleeha has her arms outstretched on either side of her body and her neck extended so far back the only view she'd be able to see is the sky above her. "Mum, are you doing it?"

"Yeah, poppet, I am."

We spin, and we spin, and we spin.

"I'm getting dizzy, princess." I giggle.

"Keep going, Mummy," she squeals.

"Oh, oh, oh." I stumble over my feet. "I'm going to fall!" I laugh.

"That's the best part!" she laughs.

And we do fall, both of us, lying side by side on the sand. Aleeha continues to giggle so much I can't help but join her, and I laugh until I cry. I cry because sometimes I think I'm dead, hidden away in an underground graveyard, and that this isn't real at all, because I never did make it home.

"Are you crying, Mummy?" Aleeha's tone is filled

with concern.

"Happy tears, baby. They're happy tears."

She kisses my cheek. "They're the best tears to have."

I rub my hands up and down my face. "They are. Come on, let's do it again."

"I'm spinning this time, too." Brax leans over the top of me.

"I bet I can out-spin you, Brax. Let's do this."

"Do you need a hand up?" Reid leans over me, right beside Brax, and I have this moment of pure happiness that rips through my body, stealing my breath.

"Thank you, kind sir."

We spin, and spin, and spin in circles on one of the most beautiful beaches in the world until we crash from dizziness, landing on top of one another. Every sound of laughter that follows is priceless—there is no value. Every arm tangled in every limb speaks of our unity.

"I love you, Mum," Brax whispers in my ear. I roll my head and kiss his cheek.

"I love you, too, Brax.

"I love you more, Mummy." Aleeha's lips peck mine.

"I love you, too, Aleeha.

"You're my forever, Morgan." Reid's fingers link with mine.

"And you're mine. Let's move here. It can be home."

"I'd like that." Reid's blue eyes sparkle above me as

he lowers his head. "I love you," he says against my lips.

And he does, and he will, until the very end of my life.

Also by Belle

Thirty Days Trilogy

Thirty days: Part One

Thirty days: Part Two

Finding the Magician

Standalones

Always You

Winner

That Guy

Acknowledgements

A massive thank you from the bottom of my heart to: Kylee Harris, Liz Lovelock, Kirsty Roworth, Caroline Dayas, Jakarra Adams, Natalya Bryan, Shaelene Adams, Donna Martin, Tracey Wilson-Vuolo, Tracey Davis Zelukovic, Serena Worker, Sarah Pilcher and Robin Yatsko. I love you guys.

A massive thank you to my wonderful ARC team. I couldn't do any of this without you. You all know who you are.

To the Tinkerbelles—you're an amazing bunch of people who light up my life and keep me smiling. I love ya faces.

To my husband, Michael, whom I love dearly. It's always been you, baby.

To my beautiful children, the keepers of my soul. I love you to the moon and back.

To my wonderful team of talented and creative people, Lauren Clarke, Jaye Cox, and Emma Wicker. You ladies have a talent beyond belief, and I'm so grateful to share this journey with you.

Lastly, I'd like to thank everybody who has helped to promote my work—all the bloggers, Enticing Journey Book Promotions for a wonderful promotional campaign, and all the readers. Without the readers, there'd be no purpose for these stories.

My dreams are coming true, and it's all because of you.

Thank you.

Belle Brooks xx

About the Author

Belle Brooks is a former business manager, wife, and mother of three, living in Queensland, Australia. For as long as she can remember, writing has been a major part of her life, bringing her peace and comfort in the arms of her fictional characters. Never planning to have her work published, she focused her attention on her career and family. That is until she finally found the courage to allow her words to become public for others to enjoy, due mainly to the encouragement and support of those who love her. Game of Life, is her Twelfth publication.

Stay Connected with Belle Brooks

Website:
www.bellebrooksauthor.com

Facebook Page:
Belle Brooks Tinkerbells

Instagram:
@bbrooksauthor

Twitter
@Bellebrooks16

11914589R00380

Made in the USA
San Bernardino, CA
08 December 2018